IN THE
AIR
TONIGHT

Also from Marie Force

Single Titles
In the Air Tonight
Five Years Gone
One Year Home
Sex Machine
Sex God
Georgia on My Mind
True North
The Fall
The Wreck
Love at First Flight
Everyone Loves a Hero
Line of Scrimmage

Ongoing Series

The Fatal Series *Romantic Suspense*
One Night With You, A Fatal Series Prequel Novella
Book 1: Fatal Affair
Book 2: Fatal Justice
Book 3: Fatal Consequences
Book 3.5: Fatal Destiny, the Wedding Novella
Book 4: Fatal Flaw
Book 5: Fatal Deception
Book 6: Fatal Mistake
Book 7: Fatal Jeopardy
Book 8: Fatal Scandal
Book 9: Fatal Frenzy
Book 10: Fatal Identity
Book 11: Fatal Threat
Book 12: Fatal Chaos
Book 13: Fatal Invasion
Book 14: Fatal Reckoning
Book 15: Fatal Accusation
Book 16: Fatal Fraud

Sam and Nick's story continues…
Book 1: State of Affairs
Book 2: State of Grace

Book 3: State of the Union
Book 4: State of Shock
Book 5: State of Denial
Book 6: State of Bliss
Book 7: State of Suspense

The Gansett Island Series *Contemporary Romance*
Book 1: Maid for Love (Mac & Maddie)
Book 2: Fool for Love (Joe & Janey)
Book 3: Ready for Love (Luke & Sydney)
Book 4: Falling for Love (Grant & Stephanie)
Book 5: Hoping for Love (Evan & Grace)
Book 6: Season for Love (Owen & Laura)
Book 7: Longing for Love (Blaine & Tiffany)
Book 8: Waiting for Love (Adam & Abby)
Book 9: Time for Love (David & Daisy)
Book 10: Meant for Love (Jenny & Alex)
Book 10.5: Chance for Love, A Gansett Island Novella (Jared & Lizzie)
Book 11: Gansett After Dark (Owen & Laura)
Book 12: Kisses After Dark (Shane & Katie)
Book 13: Love After Dark (Paul & Hope)
Book 14: Celebration After Dark (Big Mac & Linda)
Book 15: Desire After Dark (Slim & Erin)
Book 16: Light After Dark (Mallory & Quinn)
Book 17: Victoria & Shannon (Episode 1)
Book 18: Kevin & Chelsea (Episode 2)
A Gansett Island Christmas Novella (Appears in Mine After Dark)
Book 19: Mine After Dark (Riley & Nikki)
Book 20: Yours After Dark (Finn & Chloe)
Book 21: Trouble After Dark (Deacon & Julia)
Book 22: Rescue After Dark (Mason & Jordan)
Book 23: Blackout After Dark (Full Cast)
Book 24: Temptation After Dark (Gigi & Cooper)
Book 25: Resilience After Dark (Jace & Cindy)
Book 26: Hurricane After Dark (Full Cast)
Book 27: Renewal After Dark (Coming 2024)

The Wild Widows Series—a Fatal Series Spin-Off *Contemporary Romance*
Book 1: Someone Like You
Book 2: Someone to Hold

Book 3: Someone to Love
Book 4: Someone to Watch Over Me

Downeast, A Gansett Island Series Spin-Off *Contemporary Romance/Romantic Suspense*
Dan & Kara: A Downeast Prequel

Completed Series

The Green Mountain Series *Contemporary Romance*
Book 1: All You Need Is Love (Will & Cameron)
Book 2: I Want to Hold Your Hand (Nolan & Hannah)
Book 3: I Saw Her Standing There (Colton & Lucy)
Book 4: And I Love Her (Hunter & Megan)
Novella: You'll Be Mine (Will & Cam's Wedding)
Book 5: It's Only Love (Gavin & Ella)
Book 6: Ain't She Sweet (Tyler & Charlotte)

The Butler, Vermont Series *Contemporary Romance*
(Continuation of Green Mountain)
Book 1: Every Little Thing (Grayson & Emma)
Book 2: Can't Buy Me Love (Mary & Patrick)
Book 3: Here Comes the Sun (Wade & Mia)
Book 4: Till There Was You (Lucas & Dani)
Book 5: All My Loving (Landon & Amanda)
Book 6: Let It Be (Lincoln & Molly)
Book 7: Come Together (Noah & Brianna)
Book 8: Here, There & Everywhere (Izzy & Cabot)
Book 9: The Long and Winding Road (Max & Lexi)

The Miami Nights Series *Contemporary Romance*
Book 1: How Much I Feel (Carmen & Jason)
Book 2: How Much I Care (Maria & Austin)
Book 3: How Much I Love (Dee's story)
Nochebuena, A Miami Nights Novella

Book 4: How Much I Want (Nico & Sofia)
Book 5: How Much I Need (Milo and Gianna)

The Quantum Series *Erotic Romance*
Book 1: Virtuous (Flynn & Natalie)

Book 2: Valorous (Flynn & Natalie)
Book 3: Victorious (Flynn & Natalie)
Book 4: Rapturous (Addie & Hayden)
Book 5: Ravenous (Jasper & Ellie)
Book 6: Delirious (Kristian & Aileen)
Book 7: Outrageous (Emmett & Leah)
Book 8: Famous (Marlowe & Sebastian)

The Treading Water Series *Contemporary Romance*
Book 1: Treading Water
Book 2: Marking Time
Book 3: Starting Over
Book 4: Coming Home
Book 5: Finding Forever

The Gilded Series *Historical Romance*
Book 1: Duchess by Deception
Book 2: Deceived by Desire

IN THE AIR TONIGHT

NEW YORK TIMES AND *USA TODAY* BESTSELLING AUTHOR

MARIE FORCE

BLUE
BOX
PRESS

In the Air Tonight
By Marie Force

Copyright 2024 HTJB, Inc.
ISBN: 978-1-963135-12-1

Published by Blue Box Press, an imprint of Evil Eye Concepts, Incorporated

Chapter 1

Blaise
NOW

I'M LATE GETTING HOME from work and in a foul mood after another long day with my jerk of a boss, Wendall, barking orders at me that couldn't be seen to in a month, let alone a single day. But that's what he expects—everything *right now*. Six months ago, I stopped taking his calls after hours because I don't get paid to tend to him for more than eight hours a day. That's all he gets from me now.

He didn't like that.

Ask me if I care. We've reached the point where he needs me far more than I need him, and he knows it.

My friends in the city were green with envy when I landed a job as the personal assistant to the hottest star on Broadway. They don't know he's a nightmare. No one knows that but me and the people he stars with in *Gray Matter,* the top-grossing show on the Great White Way this year. As the show becomes more successful, he's an even bigger dick to everyone around him.

I'm giving him six more months and then moving on. Life's too short to work for someone I can't stand.

I've barely walked into my apartment when my phone rings with a call from my mother. I hesitate to take it because I'm in such a shitty mood, but she worries when I don't answer. I press the big green button.

"Hey, Mom." After kicking off my sneakers, I drop my bag on the sofa. It's got my laptop and the heels I wear at the theater where I spend my days.

"I'm so glad you answered, sweetheart. I tried you yesterday but got your voicemail."

I've told her—many times—I never check my voicemail and she should text me if she wants to chat, but she's never gotten the hang of texting. My siblings and I have tried to teach her. She says she has a mental block. I say she couldn't be bothered. "What's going on?"

"Teagan is pregnant again."

I'm shocked. My sister has four children under the age of seven. "Wow. Four wasn't enough?"

"I guess not. She's so happy. I could hear it in her voice when she called to share the news. Doug has a big new job that allows her stay home with the kids. She's thrilled to be a full-time mom now."

"I'm glad for her. That's a lot to juggle with a job."

"It was too much, and the daycare bills were sucking up most of her salary anyway."

"I'll text her to say congrats."

"I know she'd love to hear from you."

I hear the sadness in my mother's voice. How could I not? It's been there since the day I left home and never looked back. My family has asked over the years why I never come home, even for holidays I used to enjoy. I haven't been able to provide an answer that satisfies them. This is what works for me. Staying away from there, from the memories, has made it possible for me to have a life of purpose without guilt swallowing me whole.

Since I left for college nearly thirteen years ago, I've been home once—when my father died suddenly.

I've always been certain that if I go back there for any length of time, my carefully constructed house of cards will come crashing down.

My mother chats on about people I barely remember, kids I grew up with who are now parents many times over, her friends' grandchildren and other gossip from home.

"Was Ryder Elliott your year or Arlo's?"

The bottom drops out of my world at the mention of that name.

Ryder Elliott.

"Blaise? Hello? Are you there?"

I swallow hard. "I'm here. What did you say?"

"Was Ryder your year? Or Arlo's?"

All the spit in my mouth is gone, and I'm right back in the woods on the night that changed everything. The scent of woodsmoke is forever tied to that night as is the Steve Miller song "Jet Airliner."

"I, uh, my year," I somehow manage to say.

"He's running for Congress. Can you believe that kids you went to school with are now doing things like that?"

A roar overtakes me, so loud it drowns out every thought in my head. "No."

"What? Did you say something, honey?"

I'm screaming to myself. *No, no, no, no.* He's running for Congress? Oh no. No, he is not. That cannot happen. Something about those words, *he's running for Congress,* tips me over an edge I've hovered on for fourteen long years. I can't stay there another second.

I remember every detail of that night as if it happened five minutes ago. It's as vivid to me now as it was then, unlike other things that've faded into the ether.

"Mom?"

"You're scaring me, Blaise. What's wrong?"

"I'm coming home."

Blaise
THEN

MY MOM MADE MEATLOAF, one of the five meals we'd all eat. Tired of fighting dinner battles with four picky kids, she rotates from one meal to the other, but meatloaf is usually my favorite. I can barely swallow a bite because I'm so nervous. While my parents, sisters and brother keep up a steady stream of chatter, I try not to puke from nerves.

I'm a month shy of my seventeenth birthday and about to do something I've never done before on the first night of summer vacation—directly disobey my parents. Sure, I've told a white lie here and there, had a few beers and even smoked pot a couple of times. But I haven't taken the car somewhere they've specifically told me not to go.

My phone buzzes with a text from Sienna Lawton, my best friend. *Still good to go?*

We're not supposed to text at the table, so I keep the phone in my lap when I reply with Ya.

I'm going to be sick.

"What's wrong, Blaise?" Mom asks. "Why aren't you eating? It's your favorite."

"I had a big lunch on the way home from the beach. Can I wrap it up for later?"

"Sure, honey. That's fine."

"It's delicious, Mom. Thank you for dinner."

She smiles at me. "You're welcome."

I'm a good kid. I work hard at school, get excellent grades and generally do what I'm told, unlike my sister Teagan, who's three years older than me and gives them nothing but trouble. I fly under the radar and like it there. I'd never want the kind of attention Teagan gets from them, which includes a lot of yelling, door slamming and overall contention.

My brother, Arlo, a year older than me, is my hero. He manages to smoothly do whatever the hell he wants and get away with it. My parents think he's the perfect son. However, I know where most of his skeletons are buried. I'll take that info to my grave. He and I look out for each other. It's not something we ever talk about, but we've got each other's backs.

My little sister, Juniper—known as June or Junie—chats nonstop, which usually annoys me. Tonight, I'm thankful for the distraction she provides.

I'm taking the car to a party across the river in Land's End, where I'm most definitely not allowed to go. My parents say the long, dark winding roads leading to Land's End are an accident waiting for a teenager to happen. Plus, it's well known in our town of Hope that some of the kids from Land's End, who are bussed to our high school because they don't have one of their own, are partiers.

My parents would lose their shit if they knew my plans for the evening.

They don't track my phone because I've given them no reason to, whereas they pay extra for new technology that lets them track Teagan's every move. She calls me the Golden Child. It's not a compliment coming from the Merrick family's chief agitator. Just because I'm not constantly getting in trouble doesn't mean I don't know how to have fun. Granted, I'm not one of the super popular girls like Teagan was in high school, but I can live with that. I have several good friends, even if none of us are considered the "cool" kids.

Sienna sort of straddles both worlds thanks to her boyfriend, Camden Elliott. He and his older brother Ryder, who are both in our class thanks to Ryder being held back a year before kindergarten, are the most popular boys in our school. They're co-captains of the football team, as well as baseball (Camden) and track (Ryder) stars.

They're also Arlo's closest friends. You'd think that having a best friend and brother attached to the school's most popular kids would elevate me, too. You'd be wrong about that.

Sienna and Cam have been a couple for as long as I can recall. I barely remember her without him. However, things have been weird between them lately, which is why we're risking everything to go to spy on a party we weren't invited to. Cam pretended like he didn't know about the party, which made her suspicious and paranoid. When she couldn't get her family's car for the night, her paranoia became my problem.

Upstairs, I change into denim cutoff shorts and a halter top. In the long shot possibility that we're able to talk our way into the party, I put on makeup, focusing on the blue eyes that people say are my best feature. I run a brush through the reddish-brown hair I straightened earlier. I want to change my hair color, but my mom won't let me. Try having reddish hair when your name is Blaise. I've had every nickname from Fire Ant to Fireball. I especially hate that the boys call me Ablaze. Worst nickname ever.

As a finishing touch, I spray on some of the fancy perfume my grandmother gave me for Christmas. I'd never heard of the scent, but Gran said it's best not to smell like anyone else.

I'm ready to go, but still feel like I'm going to be sick. I knock on Teagan's door. She's only home because she's grounded—again.

"What?" She's twenty and finished her second year at community college in May, getting grades that barely kept her off academic probation. She has to do another semester to get an associate degree. Last week, she was caught at a bar in Newport, even though she's underage. My parents went ballistic and demanded she turn over her fake ID. Knowing her, she has two others hidden in her room.

"Do you have any Tums?"

She hurls the bottle at me, barely missing my head. I catch the bottle, shake out two of them and put the bottle on a desk piled high with clothes and other crap. It's never seen a school book in all the years since Mom bought desks for us at Pottery Barn Kids.

"Thanks."

She grunts something in reply but doesn't look up from the phone she earned back after the latest parental altercation by doing chores around the house.

In a way, I'm kind of thankful for her. She keeps the attention off me.

In the hallway, I run into Arlo. His light brown hair is wet from the shower, and his blue eyes give me a quick once over. "What's with you?"

"Nothing. Why?"

"You're dressed up." He leans in for a whiff. "Wearing perfume and makeup. Where're you going?"

"Nowhere." If anyone can see right through my lies, it's him, which can be comforting and annoying—at the same time.

"I'd better not see you anywhere near Land's End tonight, you got me?"

"Why would I go there?"

He gives me a withering look that big brothers have been giving their younger sisters since the beginning of time. "Stay. Away."

"I have better things to do than go to your stupid party."

"Don't tell Mom and Dad anything about it, or I'll murder you."

I roll my eyes, to say 'as if I'd start talking now'. Why would I tell them that Houston Rafferty's parents are away, and he's hosting a rager with booze? His party has been the talk of our town and LE for days. I'm surprised my parents haven't picked up the scent by now.

I land downstairs feeling moderately better after taking the Tums.

My dad is doing the dishes. She cooks. He cleans up. They get along great and only butt heads over Teagan. He's tough on her. Mom's a softie, and that infuriates my dad, who, as he says, is trying to keep her out of jail. Mom says he exaggerates, but I tend to agree with him. He's probably the only thing keeping her out of serious trouble.

Dad glances at me and smiles. "You ready to go?" His gaze takes in my outfit. He hates the crop tops that're all the rage with girls my age, but thankfully, he doesn't make an issue out of it.

I swallow the lump in my throat. "Yep."

"And you guys are going to the movies and maybe downtown, right?"

"Yes." I feel sick lying to him.

"Home by midnight?"

"I'll try. If I'm running late, I'll text you."

He hands over the keys to his Toyota SUV and kisses my cheek.

"Thank you for being so considerate. It's very much appreciated."

I come this close to spilling my guts and telling him the truth. But he'll never let me take the car to Land's End, and Sienna is counting on me.

How many times will I wish I'd told him the truth about my plans for that night?

Every day for the rest of my life.

Chapter 2

Blaise
THEN

SIENNA JUMPS INTO THE SUV before it completely stops moving, letting out a shriek of excitement that stretches my nerves almost to the breaking point. Her wild, curly brown hair is still wet from the shower, and she's taken a bath in Victoria's Secret body spray. "I honestly thought you'd chicken out." She changes the radio station from B101 to WHJY and cranks the volume on "Freebird."

"I almost did. I might throw up."

"You'll be fine. We'll go over there, see what Cam is doing and then come back. No biggie."

Right. No biggie. It's not her ass on the line if we get caught there. People know my dad's car, which is why we drive around for an hour until darkness gives us the cover I need to go through with this plan.

We head across the bridge into Monroe, the town between ours and Land's End. The kids from Land's End used to go to Monroe High School, but for reasons I'm not clear on, they ended up in school with us. School got a lot more interesting once the Land's End kids joined us freshman year, especially Dallas Rafferty.

Not that he knows I'm alive, but whatever. A girl can dream. No one knows I like him, even Sienna, who'd want to try to fix me up with him because Cam plays football with Dallas and is friends with him outside of school.

In fact, Dallas's older brother Houston—their mom is originally from Texas, and their sister is named Austin—is the one having the party tonight. I was surprised to hear Houston was having a big party, since his dad is the police chief in LE. Sienna heard his parents are on a cruise and off the grid, thus the party. Houston is a senior in college and legal, which means there'll be plenty of beer and other booze at the party. That'll draw a lot of kids from Hope across the river tonight, which is all the more reason to be scared. Someone might still recognize my dad's car and rat me out.

So many of my friends can do whatever they want. Their parents never ask them where they're going, who they're going with or when they'll be home. While part of me thinks that would be nice, I'm grateful that someone would care enough to ask where I was if I didn't show up at home. My parents would call the police if I didn't come home.

Sienna is practically bouncing in the passenger seat. "You're driving like my grandmother."

She gets hyper when she's stressed, and worrying about Cam lying to her has had her on edge for days.

"Why don't you come right out and ask him if he's going?"

"I don't want him to know that I know about the party."

"Why not?"

"He'll think I don't trust him."

I don't follow the logic. "Well, you don't…"

"Yes, I do! It's just a bump. We're solid. Always have been and always will be."

"Of course you will." I tell her what she needs to hear even if I'm not so sure lately. I've noticed subtle signs of Cam pulling away from her, even if she can't admit it.

I don't want to be around if they break up. I'll have to make up an emergency trip to Siberia or something to avoid having to deal with her if that happens. Not that I wouldn't want to be there for my best friend, but her without Cam is unimaginable. They're an institution, the longest-standing couple in our entire school, the homecoming king and queen two years in a row and the couple most likely to get married. They're even planning to go to college together in Arizona. Her whole life is tied up in him and vice versa.

I desperately hope we don't catch him doing something unforgivable at this party.

The road to the Rafferty house is lined with cars.

"Where should we park? If Arlo sees the car, I'm screwed."

"There's a back road Cam showed me once. Go past the house. You can circle around. We can walk in from the next block over."

I follow her directions to a street a block away and park in a dark spot between two streetlights. The second we emerge from the SUV I can hear the party. Music, loud voices and laughter fuel my anxiety as we walk through a thicket of trees, the noise getting louder as we get closer. The scent of woodsmoke from a bonfire fills the air. Houston is famous for his epic bonfires, or so I've been told. I've never been invited to one of his parties.

Sienna takes my arm to stop me from going any farther. "We can see from here."

The party is massive. If you ask me, every kid from Hope, Monroe and LE is there, except us.

I smack a mosquito that lands on the back of my neck. "Shit, we forgot bug spray."

She digs through the gigantic purse she takes everywhere. "I've got some."

We joke that anything we will ever need can be found in Sienna's bag.

The smell of woodsmoke and bug spray will forever remind me of this fateful night.

"There's Cam," I whisper to her.

She leans in for a closer look.

He looks a lot like Ryder with lighter hair but isn't as ripped as Ryder. Sienna says that's because he likes pizza so much.

Shit, he's talking to Brooke, who's a year ahead of us with boobs twice the size of Sienna's. "They're just talking," I whisper to her. "It's no big deal."

I venture a glance at Sienna's face and see that it's a very big deal to her. I've wanted to ask her how things are between them when they're alone, but I've been afraid to. From the outside looking in, something has changed. If I can see that, surely she can, too.

My stomach hurts like it did earlier as I pray Cam doesn't do anything that can't be undone—or unseen. The very fact that we're spying on him like this should be the biggest red flag ever for their relationship, but I'm not about to say that to her.

I see Arlo mixing with the other kids, holding court the way he always does. Everyone likes him. He's tall, dark-haired, handsome and easy going. I aspire to be more like him and less of an anxiety-ridden mess of insecurities. I'm a work in progress, and he's already arrived at his final destination. I'd hate him for that if I didn't love him so much.

"What the hell is *she* doing here?" Sienna whispers.

At first I'm not sure who she's talking about. And then I see her—the new girl, Denise Sutton, who goes by Neisy. The boys are crazy about her. The girls hate her because she's stunning, with big boobs, long sun-kissed hair and bee-stung lips. She arrived at our school last September, at the beginning of our junior year, touching down with the impact of an F5 tornado and completely upending the social order. Even the most popular girls in our class have nothing on her, and they know it, which is why they despise her.

They treat her like she's radioactive, crossing the hallway to avoid her, getting up and moving away from any table she sits at in the lunchroom and spreading vicious rumors about her, like how she fucked the entire football team after a game last fall and how someone from her old school said she had an abortion freshman year.

I've been surprised and ashamed at how girls I've known my whole life have treated her.

It's hard to know what to believe. Everyday it's something else. I wouldn't be surprised if some of the girls are making shit up just to undercut her. The boys are too dazzled to care what anyone says about her.

Oh shit. Cam's talking to Neisy now.

Sienna vibrates with outrage next to me.

He leans in closer to hear what Neisy is saying, and then his big laugh rings out so loudly, it's like he's standing right next to us.

"I'm going to fucking stab him," Sienna mutters.

"He's not doing anything wrong talking to other girls."

"He knows how I feel about her."

It's news to me that she has an opinion about Neisy. "How do you feel about her?"

"She's a slut."

"What? You don't know that."

"You've heard the rumors same as I have."

"It doesn't mean they're true!"

"Whose side are you on?"

"I'm on your side," I tell her. "Always." We've been best friends since third grade. "But we don't know her well enough to call her that."

"From what Cam says, the whole football team knows her."

"Including him?"

"He wouldn't do that."

I'm not so sure, but I keep that to myself, too. Ever since they finally had sex last winter, Sienna has been extra possessive of him.

Minutes pass as Cam makes the rounds, seemingly talking to everyone as Sienna goes silent. That's never a good thing.

My legs are starting to cramp from squatting.

"Here comes Ryder," Sienna whispers. "Don't move or he'll see us."

I've thought Ryder Elliott is hot for as long as I've known what hot meant. With dark wavy hair, dreamy blue eyes and a muscular body, he's like a god in our school, revered by everyone, scouted by colleges that want him for football and track. Every girl wants to be his girlfriend, but he's been dating Louisa Davies since ninth grade. Ryder and Louisa will be our class couple, and it's understood they'll get married as soon as they finish college—if she lives that long.

Louisa has been fighting Hodgkin's Disease since she was fourteen. Ryder has been by her side through it all, hosting fundraisers for her family and making sure she has everything she needs. They recently celebrated her remission after grueling treatments that had her out of school for most of our sophomore year and again the last half of our junior year.

Everything was looking up until recently when we heard she'd relapsed again. She's back in treatment, and her immune system is fragile, so she's not allowed out of her house. I heard how Ryder leaves flowers outside her door every morning. She's the sweetest girl, and we're all praying for her recovery. No one more so than Ryder.

We're about six feet from where he stops and turns to speak to someone.

Neisy.

Shock ricochets through me. No way. What's she doing with him? By now she must know he has a longtime girlfriend. Maybe the things people say about her are true.

I want to tell Sienna that we should go, but I can't get the words out.

I've asked myself over and over what would've been worse—what we saw or no one knowing what he did to her.

At first, all they do is talk.

We can hear everything they say.

He sips from a red Solo cup. "You know you're driving me crazy with the way you look at me in school."

"How do I look at you?"

"Like you want to fuck me."

She crosses her arms. "Well, I don't."

"Yes, you do."

"No, I really don't."

"There's nothing worse than a cock tease. That's what all the guys say about you. That you're a cock tease, among other things."

"They can say what they want. I know the truth. I thought you said you wanted to talk to me about Louisa."

As if she hasn't said anything, Ryder moves closer to her. "You don't care what they say about you?"

"Why should I? I don't even know them. I don't know you. Why would you think I want to fuck you?"

He moves so quickly she never sees it coming—and neither do we. One minute they're standing a foot from each other, the next they're on the ground, and he's on top of her, his hand over her mouth as he pulls at her clothes.

She struggles against his tight hold, fighting him fiercely, but she's no match for him.

Sienna's fingers dig into my arm.

I want out of there right now. I don't want to see this. Bile burns in my throat.

Neisy bites his hand, and he slaps her hard across the face.

She screams, but no one can hear her over hundreds of voices and "Empire State of Mind" playing at full volume.

"We need to do something," I whisper to Sienna.

"We can't. We'll get in huge trouble."

"He's going to hurt her."

His hand is between her legs.

I look away. I want to go. I tug at Sienna. "Please. Let's go."

"He'll see us if we move."

Bile burns my throat.

Neisy begs him not to do what he's already doing. "Please, I've never—" She cries out in pain.

"Shut up," he says, grunting. "Shut the fuck up and take what you've been asking for since the day we met."

I want to die.

I've never experienced anything that would've prepared me for this.

Sienna weeps silently next to me, her fingers pressed so tightly into my arm that I'll have bruises.

If we so much as move, he'll see us.

Our parents will know we were there. We'll be grounded for the rest of our lives. We'll be ruined for spying on the party. For spying on Ryder.

We barely know Neisy.

But we know him. We've known him all our lives.

I'm revolted.

After he finishes with a loud groan, he gets up, pulls up his pants and walks away from her, leaving her on the ground sobbing.

"We need to go to her," I whisper to Sienna.

"We can't, Blaise."

"What do you mean? Who cares if we get in trouble?"

"He's Cam's brother and Arlo's best friend. We *can't*."

I look at her like I've never seen her before.

Neisy is curled into a ball, still lying on the ground, her underwear around her ankles as she sobs.

Sienna pulls me toward the SUV.

"We can't just leave her there."

"We don't even know her," she says on a hiss.

"Sienna! Who cares if we know her? He *raped* her."

She drags me back to where we left the SUV. "Let's go home and forget about this."

"Are you insane? I'll never forget this."

"You have to. She's nothing to us. He's been part of our entire life. He'll be in my life forever. You can't say anything. No one will believe us anyway."

She's right, and I hate that.

People at school hate Neisy.

They love him.

It'd be our word—and hers—against him. We'd be vilified.

I lean over and puke up the meatloaf, which burns on the way out.

I'll never eat meatloaf again.

"For God's sake, Blaise, you're being so dramatic."

We ride home in stony silence. My hands shake so hard I can barely keep the vehicle in the lane. To think my biggest fear upon leaving the house was getting caught with the car across the river. Now that's the least of my concerns. I pull up to her house, a two-story colonial with black shutters.

"You can never say anything about this."

I maintain my stony silence. I feel like I don't know her at all.

"Swear to me that you won't say anything, Blaise. No one knows this, but Ryder's up for an appointment to the Naval Academy."

Hearing that, I feel sick all over again. His gilded life will go on like nothing happened while Neisy will never be the same. And neither will I.

"Blaise?"

Almost ten years of close friendship has come down to this. If I do the right thing, I'll lose my best friend and be made a pariah at school. Not to mention Arlo will hate me. Ryder has been his best friend since T-ball. I've never been more conflicted. If I tell what I saw, life as I know it will be over. People will hate me for taking Neisy's side against Ryder.

"I won't say anything."

"Good." Sienna gets out of the car and slams the door. She disappears inside the house, leaving me shaking uncontrollably. It's so bad I fear I shouldn't drive the short distance to my house. I sit there for a long time, trying to get myself together so I can get home safely.

I'm sobbing so hard I'm afraid I might vomit again.

Later I won't recall driving home. Those few minutes will be a total blank while everything I saw in the woods will exist in my memory bank in bright, living color forever.

My mother is in the kitchen when I come in through the door from the mudroom.

"You're home early," she says as she makes the sleepy time tea she says is critical to getting any rest.

"Not feeling good. My stomach."

She comes over to feel my head. "Have you been crying?"

"From feeling sick."

"You're not warm. Did you drink anything?"

"Of course not. I was driving. I just want to go to bed."

From under the sink, she produces the lime green bowl that's served as our puke bucket my whole life. "Take this with you. Just in case."

I take it from her, hoping she doesn't notice my hands are shaking. "Night."

"Come get me if you need me during the night."

"I will."

My dad is in the family room when I cut through on the way to the stairs. "What's up? Thought you'd be out for hours yet."

"Not feeling good."

"Oh, too bad."

"Yeah. See you in the morning."

"Feel better."

"Thanks."

I close my bedroom door and slide down to the floor, burying my face in my hands, sobbing harder than I ever have in my life, even after my grandpa died. Every part of me feels sick. We were wrong to leave Neisy there. I've been raised to treat others how I'd want to be treated. If something like that happened to me, I'd hope someone would help me.

What I couldn't have known then was that the sick feeling would stay with me forever.

Chapter 3

Neisy
THEN

I'M IN SHOCK. THAT has to be why my arms and legs refuse to cooperate with my brain's instructions to get up and get out of there before someone finds me half-naked and bleeding. The thought of having to explain what happened provides the impetus to sit up and try to collect myself. My hands shake violently as I pull up my underwear over thighs streaked with blood.

Ryder Elliott raped me.

Even as those words filter through my mind, I still can't believe it happened.

The hideous smell of beer on his breath made me gag. I retch into the dry leaves on the ground next to me. I hate the smell of beer, and now I always will.

I get up on shaky legs, shove my feet into the sandals that came off at some point, pull my skirt down and make my way through thick brush to the road where I parked my car. By the time I emerge onto the pavement, my arms are scratched and bleeding.

I'm numb to the pain coming from every part of my body, especially between my legs. Contrary to the rumors about me, I was a virgin.

I'm not anymore, which breaks my heart into a million pieces.

I struggle to breathe as the weight of that new reality settles on my chest. Kane's smiling face appears in my mind. He was supposed to have been my first. If I think about him now, I'll lose the composure I need to get myself out of here.

Oh God, where're my keys?

Somehow my purse is still slung across my body, but my keys aren't in it. They must've fallen out.

I can't go back there to look for them.

I just can't.

In case I got locked out, my dad put a hide-a-key under the back bumper of the white Honda Civic he bought for me. I feel around for the magnetized box he put it in and manage to knock it to the ground. I have to get on my knees to retrieve it, thankful for my safety-first dad.

A sob erupts from my chest.

He can't ever know about this. He'd kill Ryder.

Tears roll down my cheeks as I get into the car, crying out as my tender flesh connects with the seat. As I lean my head on the steering wheel, my body shakes with sobs and tears clog my throat. When Ryder said he needed to talk to me about Louisa, it never occurred to me that I shouldn't go with him to find a quiet place to talk.

Everyone knows he's madly in love with Louisa and how good he's been to her during her illness.

I start the car and pull onto the street. I probably shouldn't be driving, but I have to get out of here before someone sees me and starts asking questions. I drive slowly, which I once heard my dad say is a red flag to cops looking for drunk drivers. I'd rather think about things my dad says than about what happened in the woods.

I shift in the seat and realize my clothes are wet. Is it blood or... I can't. I just can't.

For the first time ever, I'm thankful my dad is away more than he's home. Getting by my mom won't be a problem. That wouldn't be the case with him.

I'm still shaking and nauseated as I make my way across the bridge to Hope and take the exit that leads to the split-level house my parents bought when we moved here last June so my mom could be closer to her aging parents. That seems like a long time ago after a hellish year at Hope High School with kids who hated me on sight.

I worked at my cousin's restaurant last summer with Houston Rafferty, which is the only reason I was invited to his party in the first place. I shouldn't have gone. I knew that before I went, but I refuse to hide from the assholes at school.

As I imagine myself accusing Ryder Elliott of rape, a powerful wave of nausea has me pulling off the road and leaning out to vomit. Bile burns my throat as I retch violently. I want it to stop so I can get out of there before I attract attention from the police. That's the last thing I need.

No one can ever know about this, or my life here will be even more horrific than it already is. With my dad being a high-ranking naval officer, I'm used to being the new kid in school. It's never been as hard as it is here. The other kids took an immediate, visceral dislike to me on the first day of my junior year, and that was it. My life has been a nightmare ever since.

Houston is one of the only true friends I've made here. He tells me all the time to ignore the assholes and keep being awesome. That's easy for him to say. No one has ever been shitty to him in his entire life. He treats me the same way he does his little sister, Austin, which I appreciate. But since he's been in college in Boston almost the whole time I've lived here, he isn't much help to me at school.

I want so badly to tell him what happened with Ryder, but I can't. Houston's father is the LE chief of police. If I tell Houston, he'll tell his father, and everyone will know.

No one can ever know, or my living hell will become even more so.

I pull into the driveway at the house. I never refer to it as "home," because it doesn't feel like that. It's just another in a long string of houses that've provided shelter for however long we've lived in a given place. After I turn off the car, I sit for a long time trying to get myself together before I go inside.

My mom is usually passed out by now, having consumed at least two bottles of wine since the afternoon. Normally her drinking disgusts me. Tonight, I'm thankful for it. I enter through a side door that leads to the garage and then the kitchen. I tiptoe past the living room where she's asleep on the sofa and head upstairs, going straight to the shower across the hall from my room. As I strip off my clothes, I'm alarmed by how much blood there is, mixed in with other fluid that makes me shudder.

What if I get pregnant?

That possibility has me vomiting again in dry heaves until there's nothing left in my stomach.

I throw my clothes into the bathtub and step into the shower.

Hot water has never felt so good as I scrub my body from the top of my head to the bottom of my feet, wincing at the pain between my legs when soap meets abused flesh. And then I'm sobbing again. I slide down the wall to sit in the tub as the water continues to rain down on me, washing away some of the horror.

I'm hardly naïve after living in ten different places in my first seventeen years, but I never thought something like this would happen to me. I'm careful. Street smart. Aware. My dad has made sure of it. I keep going back to Ryder asking if he could talk to me about Louisa. She was in my English class before she had to leave school. I thought she was very sweet, and I had the feeling she liked me, too.

Her kindness stood out to me because everyone else was a jerk.

I had no reason to be afraid of Ryder.

Sure, he'd been flirtatious with me in the past, but all the boys are. That's why the girls hate me so much, not that I do anything to encourage the boys. My boyfriend, Kane, is currently living in Spain. We met when our families were stationed together in Jacksonville, Florida, for four years, the longest I've lived anywhere.

We've been a couple since we were in seventh grade, which sounds bonkers, I know. But our bond was deep and immediate, and has stayed that way, even with an ocean between us.

He questioned the wisdom of me going to Houston's party, which was sure to be attended by the same kids who've made me an outcast. He knows Houston is my one good friend here, and I didn't want to miss his party because of the assholes. I should've listened to Kane.

I wrap my arms around my knees and drop my head to rest on my forearm.

Kane…

He was supposed to have been my first, my only. I've known for years that he's the love of my life and vice versa. Yes, we're young, and we've heard all the detractors advise us not to get our hopes up about each other. But when you know, you know.

How will I ever tell him about this?

I'm still in the shower quite a while later when the hot water starts to run out. The cold water is like a slap to the face that gets me up and moving again. I notice a pink tinge in the water where I was sitting and shiver from the cold as well as the trauma.

Even though it's still warm outside and my dad hates paying for air conditioning, I get dressed in my coziest sweats and a long-sleeved T-shirt before I crawl into bed, pulling the covers up and over my head. If I could, I'd stay here forever.

No one can ever know about this. Even in the midst of the shock, I know that much for certain. Ryder Elliott is the king of Hope High

School. I could scream from the rooftops about what he did to me, but no one would believe me. They've known him forever. Most of them went to preschool together. Their parents were high school classmates.

I'm an outsider in every possible way.

And they think I'm a slut, which is what they'd say about me if I accused him.

I saw a movie once about a girl who reported a rape and had her own life torn apart by the guy's friends and family. That would happen here, too. That's why I didn't go straight to the police like I should have.

It would be my word against Ryder Elliott's, even if I'd bothered to preserve the evidence.

They'd tear me apart.

Blaise
THEN

THE DAY AFTER, WE'RE due at my grandmother's house for a long-planned family reunion that I've been looking forward to for months. I don't get to see my cousins very often, and most of them will be there.

I can't get out of bed.

Teagan comes to the door, her expression stormy. "What the hell are you doing? Everyone is waiting for you."

"I'm sick."

"So am I, but I'm going."

"I can't."

"What the hell, Blaise? You helped to plan this stupid thing. And now you don't want to go?"

"I do want to. I'm sick."

"What's going on, girls?" Mom frowns when she sees me still in bed. "Get up, Blaise. We're due at Gran's in thirty minutes."

"I'm still sick from last night."

Mom feels my forehead. "You do feel a little warm."

"She's *faking*," Teagan says.

"Hush," Mom replies. "That's your thing, not hers."

Teagan makes a nasty face at me.

"Are you sure you can't go, honey?" Mom asks. "You've been so looking forward to it. The photographer is coming to take a picture of the whole family."

She's crushed when she realizes I won't be in the photo, but I can't rally, even for her.

"I'm sorry, Mom."

"It's okay. You haven't been sick in ages. I suppose you were due."

Now I feel doubly guilty for lying to her.

"Tell everyone I said hello, and I'm sorry to miss it."

"I will." She leans in to kiss my cheek. "Can I get you anything before I go?"

The thought of eating anything, ever again, makes me sick. "No, thanks."

"I'll bring you back some of Gran's brownies."

"That sounds good." I choke back more bile. "Thanks."

Mom leaves the room.

Teagan hangs back. "You're full of shit. Why're you faking?"

"I'm not."

"You are, and I'm going to find out why."

She storms out of the room, leaving my stomach in new knots at the thought of her finding out why I'm sitting out the family reunion.

Two hours later, my phone rings.

It's Sienna. "Hey."

"Are you at the reunion?"

"I'm sick."

"For real?"

"Yes."

She feels like a stranger to me after the way she acted last night. Her first impulse was to cover for Ryder, not assist Neisy. I hate her for that as much as I hate myself for being so weak that I caved to her intense peer pressure.

"Last night was fucked up."

That's one way of putting it.

She clears her throat. "I, uh… You didn't tell anyone did you?"

"No."

"Oh," she says on a long exhale. "Good. That's good."

"It's not good. None of this is good. Ryder *raped* her, Sienna."

"Don't say that! Someone might hear you."

"No one is here."

"Don't even say it out loud."

"This is wrong. You know it as well as I do."

"How is it wrong to protect someone we grew up with from someone we don't even know?"

"He did this to *her*, not the other way around."

"She must've done something to make him want to."

"Sienna…" Did I ever know her at all? "Rape is never the fault of the victim. Tell me you know that."

"How do we know they haven't been getting busy before now? Maybe that's how she likes it. A little rough."

I'm even more nauseated now than I was before. "I have to go."

"You can't say anything. You promised me you wouldn't."

I want to tell her to fuck off and to hell with whatever promise she thinks I made.

"Blaise… Tell me you understand that you can't say anything. No one would believe it."

"They would if we both said something."

"I never will. Not now or ever."

"How can you act like you didn't witness a crime?"

Her harsh laughter hits like a knife to my chest. "A *crime*? What the hell are you talking about? Two horny teenagers got busy in the woods, and you want to call it a *crime*?"

"That's what this was, and you know it."

"I'll deny I was there. If you say anything, I'll deny it."

"How can you care so little for what happened to her?"

"She's nothing to me."

I'm disgusted by her. While I've always known she could be a bit shallow, this is taking it to a whole new level. "She's a human being."

"We grew up with him. He's one of us. She isn't. It's not even worth debating. Besides, if she's smart, she'll keep her mouth shut about it. People already hate her. If she tries to go after Ryder, that won't go well for her."

"Unless a witness backed up her story."

"You wouldn't dare."

I have nothing to say to that.

"Tell me you won't say anything, Blaise. You'll ruin everything if you do! Don't you care about me at all? What will Cam say if my best friend accuses his brother of a crime?"

"His brother committed a crime!"

"It'd be her word against his, and no one will believe her. Everyone knows he's madly in love with Louisa."

"If that's true, why did he attack Neisy?"

"Who knows what she said to drive him over the edge? He's been so stressed out over Louisa. Maybe Neisy's been coming on to him for weeks for all we know. She might've had it coming."

I gasp, disgusted by my so-called best friend. "How can you say that? No one deserves to be raped, Sienna."

"You've seen how she acts around the boys. She's always teasing them and flirting with them."

"She could strut naked in front of them, and she still wouldn't deserve to be raped."

"I'm done talking about this. Keep your mouth shut or else."

"Or else what?"

"Or else there'll be trouble when everyone hates you for taking her side over Ryder's."

The phone goes dead.

I can't believe she hung up on me or the things she said.

Intense nausea has me running for the bathroom in the hallway, where I'm seized again by dry heaves. There's nothing left in my stomach but bile that burns my throat and mouth. I thought I felt as awful as it was possible to feel after my grandfather died last year. As bad as that was, it was nothing compared to this.

I hate that Sienna is right. If I say anything or come to Neisy's defense, my life won't be worth living in this town. Everyone will hate me, even the parents who've always thought of me as a good kid. No one will want to hear that Ryder attacked and sexually assaulted Neisy. And even if I came forward to back her story, no one would believe us.

Ryder is the son everyone wishes they had. When I worked at McChord's grocery last summer, I heard people say that. He'll graduate at the top of our class next June. He's the star of multiple teams and in line for an appointment to the Naval Academy. What must it be like, one of the ladies who worked with me in the deli asked, to have a son so successful at such a young age? She'd joked that her son had barely made it out of tenth grade.

Every part of me trembles as I ponder the implications of doing the right thing.

Everyone would hate me, even my own brother.

I drop my head to my knees as sobs rip from my chest.

If you'd asked me before yesterday if I was the kind of person who'd always do the right thing, I would've said absolutely.

Now I know there's no such thing as absolutes.

I hate myself as much as I hate Ryder and Sienna. I hate knowing that kids I grew up with and considered friends are capable of such things.

More than anything, I hate knowing I'll have to live with what I saw forever. I hate that a young woman is suffering after being the victim of a hideous crime, and there's not a damned thing I can do about it without ruining my own life.

Chapter 4

Neisy
THEN

THE LAST FEW WEEKS have been bad. I can barely get out of bed. I got fired from my job at the restaurant my mom's cousin owns because I missed too many shifts. For the first time ever, I'm thankful to have an alcoholic mother who's so self-absorbed she barely notices me.

However, my dad is due home later today, and he'll see what my mom has missed. He and I have always shared a tight connection, and even though I've answered all his daily texts while he was away, he'll take one look at me and know something is very wrong.

Part of me hopes he can tell that a terrible thing has happened.

The other part dreads him knowing.

What will I say to him when he demands to know what's wrong?

He's well aware that life has been hard for me here and it was probably a mistake to let my mom talk him into moving me to her hometown for my last two years of high school while he's stationed in DC. My mother hated it there like I hate it here.

I miss the friends I had in Virginia, who I'm still in touch with and hope to join in college at the University of Virginia after one more very long year in Rhode Island.

I yearn for Kane, who's deeply concerned about me. Even with an ocean between us, he can tell I'm not myself and keeps asking what's wrong. Last night he asked by text if I've met someone else and am afraid to tell him.

No! I replied. *Just the same old shit with this place. It's definitely not you.*

You're the one bright spot in my whole life.

I wish you didn't have to stay there. Why can't you go back to DC with your dad and go to your old school?

Because he's too busy to keep tabs on a teenager, or so he says. He works like 12 hours a day.

Still, you'd be better off there than where you are.

Not going to happen. I lost that battle a year ago when they insisted on moving here.

They'd had concerns about the "fast" crowd I was running with in Virginia. I tried to tell them they were wrong about my friends, that we were average teenagers. They didn't buy it. When my dad sided with my mom over the move to RI, I didn't speak to him for a month.

I could tell that really upset him, but not enough to change his mind.

If he ever knew what'd happened with Ryder, he'd lose his mind.

He can't ever know.

In anticipation of his arrival at some point today, I force myself out of bed and into the shower. For the first time in weeks, I work on my appearance by blow-drying my hair and putting on a bit of makeup to hide the dark circles under my eyes. I stare at the reflection in the mirror, as if I'm looking at a stranger. Who is that girl after what happened to her?

The injustice burns in my gut. I'm devastated, and he's off living his golden life like nothing has changed. I saw on Facebook that he hosted his annual fundraiser for Louisa's family, which attracted a massive crowd and raised close to one hundred thousand dollars. He posted photos of himself smiling widely, his arm around his beautiful, frail girlfriend as their parents stood on either side of them.

His hypocrisy makes me sick.

Did he decide to attack me because she's not able to have sex with him? Did he pick me because he knows people hate me, and I wouldn't dare speak out against him?

Kane and I had been waiting to have sex until he comes to visit next month, which is another thing Ryder took from me—my first time with someone I truly love. Now I can't imagine doing that with Kane or anyone.

Ever.

What used to be something I looked forward to with anticipation and a tiny bit of fear is now something to be avoided at all costs.

I want Ryder to pay for what he took from me.

I'm angry, hurt and terrified he might've gotten me pregnant. My period is due in two days, and if it doesn't show up on time, I don't know what I'll do.

A couple of hours later, I'm pretending to read a book while lying on top of my bed, which is made for the first time in weeks, when my dad appears in the doorway.

"There's my baby girl."

"Hey, Dad." I get up to greet him with a hug. He's tall, dark and handsome, which is how my mother always describes him.

The minute I catch a hint of his familiar scent as he hugs me I want to break down and tell him the whole sordid story.

But I can't.

I just can't.

"How's my favorite daughter?"

"Still your only daughter, that I know of."

The back and forth with him is one of the best things in my life.

His smile fades a bit. "How's your mom been?"

"A little worse than usual."

"How's that possible?"

"I'm not sure."

He runs his fingers through his hair, which he does whenever he's annoyed or frustrated. I'm sure he's both when it comes to her. "I have to get her into a program somewhere."

"There's no point in that until she's ready for it."

We've done the research. A year ago, we had a local facility ready to take her for three weeks of intensive in-patient treatment, but she refused to go. We found out we couldn't make her go. She has rights.

What about our rights, my dad asked at the time.

"Ronnie called the other day."

My stomach sinks. "He called *you*?"

Ronnie is my mother's first cousin. He owns the restaurant where I used to work.

"He was worried about you when you stopped coming to work." He leans against the doorframe. "Your mom wasn't answering his calls, and you were vague about what's going on. You didn't tell me you quit your job. I thought you liked it there."

"I do. I mean I did."

"What happened?"

"I wasn't feeling well for a couple of days, and Ronnie got mad when I called out."

"He said you never called out. You just didn't show, which isn't like you either."

Fuck, fuck, fuck. I didn't think Ronnie would reach out to him.

"I've been a little down the last few weeks."

Hearing that, he straightens out of the slouch he was in. "Like before?"

"Maybe. A little."

I had a depressive episode, as it was called at the time, in seventh grade. After more than a year of intensive counseling and medication that I still take, I started to feel like myself again.

"We have to get that checked. You might need a different dosage now that you're older. I'll make an appointment for you at the navy clinic."

"Thanks, Dad."

"You should've told me about this, Neise."

"I didn't want you to worry when you're so busy."

"I'm never too busy for you, and you know that." He gives me a more intent look. "Are things any better with the kids in town?"

"Eh," I tell him. "It is what it is."

"I'm sorry this move has turned into such a mess for you, sweetheart. I hate that."

Oh, Daddy, you have no idea... "It's okay." I want to plead with him to take me back to DC with him, but he won't. Most of the time, he splits the month between the two places and would never leave me there alone when he has to be here. "It's only one more year. I can get through that."

Can I, though? How will I ever go back to Hope High School and have to see *him* in the hallways, acting as though nothing happened? For him, nothing did. For me, everything has changed, and he did that to me.

"Neise? Where'd you go?"

"Nowhere."

"I'm worried about you, sweetheart."

"No reason to be."

"Let me go make that appointment so we can get you feeling better."

"Okay."

TWO DAYS LATER, MY dad drives me to the navy clinic. I tried to talk him out of coming, but he insisted on driving me and said we can go to lunch afterward.

I realize he took time off for this and appreciate the attention, even if I'm scared I'll crumble in front of him and confess the whole story.

I want to.

I want to tell him.

I want to watch him go ballistic and make Ryder's charmed life into the living hell that mine has become.

Because that's what he'd do.

But then he'd have to hear how all the girls at school think I'm a slut simply because their boyfriends find me attractive. He'd learn how they say I screwed the varsity football team and have my gaze set on the basketball team next or whatever crazy bullshit they come up with.

The irony isn't lost on me. I was a virgin until Ryder stole that from me, but thanks to those viperous bitches, no one would believe that.

"Do you want me to come in with you, sweetie?" Dad asks when we're in the waiting room.

"No, that's okay. I'm sure it won't take long."

"Make sure you tell her how instrumental the meds were in making you feel better the first time this happened."

"I will."

"Okay. Text me if you need me."

"Denise?"

No one calls me that, so it's weird when someone does. I get up to follow the young, male medic into the clinic.

Thankfully, he leaves the door open when he weighs me and takes my blood pressure, otherwise, I would've told him to open it. I notice his gaze is trained on my breasts as he takes my pulse.

I'm tempted to tell him that my dad, the navy captain, would end him and his career if he saw him looking at me that way.

That's a thought I never would've had before Ryder raped me. I used to low-key enjoy the attention I got from boys and men. That was before I found out what they're capable of. Now I don't want any of them looking at me or imagining me naked or any of the other vile things they might be thinking.

"Dr. Cummings will be in shortly," he says on his way out the door.

I exhale a sigh of relief that he's gone and pray that Dr. Cummings is a woman. Military doctors cycle in and out of the clinic, so you never know who you might see.

I don't want men anywhere near me, even in a place like this, which is supposed to be safe.

Is anywhere safe?

Dr. Cummings is short, blonde and very pregnant. She wears her khaki uniform shirt untucked over her round belly. I glance at the gold insignia on her collar. Lieutenant commander. My dad would be proud. I knew all the ranks by the time I was six.

"Hi there, Denise. I'm Dr. Cummings." She goes to the sink to wash her hands. "How are you doing?"

"Fine."

She uses paper towels to dry her hands and then sits on a stool. "What brings you in today?"

"I've been feeling a little low lately."

"Has this happened before?"

"When I was twelve. I've been on meds for it ever since. My dad thought I might need to have the dose adjusted."

"Let me take a look at what you're on now." She clicks around on my chart and recites the name and current dosage for my prescription. "We could try another ten milligrams a day to see if that helps."

"Okay."

"Has there been any change in your diet or exercise in the last few weeks or anything else going on?"

I've barely eaten or left my room in three weeks, but I can't tell her that. "No."

Is she trained to know what happened just by looking at me? I want to run away, but if I do, where will I go? How will I explain my behavior to the doctor or my dad? I'm on the verge of hyperventilating, and all she's done is type some stuff into a computer.

"Are you all right?" she asks, her brows furrowed with concern.

"I'm just… nervous."

I want so badly to tell her the truth, but when I think of how evil those girls have been to me, I can't. No one would believe me, and things would only get worse than they already are.

"Take a few deep breaths and try to relax. We're just going to talk, okay?"

"Uh-huh."

"I have a routine questionnaire that goes over some basic things."

I answer a bunch of questions about my health—age of first period, most recent period and a full depression screening, which I've been through before. The questions bring back memories from when I was feeling so low I wondered how I could still be alive. I hadn't known then that it was possible to go even lower.

"Is there any chance you could be pregnant?"

I want to die on the spot. Can she tell if I am, and will she know if I'm lying?

"It's okay, Denise. You can talk to me."

As if a dam has burst, I start to cry so hard I can't breathe or think or do anything other than cry.

She stands by my side, holding my hand as the emotional tsunami overtakes me. I suppose it was only a matter of time before it broke.

"I'll get you some water." She hands me another tissue. "I'll be right back."

When she returns with a plastic cup of water, she rubs my back and holds the cup while I take some sips. "I'm sorry."

"Don't be. How can I help?"

"You can't. No one can."

"That's not true."

I release a bitter laugh as I mop up my tears with a third tissue. "In this case, it is."

"I've found that it helps to talk about whatever is weighing on you. When you share it with someone who can help, it takes some of the burden off your shoulders."

Her words settle over me like a warm blanket. I want so badly to tell someone, but I'm terrified of the consequences.

"Would you have to tell my dad whatever I say in here?"

"Absolutely not. It's between us, but I may encourage you to talk to him or someone else who can help you."

"Am I pregnant?"

"I can't say for certain without further testing."

A sob erupts from my chest as my worst fears come true. "Can you get pregnant the first time?"

"Yes."

That's not what I wanted to hear. I've been tempted to ask Google that question for weeks but was afraid of the answer. The health classes that covered such things were years ago now, and I can't remember the details. Besides, I've had no need to know those details before now.

"Are you in a relationship with someone?"

"Yes, but he lives in Spain."

She doesn't respond to that, probably hoping I'll say more.

"This… What happened… It wasn't…" I can't speak or breathe over the wave of emotion that jams my throat.

"Denise, were you raped?"

Here it is. The moment of truth. If I tell her, it'll never again be just my secret—and his. Someone else will know.

She continues to run her hand in soothing circles over my back. "You're in a safe place. Whatever you tell me will remain confidential unless you don't want it to."

"W…will you have to report it to the police?"

"Only if that's what you want me to do."

Another long moment of silence passes before I can't hold it back any longer. "I was raped. Three weeks ago."

"Do you know the person who assaulted you?"

I nod. "We go to school together." I can't believe the profound relief I feel at knowing someone else is aware of what happened to me.

"And it was your first time?"

"Y-yes."

"I'm so sorry that happened to you, Denise."

"My friends call me Neisy."

"Neisy." She provides more tissues as I need them. "Were you injured?"

"I think. Maybe. It hurt for a long time after."

"Would you consent to an exam so I can check to make sure you've healed properly?"

"I don't… I don't think I can do that."

"That's fine. It can wait."

"Wh-what should I do?"

"I can't tell you that."

"What would you do?"

"I'd want him to pay for what he did to me."

"No one would believe me. He's everyone's best friend, a star athlete and student. He's supported his longtime girlfriend through cancer treatment. I'm new to the school as of last year, and they all hate me. It would be my word against his."

"If you're pregnant, the baby's DNA would back up your story."

I hadn't thought of that, and for the first time, I feel a spark of hope that I might get justice for what was done to me. But then I consider what'll happen if I accuse Ryder Elliott of raping me, and I shrivel into a ball of dread.

"I can't report it. I just can't. It would be a nightmare."

"You're the victim of a crime, Neisy, a crime that wasn't your fault in any way."

"The girls in my school would say I was asking for it. They decided on day one that I was a slut, and they've been awful saying things about me ever since."

"I'm sorry you've had to deal with that."

I shrug. "Most of the time, I don't care what they say because I know the truth. But this…this would be different. They grew up with him. They'd defend him and say it was impossible. They'd make me out to be a whore, and say I had it coming." I shudder just thinking about it.

"All those things might happen, but you'd force him to defend himself against the charges in court. Even if he's acquitted, the accusation would stay with him forever. You may also find you're not the only one he's attacked."

That possibility has never occurred to me.

"Or, you may be the first but not the last."

A surge of bile from my stomach burns my throat and makes me gag.

She hands me the cup of water, and I take several careful sips.

Someone knocks on the door.

She goes to answer it.

"Your patient's father is asking if everything is okay."

"Tell him we need a few more minutes."

"Will do."

She closes the door and leans back against it. "If you'd like, I can run a pregnancy test, so we'd know for sure one way or the other."

"What does that involve?"

"A urine sample."

"Um, okay. I guess so."

"Take a minute and then meet me in my office across the hall. I'll have everything ready for you."

"Can I ask you something?"

"Anything."

"If I'm pregnant, do I have to discontinue my medication?"

"No, we don't recommend that."

"Oh, good. Okay."

"I'll be right across the hall."

After she leaves the room, I go to the sink and splash some cold water on my face. Then I take two full minutes to breathe before I open the door and cross the hall to her office.

"Do you know how to do a urine sample?"

I nod. "I had bladder infections when I was younger."

She hands me the antiseptic wipe and the container. "The rest room is two doors down on the left. I'll wait for you here."

The possibility that I could be pregnant is too big to consider.

What if Kane doesn't believe I was raped and thinks I cheated on him? How will I ever tell him about any of this? Will he still love me when he finds out? The possibility that he won't is more than I can handle. He's been my rock and very best friend through everything for the last four years. Even with an ocean between us, we're still best friends.

I love him.

I cannot lose him.

Tears slide down my cheeks as I go through the motions of providing the sample.

I wash my hands and gasp at my ravaged reflection in the mirror.

My dad will know something terrible has happened.

One thing at a time, Neisy.

I deliver the sample to the doctor.

"Have a seat. I'll be right back."

When she returns ten minutes later, I can tell by her expression the test was positive.

My heart sinks as I'm filled with despair. "What do I do now?"

"That's entirely up to you."

"How can it be up to me? I don't know what the hell to do about any of this."

"Would your dad be willing to help?"

"He'll die if he hears I'm pregnant, and then he'll want to kill the person who did this."

"He won't, though."

"I don't know. He might."

"I have two other children, and in this situation, my first thought would be for the well-being of my child and making sure she has whatever support she needs to get through this."

"What if he doesn't believe me about how it happened?"

"Why wouldn't he? Have you lied to him before?"

"Once. In fifth grade. I said I wasn't there when kids were making crank calls, but they had my voice on a recording. It took a long time for him to get past that."

"You were much younger then. Have you lied to him since?"

"Not once ever. I was so sad that he was disappointed in me the first time. I never want him to feel that way again."

"I'm sure he's seen the effort you've made to be truthful."

Shrugging, I say, "I guess. He's often gone on deployment and stuff."

"What about your mom?"

"She has some problems. She, um… She drinks. A lot."

"I see."

"You'd never tell her I said that, would you?"

"Never. Our conversations are confidential."

"Oh, okay. Thanks. That would make her mad. She doesn't like to talk about it."

"Do you want me to ask your dad to come in so we can talk to him together?"

"You'd do that?"

"Of course. Whatever you need, Neisy. I'm here for you."

"You must have other patients." I'm looking for any reason I can find to avoid having to tell my dad. "They're waiting for you."

"I asked my colleagues to cover for me, so I could help you."

Her kindness has me in tears again. "That's very nice of you."

"It's no problem."

I'm sure that's not true, but I appreciate the kindness that gives me the courage to take the next step. "I guess I have to tell my dad at some point." It may as well be with the doctor there to help me.

"I'll ask him to come in."

"Will you…will you ask him not to freak out? That won't help."

"I'll do that."

She leaves the room and a few minutes later I hear the murmur of voices in the hallway, one of which I recognize as my dad's.

"What's the matter with her?" he asks, his voice louder now.

"She'd like to speak to you about something upsetting, and she's asked that you refrain from reacting until she's told you everything."

"What the hell? Where is she?"

"Right this way."

The doctor comes in, followed by my dad, who stops short at the sight of my red, puffy face.

"Neise. Honey. What's going on?"

"Would you please have a seat, Captain Sutton?"

He doesn't want to, but he takes the seat next to mine and reaches for my hand. "Whatever it is, honey, we'll work it out."

That sends more tears spilling down my cheeks.

"Sweetheart, you're scaring me. What's wrong?"

I look to the doctor, who nods in encouragement.

"A few weeks ago," I say softly, "I went to a party in Land's End with some kids from school. It was at Houston's house. Remember him from the restaurant?"

"Sure, I do. He's a nice kid."

"Yes, he is. Normally I don't go to stuff like that because, well, you know… But he's my friend, and I wanted to go." I take a tissue from the box the doctor pushes across her desk to me and wipe my eyes. "While I was there, another kid I know from school said he wanted to talk to me about his girlfriend, who I know from a class last year. She's been really sick, and I wanted to hear about how she's doing. I went with him down this path away from the others. I, um… He said some things about how I look at him, which weren't true. Then he pushed me down and—"

"Oh no," Dad says on a long gasp. "Neisy."

"I'm so sorry, Daddy." Sobs shake my body. "I swear I never did anything to encourage him."

His arms are around me so fast I hardly seem them coming. "Shhh, it's not your fault. You did nothing wrong."

As I breathe in his familiar scent and wallow in the warmth of his embrace, I'm relieved all over again because he knows, and he believes me.

"Who is it?"

"I don't want to tell you that."

"Denise is afraid you might harm him."

"I swear on your life I won't harm him physically."

I'm well aware there's nothing he could say that would mean more. I've always known I'm the most important thing in his life. "Ryder Elliott."

"The football player?" He sounds as shocked as I felt when it happened.

"Yeah."

To the doctor, he says, "Are you required to report this?"

"Not without Denise's consent, and her concern is that it would be her word against his. It happened weeks ago."

"So there's no evidence."

"There may be one piece of evidence." She looks to me to confirm that.

He pulls back so he can see my face. "What evidence?"

"I'm pregnant."

For the rest of my life, I'll never forget the expression on his face when that sentence registers. It's a look of complete shock I've never seen before or since.

"Pregnant."

"Yes," the doctor says, "and the baby's DNA could be used to confirm Denise's claim from about nine to twelve weeks of pregnancy onward."

Dad drops his head into his hands.

"I'm so sorry, Daddy."

He pulls himself together and looks at me with a fierce expression. "I don't want you to be sorry. This was done to you, and I'll take care of it."

"How?"

"That's not for you to worry about."

"Yes, it is! This is my life. You can't just go rogue and cut me out of it."

"I'll have a talk with Ryder's father to start with."

"If I may…"

He looks up at the doctor.

"I'd suggest you talk to the police first, but only if Denise agrees with that plan."

They both look to me.

Here it is. Another moment of truth. If I go public with these accusations, I'll be vilified like I've never been before.

But how will that be different than how they treat me now? It won't be. Houston is the only true friend I've made here, and he just graduated from college and got a job as a police officer outside of Boston. He won't be around to help me navigate my last year of high school or anything else after this blows up.

It's up to me.

Do I want Ryder to pay for what he did to me?

Hell yes.

Do I care about the consequences?

Not as much as I probably should.

"I think I'd like to report it to the police."

"Then that's what we'll do," Dad says.

Chapter 5

Blaise
THEN

I'M HALF ASLEEP WHEN my phone blows up with texts at about ten thirty. Everyone I know is asking if I heard the news about Neisy accusing Ryder of raping her.

I sit up in bed and scroll through the texts before switching over to Facebook where girls from school are already calling her a liar.

There's no way Ryder would touch her, Brooke says in an emotionally charged post. *Everyone knows he's in love with Louisa and has never looked at another girl the whole time they've been together. Neisy is lying. Don't believe her. Ryder is innocent!*

My brother is innocent of these vile charges, Cam writes. *Don't believe everything you hear from people who are always looking for attention. #JusticeforRyder*

Seriously? Sienna writes. *She must be delusional to think he'd go anywhere near her. #JusticeforRyder*

Her words hit me like a spike to the heart. She *knows* Neisy is telling the truth, but is publicly backing Ryder, even after what she saw him do.

I'm sick all over again, like I was when it first happened, especially as other kids weigh in with cruel words about Neisy.

The door to my room bursts open, and Arlo comes in looking wild eyed. "Did you hear?"

"Yes."

"What the actual fuck does she think she's doing?"

"I, uh, I don't know." I want so badly to tell him I saw it.

For years, I'll wonder why I didn't.

In the moment, I can't get words that would change everything for both of us past the boulder in my throat.

"She's full of shit! Everyone knows how he feels about Louisa. God, what she must be thinking. Did you hear Louisa is going into hospice? She's not responding to the treatment, and there's nothing more the doctors can do for her. Like she and Ryder don't have enough to deal with."

My heart sinks. "I hadn't heard. That's terrible."

"I honestly don't know how much more they can take. Cam says Neisy's dad is raising hell with the police, demanding they arrest Ryder."

"Are they going to?"

"I'm not sure. I heard there may be some sort of evidence, but I don't believe it. I'll never believe it." He looks at me now with fire in his eyes. "We'll defend him every way we can, starting with a rally at the school tomorrow for everyone who believes in him. There's no way we'll let someone like her ruin him. I'll let you know the details when I have them."

Arlo is gone as fast as he came with things to do in support of his best friend.

I run to the bathroom to vomit, which has happened almost every day since that night. I've lost thirteen pounds I didn't have to lose, and my mom is asking what's wrong.

Everything is wrong.

Every single thing.

I don't know how to live with this knowledge I can do nothing with. If I tell the truth, everyone will hate me, including my own brother and now-ex best friend. I haven't heard a word from Sienna since the night she called and told me again to keep my mouth shut or else. That's fine because her behavior is revolting to me, but I miss having someone to talk to, especially right now. There's certainly no one else I can talk to about this.

I've thought about going to Teagan. There was a time, not that long ago, when we were close. That was before she decided that being a rebel was more important than being a good sister. She barely gives me the time of day now, but if I went to her and told her what happened, I have to believe she'd be there for me.

But what if she isn't? What if she turns on me and calls me a liar or tells people I made up some crazy story about Ryder? Then what?

I can't take the chance. I have one more year to get through at HHS, and being a social pariah is not how I want to spend my senior year.

Just that quickly, my thoughts return to Neisy and what she must be going through. I feel sick again. I wish I was strong enough to sacrifice myself and my relationships with family and friends, not to mention the trouble I'd be in if I confess to where I was that night, to do the right thing.

I'm not.

A good person would speak up, would tell the truth regardless of the consequences for herself. My soul is heavy with the realization that I'm not a good person like I always thought I was. Prior to this, it never once occurred to me that I might witness a violent crime and tell no one what I saw.

I wonder why Neisy decided to report it so many weeks after the fact. Did something else happen? And how did her dad find out? I hope the police arrest Ryder. That would make me feel much better, even if it would still be her word against his. Arlo said something about evidence. I'd love to know what that is.

Nothing would make me happier than to see her prevail against him.

I pick up my phone when I get back to my room to scroll through the vitriol online, all of it directed at the outsider who's accused one of our own of an unspeakable crime.

The comments are one hundred percent in favor of him and the outsized role he's played in our class and our lives. He's been our class president since we were in eighth grade, not to mention his many victories on the field and in the classroom.

Everyone knows now that he's bound for a career as a naval officer.

Will Neisy's accusations derail his appointment?

Teagan knocks once before she walks into my room. "Do you know this girl who's accusing Ryder?"

Those are the first words she's said to me in days.

"A little. She's in our class."

"You think he could've done it?"

I shrug, having already decided I can't trust her.

"He's probably all pent up because Louisa's been sick for so long."

"That's disgusting, Teagan."

"It's true. I wouldn't be surprised if he was getting busy with a lot of people behind her back."

"Rape isn't getting busy."

"So you think he did it?"

"How would I know?"

"He didn't do it, Teagan," Arlo shouts from behind her. "And I'd better never hear you say that again."

"Take it easy, little brother. I was simply asking Blaise what she thinks."

"It doesn't matter what anyone thinks. *I know him.* I know the truth. Anyone who says otherwise is dead to me, you hear me?"

"I hear you," Teagan says in a blasé tone. "What do I care anyway? He's nothing to me."

"He's my *best friend*, and this could ruin his life. So excuse me if I care."

"What's going on?" Mom asks from the hallway.

Arlo glares at our sister. "Teagan is talking out her ass about things she knows nothing about."

"Shut up, Arlo. I simply asked Blaise if she thought he did it."

"And I simply said to shut your mouth."

"That's enough, Teagan. This is upsetting for Arlo and Blaise. They're friends with Ryder."

"I'm not." It's important to me to put that out there to anyone who'll listen.

Arlo looks at me with disbelief. "You grew up with him, Blaise. You may not be best friends with him, but you're obligated to defend him against an outsider who'd try to ruin his life."

"No one is obligated to do anything, Arlo," Mom says. "You do what you need to, and Blaise can do what she wants."

"You've preached to us about loyalty all our lives, Mom." Arlo is on the verge of tears. "He's *one of us.* He practically grew up in this house. How can anyone doubt him for a second?"

"I don't doubt him," Mom says, "but I also don't know him as well as you do, so you can't expect me to be as certain as you are."

"You know him! You helped to raise him and Cam the same way his parents helped to raise me."

"Indeed I did, but I have no idea how he behaves when the parents aren't looking."

I want to give that statement a fist bump. Rather, I roll my hands into fists and give the bump in my head.

"I can't believe this," Arlo says. "I'm very disappointed in you guys."

"You need to take a deep breath, Arlo," Mom says, "and think about why this young woman would say such a thing if it wasn't true. What does she stand to gain?"

"Revenge." Arlo's low, sinister tone sends a chill down my spine. "People have treated her shitty since she showed up at school out of nowhere, and this is her way of making us pay."

The three of us stare at him aghast.

"That's insane," Mom says. "This will ruin her life right along with his. Why would she put herself through accusing him of such a thing simply to exact revenge on people who were disparaging to her?"

"Because she knows by now what he means to us," Arlo says fiercely. "If you guys can't support him the same way you would if this were happening to me, then I've got nothing else to say to you."

He storms off toward his room, slamming the door closed.

"He's right," Teagan says. "Ryder did grow up in this house, and we owe him our support and loyalty."

Mom doesn't seem so sure, but she doesn't say so.

Teagan goes to her room and closes the door.

"I want to talk to you." Mom comes into my room and closes the door. "What's going on, Blaise? And don't say it's nothing. You've barely left your room except to go to work, and you're not eating. You know how I feel about that."

She battled anorexia as a teenager and has been vigilant with us.

"I've just been feeling off lately," I tell her. "I'm not sure why."

"If you don't start eating and participating in life again, I'm getting the doctor involved. Even Junie is worried about you. I won't allow this to happen to one of my girls. Do you hear me?"

"I do. I'm sorry to worry you." And I'm sorry to hear my little sister is concerned about me.

Mom kisses my forehead. "You've never given me a moment's worry. Don't start now, okay?"

I force a smile. "Okay."

"Love you, sweet girl."

"Love you, too, Mama."

"Get some rest. I'll see you in the morning."

After she leaves, I get back in bed and return to scrolling, reading one nasty comment after another about Neisy, her motives, her reputation as a slut and every other hideous thing people can think of to say about her.

I always knew she'd do something like this, one of the mean girls named Abby writes. *You could see it coming a mile away. She picked the wrong crew to mess with. We've got your back, Ryder. #JusticeforRyder*

My heart aches for Neisy.

I wish I had someone to tell me what to do.

I could go to a school counselor or therapist, but I remember a unit we had on the role of counselors in seventh or eighth grade. They'd be obligated by law to report that I witnessed a crime, so that's not an option.

There's no one I could talk to who would keep this information confidential, and since I couldn't bear for everyone I know to hate me more than I already hate myself, I have to stay quiet.

Even if it kills me.

Neisy
THEN

NOTHING IN MY LIFE, even the hell of the past year, could've prepared me for what happens after we report the attack to the police. Before I have the chance to tell Kane what's going on, my phone blows up with texts from numbers I don't recognize, calling me everything from a whore to a liar and threatening harm to me and my family.

One of them encourages me to kill myself before someone else can do it for me.

My dad reports the threats to the police.

They bring Ryder in for questioning and release him when they realize this is a matter of his word against mine. He denies he attacked me and claims I'd been coming on to him for months, and that he's far more concerned about his girlfriend's declining health than he is about seeing other girls.

Facebook is on fire with how I lured him away from Louisa during her time of need, which makes me even more of a whore than I was before.

My mother's closest cousins, who are friends with the Elliotts, text to tell her she and I are dead to them after this and how dare I make up such a lie about Ryder. Mom has been drunk for days since she got that text.

I feel oddly removed from it all, like I'm floating above the fray watching it happen to someone else. If there's any good news, my dad has agreed that I can never go back to Hope High School after this. He said he's working out a plan for me to return to my old school in Virginia for my senior year. Although even that might not be possible as I'm sure word of my troubles here will follow me wherever I go.

And then there's the matter of the baby I'm carrying, which will prove I didn't lie about what Ryder did to me once I get to the nine- or ten-week mark. I don't want to think about what will be involved in getting DNA from a baby in utero.

Kane texts me overnight. *Neisy… What the hell is happening?*

Can you talk?

Yes.

I call him on Skype, which allows us to talk for free.

"Hey," he says. "Are you all right?"

I love that that's his first question.

"I've been better."

"Neise… Why didn't you tell me?"

He looks heartbroken.

Tears flood my eyes and spill down my cheeks. "I didn't tell anyone."

"I'm not anyone."

"I thought you'd be mad."

"What? *Why?* You didn't do anything wrong."

"Maybe I did. Maybe I did tempt him and—"

"Neisy, no. Absolutely not. He did this to you. Are you… I mean, were you hurt?"

"For a while. But I'm better now. There's something else I should tell you…" I feel like I'm going to hyperventilate. "I, um, I'm pregnant."

"Oh, honey. Oh, no."

"It's actually a good thing. The baby's DNA will help to prove I'm not lying about him attacking me."

"I'm so, so sorry this happened to you. I want to come there and strangle him."

"I can't wait to see you, but no strangling." I hiccup on a sob. "Do you…"

"What, sweetheart?"

"Do you still love me after hearing about this?"

"I'll love you forever and ever amen."

We've been saying that to each other for years, and hearing it now breaks me. "It was supposed to be you," I say between sobs. "Y- you were supposed to be my first."

"And I will be. What he did doesn't count."

I'm crying so hard I can't speak.

"Shhh, it's okay. Everything is all right."

"It's not."

"It will be."

I don't know if that's true. I feel like nothing will ever be all right again. "I'm sorry I didn't tell you."

"Don't be. You were traumatized."

"I'm not sure this is the best time for you to visit. Everything is a mess."

"That makes it the best time for me to come and support you. I've been so worried. I knew something wasn't right. I thought maybe you'd met someone you like better."

"That'll never happen."

"You're all I think about, all I want, all I need. I can't wait to see you."

"Even now that you know I'm an emotional wreck?"

"Especially now."

"I'm worried my dad will do something that'll get him in trouble. He's so angry."

"He won't. He's too smart for that."

"I don't know… I've never seen him so worked up. And he's outraged that my mother didn't realize something was wrong while he was away. I heard him tell her he's had it with her and her drinking and her obliviousness. He told her if she doesn't get help—soon—he's leaving her and taking me with him."

"That's been coming for a while, though, right?"

"I guess. He's just so angry that this happened when I was home alone with her, and she didn't notice anything was wrong. There's been a lot of yelling."

"I'm sorry it's been such an awful summer. I'll be there soon to do what I can to make it better for you."

"I was so afraid you'd hate me for this."

"Never. I love you more than ever. Hang tough. We'll get through this together. I promise."

We talk for a while longer about a vacation he took with his family to the south of France and a visit with his cousins who came from San Diego.

It's a relief to think about something other than my own situation for a few minutes, but the second we say goodbye for now, I'm right back in hell. My boobs ache, and I'm nauseated. I've read that both are normal in early pregnancy, but nothing about this pregnancy is normal.

A knock at the door has me sitting up in bed. "Come in."

My dad comes in and shuts the door. He looks like hell, as if he hasn't slept in days. His face is haggard from the strain, and his chin covered in scruff I've rarely seen on him. He's always clean shaven and squared away, so it's upsetting to see him this way. "Were you talking to Kane?"

"Yeah, I finally told him everything."

Dad sits on the end of my bed. "How'd he take it?"

"He's upset, of course, but he said all the right things."

"I'm glad you have his support. Is he still coming next week?"

"That's the plan."

"I've been thinking…about the baby." His expression is gut wrenching.

"What about it?"

"It's not right that you should have to carry a baby conceived this way. If you want to seek out alternatives, I'd support whatever you decided to do."

I've heard both my parents say that abortion isn't something they would've chosen to do, but they'd never make that decision for someone else. So I know it's a big deal for him to present that option to me.

"Would we still be able to check the baby's DNA if we did that?"

"Yes, I believe so. I just want you to have all the options. In the end, it's your decision."

"Thank you for the support."

"I feel sick that you were alone with this for weeks, Neise. You should've called me. I would've come right home."

"I knew that. I needed some time to process it. I keep going over it and over it, looking for the point when he might've thought it was okay to do what he did. He said he wanted to talk to me about Louisa, so I went with him, away from the others. It never occurred to me…"

Dad's warm hand lands on my cold one. I'm cold all the time lately. "You didn't do anything to encourage him. Nor did you do anything to deserve what he did. A real man doesn't attack a woman and force her to have sex with him."

"Daddy…" I squirm as his hand clamping down on mine starts to hurt.

He immediately releases me. "I'm sorry, baby. I'm just so upset. I want to go over there and wrap my hands around his neck and show him what happens to animals who rape women."

"Please don't do that or anything like it. We have to let the police handle this. Don't risk your career and your pension over him. He's not worth it."

"I heard he's up for a commission to the Naval Academy. I can sure as hell do something about that. We don't need his kind in the navy."

"Promise me you won't go to his house."

He looks down at the floor, seeming to wage some sort of private battle. "I want to kill him for hurting you."

"I know, and that means everything to me, but please, Dad. Promise me you won't do anything to make this worse."

After a long pause, he says, "I won't do anything to physically harm him, but I'll do everything within my power to make sure he pays for what he did to you."

Chapter 6

Camden
THEN

EVEN WITH A FULL day to absorb the news, I can't believe it. Neisy Sutton has accused Ryder of raping her. As if Ryder would ever do something like that, especially since he's madly in love with Louisa and has been for as long as anyone can remember.

The police have asked Ryder to come in for another interview.

My parents are losing their minds. They've called in a high-powered attorney from Boston, who advised Ryder to stay away from the police station.

"You don't want to give them a chance to trap you into saying something that isn't true," the lawyer said when he came to the house earlier. "Let me handle the police. You sit tight and don't talk to anyone."

"He has football practice," Dad says. "He's a team captain. He can't miss it."

"Go to practice," the lawyer says, "and come straight home. Don't discuss the case with *anyone*. I need you tell me you understand me when I say *no one*."

"I get it," Ryder says.

"You have to make this go away." Mom sounds frantic. "That someone could accuse him of such a heinous crime... His entire future is at stake."

"I'm well aware of what's at stake, Mrs. Elliott. I'll do what I can."

The lawyer goes through everything about the night in question, writing down the names of friends who can attest that Ryder was at

Houston's party, that he didn't go near Neisy, that what she's accusing him of couldn't be possible.

The party was weeks ago. Details are difficult to recall. So much has happened since then—Louisa's entrance into hospice care and the associated trauma, gatherings with friends, Fourth of July celebrations, two-a-day football practices.

The lawyer asks Ryder to recount every conversation he's ever had with Neisy, which is three that he recalls, all in passing.

"Did you ever hit on her, ask her out, say anything inappropriate to her or about her to someone else?"

"No, never. I have a girlfriend. We've been together since middle school."

I ache for him and for Louisa, who has enough to handle after hearing there isn't anything more that can be done for her. I can't imagine life without her. I can't begin to know how Ryder must feel. The news devastated him, and that was before the police came to the door.

The lawyer leaves, promising to be in touch shortly.

Mom and Dad are shattered, and Ryder... He's pale as a ghost and shaking.

I tip my head, telling him to come with me. We go outside to the backyard oasis my parents put such care into creating. We love being out here, but it brings no comfort to us now. Both our older sisters, who live out of state, have been texting nonstop since the news broke online.

"What can I do?" I ask my brother, my closest friend and confidant.

"I don't know."

"You want a drink?"

He shakes his head. He never drinks during football season, but there's a first time for everything.

We sit in the Adirondack chairs that encircle the stone firepit Dad built himself.

"If you want to talk, you know I'm always here."

"I do. I know that."

"The girls were right about Neisy. She's been trouble from the get-go."

Ryder stares straight ahead, transfixed the way he would've been if a fire had been lit.

I ache for him. I'd give anything to make this go away. Both our phones are buzzing with texts we ignore. Our friends are rallying around us, offering whatever help they can, expressing their shock and disbelief.

No one believes her.

They grew up with Ryder. They know him. They know he'd never do something like what she's accused him of.

"Cam."

"Yeah?"

"I need to tell you something."

"Okay."

"You have to take it to your grave."

"What is it?"

"Swear to me. No matter what happens, this stays between us."

"You have my word."

He says nothing for the longest time as his foot pokes at the grass. "What she said…"

Everything around us goes quiet. Even the crickets are silent.

I hold my breath, equal parts interested in whatever he has to say and terrified of how it will change everything.

"It happened like she said."

The whooshing sound inside my head is like a tsunami overtaking me as I struggle to process the words, the implications, the horror…

"Ryder, no. You wouldn't have done that."

"I wasn't in my right mind. I'd heard about Louisa going into hospice. I mean after all this time, the war she'd fought, that we'd fought, she was still going to die? I'd been drinking all day, ever since I heard that news. Everything was a mixed-up mess, and Neisy was just there, you know? No one likes her… I don't even know how it happened. It just did."

"You…you raped her?"

"I didn't mean to. She's always looking at me like she's interested, so I asked her if we could talk, and one thing led to another. It was like I was possessed or something. Louisa has been so sick… I haven't been with her in a long time. Tell me you understand."

I don't. I don't understand. He could have any girl he wanted. He doesn't have to attack anyone.

"Camden, please. Tell me you get it. I wasn't myself after hearing about Louisa. She's going to *die*." He sounds desperate and unhinged— and he's using my full name. I've never seen him like this. He's the one who's always in control. I'm the emotional one. "I need you."

The weight of his confession is already unbearable, and I've only known for a few minutes. I want to go back to before we came out here, before he unloaded on me. "Why'd you tell me this?"

"I needed someone to know. I feel sick about it."

I feel sick, too. "Because you did it or because she's got the cops involved?"

"Because it happened in the first place!" He tears at his hair as he breaks down. "That girl has driven me mad since the first day she showed up at school."

That's another thing I'd rather not know. "Wh...what about Louisa?"

He looks up at me, torment etched into his tearful expression. "I love her more than anything or anyone. I always will. But her illness... It's been a lot. The not knowing what's going to happen, and then hearing that after everything she's been through, that *we've* been through, she's still going to die... I was drunk and devastated, and I fucking snapped. That's the only explanation I have. You've got to help me, Cam. I don't know who else to turn to. The guilt is eating me up inside. That I cheated on Louisa. That I hurt Neisy. That any of this happened in the first place." He drops his head into his hands. "I don't know why it happened."

I swallow hard. I'm seventeen years old. He's a year older—a legal adult who'd do hard time for a crime like this. I have no idea what to do with this information or how to help him. I want to beat the shit out of him for doing something that could ruin all of us. Our parents are stressing out about having to get another mortgage on the house to pay for the attorney on top of college tuition for four kids. And then to find out he *did* attack Neisy... Jesus. I swallow the bile that surges into my throat.

"Camden."

He never calls me that, and now he's said it twice in five minutes.

I force my gaze back to him. "What?"

"Please help me."

I'm not sure what exactly comes over me. A wave of certainty or whatever you want to call it, but I realize that few things in my life will matter more than whatever I do right now. Ryder is my brother. My closest friend. My soulmate, if you believe in such things. I'll do anything it takes to protect him.

"You can't tell anyone else. No one. Not even Louisa. Do you understand me?"

"Y-yeah. Okay. No one."

I look him dead in the eyes. "Not even Louisa."

"Not even Louisa."

"You can't have another weak moment where you feel the need to unburden yourself. As far as we're concerned, nothing happened. She's lying. The girls at school hate her, so she decided to get even with all of us by accusing one of the most popular guys of the worst possible thing. No one will believe her. They'll believe you. They *know* you."

As I speak, he nods like a bobble head, hanging on my every word.

"Tell me you understand what you have to do."

"I have to say she's lying. That nothing happened."

"You must never, ever, *ever* deviate from that story."

He looks me in the eye as we form this unholy alliance. "I won't."

"If you need to talk, you come to me. Only me."

"Only you."

I reach out my hand to him. He clasps it and holds it tightly as we lock eyes.

Whatever happens next, we're in it together.

Chapter 7

Blaise
NOW

I DRIVE WITH SINGLE-MINDED determination in a pricey rental car that put a serious dent in my always-tight budget. Whatever. It was the fastest way to get to Rhode Island, and I'll need a car when I get there anyway. People have asked me, upon hearing I'm from the smallest state, if we need cars to get around there. It's not *that* small.

Thinking about trivial things like that helps to keep me from obsessing about where I'm going and what I plan to do when I get there.

Through Rye, New York, into Connecticut, past Greenwich, Norwich, Stanford, New Haven and New London, I get more anxious with every minute and every mile that goes by.

I haven't driven in a long time. Normally, I enjoy it. Nothing about this trip is normal or enjoyable.

I cross the state line into Rhode Island at two o'clock and press the accelerator, anxious to get where I'm going before it's too late. I don't want to have to wait another day.

One more day is too many. It's already been too long. I can't take this for another second, not another hour or another night or another morning.

It has to happen today.

Before I lose my nerve.

Again.

I almost did it once before, a couple of months after it happened, when I feared I might have some sort of serious breakdown if I didn't do the right thing immediately.

I'd planned to go to the Land's End Police the next day and tell the truth, to hell with the consequences. I'd resigned myself to becoming a pariah in my own life. Anything, I thought, was better than the purgatory I was stuck in while the kids I grew up with called Neisy every foul name under the sun to discredit her.

I couldn't take it anymore.

And then Louisa died, and I couldn't do it.

I told myself I was staying quiet for her, for Louisa. I was honoring her memory with my silence, but that was bullshit.

The only person I was protecting was myself.

I knew that then, and I've known it every day since.

I've hated myself for fourteen years for keeping this secret.

That ends today.

Hearing Ryder is running for Congress was the catalyst. I actively loathe myself for not doing this before now. Not a day has gone by that I haven't thought of that night, that I haven't thought of Neisy and what she went through or how I could've helped her and didn't—not just after it happened, but every day since then.

I simply can't live with it anymore.

While I'm certain the consequences will be every bit as devastating for me as they would've been then—my brother is still best friends with both Elliott brothers, who are now married with children and successful careers—I don't care what happens to me.

I love Arlo.

I truly do. I feel terrible about rupturing our relationship, perhaps beyond repair. I hate that it'll put a terrible rift in the center of our family, that my mother and siblings will be looked down upon, that I'll be called out, judged, denigrated.

I don't care.

As I crest the Newport Bridge—I'll never call it the Pell Bridge—a flood of memories come over me as I take in the island I called home for the first eighteen years of my life. My childhood there was idyllic, made up of long days at the beach, sailing on Narragansett Bay, cozy Christmases, football games and pep rallies and a feeling of belonging that comes with living in a small town, where everyone knows you and your family. Parents look out for all the kids, not just their own.

When I say words that can never be unsaid, I'll tear apart the fabric of that town where Arlo, Ryder and Cam now live with their families. I know from social media that Cam married Sienna, and they have four kids under the age of seven. Ryder took a long time to recover from the loss of Louisa. After his appointment to Annapolis was revoked, he went to the University of Rhode Island, got an engineering degree and served eight years in the navy after graduating from college.

After an honorable discharge from the navy, he landed a big job with a prestigious engineering firm in Providence.

Now he's running for Congress, representing the district where we grew up.

Not if I can help it.

I feel sick.

My stomach churns with nausea that burns my chest and throat, a feeling reminiscent of that awful summer. I was so nauseated all the time that I couldn't eat. I lost twenty pounds. People told me I looked good when I went back to school for my senior year. They also talked about the apparent rift between me and Sienna, speculating endlessly about what'd come between best friends since the third grade.

Neither of us ever said.

"People grow apart," I told my mother when she asked me about it.

I withdrew from all my friends. I didn't go to football or basketball games. I kept to myself in school and out. In the spring, I refused to attend my prom and only walked the stage at graduation at my parents' insistence. I wouldn't allow them to have a graduation party for me, preferring to count the days until I could get out of there once and for all.

When I arrived at my college dorm at NYU, I exhaled for the first time in more than a year. I'd survived. Somehow. And now I had a whole new life ahead of me in a city where I could disappear amongst the masses.

However, the thing about moving away and bringing a devastating secret with you is that nothing changes. If anything, it gets worse when you're removed from daily contact with the people you were trying to protect by staying silent.

My health declined precipitously that first semester. I battled eating disorders and mono, and nearly flunked out of school. Only because the thought of going home was so revolting did I rally at the end of the semester and end up with a fairly respectable two-point-eight GPA. But the health issues didn't let up. I developed vexing skin conditions and have had ongoing difficulties with eating.

I continued my pattern of keeping to myself, which made for a lonely existence.

I told myself the isolation was for the best, but even then it felt unsustainable.

No one can stay completely removed from others long term. Eventually, I had to reengage with the world, if for no other reason than to support myself, but the shame was always with me. I thought of it as a tumor that wouldn't kill me but would make me sick for as long as it was inside me.

The tumor comes out today.

I drive through the familiar town of Hope, past endless stone walls and the grassy fields where my siblings and I played soccer, lacrosse, baseball and softball. As I go by the street that led to Sienna's childhood neighborhood, I experience a pang of longing for the long-ago time when I thought a friendship like ours would last forever.

I know better now.

Passing by the entrance to my own neighborhood, I give it a passing glance as I stay focused on the road ahead of me, the road to Land's End, where I'll come clean to the man who hosted the now-notorious summer party.

Houston Rafferty is now the chief of police there and is the one I'll share my story with.

No one but him.

I only know him by reputation, but I trust him to do the right thing with the information I'll give him.

I'd forgotten how long the ride from Hope to Land's End is, how winding the roads are on the way to the remote little town. I recall the anticipation when the LE kids, as they were known, joined us for our freshman year of high school. The infusion of fifty new kids into our class was the most exciting thing to happen to us in years.

Many of them were a bit wild compared to us. They lived way out in the middle of nowhere and had to take an hour-long bus ride to get to school. Their older siblings had the best parties, and their parents were super chill. It was like a whole new world had opened to us, and we loved it. We could look across the river and see their town, but it was as if they'd come from another country.

With Teagan and Arlo having experienced this influx of new friends from across the river before I did, my parents had learned to be wary of what went on "over there" until they had a chance to get to know the kids and their parents. I had a few friends from LE, but I wasn't super close to them. Wouldn't you know that the first party I attended "over there" was the night that changed my life forever.

I haven't been back here since. My skin feels clammy, and my stomach churns relentlessly as the GPS takes me closer to the police station and my date with destiny.

For a full fifteen minutes after I park in the lot outside the station, I sit staring at the building, which is painted a cheerful yellow with blue shutters and flower boxes. It doesn't look like a police station, not that I know much about how they should look.

As I get out of the car and walk toward the main entrance, I tell myself everything will be better when I share this burden with someone who can do something about it.

But I don't know that for sure.

Maybe telling my secret will make everything worse.

How is that possible?

Nothing could be worse than sitting on this horrible information for fourteen endless years.

I pull open the door and step inside, determined to get this over with. Whatever the fallout, I'll take it to be free of this heavy weight.

"May I help you?" a young female officer asks.

"I'd like to see Chief Rafferty, please."

"He's gone for the day. He'll be back by eight in the morning."

"I need to see him today. It's an urgent matter."

"Your name?"

I lick my lips. Here it is. The do-or-die moment.

"My name is Blaise Merrick, and I'd like to report a crime."

Chapter 8

Neisy
THEN

EVERYTHING IS BETTER ONCE Kane arrives. Sensing my precarious mental health, my dad doesn't object to Kane staying in my room, which would've been unthinkable before recent events. Having Kane's arms around me takes me away from the hell of the last few weeks. I had to delete Facebook and stay completely away from the internet due to the viciousness directed at me since the charges against Ryder were made public.

A photo of him appearing at his arraignment was on the front page of the *Hope Times* and other local papers. Only because my father had been so adamant was Ryder charged in what the prosecutor has called a he-said, she-said case. They're leaving it up to the judge to determine if the case should go forward.

In the article, it was reported that his longtime girlfriend, Louisa Davies, had recently entered hospice care after a long battle with Hodgkin's Disease. The inclusion of that detail infuriated me. What does that have to do with the fact that he raped me? Even the media is taking his side or so it seems to me.

"Let's take a road trip and get out of here for a while," Kane suggests deep in the middle of his second night in my bed. I thought it would be next year in college before we'd ever get to spend a night together in a bed. What did I know? "You need a break from this madness."

"That sounds like the best idea I've ever heard. Where should we go?"

"We'll get in the car and drive. We'll figure it out on the fly."

"I'd love to do that."

"Good. We'll leave tomorrow."

"I'm sorry your time here isn't what we hoped it would be."

He caresses my back. "You have no reason to apologize. All I need to be happy is you."

"Same." I rest my head on his chest and fall asleep to the sound of his heartbeat. I wake sometime later to a disturbance downstairs. Someone is pounding on the front door. I hear my dad running down the stairs.

"What's happening?" Kane asks.

"Someone's at the door."

The clock on the bedside table reads three ten a.m.

I get out of bed and go to the door.

Someone is shouting at my father. "What're you *doing*? This will *ruin his life*! Don't you care at all that your daughter is *lying*? My son doesn't need to rape anyone. He could have any girl he wants!"

"You need to get out of here before I call the police," my dad says in a cold tone I've never heard from him before.

"*Please.*" Mr. Elliott sounds as if he's crying now. "Father to father. Can't we work this out? Is it money you want? I can give you money."

"*Get out of here,*" my dad says.

When Kane approaches me from behind and puts his hands on my shoulders, I startle.

"Easy, honey. Just me."

I relax against him as my heart pounds like a jackhammer.

"I won't let her ruin his life! I'll ruin hers before she ruins his. She's a liar! Everyone who knows her says that. We could end this right here, father to father."

"I'm calling the police," Kane says.

I want to tell him not to, that it'll only make everything worse, but I'm afraid Mr. Elliott might hurt my dad.

In a matter of minutes, cars with blue-and-red flashing lights line our street.

Mr. Elliott screams obscenities as he's taken into custody. "She's a fucking liar! My son didn't touch her!"

I realize I'm crying when Kane turns me into his embrace. "It's okay, honey. He's gone now."

"It's never going to be okay again."

"Yes, it is. We'll make sure of it."

"How?"

My dad comes up the stairs, his face the picture of rage. "I'm sorry you had to hear that. He doesn't want to believe his precious little boy is capable of such an atrocity."

"I want to get her out of here," Kane says. "Right now."

"Where will you go?" Dad asks.

"Somewhere far, far from here."

Dad is visibly undone.

My mother probably slept through the whole thing in a wine-fueled daze. I'm envious of her ability to punch out of life that way. If I hadn't had such an up-close view of where it would lead, I might've started drinking this summer, too.

"I think that's a good idea. Just drive away. We'll figure out the rest later."

"We might need you to reserve a hotel room for us," Kane says.

Dad runs a trembling hand through his hair. "I'll take care of whatever you need. Neisy has my card for emergencies. This certainly counts."

"I can't come back here, Dad."

"I know. I'll figure out a plan. Don't worry about anything."

He hugs me. "We'll get through this together. I promise."

"I'm staying with her," Kane said. "I told my parents what happened. I think if you talk to them, Captain Sutton, we could make a case for me doing my senior year with Neisy. They're due to move back to the states at Christmas anyway, and they were upset about disrupting my senior year. If you're with us, they'd probably be okay with me staying."

"I'll talk to them. We'll work it out."

My heart takes flight at the possibility of Kane staying with me for this next school year. What was once so daunting now becomes manageable.

"Go ahead and pack. I want Neisy out of here."

No one wants me out of here more than I do.

Kane and I take thirty minutes to pack clothes for a variety of weather along with swimsuits and sweatshirts. He said we may as well have some fun while we're away, and I couldn't agree more.

When we drive away from the house at four thirty that morning, I don't look back. I hope to never be in this town again, except to testify against Ryder when that time comes. I look forward to that day. I'll do whatever it takes to make sure he gets what's coming to him, even if the thought of testifying makes my legs go weak and my palms get sweaty. I also realize that if I stay away, I may never see my beloved grandparents again. Fortunately, there're plenty of other ways I can keep in touch with them from afar. I've taught them how to use an iPhone, and they're hilarious with their texting.

My mom gently told them what's going on, and they've been nothing but supportive—and devastated for me.

Kane reaches for my hand. "Take a deep breath, honey. Just keep breathing."

"Thank you for this. You'll never know how badly I needed you."

"I'm here now, and I'm never leaving you again. Whatever happens next, we're in this together."

"We…we should talk about the baby."

"We don't need to talk about that right now. Let's get out of here. There'll be plenty of time for talking about the tough stuff later."

I give his hand a squeeze and exhale for the first time since Mr. Elliott woke us earlier. If they don't know where I am, they can't touch me.

Or so I think.

Cam
THEN

THE ARRAIGNMENTS OF MY brother and father are surreal. Ryder is charged with first-degree sexual assault and my dad with harassing Neisy's family. I couldn't believe when he called me from jail and said he needed me to withdraw cash from the ATM to bail him out.

Ryder is pale and pinched as he stands before the judge. We were told he wouldn't be required to enter a plea because the charge is a felony, punishable with more than fifteen years in prison. The next step is a probable cause hearing in a month at which the prosecutors will present their case. Witnesses can be called, and the judge will determine if there's adequate evidence to proceed to trial.

The evidence thing worries me. What if Neisy had a rape kit done or saved her clothes or can somehow tie Ryder and his DNA to her?

Those worries keep me awake at night as I ponder the very real possibility of my brother going to prison. He was supposed to be headed to Annapolis. Now he could be looking at spending a big chunk of his life locked up if Neisy can convince a judge and jury that he raped her. Since I've known the truth of what really happened, I find myself thinking of her almost as often as I do him.

How could he have done such a thing when we were brought up to respect women and to treat girls the way we'd want our own sisters treated?

These last few weeks have been the worst of my life, and I fear it could be just the start.

Sienna reaches for my hand.

I'd forgotten how she came to the courthouse to support me without checking with me first. I would've told her not to come.

I think she's mostly here to be on the front lines of the salacious details more than anything.

Maybe that's not fair to her, but whatever. I don't care about anything other than freeing my brother—and now my father, too—from this horrific situation.

My dad is arraigned next and pleads not guilty to a misdemeanor harassment charge. The lawyer told us he'll probably be convicted since the police arrested him outside of Neisy's home at three in the morning.

As a respected naval officer, Captain Sutton's testimony will carry weight with the judge.

Following his arrest, Dad was put on administrative leave—without pay—from his job at the worst possible time. Lawyer bills are adding up for Ryder, and now dad is out of work and has added to the legal bill. In his case, the sentence for harassment is a five-hundred-dollar fine, up to a year in prison or both.

It's just our luck that the statewide media has taken an interest in the case of the young woman who accused the athletic and academic standout of rape while his longtime girlfriend was dying of cancer. To an outsider looking in, it must sound like a movie of the week.

To us, it's a nightmare that's overtaken almost every waking moment.

When we emerge from the courthouse, we're swarmed by media wanting a statement from Ryder or dad or even me. I can't believe it when one of them calls me by name, as if we know each other, asking if I plan to stick by my brother.

I want to tell him to fuck off.

Rather, I tighten my grip on Sienna's hand and head for my Jeep. We'll deal with her car later.

Ryder gets in the back seat.

The ride home is silent and full of unbearable stress.

I'd give anything to go back to that night at Houston's party. I would've stuck like glue to Ryder, making it so he couldn't sneak off with Neisy and commit a felony.

I've gone over it and over it in my mind and have no recollection of him or Neisy leaving the party. There were a lot of people there. Hundreds, if I had to guess. It wasn't possible to track what people were doing. The police are talking to everyone who was there. If even one person says they saw Ryder leave with her or follow her or do anything with her, we're totally screwed.

I glance at my brother in the mirror. He's staring out the window. "Are you okay, Ry?"

"Sure, never better."

"She'll have to prove it," Sienna says. "How will that happen?"

We have no answers, so neither of us replies.

We're too busy praying she can't prove it.

Chapter 9

Neisy
THEN

THE TIME AWAY WITH Kane is blissful. It's everything I need after the hell of the last few weeks. Other than to check in once a day with my dad, I never look at my phone.

We end up at a lake in upstate New York, where my dad rents us a small cabin a few steps from the shore. That's another thing that would've been unthinkable a few months ago. But what does my dad have to worry about now that I've been raped and made pregnant by a boy I went to school with?

Kane went to the grocery store to stock up on essentials, so we wouldn't have to go anywhere. I don't want to have to see anyone. I'm raw from the events that sent us on this trip.

I still can't believe Mr. Elliott actually came to our house to confront my dad.

Thankfully, Dad kept his cool and stayed out of trouble.

Dad told me Mr. Elliott was charged with misdemeanor harassment or something like that.

I'm sure everyone blames me for that, too.

Kane returns from a run to find me sitting in one of the wooden chairs that overlooks the scenic lake. He kisses my cheek. "How're you doing?"

"Okay."

The nausea and overall exhaustion have been hard to take. I'm not used to feeling sick and tired all the time.

"I'm going to take a swim, and then we need to talk."

"Why? Did something else happen?"

"Not that I know of. But we have some decisions to make."

About the baby.

We've danced around the topic in the two weeks since we left town, but we haven't decided anything. Soon, the baby will be far enough along to help me prove that Ryder raped me.

In early September, we'll start our senior year at the high school in Fairfax County where I attended ninth and tenth grades. My friends there are thrilled I'm coming back, which was a huge relief. And yes, they know what happened to me and that I'll have to testify against Ryder at some point. They've been nothing but supportive and concerned for me.

It's also a relief to be away from the town where I was so unhappy long before Ryder attacked me. If I had it do over again, I would've gone to my dad and begged him to get me out of that school and that town before disaster could strike. He knew I was unhappy there, but he didn't know the full extent of it until the Facebook outrage appeared after we went to the police.

Now he knows how bad it was, and it's broken him to find out what I endured without any support. It's also made him even angrier at my mother. He's given her an ultimatum—quit drinking and go to rehab, or he's filing for divorce. His anger at her runs deep after she failed to notice something was very wrong with me. He's not staying with her unless she makes some changes.

I really hope she does. She's wasting her life by drinking herself into oblivion, even if I understand that alcoholism is a disease. I want to be sympathetic toward her, but I'd also like to have a mother again. I'm not sure if she'll stay in Rhode Island or join us in Virginia. That it doesn't matter to me whether she comes with us says a lot about how removed she's been from me in recent years.

"Can we talk about it?" Kane asks, making me realize I've zoned out on him.

"Not today. I'm not feeling great."

"What's wrong?"

"My back is hurting for some reason, and I just feel blah."

"Do you want to lay down?"

"I'd rather go out on the boat." The place we rented has a wooden rowboat that we've taken out on the lake almost every day we've been here. It's so relaxing to float on the water and not think about anything other than what we might have for dinner.

"I'll pack the picnic today."

That's usually my job. "Thank you."

"You don't have to thank me."

"Yes, I really do. You put your life on hold to come here, to run away into the unknown, to stay with me in this hellish situation. I owe you so much."

He squats down next to my chair and takes my hand. "I love you, Neisy. I've loved you so long I don't remember what it was like *not* to love you. Being away from you was torture. As much as I hate what happened to you and all the pain and worry you're dealing with, I'm so happy to be with you again and to know I don't have to leave you ever again." He kisses the back of my hand. "So no, you don't owe me anything."

Before I can come up with a reply to the sweet words that leave me with a lump of emotion in my throat, he stands and walks toward the cabin.

We're lucky to have found each other so early in our lives. Both sets of parents warned us about getting so involved at such young ages, but we didn't want to hear it. We know what we know, and I don't have the slightest doubt about fully committing to him for a lifetime. The certainty that he feels the same way is the ultimate reward.

He returns a few minutes later with the picnic basket we found in a closet in the cabin, sweatshirts and towels for both of us and the bag that contains my sunscreen and the new e-reader my grandparents bought me for Christmas. He's teased me about loving that device more than I love him. Reading has been my favorite pastime since I first learned how. Over these recent tumultuous weeks, I haven't had the attention span to do anything, even my favorite thing. Being here, though, has calmed my mind to the point where I can enjoy reading again.

Kane helps me into the rowboat before he shoves it off the beach and then jumps in as we float away from the shore.

The cushions and umbrella are right where I left them yesterday.

I relax into their comfort, enjoying the play of his muscles as he rows.

He's so gorgeous with his dark silky hair, olive-toned complexion, brown eyes and smooth skin. I tell him all the time that it's not fair he hasn't had so much as a blemish while I've battled acne since I was thirteen. I've been on medicine for it that's helped, but he's had no such issue.

This would be such a perfect day if my back didn't hurt so badly. I wish I could take the ibuprofen that usually works for me, but I read that it's better not to take any pain meds while pregnant. I can't bring myself to do anything to hurt an innocent child, which is why I've more or less decided to carry the baby to term and put him or her up for adoption. I haven't discussed that with Kane yet, but I will. Soon.

Kane rows for a long time, until we're so far from where we started that our cabin is but a speck in the distance. The sun is warm, the air crisp and the lake placid and calm.

"It's so beautiful here," I say after a long period of contented silence.

That's one of the things I love best about being with him. We're so happy to be together that we don't feel the need to constantly fill the empty spaces with conversation.

"I do, too. We'll have to come back every summer, unless it would remind you of things you'd rather forget."

"I've felt so much better since we ended up here. I'd love to come back." I shift on the cushions, seeking a comfortable position as my back pain intensifies.

"What's wrong?" Kane asks.

"Just this weird pain in my back that's been getting worse all day."

"Why didn't you say something?"

"I thought it was just a pulled muscle or something, but it's—"

The breath is stolen from my lungs by a sharp pain that radiates from back to front and a gush of fluid between my legs. I gasp as I lean forward.

Kane releases the oars and reaches out to me. "Neisy, you're bleeding."

"No! The baby!"

If I lose the baby, I'll also lose the proof that Ryder raped me.

"I'll get us back to shore."

He rows like an Olympian, stopping only to pull his phone from his pocket. "Damn it, there's no service out here." He goes back to rowing.

The pain is ridiculous, unlike anything I've ever experienced, even the appendicitis I had when I was ten.

"Are you okay, Neise?"

"Uh…" I can't seem to form a coherent thought.

The bottom of the boat is covered in blood.

When we get closer to the shore, Kane again tries his phone. "Thank God we have service now."

The next hour is a blur as I'm loaded into an ambulance with Kane by my side and transported to the hospital. I want to remind him that we need the baby's DNA to convict Ryder, but I can't form words around the pain that's ripping me apart inside. I black out at some point and come to in a brightly lit room with people all around me. Where's Kane? I want to ask for him, but I can't speak. I can't do anything other than experience this searing pain.

When a needle is inserted into my hand, the pinch barely registers, but the relief is immediate.

My eyes become heavy. I can't keep them open.

The next time I open them, I'm in a darkened room.

Kane is there, sitting next to my bed holding my hand.

I lick lips that are so dry they feel like sandpaper. "What happened?"

"You had a miscarriage."

"Oh."

"You lost a lot of blood. They had to give you a transfusion."

I try to process what he's saying, but it's like my brain is made of cotton. Nothing makes sense.

"You scared me."

"Sorry," I whisper.

He strokes my face and brushes hair back from my forehead. "Don't be sorry."

"Can I…" I force my unfocused eyes to look at him. "I can have others?"

"Yeah, you can."

I blow out a sigh that becomes a sob, ripped from the deepest part of me. The baby I didn't want is gone. I should be relieved, but all I feel is shattered over the loss of an innocent bystander in this tragic situation. Tears spill down my cheeks.

Kane sits on the edge of the mattress and wipes them away with a tissue.

"I don't know w-why I'm crying."

"You've been through a traumatic ordeal."

"Did you call my dad?"

"Not yet. I figured it would be better if you called him so he could hear your voice."

"Thank you for thinking of that."

"No problem."

I have one more question for him, the biggest and most important of all. "Were they able to get DNA from the baby?"

"No, honey. It was too late by the time we got here."

The disappointment is gut wrenching. How will I ever make Ryder pay for what he did to me without the baby's DNA for proof? It'll be my word against his, and they'll believe him because of how accomplished he is. I'm nobody next to him. Maybe that's why he chose me to attack in the first place. He knew he could crush me in every way that matters.

Kane stretches out next to me and holds me while I cry. "I know it doesn't seem like it right now, but you're going to be okay. I promise."

He smells like fresh air and sunscreen.

I realize he has tears running down his face, too. As I pull back so I can see him, I'm struck by his obvious devastation. "Kane…" I brush away his tears. "What is it?"

"There was a nurse in the ER… She was so nice and caring. She… she said we're young and we can try again. That we'll have lots of babies when we're ready for them."

"Oh, God, I'm so sorry." Of course she thought the baby was ours. Why wouldn't she?

"It's true, you know. We are young, and we'll bounce back from this and have lots of babies and a happy life. We won't let this ruin anything for us, do you hear me?"

"Yeah, I hear you."

"As awful as this is, we'll get through it together and be stronger for it."

"I often wonder what I did to get so lucky to meet you when I was so young, to know I wanted to be with you forever, no matter what."

"Same, honey. We're so lucky, and we're going to stay that way."

He holds me as close to him as he can possibly get me, which is right where I want to be. Like always, he makes me feel so much better than I would've without him by my side. When he tells me we're going to be all right, I believe him.

The next day, my father calls to check on me after I'm released from the hospital with orders to take it easy for the next four to six weeks. We texted him the news last night and said I wasn't up for talking but to call me the next day.

"How're you feeling, sweetheart?"

"Tired and sore, but otherwise okay."

"I'm so sorry you went through another traumatic ordeal."

He sounds tearful, which breaks my heart. My dad is the strongest person I know, and I hate to hear him broken because of me. "I'm all right, Dad. I promise. But what happens now that we can't use the baby's DNA to prove he attacked me?"

"I'm not sure. I have a call with the prosecutor later today to update him."

"I still want to testify against him. Even if we lose, I want people to know what he did to me."

"I'll pass that along. You amaze me, Niece. I'm so proud of you."

"I get my resolve from you."

"I suppose you do, but I wasn't strong like you are now when I was your age."

"What is it you always tell me? That people step up to the moment when they need to? That's all I'm doing."

"I'm very proud."

"That's all that's ever mattered to me. You know that, don't you?"

"Yeah, sweetie. I know. Do you want me to come up there?"

"There's no need for that. We're fine. Kane is taking very good care of me."

"Tell him thanks from me."

"I will. How's Mom?"

"She hasn't had a drink in a week, and she went to an AA meeting with Mrs. Dalton. Do you know her?"

"The neighbor down the street?"

"Yes. Mom had heard she was in recovery and reached out to her. Mrs. Dalton offered to take her to her first meeting and to be her sponsor."

"That's progress."

"I guess. We'll see if it sticks without some sort of in-patient rehab."

"I hope it does."

"Me, too."

"Do you still love her, Dad?"

"That's a complicated question. If you'd asked me that before this happened to you, I would've said yes. Now… I don't know. I'm furious that she let you suffer in silence for weeks after you were attacked. How could she *not* know you were going through something so awful?"

"She's got an illness. I don't blame her for that, and you shouldn't either."

"I'm trying. Mrs. Dalton suggested Al-Anon for me, and I'm thinking about it. I've heard great things."

"I think you should try it. Can't hurt, right?"

"That's what Mrs. Dalton said, too. Let me know how you're doing later?"

"I will. Thanks for checking on me."

"Love you so much, honey. I hope you know…"

"I do. I've always known that. Love you, too."

"How's he doing?" Kane asks as he delivers a cup of tea to me.

I sit up on the sofa and take the mug from him. "Thanks. He's doing okay. Upset, of course. I feel like that's the word of this summer. Upset."

"I prefer something more like resilient or courageous or inspiring."

He makes me smile when I would've thought that was impossible today.

"Is it strange that I'm sad about the baby despite everything?"

"I can see why. He or she had nothing to do with any of this and deserves to have someone mourn for them."

"It helps me that you understand."

"I do. I feel sad about it, too, and not just because the baby would've helped you get justice."

"That'll be much more complicated now."

"All you can do is tell the truth and hope for the best."

As I try to imagine taking the stand to testify against Ryder, my whole body goes tense.

"Don't worry about that now." I should be used to how he can always tell what I'm thinking. "There'll be plenty of time for you to prepare for that later. Right now, you need to focus on resting and healing. Okay?"

My gaze meets his, which is full of concern and love. So much love. "Okay."

Chapter 10

Neisy
THEN

TWO WEEKS AFTER MY miscarriage, Kane and I return to Rhode Island for a hearing in the case. Ryder's defense attorney has filed a motion to dismiss the charges due to a lack of physical evidence. The judge has asked all parties to be present and prepared to answer her questions.

After this, we'll head to my father's apartment in Virginia, where he stays when he's there. He's working on renting a house in our former district for our senior year.

I'm still not sure if my mother will be joining us, but I'm not asking any questions. As long as I don't have to go back to school in Rhode Island, I'll be fine.

Kane is worried about whether I'm strong enough for the hearing.

I'll have to recount what happened in open court, with Ryder, his family and friends in the room. The thought of seeing him again makes me as sick as I've felt since the miscarriage, but either I show up to this hearing or he gets away with what he did.

It will all come down to the judge.

The prosecutor, a very kind assistant attorney general named Neil DeGrasso, has told me it could go either way. Neil said it will depend on which one of us the judge believes, and whether she thinks we have enough to convince a jury of Ryder's guilt.

With no evidence or witnesses to back up my story, it's possible the judge will decide my testimony isn't enough. I have no doubt his attorney will make sure Ryder's many accomplishments are taken into consideration. Neil warned me that the defense attorney would ask why a well-liked, accomplished young man like him would need to rape anyone. It isn't a fair question, Neil said, but he wanted me ready for it.

We arrive at my parents' house at eleven o'clock the night before the hearing.

My dad is waiting at the door to greet me. I feel like he's aged ten years since he heard I'd been attacked.

He hugs me tightly.

When he steps aside to let us come in, I'm surprised to find my mom standing there, nervously awaiting the chance to greet me.

I hug her. "Hi, Mom. It's nice to see you."

"You, too. It's good to have you home."

"Thanks." I want to tell her this will never be my home, but she doesn't need to be reminded that all my problems began when she brought me to her hometown, where I never stood a chance of assimilating with kids who'd been together their whole lives. At least at my old school there were tons of military kids like me, so it wasn't as complicated to be new. There were some military kids in school here, but for whatever reason they had none of the problems I did.

Maybe it's me. I must've done something to cause them to take an instant dislike to me. I've thought a lot about that over the last few weeks, picking over every second of those first weeks in a new school. For the life of me, I can't think of anything that would've caused them to hate me so much.

Kane says it's because they were intimidated by how pretty I am.

I think that's silly. A lot of them are prettier than I am.

He said he doubts that.

I told him he's biased, and I refuse to believe that the kind of things I experienced could be caused by something so superficial as how someone looks.

Being back in my old room triggers the trauma. I'd give anything to not have to spend even a single night in that room, but since Kane is with me, I get through it.

When I walk into the courtroom the next morning, the trauma hits like a tidal wave when I see Ryder sitting at one of the tables in the front of the room, next to a man with gray hair who is leaning in to hear what Ryder is saying.

I feel the eyes—or I should say the glares—of everyone in that room on me as I walk to my seat in the front where Neil told me to sit.

Kane's hand on my lower back reminds me to keep breathing, to get through this so I can get out of here as soon as possible.

My parents follow us in and sit next to me. Kane holds my right hand while my dad has the left one.

The sheriff's deputy tells us to stand when the judge enters the room.

"The Honorable Judge Morgan Denton presiding."

"Please be seated," Judge Denton says.

She's younger than I thought she'd be, forty at the most, with brown skin, dark eyes and a no-nonsense expression on her pretty face.

"We're here today to consider the defense motion to dismiss this case due to a lack of evidence. Before I can consider the merits of the motion, I'd like to hear from Ms. Sutton."

Kane gives my hand a squeeze before he releases it.

I thought a lot about what to wear today and decided on a navy dress I wore to my cousin's wedding right before school started last year. I left my hair down and other than lip gloss, I'm not wearing any makeup. I was surprised when Neil asked me about what I'd wear and suggested I keep it as simple as possible.

When I'm seated in the box next to the judge, the bailiff appears with a bible and swears me in.

"I appreciate you being here today, Ms. Sutton," the judge says. "I requested you be sworn in because it's a crime to lie under oath. You're accusing Mr. Elliott of a very serious crime. I want to hear your story from you before I rule on the defense motion. Do you understand?"

"I do."

Over the next half hour, Neil leads me through the events of that evening, guiding me in the telling of my story. I try very hard to remain unemotional, but when I get to the part where I have to describe the attack in detail, I can't help the tears that spill down my cheeks.

"Ms. Sutton," the judge says, "what contact had you had with Mr. Elliott before that night?"

"I only knew him from school. I mean everyone knew him."

"Had you spoken with him or had any direct interaction with him?"

"Once or twice, but just to say hello."

"And yet he said you'd been looking at him like you wanted to fuck him? Was that the way he said it?"

I nod.

"I need you to say the words for the court stenographer."

"Yes. That's what he said, but it's not true. I have a boyfriend I love very much. We've been together for years. I've never wanted anyone but him. Everyone in school also knew that Ryder was involved with Louisa, so it was shocking to me when he said the things he did."

"Objection." The defense attorney leaps to his feet. "The witness is editorializing."

"Overruled. The whole reason we're here is to determine what happened that night and whether we have grounds to go to trial. I want to hear what Ms. Sutton has to say."

The defense attorney sits down, but he's pissed.

I refuse to look at Ryder, but I can feel him and everyone else staring at me with barely concealed hostility.

"Ms. Sutton," Neil says, "when Mr. Elliott asked you if he could speak to you in private, were you afraid to leave the party with him?"

"No. I had no reason to be. He'd said it was about his girlfriend, Louisa. We'd had a class together before she left school. I liked her and felt like she liked me, too. And when he said the things he did… About the way I looked at him… I was shocked."

"What happened after that night?"

"A couple of weeks later, I learned I was pregnant."

The courtroom erupts in pandemonium as the judge bangs her gavel and calls for order.

"Who was the father of your child?" Neil asks.

"Ryder Elliott."

"Objection!"

"Overruled."

"Are you still pregnant?"

"No, I miscarried at five weeks."

"Have you told the truth today about what happened that night?"

"Yes."

"Nothing further," Neil says.

The defense attorney stands. "Is it true that you had a reputation at school for being promiscuous?"

"I did nothing to earn that reputation."

"But is it true that people said that about you?"

"They said a lot of things about me, but they didn't know me."

"Please confine your answers to the questions you're asked. Is it true that you had intimate relations with members of the football team?"

"No, that's not true."

"Your honor, we have a sworn affidavit to the contrary from ten members of the team."

"That's a lie!"

"Ms. Sutton, please control your outbursts in my court."

"They're lying! I never slept with any of them!" What if Kane believes them? How can they swear I did that when it's not true? I look to Neil, hoping he'll do something about this vicious smear. I shouldn't be surprised that Ryder's friends came together to defend him this way, but still... I'm shocked that they'd lie under oath.

"Objection!" Neil says after he's handed a copy of the document. "They are the defendant's brother and closest friends. Of course they'd lie to protect him."

"That's a very serious accusation, Mr. DeGrasso. These young men made sworn statements and were informed of the consequences of lying under oath."

"We have statements from Camden Elliott, Arlo Merrick..."

He continues to recite names that're familiar to me, but it's all lies. I never went near any of them.

Neil glances at me. As his gaze collides with mine I realize he's not sure who to believe.

"Ms. Sutton," the defense attorney says, "is it true that you were sexually promiscuous while attending Hope High School?"

I shake my head. "No, it's not true. I'd never had sex before Ryder Elliott raped me."

"Ms. Sutton, please confine your answers to the questions you're asked," the attorney says testily. "One final question. Were you disappointed when you asked Ryder Elliott to go out with you and he declined?"

My mouth falls open in shock. "That never happened."

"It's a yes or no question, Ms. Sutton. Were you disappointed?"

"No, I wasn't, because I never asked him any such thing."

"No more questions."

"Ms. Sutton, you're dismissed."

I look up at the judge, feeling incredulous that she'd allow them to smear me this way.

She won't look at me.

That's when I know she's going to let him off, that the lies Ryder and his friends have told will take precedence over the truth.

I'm so devastated I can barely find the strength to stand and walk back to my seat. The devastation is compounded when Kane doesn't take my hand. He can't possibly believe I'd do that to him. Can he? What if he does?

If I lose him, I'll never get over it.

"This is a very difficult situation," the judge says.

The room is eerily silent and thick with tension as we wait for her to render judgment.

"Ms. Sutton, I believe something happened that night, but without the physical evidence to tie Mr. Elliott to a crime, I can't allow this case to go to trial. The charges are dismissed. Mr. Elliott, you're free to go."

His supporters erupt in cheers as he hugs his attorney and then his parents.

He's surrounded by the same group of boys who lied for him as they cheer for his exoneration.

"Please get me out of here," I say to my dad.

He puts an arm around me and has me out of there in a matter of seconds.

I'm so cold, I feel like I'll never be warm again.

We ride back to the house in complete silence.

Kane looks out the passenger side window.

What is he thinking?

In the driveway at the house, my parents get out.

Kane and I don't move.

"Are you coming?" Dad asks, his expression full of utter devastation.

"In a minute." I can't go another second without knowing what Kane is thinking. The second the car door closes, I turn to him. "Say something! None of that was true! You're the only one I love, and you know that."

"They swore it was true."

"They were *lying*! I swear to God. I've never even met Arlo Merrick or Camden Elliott or most of the other guys who signed that *lie*!"

He stares straight ahead as his cheek throbs with tension.

And then I realize he's weeping.

"Kane…"

"I thought I understood what you went through with these people… But until today, I didn't realize how bad it was."

I reach for him.

He wraps his arms around me. "I'm so, so sorry, Neise."

"It's not your fault."

"I want to kill them for daring to lie about you."

I'm sick with relief that he believes me.

We hold each other for a long time, and when we pull apart, our faces are wet with tears.

"Let's get out of here."

"Yes, please."

"And never come back."

Chapter 11

Blaise
NOW

I WAIT FOR A long time before Houston comes into the station, wearing jeans and a long-sleeved T-shirt. His hair is windblown and his cheeks red as if he's been exerting himself. He's taller than I recall, with dark blond hair and blue-green eyes. His brother, Dallas, the boy I used to have a big crush on until he lied about Neisy, is built like him but with darker hair and eyes.

I stand to greet him.

"I came as soon as I could, Blaise. Sorry to keep you waiting."

"It's okay."

"Come in."

He leads me past the officer who helped me track him down to an office in the back of the building. After he gestures for me to go in ahead of him, he closes the door and takes a seat behind the desk.

My heart beats so fast and so hard I'm afraid I might pass out before I can say the words I've kept buried inside me for fourteen torturous years.

"What's going on? I thought you lived in the city now."

I'm shocked that he knows anything about me. I'm four years younger than him. He graduated before I ever stepped foot into high school, but he knew Teagan and Arlo. "I am. I mean, I do. I live there."

"I give you credit. That place would drive me crazy. I can barely stand a weekend there."

"When you're used to LE, anything seems crazy in comparison."

He grunts out a laugh. "That's true. I was coaching my niece and nephew's soccer team, or I would've been here sooner. They said you wanted to report a crime?"

"I do."

"I guess I'm confused since you don't live here anymore."

"It happened fourteen years ago."

"Oh. Okay…"

"It happened at the party you had."

He sits up a little straighter, his eyes going wide. "Are you talking about Ryder and Neisy?"

This is it. My mouth is so dry I can barely swallow. All the moisture in my body has collected in the palms of my hands, which are pressed tightly together. "Yes."

"What're you saying, Blaise?"

"I…I saw him attack her."

For a long moment, he's still and silent, his stare unblinking. "You saw Ryder rape Neisy."

"I did."

"Blaise…" He says my name with an expression of disbelief. "Why didn't you come forward sooner?"

I tip my head to give him a "come on, you know why" look. "It was wrong of me not to. I've always known that. I lacked the courage to upset my entire life then, and it's haunted me ever since. I'm as sick over it today as I was the day it happened."

"So why come forward now?"

"I heard he's running for Congress, and I couldn't sit on it for another second."

"It can be a crime to conceal evidence of another crime."

That hadn't occurred to me, and for a second I'm not sure how to reply. But then I know what I should say. "I'm willing to take whatever punishment comes my way to do what I should've done fourteen years ago." My voice wavers on "whatever punishment comes my way," but my resolve is firm. I simply cannot live with this any longer.

"Did anyone else witness this crime?"

"I'm speaking only for myself."

"So that's a yes?"

"I can neither confirm nor deny."

He expels a deep breath and seems to become very interested in the far wall as he fiddles with a pen on his desk. "Do you understand what'll happen when I notify the attorney general that a witness has come forward?"

"I think so."

He leans forward, arms propped on the desk, gaze intense and fixed on me. "It'll be a nightmare, Blaise. People will attack you for not reporting it at the time. They'll question your motivation for coming forward now. They'll tear apart every aspect of your life. Old crap from high school will be resurrected. The Elliotts will fight back—hard. Are you sure you're ready for that?"

"In other words, the same thing that would've happened fourteen years ago will happen now, only worse because I'll be vilified for waiting so long to report it. Do I understand you correctly?"

He never blinks when he says, "Yes."

"I can handle it."

"Are you sure?"

"No, I'm not sure! Would you be if you were me?"

"I wouldn't have sat on this for more than a decade."

"Really? You're so certain of that? You would've had the stomach to have an entire town of people you've known all your life turn on you for daring to accuse one of your own of such a thing? You would've had the fortitude to have your only brother hate you because you were accusing one of his closest friends of a monstrous crime? You would've been okay with being a social outcast, a pariah, a Facebook target, when you were seventeen?"

"Maybe not," he concedes, "but there're a lot of years between seventeen and thirty-one."

"I realize that, and it shouldn't have taken this long. I don't know what else I can say other than I was wrong. I knew it then, and I know it now. I want to fix it."

"I'll need to bring this new information to Neisy. We'd need her onboard to reopen the case."

"Do you know where she is?"

"No, I don't. I'll have to find her. Her cousin still runs the restaurant where she and I worked together. I'll start there."

He takes down my phone number and promises to get in touch after he talks to her and the AG.

"Do you believe me, Houston?"

After a long pause, he says, "I believe you'd have no reason to make up something that'll turn your life upside down as much as it will Neisy's and Ryder's."

"Thank you."

"I want you to be prepared, Blaise. If we go forward, it'll be ugly."

"I understand."

"You need to find somewhere safe to stay."

"I can go to my mother's house."

"No, you can't." He writes something down and then hands me a sticky note. "Go see my friend Jack Olsen and tell him I sent you. He's got a couple of cottages for rent on his property. No one would think to look for you there. I want you to go there and stay there until you hear from me."

"You really think that's necessary?"

"I really do."

Houston
NOW

AFTER BLAISE LEAVES, I sit for five full minutes, trying to wrap my head around what she told me.

Ryder Elliott *did* rape Neisy Sutton.

And he's gotten away with it for fourteen years, during which he attended college, graduated with honors, served eight years in the navy before separating with multiple awards and other honors. An engineer by trade, Ryder has worked for a top company in Providence since his separation from the military. He's married with three young children and has a house on the same street in Hope where he, Cam and their sisters grew up.

Dallas and I play poker with him and Cam as well as Blaise's brother, Arlo, on the third Saturday night of every month.

I'm revolted to think I've considered him a friend.

All this time…

No one believed Neisy when the allegations first came to light. Not one supporter stepped forward to say she'd never make up something like a rape charge, because no one knew her well enough to vouch for her. Even I, who'd been one of her few friends in the area, had failed to step up, to say there's no way she'd fabricate such a thing because I wasn't entirely sure. Even though he was three years younger than me, I knew Ryder and his family much better and for much longer than I'd known her.

I never came right out and said it to anyone, but I'd sided with him.

Everyone had sided with him, including the teammates who'd sworn that she'd slept with all of them. One of them was my own brother, a realization that makes me sick in light of what Blaise told me.

Neisy hadn't stood a chance.

I go to filing cabinets in another room to find the original case file. I take it with me to my office and close the door. I pour my fourth cup of coffee of the day and open the file, which dates back to my father's era, before the department was fully computerized. My dad was meticulous. We've always said his handwriting could've been a font.

Responded to a phone call from Navy Captain Rick Sutton, who reported his daughter, Denise, was sexually assaulted by Ryder Elliott in the woods near my home three weeks ago. The alleged assault took place at a party hosted by my son, Houston, while my wife and I were out of town. Captain Sutton brought his daughter to the station the next day. She gave the following account:

I attended the party hosted by my friend Houston Rafferty, who I worked with at The Daily Catch the previous summer. During the party, Ryder Elliott asked me if he could talk to me about his girlfriend, Louisa, and led me away from the group, down a pathway to an area with a lot of trees and brush. I asked him what he wanted to tell me about Louisa, and he said I knew what he really wanted. I didn't know. I'd never spoken to him before, except to say hello a couple of times. I knew he played several sports and about him and Louisa and that she'd been ill. I was in a class with her and his brother Camden, but I'd never had any other interactions with either of the Elliott brothers. I asked Ryder to explain what he meant, and he said I'd been driving him crazy with the way I looked at him at school. When I asked him how I'd been looking at him, he said like I wanted to fuck him. I said I didn't, and we argued about that. He insisted it was true and said the other guys call me a cock tease. I told him I barely knew him so why would I want to fuck him. Then he moved so quickly that he caught me by surprise, knocking me over. He came down on top of me and pulled at my clothes. I was wearing a dress. He tore at my underwear and pulled it down. I screamed at him to stop and for help, but no one could hear me. The music was loud and there were so many people that no one could hear.

The rest is almost too much to bear. When Ryder was finished, he got up and walked away, leaving her there bleeding and crying. She reported how she eventually was able to get herself up and back to her car, which had been parked a quarter mile or so from the house.

I finally get up to leave the office, feeling weighted down by guilt and regret. Neisy was my friend. Why didn't I come to her defense when she needed me? I worked with her for a full summer, had a fun rapport with her and would've asked her out if she hadn't been so much younger than me. Rather than date her, we'd had a big brother-little sister vibe. When she accused Ryder of rape, my first thought was no way, especially since he'd been with Louisa for years by then and had seen her through a terrible illness with loyalty and faithfulness.

I couldn't reconcile that guy with the person Neisy described in her complaint, which I was privy to because I asked my dad to share it with me. I'd been deeply upset to learn weeks later that someone might've been sexually assaulted at my party. I remember thinking at the time that if the perpetrator had been anyone else, I would've believed her.

But Ryder Elliott? No. I refused to believe it was possible, and my brother and our other friends felt the same.

Dallas knew him well and was adamant he never would've done such a thing. I remember him having a screaming fight in defense of Ryder with my dad, who'd had no choice but to investigate the charges.

Dad had been furious with me for hosting a party with underage drinking while my parents were away on a badly needed vacation. That was the one time my dad and I were seriously at odds. His disappointment had crushed me.

I remember being a little pissed at Neisy for making trouble for me with my dad by reporting something that'd happened at a party I wasn't supposed to have had. My parents never would've known about it if she hadn't accused Ryder, which I knew then was deeply unfair, but I couldn't help how I felt.

That was a difficult time for everyone involved, but no one more so than Neisy, who'd left town shortly after and as far as I know, had returned only for the preliminary hearing that resulted in Ryder walking free.

I want to talk to my dad about this new development, so I head to the house where I was raised with my brother and sister. The drive home is short, through the winding rural roads that make up my hometown. Not much has changed here, and we like it that way. You won't see any sort of chain businesses mixed in with the farm stands, antique stores or coffee shops. We're all about bucolic beauty in Land's End, which has become an exclusive enclave in the last ten years. Many of the coastal homes are owned by summer people and sit empty the rest of the year.

Being a police officer in this town can be boring at times. Not so much for me now that I'm the chief, which happened four years ago. Many of the younger officers don't last long and go looking for something more exciting than our corner of the world.

I don't blame them for moving on. After I finished college in Boston, I worked for two years in a suburb outside the city. Then I came back here. I've never wanted to live anywhere but LE.

It's home.

I take a left turn down a winding dirt road that leads to my original home, where my parents still live after retiring years ago—my dad from the police department and my mom as principal at the town's elementary school.

These days, they tend to their horses, their garden and the five grandchildren my brother and sister have provided.

I park my department-issued SUV behind my dad's old Ford truck and head inside.

"Knock, knock," I say as I step inside.

"No need to knock," my mom says as she does every time I come by and insist on knocking. She raises her cheek for a kiss. "This is a nice surprise. Are you hungry?"

"Always."

"We had pot roast tonight. I'll fix you a plate."

"Is he eating my leftovers again?" Dad asks as he comes into the room.

"Hush, Chuck. There's plenty left for you."

Their banter has always amused me and made me want what they have. I haven't found it yet, but I haven't given up. As I cruise into my late thirties, however, the prospects seem to be dimming.

Dad cracks open beers for each of us. "What's going on?"

"I wanted to run something by you."

"I can go watch 'Jeopardy' if you want to talk to Dad in private," Mom says as she wipes down the counters.

"You can stay. I'd welcome your take on it, too, but as always, it's highly confidential."

"We won't breathe a word," she says.

I know they won't because they never have, and I've shared a lot with them.

I take a few bites of the delicious meal and wash them down with the beer. "Do you remember when Ryder Elliott was accused of rape?"

"Oh Lord," Mom says. "I sure do. That was such an awful thing. I felt terrible for Mary and Dave. They were so upset."

"What about it?" Dad eyes me as a fellow law enforcement officer who worked on the case when it first happened. It took a long time for he and I to get past what he felt to be a major violation of his trust, so bringing this up to him is the last thing I want to do. But I need his input.

"Someone came forward today claiming to have witnessed it."

Their faces go flat with shock.

"What?" Mom says softly. "It's been *years.*"

"Fourteen years."

"And the person is just now coming forward?"

"Yes. She said she'd been sick over it since the day it happened, and after she heard he's running for Congress, she couldn't stay quiet another minute."

"Do you believe her, son?" Dad asks.

I rub the back of my neck where all my tension lands. "Yeah, I do. She'd have nothing to gain other than clearing her conscience and a lot to lose, including her own brother, who's still close to Ryder."

"As are you," Mom says.

"I wouldn't call us close. We play cards once a month."

"Still, he's a friend."

"Yeah, he is."

"What're you going to do?" Dad asks.

"I guess I'll find Neisy and let her know a witness has come forward. It'll be up to her to decide what she wants to do because I can't do it without her, even with a witness."

"There's a sworn statement from her," Dad reminds me.

"I'm not sure that'd be enough without her willing to testify in a reopened case."

"So you'd let it go if she isn't willing to cooperate?" Dad asks.

"What would you do?"

"That's a tough one. On the one hand, you have new evidence in an old crime, but without the victim's cooperation, I'm not sure how you'd be able to make a case other than to use the sworn statement we took from her at the time. But there's also the matter of your witness taking fourteen years to come forward. That speaks to her credibility."

"From her perspective, she had good reason to keep quiet with the way everyone rallied to his defense. Put yourself in her place as a seventeen-year-old going up against every kid she grew up with, not to mention that Ryder was her brother's best friend. That'd be a lot for anyone, especially in a close-knit town like Hope."

"I can't help but think about the poor girl who was attacked," Mom says. "Didn't this witness have a scintilla of concern for her?"

"I think she had tremendous concern for her, but when weighed against her own well-being, she chose herself. That's what kids do."

"She hasn't been a kid for a long time," Mom says a little more sharply. "Why didn't she do something about this before now?"

"Only she can know that, but people have their reasons, Mom. I get that, even if I don't agree with it. She asked me what I would've done in her place, and I honestly can't say I would've handled it differently."

"You would have," Dad says. "You've always done the right thing."

"Not always. I had the party in the first place, when you guys were away."

"You wouldn't have sat on something like this for all that time."

I release a deep sigh. "We all like to think we'd do the right thing in any situation, but honestly, until we're in it with all the various consequences staring us in the face, we can't say for sure what we'd do."

"You're right," Mom says, frowning. "People always like to think they know what they'd do if such and such thing happened to them. But we can't know for sure until it does."

"That's why I want to give her the benefit of the doubt. It's not easy to come forward to accuse a kid you grew up with of a heinous crime. I think it matters more that she came forward than it does that she waited."

"The AG may not agree," Dad says. "Before you get too far down the road with this thing, make sure you consult with them."

"Of course. That's on the list for first thing tomorrow morning. If they're on board, my next move will be to track down Neisy."

"I don't envy you this, son," Dad says. "If you decide to move forward, it's not going to be easy. People think the world of Ryder."

"I know they do. Hell, I always have. But I can't un-ring this bell now that I know there's a witness."

"No, you can't."

Chapter 12

Blaise
NOW

I FOLLOW THE DIRECTIONS to the place Houston told me about and drive down a long driveway lined by stone walls on both sides to a large Colonial-style house painted white with black shutters. As I park the car, a man comes out of the house wearing faded jeans and a flannel shirt. I notice he's barefooted.

"Help you with something?"

I get out of the car. "Houston Rafferty sent me. He said you have short-term rentals."

"I do." He extends a hand. "Jack Olsen."

I shake his hand as I realize he's handsome with golden brown eyes to match dark blond hair that needed to be cut weeks ago. "Blaise Merrick."

"Pleasure to meet you." He gestures for me to follow him around the house, which gives me pause until I remember that Houston sent me here. That hesitation comes straight from what I witnessed on that long-ago night. Trust issues have caused me no end of difficulty in my sporadic dealings with men.

"Are you coming?" Jack asks, glancing over his shoulder.

"I'm coming."

He leads me to the back of the property where three shingled cottages are positioned in a row along yet another stone wall. "Each has a bed, sofa, kitchen and bathroom. Our season is over now, so you can have your pick."

"How much?"

"A hundred a week?"

I do some quick math to determine if I can swing that and my rent in New York without working for a while. I've got some savings, but it won't last long. Thank goodness for credit cards.

"That sounds great, thank you."

"Any friend of Houston's is a friend of mine," he says with a warm smile. "Never hurts to have the police chief owe me a favor."

And he's a bit charming, too, not that I care about such things. "I'm not sure how long I'll be here."

He shrugs as he unlocks the door to the middle cabin. "Doesn't matter. I don't have bookings until Thanksgiving, and it's only for one of them. Take a look."

As I cross the threshold, I'm greeted by the scent of lemons. "This is very cute."

"My best friend from high school gets the credit for decorating. She's a professional interior designer. Gave me a great deal."

"She did a nice job."

The navy-blue patterned quilt on the bed matches the navy sofa.

I turn back to him and startle when I realized he's followed me into the small space.

"Easy." He holds up his hands. "Nothing to worry about here."

"Sorry."

"It's okay. What do you think?"

"I'll take it."

Jack peels a key off his ring and hands it to me. "Make yourself at home. I'm right across the yard in the big house if you need anything. Do you know the area?"

"I'm from Hope but didn't spend much time over here back in the day."

He tells me where the grocery store is and mentions a fun, new coffee and garden shop at the Monroe four corners.

"Thank you very much. I'll pay you in the morning for this week if that's okay."

"Sounds good. Let me give you my number in case you have questions."

As he recites the number, I punch it into my phone.

"Text me so I have yours."

After I send the text, he heads out through the door he left open when he followed me in. Something about that feels reassuring, as if he knew I wouldn't want to be enclosed in that small space with a man I only just met. I've been called aloof, cold and distant by men who were offended by my need to feel safe. They say I take it too far.

I know better than most people that you can never take such things too far.

Jack has earned hard-to-get points with me for the small gesture of leaving a door open. "You can drive around the house if you take a right off the driveway," he says over his shoulder. "It'll be a left on the way in."

"Good to know. Thanks again."

"No problem."

I wonder if he lives alone or if there's a Mrs. Jack.

What does it matter? I'm here only until Houston has a chance to figure out the next steps. I'll be back in New York in a matter of days.

My phone rings with a call from Wendall that I take only because I need to tell him I'm taking some time off.

"Damn it, Blaise, where the hell are you?"

"Rhode Island."

"What? Since when?"

"Since my mother called about a family emergency. I was going to text you later."

It would be just like him to tell me that's no excuse for missing work. Luckily for him, he doesn't say that. "What am I supposed to do without you?" I can picture the pout that goes with the words.

"I'm sure you'll be fine for a few days. I'll send you the schedule for tomorrow shortly."

"Fine."

I wait a minute to give him a chance to add a thank you, but he doesn't. Sometimes I wonder if those words exist in his vocabulary.

"I, uh, hope everything is okay with your family."

I'm shocked he said that much. "Thank you."

I end the call before he can say something that'll ruin the goodwill he earned by showing the most basic kindness.

Returning to the driveway, I start the car and follow the directions Jack gave me to drive the car around to my cabin. After I unload my suitcase and computer bag, I send Wendall his schedule for tomorrow, so he won't have a meltdown, and then contemplate what to have for dinner.

My phone rings with a call from my mother. "Hi, Mom."

"I thought you were coming home?"

"I'm in Land's End."

"What're you doing over there?"

"Taking care of some business."

"What business, Blaise? What's going on?"

I want so badly to tell her, but first I want to wait to find out what Houston plans to do with the information I gave him. There's no point in exploding my life if Neisy or the AG decide not to pursue the matter.

"I'll tell you when I can, Mom."

"This is all very unsettling. First you stay away for years, then you come running back when you hear Ryder is running for Congress, and now you're staying over there rather than here with me."

"It's for the best right now. I'll come see you soon, okay?"

"And you'll tell me what's going on?"

"When I can."

"Are you safe?"

"I am. Don't worry."

"That's like telling me not to breathe."

"I know, Mom. I'm sorry. I wish I could say more."

"Call me tomorrow?"

"I will."

"Love you, Blaise."

"I love you, too, Mom."

I'm still holding the phone when I land on the sofa, exhausted from the turmoil of this day. But more than anything, I'm relieved. Someone else knows my terrible secret. It's been released into the world, and no matter what happens next, that's better than holding it inside me for all this time.

Or so I think.

Houston
NOW

MY FIRST CALL THE next morning is to the longest standing assistant attorney general, the one most likely to remember the case from fourteen years ago. Neil DeGrasso retired five years ago.

"Vaguely," Joshua Spurling says after I ask if he recalls the case brought against Ryder Elliott and dismissed at preliminary due to a lack of evidence.

"A witness has come forward."

"A witness."

"That's right, someone who saw Ryder Elliott rape Denise Sutton."

"And where has this witness been for the last fourteen years?"

"She was a teenager at the time, with deep ties to Elliott and his family after having grown up with him. She was scared to come forward then but is willing to do so now."

"Why now?"

"After she heard he's running for Congress, she couldn't keep the secret any longer."

"I don't know about this, Houston. A defense attorney would shred her on the stand."

"She understands that and had good reason for keeping quiet before. Or at least it made sense to her at the time, but to hear her tell it, she's been sick over this incident since the day it happened."

"Are you angling to reopen the case?"

"That depends on whether I'd have the support of your office."

"I'll talk to Roberts about it, but no promises." The AG, Victor Roberts, has been in office just under three years, so he had nothing to do with the original case. "It might be too little too late at this point. Do we even know where the victim is?"

"No, but I could find out pretty easily."

"Work on that while I pitch this to Roberts."

"Will do."

"I'll be back to you with an answer as soon as I can."

"Thanks, Josh."

My next move is to find Neisy. After she left the area, we lost touch with each other. I start with social media, combing through Facebook and Instagram but find no sign of her. I move on to Google, which is just as frustrating. There's no mention of a Denise Sutton after her graduation from a Virginia high school one year after the alleged incident.

People are easy to find in this day and age, unless they choose not to be, which she probably has. I wouldn't blame her after the way people savaged her when she accused Ryder.

I wanted so badly to believe her back then, because she wasn't the kind of girl who'd make up something like that to get attention. Her life at HHS had been rough, and I remember thinking at the time that there was no way she'd do anything to make it worse than it already was, but I couldn't get past the feeling that Ryder wouldn't do something like that. I told my father that, too.

One thing was for certain, she'd definitely lost her sparkle since we'd worked together the summer before she started school in Hope and had her whole life go to shit.

The restaurant is owned by her mother's cousin, so I'll stop in to see what he can tell me.

I grab my portable radio, tell the sergeant working the desk that I'm heading out for a bit and get into my SUV to drive to the seafood restaurant where Neisy and I worked together the summer before she started at HHS.

As I drive to the waterfront restaurant in Monroe, I remember the first time I ever saw her and how dazzled I'd been by her. She was far too young for me at sixteen, but you'd have to have been blind not to notice how beautiful and sweet she was. It was the first time in my life I'd yearned to be younger. A twenty-year-old college junior didn't ask out a high school junior, no matter how mature they were, especially when she was the boss's cousin.

Instead, I'd befriended her and later learned about her long-distance boyfriend, Kane, and how much she loved him and couldn't wait for him to visit that summer.

A year later, when her dad came forward to report that she'd been raped by Ryder Elliott at my party, I'd been devastated. That something like that might've happened at my party and to someone I truly cared about… And Ryder Elliott… My brother, Dallas, had played football and run track with Ryder. They were close friends. So while Dallas had defended Ryder and called the charges preposterous, I'd made a lame attempt at defending Neisy as I'd come to the realization she'd have nothing at all to gain by making up such a thing. That was the first time I was ever seriously at odds with Dallas.

After the case was thrown out for a lack of evidence, it took Dallas and me a long time to get our relationship back on track. He never forgot that I doubted his friend, and I never forgot that he doubted mine. Eventually, we got to the point that we stopped talking about it and agreed to disagree, but that took years, and things were never quite the same afterward.

Dallas and Arlo recently left high-paying jobs, as did Ryder's brother, Cam, to help get Ryder elected to Congress.

My stomach hurts when I think about the potential ripple effect of Blaise's admission and what it could do to the lives of people I care about.

It would be easier to forget I ever heard what she said.

But then I think of Neisy and what she went through after the accusation became public, and I can't go back to yesterday when I didn't know there was a witness.

I pull into the lot at The Daily Catch and park as a million memories of summers spent hustling fried seafood come flooding back to me, including how my family used to make me undress outside because I stunk so badly after a shift.

As I walk inside, the bell jingling on the door sparks even more memories as does the smell of fried fish.

The owner, Ronnie, is working at the counter with a stack of paper, a pen and calculator. He looks up and smiles when he sees me. "This is a nice surprise."

I reach across the counter to shake his hand. "Good to see you."

"You, too. How're things in LE?"

"It was a busy summer, but it's gone quiet now."

"I'm sure it has. Coffee?"

I slide onto a stool at the counter. "I won't say no to that. How's business?"

"Busier than ever, year-round these days."

"Glad to hear it." The restaurant is located on the shore of a placid inlet off the river, with picnic tables and a dock that make it a go-to spot for boaters looking to pull up and grab a meal.

"What brings you by, Houston?"

"I was thinking about Neisy the other day and wondered how she's doing."

"She's great. Married to Kane with four kids, last I heard."

I'm thrilled to hear things worked out for them. After seeing them together, I'd had no doubt they were the real deal. "Is she still living in Virginia?"

He nods. "They're in Norfolk. Kane's a lieutenant commander in the navy. They got back from a three-year tour in Italy about six months ago. Had a great time over there."

"I'm glad to hear they ended up together."

"Never had a doubt. He was it for her since they were kids."

"Yes, he was."

"What about you? Never got married, did you?"

"Nope. I still haven't found someone I can't live without."

His guffaw of laughter makes me smile. "I hear you, brother. My Claire is a doll, but sometimes she makes me want to muzzle her."

That makes me chuckle. "As I recall you couldn't run this place without her."

"That's the truth, and she keeps our three teenagers in check. I got lucky, and I know it. You will, too. I'm sure of it."

"I guess we'll see. It's good to see you, Ronnie." I put a couple of singles on the counter for the coffee that he pushes back at me.

"My treat. Don't be a stranger. Bring the folks in for dinner sometime soon."

"I will. Thanks for the coffee."

"Come by for a cup any time."

"Will do." I shake his hand and head out with the info I came for, feeling a bit guilty for deceiving Ronnie by not telling him why I was really asking about Neisy. He was good to me during the four summers I waited tables for him and his parents, who ran the place before he took over.

Now that I know Neisy married Kane and they live in Norfolk, it takes about four seconds on my phone to track down an address for them, even before I knew his last name was Messner.

Denise Messner.

Who is she these days and does she still think about what happened on that long-ago summer night? What would it mean to her to hear there'd been a witness? Would she want to reopen the case or keep it in the past? If the AG is willing to go forward based on Blaise's eye-witness testimony, it'll come down to what Neisy wants to do.

I send an email to Josh letting him know I've located the victim.

I'm back at the station when he replies. *I'm meeting with Roberts at two. Will get back to you after.*

I call Blaise to update her and to make sure she isn't having regrets the day after her confession.

She answers on the first ring. "Hi."

"How're you doing?"

"Okay. I think. Jack's place is great. Thanks for the recommendation."

"I'm glad it worked out. I wanted to update you on what's going on. I've notified the attorney general's office that a witness has come forward. The assistant AG is meeting with the AG today. I've also located Neisy in Norfolk, Virginia, where she lives with her husband and four children."

"Wow, she's married with four kids."

"She married her childhood sweetheart, Kane. He's a lieutenant commander in the navy."

"I'm glad she's happy."

"What about you?" I ask the question before I take two seconds to think about whether I should. "Are you married?"

"No. That hasn't been in the cards for me. I've barely dated." She pauses before she continues. "I want you to know... What I saw that night has haunted me in ways I can barely fathom let alone describe. I've had health problems, trust problems, emotional issues, anxiety... It messed me up badly, Houston."

"The AG will ask why it took you so long to come forward."

"And that's a fair question. The only answer I have is that so many people I loved would've been hurt by me coming forward at the time, so I chose not to. I own that choice, but it was the wrong thing to do. My only excuse is I was seventeen, and the person being accused was someone I grew up with. He was my brother's closest friend. My best friend was dating Ryder's brother and is now married to him. All I could see at the time was everyone I loved turning on me for telling the truth. And that doesn't account for the fact that I was expressly forbidden from being in LE that night. If my parents found out I was there, I would've lost their trust."

"I understand all that, but it's been fourteen years, Blaise. Surely you could've come forward at some point after you left home."

"I almost did once."

"What stopped you?"

"Ryder's longtime girlfriend, Louisa, died. I lost my nerve after that."

"I guess I can understand that."

"I wish you knew how many nights I stared at the ceiling thinking about telling the truth. I have no defense for why I haven't done it sooner. Maybe I wasn't ready to blow up my life. I'm still not, but I can't live with this anymore. I just can't."

"If the AG decides to reopen the case, I'm worried about it getting ugly. I want you to be prepared for that."

"I tell myself I'd prefer that to the purgatory I've been in all this time."

"You know how people are around here. They close ranks around their own, and Ryder is one of their own."

"I know," she says, sighing. "All I can do is tell the truth and let the fallout be what it is. I saw him rape her, and I've been sick with guilt over my own inaction ever since."

"One thing you haven't said is if you were alone when you saw what you did."

"I'm not going to comment on anything other than my own story."

I note how she answers the question without actually answering. "So you weren't alone, and the other person is unwilling to come forward."

"I'll only comment on my own story."

"The AG will ask who else was there."

"I'll only comment on my own story."

"It'd go easier for you if someone could corroborate your story."

Her silence speaks volumes.

"Okay, Blaise. We'll play it your way. I'll let you know what the AG says."

"Thank you, Houston."

I stare out the window for a long time, thinking about this case and the absolute shit storm that will ensue if the AG moves to reopen the case. I receive an email that afternoon from Spurling that the AG wants twenty-four hours to review the case files and decide whether to proceed.

In the meantime, I need to see Neisy and warn her of what might be coming. If she's unwilling to participate, it'll all be for naught anyway. But there's no way I can let her be blindsided.

I fire up my computer and buy a ticket to fly to Norfolk tonight with a return tomorrow afternoon.

Chapter 13

Neisy
NOW

"LEVI, GET YOUR SHOES on. We're going to be late." That kid will be the absolute death of me. He moves in reverse, especially in the morning. Kane and I joke about giving our six-year-old coffee for the jolt of caffeine. We look forward to him becoming a teenager so that'll be an option. In the meantime, every morning is a struggle with him.

"He's still in the bathroom, Mom," my eldest, Charlotte, tells me when she comes downstairs ready to rule the fourth grade.

"Seriously?"

"Would I lie to you?"

"Never. Watch the twins while I fetch him." I kiss the top of her blonde head and take the stairs two at a time. "Levi! Let's go."

"I'm coming."

"Not fast enough."

"Dad says these things cannot be rushed."

I roll my eyes because that's absolutely true. Kane takes forever in the bathroom, and his son is him all over again in more ways than one.

"If I have to come in there…"

"You do *not* want to come in here."

"You're going to miss the bus." I drove Charlotte to school every day until the twins arrived and made it impossible to get four kids out the door by seven forty-five every morning. The bus is the best thing to ever happen to me since the twins were born.

"I haven't missed it yet, and I'm not gonna start today."

"Please, buddy. Hurry up."

"I'm coming."

The sound of the toilet flushing gives me hope that I won't be trucking four kids to the elementary school this morning.

"I've got your stuff." I go back downstairs with his sneakers and sweatshirt. The mornings are still cool, but it'll be in the seventies by midday. I love the fall, but not as much as I love the lazy days of summer when no one has to be anywhere until cheerleading starts up for Charlotte in late August.

I'm in the kitchen closing lunch boxes when my phone rings. When I glance at it and see that it's Kane, I grab it. He's been deployed on the U.S.S. *Dwight D. Eisenhower* aircraft carrier for two weeks and is due home later tonight. I'm thrilled to realize he's back in cell range.

"Hey there." I hold the phone in the crook of my neck to keep my hands free.

"Hey, yourself. How goes it there?"

"Usual morning chaos thanks to your son."

"I love how he's my son when he's causing chaos and your son when he makes the honor roll."

"What's your point?" I ask, smiling. I can't wait to see him. Everything is better when he's home.

"No point. Just sayin'. I miss you guys. How're my babies?"

"They're wonderful. Charlotte is in charge while I smoke Levi out of the bathroom."

Kane laughs.

"It's not funny, and it's all your fault for telling him a man needs time to himself in the morning."

"That's the truth."

"If you teach Hayes and Hudson that, too, we're going to have a problem."

"I can't wait to see you guys."

"Same."

"Date night after bedtime?"

"It's on."

We've become experts at date nights in our own home, since finding a babysitter for four kids under the age of nine, including nine-month-old twins, isn't a simple proposition.

"What time will you be home?"

"Should be there by late afternoon. I can see land."

"They'll be so excited." I never tell them he's due home until he's back in port, lest something happens to delay him. That doesn't seem likely today, so I feel safe telling them.

"Same. I'll take them to the park to give you a few minutes to yourself before dinner."

"I won't say no to that."

"See you soon. Love you."

"Love you, too. Hurry."

"I'm hurrying."

"Was that Dad?" Charlotte asks.

I hand her lunchbox to her just as Levi finally appears in the kitchen to down a protein bar.

I point to his shoes. "Yes, that was him. He'll be home this afternoon."

"You get all silly when he calls after deployment," she says, batting her eyelashes as she mocks me.

I sputter with laughter. "Are you having a seizure or something?"

"Haha, nope. That's you when Dad comes home."

I bop her playfully on the head, retrieve the twins from their high chairs and step outside the front door just as the bus lumbers down the street. Another close call. Somehow I manage to juggle the twins and blow kisses to Charlotte and Levi and get myself back into the house without disaster.

I put the babies down on their mat in the playroom and run into the kitchen to grab my coffee without taking my eyes off them. They're quick these days.

When I return to the playroom, Hayes has Hudson's foot in his mouth.

I don't stop that until Hudson starts to protest and then I separate them. But like the proverbial magnet and steel, they're right back on top of each other a minute later. They hate being separated for any reason.

I've just put them down for their morning nap when the doorbell rings.

It's probably my neighbor wanting me to try her latest confection. She's working on getting a home baking business off the ground, and I've been assisting with social media.

I swing the door open, but it's not Gretchen.

The sight of Houston Rafferty brings back a thousand painful memories in one big rush of emotions from a time I'd much rather forget. What the hell is he doing here? "Houston?"

"Hey, Neisy." And that name… I haven't gone by that since the summer from hell.

"Wh-what're you doing here?"

"Could I come in for a minute?"

I realize I've been frozen in place since I realized who was at my door. "Of course." I unlock the storm door and open it for him.

As my old friend steps into my house, I'm screaming on the inside. Houston was always so good to me, but he's a reminder of a time I've worked so hard to leave in the past.

"Beautiful home."

"It's a mess. Four kids." I shrug. "I gave up years ago."

"I was happy to hear you and Kane were still together."

"H-how did you find me?"

"I saw Ronnie."

My mom's cousin, who owns the restaurant where I worked with Houston. I haven't seen Ronnie in years, not since...

I cross my arms, wishing that could protect me from the onslaught Houston's unannounced arrival has unleashed.

"Could we sit?"

If he hadn't been the one person from that time who was good to me, I would've said no, we can't. I would've asked him to leave. But because it's him asking, I sit on the loveseat while he takes the sofa in the one room that's not been completely overtaken by kids.

"Why are you here?"

"I have some news about your case."

Those words make me go cold all over with dread. "My case? There is no case. It was dismissed for a lack of evidence."

"A witness has come forward."

It takes what seems like a full minute for his words to register. "A witness."

"Yes."

"Someone saw him..."

"Yes."

He never blinks.

I look away. I can't bear this.

"Neisy—"

"Please don't call me that. I'm Denise now." I want to tell him Neisy died a long time ago. Denise was forced to pick up the pieces of her life and carry on, to find love, meaning and joy, things Ryder Elliott tried to take from Neisy.

"I'm sorry, Denise."

"What do you want from me?"

"I'm the police chief in LE now. The attorney general may be willing to reopen the case based on this eye-witness testimony."

"No."

"No?"

"I'm not reopening the case. The first time almost killed me. I can't go through that again."

"I understand how you feel, but—"

Rage, the kind I haven't felt since that summer, boils up inside of me. "Unless you were attacked, assaulted and robbed of your virginity by the local hero and called a slut by his friends, you can't *possibly* understand how I feel. Unless you miscarried the baby you were left with after that night, you can't possibly know the journey I was forced to take to get my life together or how long that journey took. It took *years*, Houston. I can't go back to that place again because someone who failed to do the right thing then wants to clear their conscience. There's nothing in this world that could make me revisit that time."

"Not even to get justice?"

I shake my head. "Who's the witness?"

"I suppose it doesn't matter because if you're not willing to participate, we have no case."

"It matters to me. I want to know who left me in the woods after I was raped and then sat on that for all these years."

"Blaise Merrick."

It takes me a second to put a face with a name. I remember Arlo Merrick because I had a class with him, and he was one of the boys who signed that hideous affidavit full of lies. Blaise didn't stand out to me, which means she wasn't one of the tormentors.

"Why didn't she come forward?" As soon as I ask the question, I hold up my hand. "Never mind. I know why. She grew up with him. I was nothing to her."

"You weren't nothing to her. I took her statement. This has weighed on her soul every day since it happened. She explained that she had close ties to him through her brother, who's still one of his best friends. Her best friend at the time was dating his brother. And she wasn't allowed to be in LE with the car. A lot of things conspired to keep her quiet, and she regrets that very much."

I find that hard to believe. "So why now?"

"Ryder is running for Congress. Blaise said she couldn't bear to think of him running for office, knowing what she did about him. She said the minute she heard about his campaign she couldn't hold on to this secret for another second. She drove straight from her home in New York City to LE and asked to see me."

My insides twist into knots.

Ryder is running for Congress.

Blaise saw him rape me and is willing to testify to that or Houston wouldn't have come all this way to find me.

Houston puts a business card on the table in front of me and then stands to leave. "Think about it. If you change your mind, give me a call."

I want to tell him I won't change my mind.

As I walk him to the door, my mind races with thoughts, emotions and memories that've been buried for years. It took a long time, a very long time, not to think of that summer every day anymore. I can't revisit that dreadful time and continue to care for my family. I know that as sure as I'm breathing. It would undo me all over again. I survived it once. I can't do that a second time.

"I'm sorry to show up out of the blue this way and upset you, but I didn't want to call you with this news."

"You're only doing your job. Congratulations on becoming chief, by the way."

"Thanks."

"Your dad must be proud."

"He is."

"The rest of your family is well?" I force myself to ask even though I don't care about anyone from that time except for him, the one friend I had.

"Yeah, Dallas lives locally with his wife and three kids, and Austin is in California. She's married with two little boys."

I feel rage at the mention of Dallas, who also lied about me to save Ryder. "What about you?"

"Not married and no kids. I guess you could say I'm married to the job."

"Thank you for coming, Houston. I'm sorry if it was a wasted trip."

"It wasn't wasted because I got to see an old friend. I'm glad to see you happy and doing well, Denise. You deserve that."

"We all do. Don't give the job too much."

"I'll try not to." He gives me the tender look of an old friend. "Take care of yourself."

"You do the same."

KANE'S HOMECOMING IS THE usual circus with the kids wanting every second of his attention after missing him for two weeks. He takes Charlotte and Levi to the park and then helps with homework and baths while I go through the motions of making dinner.

"What's going on?" he asks when he catches me zoning out for the third time.

"We'll talk after they're in bed."

"Are you okay?"

"I think so."

He gives me a curious look before scooping up the twins to get them to bed first.

Charlotte and Levi take longer to settle down and require multiple stories from daddy.

He comes downstairs more than an hour after he went up.

I'm waiting for him with a glass of the Cab he loves.

"First things first." He sits next to me and leans in for a lingering kiss. "Hi there."

He makes me smile even at the most difficult of times. "Welcome home."

"These deployments get harder all the time. I want to be here with you guys."

"Does that mean you've made a decision about staying in?" As he nears the eight-year mark, he's torn about whether he wants to make the navy a career.

"Maybe, but we'll talk about that later. What's going on with you?"

"Houston Rafferty came to see me earlier."

That name and the memories that go with it shock him as much as Houston's visit shocked me. "What'd he want?"

"To tell me a witness has come forward who can back up my story about what happened that night."

He stares at me, his expression conveying shock and anger. "A witness has come forward *now*? Where've they been all this time?"

"She had close ties to him. Apparently, she couldn't live with it any longer after she heard he's running for Congress."

Kane blinks and looks as angry as I've seen him since that summer. "He's running for Congress."

"That was a surprise to me, too, but the witness told Houston there was no way she could let that happen."

"But she had no problem watching you be savaged when this first happened? She didn't have the decency to step forward when her testimony would've sent him to trial?"

"It was complicated for her."

"Complicated for *her*?"

"Shhh, Kane. Keep your voice down."

"I'm sorry, Dee, but I don't want to hear how this was complicated for her. You went through hell, and she could've helped you but chose not to."

"Houston said her brother was best friends with *him*." We never say his name in this house. "Her best friend was dating his brother. She wasn't supposed to be there that night and would've gotten in big trouble at home. Not to mention she grew up with him and didn't know me from Adam."

"She saw you being attacked and assaulted and said nothing. I don't care what reasons she thinks she had. There's no excuse for sitting on something like this for *fourteen fucking years*. And that *son of a bitch* is running for Congress?"

"Kane…"

"I'm sorry, but this is infuriating."

"I know."

He softens, puts his arms around me and holds me close. "Of course you do. What did you say to Houston?"

"I said I wasn't interested in revisiting that time in my life."

I wait for him to respond, but he doesn't, so I pull back to look at his face, which is set in a stormy expression that's so unlike his usual chill demeanor it's unsettling. "Tell me what you're thinking."

"I want you to nail that mother fer to the wall. He's *running for Congress*? Fuck that shit, Dee. He doesn't deserve that kind of job. He doesn't deserve *anything* after what he did to you."

"I don't know if I can do it. The first time almost killed me."

"It'd be different this time. You'd have someone backing up your story, and you're not seventeen anymore, having to deal with other kids defending him."

"The same people will still defend him, especially the ones who lied under oath to defend him the first time."

"So what? They can't touch you. You've got a whole life that has nothing to do with them."

"I don't want everyone in my new life to know about this. I don't want to reopen that wound. I'm afraid it'll change everything and undo all the hard work we've done to move on from it."

"Those are reasonable concerns, but let me ask you this. What if it's not just you he's done this to? What if there're others?"

"Don't put that on me! I can't be responsible for what he's done to other people."

"I'm not saying you're responsible. I'm saying if you testify, maybe you can stop it from happening to someone else."

I get up because I can't bear to sit still. "I don't want anything to do with it."

"It's your call."

"Will you support me if I decide I can't do it?"

"I'll always support you, and you know that."

"It may not even happen. Houston is talking to the AG's office. It'll be their call about whether to reopen the case after so much time has gone by."

"Whatever you decide to do, I'll be right there with you."

"Thank you."

"Come back over here." He holds out his hand to me. "I missed you so much."

I take his hand and sit next to him. "I missed you, too."

As I lean into his warm embrace, I'm determined not to let the past interfere with my happy, contented present. But that's easier said than done. Ever since Houston showed up on my doorstep, the memories of that time are as fresh as they were then.

"Have you told your dad about this?" Kane asks.

"No, I wanted to talk to you first."

"You need to tell him."

"I'm afraid Dad will kill *him* when he hears *he's* running for Congress."

"He won't do that, but he'll want to. Just like I do."

"I can't talk about this anymore if I'm to have any chance of sleeping."

"What can I do?"

I wrap an arm around his waist and snuggle in closer. "Just this."

"*This* is my favorite thing in the whole world."

Chapter 14

Blaise
NOW

I'M AWAKENED FROM AN unusually sound sleep by a dog barking in the yard. It takes a second for me to recall where I am and why. The events of the last two days come flooding back to me. I told Houston what I saw. He's contacted the AG about reopening the case against Ryder, and he's working to locate Neisy.

I wait for my stomach to turn at the thought of people finding out about what I've done, but the only thing I feel is resolve and relief. I want everyone to know what he did, and I want him to pay for it. I don't care anymore who might hate me for coming forward. I have to live with myself, and it's a lot easier now that I've taken the first step toward making this right.

My phone buzzes with a text—the eighth of the day from my boss.

I ignore the texts. Whatever he wants can wait while I start my day.

I use the Keurig in the kitchen to brew a cup of coffee that I take with me when I go outside to see what's going on.

Jack is throwing the ball for a gorgeous Golden Retriever. The dog sees me and loses interest in the ball as she charges over to greet me.

"Watch out for the lethal tongue from hell," Jack says.

I sit on the stairs and find he wasn't kidding as I'm bathed in dog spit, which makes me laugh for the first time in longer than I can remember. It takes about two seconds to be completely covered in dog hair and spit.

Jack rushes over to rescue me. "I'm sorry. I keep thinking she'll grow out of her puppy behavior, but she's three."

"She's beautiful. Where was she yesterday?"

"Having her teeth cleaned at the vet."

"What's your name, gorgeous?"

"Fenway."

"I love that. A tip of the hat to the Red Sox."

"Yep. Are you a fan?"

"Of course. And let me tell you, that's not an easy thing to be in New York City."

"I'll bet it's not." He tosses a tennis ball that has the dog sprinting toward the main house. "Did she get hair in your coffee?"

"I don't think so."

"Sorry if we disturbed you."

"You didn't."

The dog comes back with the ball, which she drops at his feet. She waits expectantly for him to throw it again.

"How many times do you have to throw it for her?"

"Two to three hundred a day?"

I laugh at his grimace. "My brother has a bat he uses to wear out his dog faster." I know this because I've seen video of Arlo playing with his dog, not because I've ever met the dog.

"That's a great idea. I need to get out my Little League slugger."

I sip my coffee as I watch them play while wondering what he does for work.

He's good with the dog, laughing at her antics and praising her for rare seconds of good behavior.

Though I hardly ever give much thought to men or dating or any of the baggage that comes with such things, I can't deny that Jack is truly adorable and sexy in a rugged sort of way. His faded jeans fit him just right, and his flannel shirt is mostly unbuttoned, revealing a muscular chest and abdomen, as he wanders the yard barefooted. I want to ask if his feet get cold, but he speaks before I can.

He throws the ball for what must be the hundredth time. "How long are you in town?"

"I'm not sure."

He waggles his brows at me. "You're a woman of mystery."

"Not so much."

"We don't get a lot of visitors around here who aren't vacationers, and we don't get much of those this time of year."

I know that because I grew up across the river. The area is quieter in the fall, winter and spring before the busy summer season kicks in.

"How long have you lived here?" I ask, hoping to put the focus on him rather than me since I have no idea how to answer questions about what I'm doing here.

"All my life. This was my parents' place. They passed a while back and left it to me. I added the cottages to help pay the taxes, which are substantial."

"I'm sorry about your parents."

"Thanks."

"Were they sick?"

He nods as he throws the ball again. "Both had cancer and died six weeks apart. That was two years ago."

"Oh God, Jack. I'm so sorry. That must've been awful."

"It was pretty shitty. I was their only child, so it was a lot."

Hearing his story makes me see how everyone is dealing with something heavy. I've carried around my own heavy load for so long that sometimes I forget that. For the first time in fourteen years I feel less burdened. Houston knows what I witnessed, and he's doing what he can with the information I gave him. Whatever happens from here is not up to me, and there's relief in that.

My phone rings, and Houston's name pops up on my screen.

I take the call and go inside with a wave to Jack. "Hi."

"Hey. How's it going?"

"All right. You?"

"I have a few updates for you. First, I went to Virginia yesterday to see Neisy, who now goes by Denise. I told her a witness has come forward who can corroborate her story and that the AG is considering reopening the case. She's not interested in revisiting it."

I feel strangely deflated at hearing that. But what did I expect? "Oh. Well… I can understand that."

"As can I. However, we may not need her to proceed. I'm talking to the AG's office this afternoon to go over the particulars. Your testimony may be enough added to Denise's sworn statement from when the charges were originally filed."

The thought of being the sole reason for the case being sent forward is daunting, but I'm undeterred. "Whatever's needed, I'll do it."

"I'm sure the AG will want a statement from you, taken under oath, before they decide whether to go forward."

My mouth goes dry at the thought of having to relive the excruciating details of that night, but I'm determined to do whatever it takes to make this right. "That's fine."

"I know I keep saying this, but I want you to be ready for a firestorm."

"I appreciate your concern, and I'm as prepared as I can be." As I say that, I notice my hands are trembling and my mouth has gone dry. Deep inside, that intimidated seventeen-year-old is still there and still afraid of people hating her.

"I think you should tell Jack what's going on."

"Why?"

"I want to make sure you're safe. If and when the case is reopened, I'll increase patrols around his place."

His concerns about my safety send my anxiety into the red zone. "How long do I have before people will know?"

"That depends on what the AG decides. I'll get back in touch after our meeting. It's a different proposition without Denise's testimony."

"Did you tell her who'd come forward?"

"I did. She wasn't sure she remembered you, but she knew Arlo."

"She must've been angry."

"She was confused and disappointed."

"I hope you told her I hated myself then and now for not doing the right thing."

"I told her. I'll get back to you after I talk to the AG's office."

"Do you think I should give my family a heads up about what's going on?"

"You might want to wait until after the meeting today. If the AG decides not to pursue it, there'd be no need to tell anyone."

"I understand. Thank you, Houston. I appreciate all you're doing."

"Just doing my job."

After he signs off, I sit for a long time thinking about what he said and how I should handle my mother, who wants to see me today.

I decide I'll tell her—and only her—what's going on. I text to ask if I can come by.

She responds right away. *Of course. I'll make lunch. Can't wait to see you.*

Be there soon.

Denise
NOW

I SPEND THE MORNING in bed with coffee Kane brought me, listening to him deal with getting Charlotte and Levi to the bus stop and the twins down for their morning nap.

I giggle more than once at the frustrated tone of Kane's voice as he deals with Levi.

He comes into our room, crawls onto the bed and lands face down. "I want to go back to sea."

Laughing, I stroke a hand over his dark hair, which is prickly from being cut to military standards.

He turns his head so he can see me. "How do you do this day after day and not kill one of them?"

"I never think about killing them."

"I know," he says with a big grin. "You think about killing me for gifting you with four little angels."

"You weren't supposed to know that!"

"Ah-ha! While I'm off protecting our country, you're having homicidal thoughts about me."

"Every day, and yet, I still can't wait for you to get home."

He puts his arm around me and snuggles in close, resting his head on my chest. "I couldn't wait either. I miss you all so much when I'm away."

I wrap my arms around him, giving thanks as I do every day for him and our life together. I give him full credit for putting me back together after that traumatic summer with his steadfast love. We were just kids, but he knew exactly what I needed and how to provide it. I'll never forget that. We got married right after we graduated from high school with only our parents in attendance. No one at UVA knew we were married, and we liked it that way. It was our little secret.

"Dee?"

"Hmm?"

"I've been thinking."

"About?"

"Houston's visit."

Every muscle in my body goes tense. The news Houston brought overshadowed the usual thrill of Kane's homecoming. "What about it?"

"I keep thinking about that son of a bitch out there living his life like nothing ever happened and running for *Congress* like the arrogant asshole he is with no fear of his past coming back to haunt him. He has no idea the full extent of what you endured because of him. And now there's a chance to make him pay for it." He raises his head off my chest and gazes at me imploringly. "I want him to *pay*."

"It's all I can think about."

He cups my face and compels me to look at him. "I can't even imagine what you must be feeling. To have your nightmare resurrected after all these years, to learn there was a witness who didn't come forward at the time... It's the worst kind of betrayal."

"I want him to pay for it, too, but I'm afraid."

"Of what, honey?"

"What if I tear open that wound and it wrecks me again? What if I can't take care of the kids?"

"I'd be right there with you through the whole thing."

"You have work. Who knows where you'd be if this went to trial?"

"I'm going to separate from the navy. I love my job, but I love my family more. I want to be here for everything with you and the kids. I don't want to miss soccer or dinners or game nights. I want to be with you guys."

"We want you here with us, too, but only if it's what you really want. I know how much you love being in the navy."

"I do, but not as much as I love you and the kids."

"What'll you do for work?"

"I've got some feelers out for jobs. How would you feel about going back to the DC area?"

"I'd miss our friends here, but most of them will be moving in the next few years anyway, and DC is home."

"I was hoping you'd say that. This means I'd be right there by your side when or if the case went to trial. We'd be near your dad and my parents, who'd help with the kids."

My parents divorced years ago. My mom, who succeeded in getting sober after years of stopping and starting, lives in Denver now with her second husband. Dad has a longtime girlfriend that we all love and is enjoying being retired.

"You really think I should do this?"

"I think you should do whatever works for you. If the answer is no, it's no. But I want you to know that if you choose to go forward,

I'd support you every step of the way—and I'd be around to do that in person, not remotely."

"That makes all the difference. Everything is better when you're here."

Smiling, he leans in to kiss me. "That's how it is for me, too. Funny how that worked out, huh?"

"It's the best thing in my whole life. I wouldn't have survived this the first time without you."

"Yes, you would have because you're tougher than you give yourself credit for being."

"No, I'm not."

"We'll have to agree to disagree on that, but in my opinion, you're the strongest person I've ever known."

"You need to get out more."

"Haha, you know there's nowhere else I want to be than right here with you." When he kisses me again, I wrap my arms around him and let all my worries fall away for now. They'll still be there after this stolen interlude with my love.

"There was a tradition we forgot when I got home last night," he says against my lips.

"I didn't forget. I was hoping you'd let me make it up to you this morning."

"You don't need to make up anything to me."

"What if I want to?"

"Are you sure?"

"I refuse to let *him* or Houston or any of this set me back to where I was then. We worked too hard to get past it to let that ruin anything now."

"And I hear you. I really do. But I want you to be certain."

"I'm certain that I know exactly who I'm in bed with—the love of my life."

Smiling, he kisses me and touches me and takes me away from all my worries and fears the way he has for as long as I've known him. It took a long time, more than two years and several unsuccessful attempts, before I was able to finally make love with him and not experience anything other than pure happiness and excitement.

He never wavered in his devotion to me or his determination to wait until I was ready for more. I credit him with saving me in more ways than one. After the twins were born, he had a vasectomy, which has freed us to enjoy being together without worries about more babies. We got twice what we bargained for when we decided to have a third child. Now our family is more than complete.

I want so badly to enjoy this reunion with him, but my brain is stuck in the past, which makes it impossible to do anything other than go through the motions with Kane.

"Dee."

I look up at him as he moves inside me.

"Where'd you go?"

"Nowhere."

He tips his head as he studies me. He knows me better than anyone and is fully aware of what's going on in my mind. "It's you and me, sweetheart. Just you and me."

"I know."

"Stay with me."

"I'm here."

"I love you so much. You're my whole life."

His sweet words bring tears to my eyes. "You're mine, too."

"And as long as we have this, we have everything. Don't forget that."

"I won't. I never could."

He gathers me into his warm embrace as we chase the finish that doesn't happen for me. I'm just too distracted as much as I wish I wasn't.

After a long moment of silence as we catch our breath, I say, "I'm sorry."

"Don't be, love. I know what this situation does to you, and I don't blame you at all."

"I'm thinking about what you said before… About not letting him get away with it."

He gazes down at me as he brushes the hair back from my face with his index finger. "It's totally up to you, and I'll respect whatever decision you make."

"I'm afraid of what it'll do to me and us and our family. But when I think of him out there living his life—and running for office, of all things—like he's done nothing wrong… I want justice. I want people to know what he did to me. I want them to know about the baby he left me with and how I had to suffer through losing it while he went on with his life like nothing had happened. And I want to say again, in open court, that the other boys who swore they'd slept with me were liars."

"I'll be right there with you, Dee. Every minute of every day for as long as it takes to get justice."

"That's the only reason I can do this, because we'd be doing it together."

"Like always."

"I'll call Houston today."

Chapter 15

Blaise
NOW

I SHOWER AND CHANGE into jeans and a sweater before heading out to return to my childhood home for the first time since my dad died of a heart attack seven years ago. That's the only time I've been home since I left for college, a stance that's caused significant friction in my family. They've asked for years why I stayed away until they quit asking and stopped reaching out. I still talk to them, but we're not close. I have nieces and nephews I barely know. That's how I wanted it, for reasons that made sense to me for all this time, but now... If everything comes out, will it drive us further apart or bring us closer together?

I don't know how that'll go, and the not knowing only adds to my anxiety as I drive across the bridge into Hope.

Every nerve in my body is on full alert as I take the familiar roads to home, traversing the same route I did on that long-ago night after witnessing the crime that changed everything.

I park behind my mother's silver Toyota Camry and take a moment to look at the two-story Colonial home where I was raised. It's been painted a darker shade of grey, and the shutters are now black. They were red when I lived there.

Mom comes out of the house, smiling with excitement that's been sorely lacking in her since Dad died. She's visited me often in the city, but I know she's yearned for me to come home.

I hug her on the sidewalk.

"It's so good to have you here, my sweet girl."

"It's good to be home."

As I walk inside with her, the familiar scents of candles and the cleaning products she favors spark a million memories of good times and bad. There was far more good than bad, but the bad eclipsed everything else, which is another thing I feel guilty about. I hurt my parents and siblings by turning my back on them and this place where we lived as a family.

On the wall of the living room, our four senior pictures are framed in a square with Teagan and Arlo on top, and me and Junie on the bottom. I'm the only one who isn't smiling. My senior year was a nightmare to be endured not celebrated.

I recall my mother being annoyed that I'd refused to smile for the photographer. *Honestly, Blaise,* she'd said at the time, *I don't know what the hell is wrong with you these days.*

I haven't thought of that in years.

She leads the way into the kitchen, which has been updated. I've seen the photos, so I'm prepared for the change. What still strikes me as too painful to believe is that my dad isn't here anymore.

I take a seat at the table while she bustles around getting me a tall glass of iced tea with lemon, just the way I like it. She brings plates with chicken salad sandwiches, a bag of chips and my favorite sweet gherkin pickles. "Thanks, Mom. This looks delicious."

"It's so, so nice to have you over for lunch, Blaise. I've missed you so much."

"I've missed you, too."

What remains unspoken between us is the same thing that's been unspoken all this time—why I left and never came back, except for the one time I absolutely had to. After my dad died, I mourned the loss of the many years of holidays and other occasions I should've spent with him and the others. It just seemed easier at the time to stay away.

Now, I'm not so sure that was the right thing to do.

I give my mom credit. She shows amazing restraint by not immediately grilling me about why hearing Ryder is running for Congress brought me running home when nothing else has, except my father's death, for fourteen years.

She fills me in on all the family news while we eat. Teagan's pregnancy has been the most difficult one yet, Arlo's four-year-old daughter—a niece I've never met—is playing soccer and Junie landed a marketing job she's excited about.

After an hour of chitchat about family, friends and neighbors, we finally run out of things to talk about.

I wipe my mouth with a paper napkin as I work up the courage to tell her the truth. "I'm sure you're wondering why I came running when you told me what you did the other day."

"About Ryder running for Congress. I can't for the life of me imagine why that would be the thing to bring you home when nothing else but losing Dad has, even your siblings having babies."

I hear the hurt her in her words, loud and clear. "I had a good reason."

Again she shows restraint by waiting for me to say it.

"Do you remember when Ryder was charged with raping Neisy Sutton?"

"I do, and as I recall it never went anywhere."

"Because of a lack of evidence."

"It was such a relief when it was thrown out. Ryder was a good kid who didn't deserve what that girl did to him."

"Yes, he did."

"What?"

"I saw it, Mom."

She sits back in her chair. "You saw what?"

"I saw him rape her."

"Oh Blaise. Oh my goodness." She pauses and then directs a penetrating stare my way. "This is why."

"Why what?"

"Why you changed overnight from a happy, well-adjusted teenager to a sullen, withdrawn shell of your former self."

"Yes."

"And Sienna! Your friendship with her ended so abruptly. Was she part of this?"

"In a way."

"Was she with you?"

"She was the reason I was there. She thought Cam was cheating on her and wanted to spy on the party we weren't invited to."

"So she saw it, too?"

"Yes, but no one can know that. She wasn't willing to help Neisy or come forward. She's the one who made me keep quiet—or else."

"Or else what?"

"Everyone would hate me, including my own brother."

"Oh, Blaise… Honey…" Her voice is laced with agony. *"Why* didn't you come to me?"

"Because! I wasn't supposed to be there, and I was afraid of getting in trouble. I never wanted to cause problems like Teagan did."

"I would've moved heaven and earth to help you."

"You would've made me report it, and Sienna was right. Everyone would've hated me, including Arlo. At seventeen, that would've been worse than living with the truth, or so I told myself." I look down at the table, which is nicked and scarred from years of homework and projects and family dinners. "In fact, living with the truth stuck inside me was hell. I've thought of it every day. Every single day."

"I'm so sorry you've been through such an ordeal."

"I don't deserve your sympathy. I disobeyed your rules and did the exact wrong thing when I saw someone in need. I've been so ashamed of myself."

"You were a kid, Blaise."

"I was seventeen. Old enough to know better."

"You witnessed something traumatic. Your best friend demanded you stay quiet and told you everyone would hate you. I don't think you should be so hard on yourself."

"Too late."

"So when I told you he's running for Congress…"

"I couldn't take it anymore. I reported it to Houston Rafferty yesterday."

"Oh God," she said with a deep sigh.

"Oh God, what?"

"Arlo quit his job to run the campaign."

"No. When?" This is devastating news. Arlo has a family to support.

"Last week."

I drop my head into my hands. "He'll never forgive me."

"Yes, he will."

"He won't, Mom." I take a breath and release it slowly as the ramifications cycle through my mind at lightning speed. They're even bigger now than they were then. "But I'm not taking it back. I simply cannot live with this for another minute. Whatever happens now is out of my hands."

Houston
NOW

I WAIT ALL DAY to hear something from the AG's office. Josh Spurling finally calls at four thirty. "I met with the AG, and he has questions."

"Okay…"

"Is the victim willing to cooperate?"

If I say no, this whole thing probably goes away right now. So I decide to hedge in the hope that Denise will come around. "I'm not sure yet. I've reached out to her, and I'm waiting to hear. In the absence of her cooperation, we have a sworn statement from her that was taken several weeks after the incident."

"That's not ideal, but it's better than nothing. He also wants to know if the witness is willing to sit for a sworn statement before he decides whether to pursue this."

"I've mentioned that possibility to her, and she said she'll do whatever is needed."

"He asked if there were other witnesses."

"She would only speak for herself. That was a hard line."

"So there were others."

"She didn't confirm or deny that but was adamant she's speaking only for herself."

"It would make for an easier sell if there were multiple witnesses."

"I understand, but this is what we have. I think it's safe to describe it as a take-it-or-leave-it situation."

"Understood. Let me talk to him and get back to you. In the meantime, let's get your witness in here for the sworn statement this week."

We agree to talk again in the morning.

I call Blaise. "Hey, it's Houston."

"Hi."

"I wanted to let you know that I've spoken to the AG's office, and they've requested the sworn statement I mentioned before."

"What would that entail?"

"You'd be sworn in like you'd be if you were testifying in court, and then walked through the sequence of events, also like what would happen in court when you testify. Basically you'd tell them the same story you told me, but you'd do so under oath this time in the presence of a court stenographer. I should also add that if it's later determined you lied about any of it, you could face perjury charges."

"I'm not lying about any of it, and I'll make the statement. Just tell me when and where."

"I'll find out in the morning and let you know."

"Would you be there?"

"If you'd like me to be."

"I think I would."

"Then consider it done."

"Thank you for your support, Houston. I really appreciate it."

"I'm just doing my job, but I understand how difficult this is for you."

"It's not about me. It's about Denise and what was done to her."

"It's also about you and what this will do to your life."

"My life has been a mess since the night I witnessed a crime and failed to do the right thing. I want to fix this, no matter what it costs me personally."

"I'll call you tomorrow with the details about the statement."

"All right. Thank you again."

"No problem."

Shortly after I end the call with her, my brother, Dallas, calls. "Hey, do you want to play cards tonight? We're getting together at Ryder's around eight."

I close my eyes for a beat. "I can't tonight, but thanks for the invite."

"Haven't seen you since soccer practice, bro." We coach his kids' team together. "What gives?"

"Nothing. Just busy."

"Let's do something this weekend."

"Sounds good."

After he signs off, I sit staring into space for a long time wondering how this bomb Blaise dropped in my lap will screw up my own life. Will my brother still want to hang out with me if I help to convict his longtime friend—and now boss—on rape charges? Those charges will send shock waves through two towns and multiple families. Not to mention the legal exposure for Dallas and the other men who signed the affidavit that Denise always said was complete bullshit.

Ryder married a woman he met in college named Caroline. After he left the military, they moved back to Hope where they live with their three young kids. He still holds an annual fundraiser on Thanksgiving weekend in honor of Louisa, who's been gone fourteen years. I try to reconcile that version of Ryder with the version that Blaise described to me, and the one I read about in Denise's sworn statement.

Her statement and Blaise's are nearly identical in their description of what transpired that night.

That's how I know Blaise is telling the truth. She'd have no way to know what Denise reported at the time.

I'm wrapping up my day when my personal cell rings with a call from Denise. I take the call and hold my breath, waiting to hear what she has to say.

"Hi, Houston."

"What can I do for you?"

"I um… I've been thinking a lot about what you said when you were here."

I can barely move. My heart beats fast and my palms are sweating.

"If it's not too late, I'd like to change my mind about testifying."

"It's not too late." I'm not sure whether to be relieved or terrified. "The AG will appreciate your participation."

"What will the timeline look like?"

"That's up to the prosecutor. I'll update him on this development right away and get back to you when I know more."

"I want you to know… Your involvement makes all the difference in my willingness to be part of this. You were the only friend I had there, and I've never forgotten your kindness to me."

"I'll do everything I can to make this as easy as possible for you, knowing nothing about it will be easy."

"No, it won't, but the thought of *him* going on like nothing ever happened, and running for Congress of all things, haunts me. Now that Blaise has come forward, I won't be alone in accusing him like I was last time."

"I think you're very courageous, but I thought that long before any of this happened. It's not easy to be the new kid in a group that grew up together. You always handled yourself with dignity, and I admired that then—and I still do."

"Thank you, Houston. There're two other things I wanted to mention."

"Okay."

"Do you remember the first time around when that group of Ryder's friends signed the affidavit swearing I'd slept with them?"

"I do." Years later, I'd gotten Dallas to admit it was a goddamned lie and had wanted to beat the shit out of him for being part of that. "What about it?"

"They were lying about me to protect Ryder. I want them to pay for that. I know one of them was your own brother, so if you want me to deal directly with the AG on that, I'll understand."

I experience a second of panic on Dallas's behalf. "I'll pass it on to the AG. They'll want to speak to you about it. What's the other thing?"

"The night of the attack, I lost my Honda car key in the clearing where it happened. I forgot to mention that when I first reported it, but the key may still be there. I never went back to look for it. I'm not sure if that would help, so I figured I'd mention it."

I make a note about the key. "It can't hurt. I'll see if I can find it, and I'll be in touch."

"Thank you, Houston."

I end that call and immediately reach out to Josh Spurling.

"Hey, it's Houston. I got your text about the date and time for the witness statement, and I have another update. The victim is fully onboard."

"Well, that's a game changer."

"She has a caveat."

"What's that?"

"After the original charges were filed, Ryder Elliott's brother and a number of their friends signed an affidavit claiming Denise, the victim, had slept with all of them in the last year. That was a lie, and in the absence of hard evidence, it most likely swayed the judge who initially heard the complaint. Denise wants that addressed."

Josh's deep sigh speaks volumes.

"In the interest of full disclosure, one of the people who signed was my brother."

"That could get messy, Houston."

"I know, which is why I won't have anything more to do with that part of it. If your office wants to pursue that, I can't be involved, but Denise made it clear. Dealing with that is a condition of her coop-eration."

"Understood. I'll speak to the AG today and let you know next steps."

"Blaise Merrick and I will be there at ten the day after tomorrow for her sworn statement."

"See you then."

I call Blaise. "Can you come by the station tomorrow afternoon? I want to go over your statement again to prepare you for the AG the next day."

"What time do you want me there?"

"Would two be okay?"

"I'll see you then."

I appreciate that she's clearly invested in seeing this through, no matter the consequences for herself. While I don't condone what she did by not reporting what she saw for fourteen years, I understand the psychology behind being a teenager from a close-knit town fearing the fallout of doing the right thing.

We like to think we'd always do what's right.

Life isn't that simple.

Blaise knows that better than anyone.

Chapter 16

Blaise
NOW

IN THE MORNING, I'M awakened again by Fenway barking in the yard and Jack telling her to hush before she wakes their guest.

The dog just keeps barking like he didn't say anything.

I'm smiling when I haul myself out of bed and make a beeline for coffee. Since I told my story to Houston, I already feel so much better than I have in years. I honestly don't care what happens next. Anything—and I do mean *anything*—is better than knowing about such a thing and not speaking up.

I pull on a zip-up sweatshirt and take my coffee out to watch the Jack and Fenway show.

"I'm sorry," he says when I appear in the doorway. "She's incurrigible."

"Don't worry about it. There are worse sounds to wake up to than puppy joy."

"That's a nice way of looking at it. I hope you don't give me a crappy Yelp review."

I laugh at the goofy face he makes to go along with the comment. "I've never written a Yelp review in my life, and I'm not going to start with you."

"Oh, thank goodness."

He's so cute and funny, and I appreciate that he shared his painful past with me. Losing both his parents in a matter of weeks had to have been a devasting blow. That he turned lemons into lemonade by adding the cottages to help pay the expenses so he could keep his childhood home is also admirable.

But I have other questions.

"So what do you do with yourself other than walk around barefooted, play with your dog at the crack of dawn and manage your property?"

"Hello, nine o'clock is *not* the crack of dawn. It's like noon for those of us who know how to make the most of a day."

"I'm on vacation. Why do I feel judged?"

He laughs, and a little shiver of excitement travels down my spine. When was the last time that happened? How about never? I was a late bloomer in the boyfriend department, which is why what I witnessed at seventeen set me back even further. I've dated here and there, had some sex I kind of enjoyed, but nothing special.

My newfound sense of freedom from the terrible burden has created space inside me to imagine things such as dating a guy like Jack, who's fun, funny, handsome, sexy and he has a very cute dog. That's definitely a plus. I've always loved dogs but never had an apartment that allowed pets.

Fenway comes rushing over to where I'm seated on the front step, drops her spitty ball at my feet and gives me a wet kiss before I have a second to prepare for any of it. "Damn, she's quick."

"The tongue is like lightning. It's a weapon of mass destruction."

I can't believe the way I giggle like a young girl as the dog accosts me while her sexy owner says funny stuff about her.

"Fenway! That's enough. Leave Blaise alone. She's our guest."

Fenway responds to his sterner tone of voice, plopping her rump down as she continues to pant and smile at me.

"She's *so* cute."

"And she knows it. That's what makes her a holy terror."

"You love her."

"Desperately. She's my best girl."

"How's a guy like you calling his Golden Retriever his best girl? And granted, she's an exceptional Golden Retriever."

"Are you asking why a sexy devil like me is single?"

I sputter with pretend outrage. "I never said that!"

"You didn't have to. I know how it is."

Rolling my eyes, I can't help but laugh. "Whatever you say, stud."

"I'll have you know that I've had several girlfriends in my life that didn't work out for one reason or another. Lately, I've decided single life is appealing, especially since Ms. Fenway came along and gave me someone other than myself to focus on."

"I get that. Sometimes it's just easier to stay uninvolved."

"Sure is. You asked what I do. I'm an illustrator."

"What does that entail?"

"I work with several children's book publishers as well as ad agencies and others in need of original art."

"Oh, wow. That sounds like the most fun job ever."

"It's pretty cool, and I get to work from home." He gestures to the house. "The entire third floor is my studio."

"Could I see it sometime?"

"Sure. Anytime you want."

A crackle of something passes between us. I know he feels it as much as I do because he stares at me without blinking long enough that it would be awkward if it wasn't for the crackle. "You want to come by later and check it out?"

"I'd love to. I have an appointment this afternoon, but I should be back before dinner."

"Come find me. The door is always unlocked. Take the stairs to the top floor."

"Are you sure I won't be disturbing you?"

"Positive. Fenway and I like the company."

"I'll bring snacks."

Hearing that word, Fenway launches from resting to full alert in one second flat.

As we laugh, Jack's gaze collides with mine, and there's that crackle again.

"You have to watch out for certain words around her."

"Maybe you can give me the list."

"We'd be happy to, but just so you know, I think she can spell, too, so that's been a problem."

"A dog who can spell. That's a heck of a challenge."

"You have no idea."

I'm excited to have something to look forward to after reliving the horror of that long-ago night again with Houston. "Well, I'd better get myself together. See you guys later."

"We can't wait."

"Neither can I."

I'm nearly floating on air when I go inside to shower. As I dry my hair, I relive every second in the yard this morning, right down to his perpetually bare feet. Something about that strikes me as so endearing. It shows how comfortable he is in his home, and I like that about him. I like a lot of things about him, and for the first time in forever, that doesn't scare me the way it would have only last week.

I've had such a strange relationship with men and dating and sex. It doesn't take a rocket scientist to tie that anxiety back to the trauma that changed my life forever. The first time I had sex, I cried the whole time as I pictured such a thing being forced on Neisy against her will. The poor guy didn't know what to do with me. He left, and I never saw him again. I remember being relieved to have gotten that first time out of the way, but when I thought about the encounter, it was mixed with images of horror.

Maybe later I'll tell Jack why I'm in town. Houston wants me to fill him in, and something tells me I could trust him with my deepest, darkest secret.

HOUSTON AND I SPEND two grueling hours going through every aspect of my statement. He picks it apart for holes he says the AG will ask me about, but I have an answer for everything. Whether those answers will satisfy the prosecutor is anyone's guess. We'll find out tomorrow.

Feeling battered, I leave the police station and head to the grocery store to pick up a few things I need as well as the snacks I promised to bring to Jack's. I keep replaying the meeting with Houston and the emotions it resurrected. It's overwhelming to tell my story for the third time in as many days after keeping it bottled up for so long.

I leave the windows down to let in the scents of autumn. That was my favorite time of year when I was a kid. I loved the fall colors and have always had an interest in gardening, although I've not been able to do much of that since I live in the city. My grandmother taught me the names of all the flowers, bushes and trees. I love that I can identify any of them on sight.

It's nice to think about things other than why I'm here. With a week to ten days until we'll hear from the grand jury, I could go back to New York. I should do that. Wendall is texting me nonstop, and I've heard from others at the theater that he's been more unmanageable than usual since I left.

Call me crazy but going back to that doesn't appeal to me at all.

I pull into a spot at the grocery store. Before I can lose my nerve, I text Wendall. *The family situation is complicated. I'd like to work remotely for the next month. If you can't allow that, I'll understand. Let me know.*

I'm coming out of the store carrying a brown bag when my phone chimes with a new text from Wendall.

Family is everything. I understand. You can work however you want. I need you to keep me sane, Blaise, the goddess of organization. Please don't leave me.

I laugh out loud at his over-the-top-ness. That's the nicest thing he's ever said to me. I should've had a "family crisis" sooner so I could find some humanity in him. My friends at the theater will be shocked by his kindness, but they also know how much I do for him.

As I'm getting ready to pull out of my parking space, the phone chimes again. Assuming it's Wendall with more drama, I glance at the screen.

Sienna. I never did take her out of my phone contacts, even though I should have a long time ago.

I heard you're back in town. I just hope you're not running your mouth about things that don't matter anymore.

A chill goes down my spine. Is that a threat? How did she hear I'm home? I haven't seen anyone but my mother, who'd never tell a soul because I asked her not to.

As I drive to Jack's, I keep an eye on the rearview mirror to see if I'm being followed. I'm the only car on the road, but I can't escape the feeling that someone is watching me. That people have heard I'm back in town. That Sienna is the only other person on Earth who knows what we saw that night unless she eventually told Cam.

I doubt she did.

The anxiety her text arouses in me is tinged with sadness for a friendship that was destroyed on that momentous night. At one time, she was the most important person in my life. We told each other everything. And then that was gone, along with my innocence, my peace of mind, my sense of worth and so many other things suddenly lost because of one person's actions.

I'm shaken by Sienna's text and think about texting Jack to ask if we can get together another time. But as appealing as crawling into bed and pulling the covers over my head might seem, I don't want to be alone.

So I arrange the crackers, cheese and fig spread I bought on a plate and then wash the grapes I got to have with it. I tuck a bottle of Chardonnay under my arm and head across the yard to Jack's back door. From outside, I see lights on in his third-floor studio, so I follow his directions to the stairs. The beat of loud music gets closer as I go up two flights.

The door to the studio stands open, and Jack is singing along to "Gimme Shelter" by the Rolling Stones.

I stand back and watch him as he studies something on a huge drawing board, hands stuffed into the back pockets of his jeans, feet bare as usual and Fenway asleep on a bed by the window.

She senses me there first, and shoots to her feet, barking happily as she comes to greet me.

Jack turns to me, smiling, and cuts the volume on the music. "There you are. We'd about given up on you."

"My meeting took longer than expected."

"No worries. Come in." He takes the plate and bottle of wine from me and puts them on a table, out of the dog's reach.

"So this is where the magic happens, huh?"

"That's what I'm told. I'm sorry it's such a god-awful mess. It makes sense to me."

Chaos is definitely the word I'd use to describe the colorful drawings tacked up on every available space on the wall, the works-in-progress on just about every surface as well as the paint and ink that stain the floor.

I point to a vivid illustration tacked up on a far wall. "May I?"

"Please. Make yourself at home while I check out the snacks you brought. I was just starting to get hungry."

The color and detail are striking. He's done everything from super heroes to fiery dragons to gentle scenes from a children's story. Animals seem to be his specialty. I gasp at the drawing of Fenway that perfectly captures her, right down to the active tongue.

His talent is truly dazzling. "I'm seriously impressed."

"I used to get in trouble in school for doodling nonstop." He shrugs as he grins. "I showed them, right? Making a living out of coloring."

"You sure did. I can't believe the sheer breadth of it. You do it all."

"But you can see where my interest lies." He uses his chin to point toward the animals as he eats a cracker and cheese. He brings me a coffee mug with wine in it. "Nothing but the best in my studio."

I touch my mug to his. "Cheers. Thank you for inviting me to the inner sanctum."

"My pleasure. When you tell someone you're an illustrator, they tend to look at you with skepticism. It helps to show them what that means."

"Was I skeptical?"

"Not at all, which is why I liked you right away."

"Oh, well, that's good." He's flirting, right? I'm so out of practice, I'm not entirely sure.

"It's very good. I appreciate people who aren't skeptical of things they don't understand or actually say things like, 'oh, so you color for a living' in an insulting tone."

I laugh at the way he says that. "Do people really say that?"

"More often than you'd believe. My cousin tells everyone that's what I do."

He makes me laugh twice in two minutes, which has to be a record. It's been such a long time since I felt like laughing or smiling.

He holds up the jar. "What's this stuff?"

"Fig spread. Try it. It's good."

"Hmmm, I'll be the judge of that." He spreads some on a cracker and takes a bite. "Wow, that is good."

"Told ya."

"I never would've pictured figs in a spread."

"You learn something new every day."

"So it seems. Do you like pizza?"

"Doesn't everyone?"

"I have a really cool pizza oven and every imaginable topping since I didn't know what you'd prefer."

"So you, like, planned ahead for my visit?"

"Something like that."

"I'm impressed."

"Don't be. Pizza is the high-water mark when it comes to me and cooking. But my pizza is extraordinary. People come from all over for it."

"If you're going to do one thing well, you may as well kill it."

"That's my philosophy for all things that I do well. Which is draw and cook pizza."

"You're a great dog dad, too."

"Okay, three things."

"I bet there're more."

He waggles his brows at me. "Wouldn't you like to know?"

I feel my face turn bright red, which is mortifying.

"Adorable," he says with a chuckle.

I grimace. "Awful."

"Super adorable."

"Who blushes at thirty-something, especially when their name is *Blaise*?"

"You do, and I'm digging it. What else can I say to make it happen?"

"Don't you dare!"

His grin lights up his face with a mischievous glee. "I do so love a challenge."

"I urge you to decline that challenge."

"If you're going to be that way about it."

"I am."

"Fine."

"Fine."

"So," he says with the grin I'm coming to like more and more, especially when he's not trying to embarrass me, "how about that pizza?"

"Lead the way."

We gather the treats I brought and the open bottle of wine and head downstairs.

"Watch out for Fenway. She's an underfootnik."

"Is that a word?"

"My own personal creation. I almost fall over her at least once a day because she tries to rush past me on the stairs."

Just as he says that, the dog darts between us, forcing him to grab me so I don't fall.

"Case in point. Sorry about that."

"It's fine. I love her. She's adorable."

"She's a demon."

"Don't say that about your little girl!"

"It's the truth. I love her madly, but she's going to be the death of me. Literally, if she knocks me down the stairs."

I stop on the second-floor landing to study photos on the wall that I missed on the way up. Young Jack with his parents, with other dogs, with groups of kids, birthday parties, soccer games, baseball, proms, graduations.

"My mom did that in case you're wondering if I'm in love with myself."

Again, he makes me laugh. I've laughed more in the last half hour than I have in years. It feels good.

"I didn't have the heart to take it down."

"Why would you ever take it down? It's the sweetest thing."

"If you say so. There's nothing more precious than the only child of a mother who yearned for kids all her life and finally got me when she was thirty-eight."

"Aw, she must've been thrilled."

"That's one word for what she was."

His affection for her comes through loud and clear.

"Where'd you go to high school and college?"

"Bishop Stang and RISD."

The Rhode Island School of Design in Providence is one of the nation's premier art schools.

"Oh wow. RISD is amazing."

"I loved every minute of being in school with people who understood that there're worse things than wanting to doodle for a living."

"I'll bet."

"Took a long time to convince my folks I could actually make a living out of doodling."

"I bet they were very proud."

"They were, especially when I started making some money at it."

"That does tend to get the parental attention."

"Right?"

We land on the first floor, and he leads me to a spacious kitchen in the back of the house that's been fully renovated. The cabinets are painted a rich navy blue with a matching tile backsplash, white counters and high-end stainless-steel appliances.

"This is gorgeous."

"It was my first project after I inherited the house. I couldn't very well tell them their kitchen was hideously outdated while they were still alive."

"True. That would've been rude."

"I couldn't wait to get my hands on it, though. Do you watch HGTV?"

"God, yes. I'm addicted."

"Me, too, and I did this myself based on my HGTV degree."

"You did not!"

"I did and let me tell you—watching it done on TV is nothing *at all* like doing it yourself. I was very quickly humbled."

"I can't believe you did it yourself."

"It took almost a year because I was determined not to ask anyone for help."

"Why didn't you list renovation on your list of talents?"

"Because if it takes a year, that's not a talent. That's a fool's errand. I got really good at microwaving during that time."

"I'll bet, but the final product is amazing. I'm impressed."

"That was my only goal for this project. To someday impress an important new friend."

I roll my eyes at him.

He's too cute for his own good—and mine. And it occurs to me that before he decides he might like me, he needs to know why I came to town in the first place. Hearing my story might make him never want to see me again.

After he washes his hands, he dries them on a towel as he studies me. "Hey. What's wrong?"

I shake it off and force a smile. "Nothing."

"Something…"

"I want to tell you why I'm here, but I'm afraid you won't want to be friends with me anymore."

"And it would bother you if we weren't friends anymore?"

I think he might be asking about more than just basic friendship. "Yeah, I think it would."

He surprises me when he tosses the towel aside, takes my hand and leads me into a cozy living room with a wood-burning stove and two full walls of bookshelves.

I scan the shelves stuffed with books. "All this, *and* you read."

"I saw a thing once advising women to quickly run for their lives if they come to a guy's house and he has no books. So I bought these at a yard sale."

"You did not."

Laughing, he says, "Made you wonder, though, didn't I?"

He's fun, funny, handsome, talented, smart, sexy, sweet and kind. He's all the things. And he deserves to know what I did before he decides if he wants to spend more time with me.

When we sit next to each other on the sofa, he doesn't release my hand.

I'm one hundred percent sure that if I give even the slightest tug, he'll let go instantly. The only fear I have of this man is the possibility of losing my heart to him. I've never experienced this kind of connection before, and I'd be sad to lose him before I ever got the chance to really know him.

"Whatever it is, it can't be that bad."

"It is. It's terrible."

He turns to face me. "Tell me."

I fix my gaze on the far wall, so I won't have to see his revulsion when I confess my sin to him. "When I was almost seventeen, I witnessed a crime. For many reasons that made sense to me at the time, I didn't report what I saw. Keeping that secret for fourteen years has all but wrecked me, and this week, I finally reported it to Houston. That's why I'm here."

"Are they pursuing the case?"

"Houston thinks it'll be presented to a grand jury in the next couple of weeks."

"How do you feel since you came clean?"

"I feel free of a horrible burden but still ashamed that it took so long to do the right thing. For what it's worth, I always knew it was wrong not to say anything."

"It's worth a lot. You were really young, Blaise. We all did things back in the day we're not proud of."

"This was a big one."

"What was the crime?"

"I saw a guy I grew up with rape a girl who was relatively new to our school and who'd had a hard time there. She was beautiful, so of course she was treated as a threat by the other girls. It was a party I wasn't supposed to be at here in LE, where I wasn't allowed to go with the car. He's my brother's best friend. His brother had been dating my best friend for years by then. Those are my excuses, but at the end of the day, I stayed quiet while the victim was savaged online after she reported the crime a few weeks later, and I was afraid that would happen to me, too. The whole thing was horrible."

"Were you the only one who saw it?"

I shake my head. "But I'm the only one coming forward. She's married to the guy's brother now. There's no way she'd back me up. She was the one who told me how everyone would hate me if I confirmed it'd happened."

"What a terrible spot to be in. I'm sorry that happened to you."

I finally look at him. "It didn't happen to me. It happened to her."

"And to you because you witnessed a violent crime long before you had the maturity to handle it the way you should have."

"How do you account for the last fourteen years when I was old enough to know better?"

"Is your brother still friends with him?"

Fenway nudges me, so I scratch behind her ears. "He is, and he recently gave up a great job to go to work for him."

"Which is why you kept your mouth shut. Your friend is married to his brother. Your brother is tight with him. The ties still run deep, even if you removed yourself from the scene."

"They do run deep. She's not my friend anymore. I haven't spoken to her since that summer, until she texted me today out of the blue to say she heard I was back in town, and I'd better not be running my mouth about things that don't matter anymore."

"Wait. She said that? In those exact words?"

"She did."

"That sounds like a threat to me."

"It did to me, too."

"What're you doing about that?"

"What can I do without revealing who else was there that night? I don't feel it's my place to force her to testify against her own brother-in-law."

"Do you think you'll be in danger when it gets out that you're willing to testify against him?"

"Possibly. Houston told me I should tell you about this so you're aware. He plans to increase patrols around here as needed. If it's too much, I can relocate to—"

"Stop. You're not going anywhere."

"You don't hate me after hearing what I did? Or I guess I should say what I failed to do?"

"Not at all. But why'd you decide to tell Houston now?"

"Because the man who did it is running for Congress. After I heard that, I couldn't take it anymore."

His face goes flat with shock. "Is it Ryder Elliott?"

I hesitate to confirm it, which answers his question.

"God, Blaise. Seriously?"

"Yeah. Do you know him?"

"Not personally. But I know of him."

"You can't say anything about this, Jack."

"I never would, but you're right that he's well connected."

"Always has been. He was the *it* guy in high school."

"Why would he do something like that?"

"I've thought a lot about that. There's never an excuse for sexual assault, but if there's a reason he snapped it probably was tied up in his longtime girlfriend about to enter hospice care after a terrible battle with cancer. Who knows what that kind of stress does to someone, not that I'd ever in a million years try to justify what he did. It's just hard to make the leap that someone you grew up with is truly evil, you know?"

"I get it, and I agree there's no justification for what he did. I didn't know he lost his girlfriend way back when."

"It was very sad. Louisa was a wonderful person, and she fought so hard. Ryder was right by her side the whole way. He also raised a lot of money to help her family with medical bills. It was difficult for me to reconcile that Ryder with what I saw him do that night."

"I'm sure it was."

"Thank you for listening."

"Thank you for sharing it with me. I know it can't be easy to talk about."

"It's not. I've never talked about it with anyone before I told Houston, and now I've told the story to Houston twice as well as to you and my mom."

"That's a huge load to carry around for such a long time."

"It's been horrible. I was happy to hear this week that Denise, the woman he raped, is happily married with four kids. It's good to know she found happiness."

"You deserve that, too, you know."

"Do I?"

"You do. I get why you feel awful about this, but you're a good person."

"How do you know that? I just told you I'm not a good person."

"A bad person wouldn't have cared so much for all this time. A bad person wouldn't have eventually done the right thing, even knowing it could cost her a lot. You're not a bad person, Blaise. You're a good person who made a bad mistake at a time in her life when she didn't have the wherewithal or maturity to do the right thing."

"I've regretted that every day since."

"Which is another thing a bad person wouldn't have done."

"A lot of people will hate me for this, including my own brother."

"Probably. How do you feel about that?"

"I think it'll be easier to live with that than it was to live with the secret."

"I'm sure it will be."

"Listen, this is a lot. If you want some time to think about whether you want to be friends—"

He shocks the shit out of me when he kisses the next words right off my lips. "I want to be friends, and I hope it was okay to tell you that way."

I smile because how can I not? "It was okay."

"Just okay? I can do much better than just okay."

With my hand on his chest, I stop him from proving that right now. "Slow your roll, cowboy."

"Fine, be that way, but just know I'm capable of way better than just okay."

"Got it." I'd really like to find out what he means by that, but not tonight. This is more than enough for right now.

"How about that pizza I promised you?"

I'm so relieved to have shared my story with him and not been tossed out on my ass. At least now I know for sure he's interested in me as more than a friend, which is good news. Because I'm interested, too. "Let's get to it."

Chapter 17

Houston
NOW

I PICK UP BLAISE at Jack's and head for Providence, so Spurling can take Blaise's sworn statement. "How's it working out at Jack's place?"

"It's great. I love it."

"He's a good dude. Did he tell you what he does?"

"He did. It's very interesting."

"He's won a ton of awards and other accolades, not that he'd ever tell you that."

"I saw his work last night. It's impressive.

"It really is. He does a little bit of everything, from kids' books to cartoons to sci-fi. He's incredibly talented."

"I can't draw a straight line with a ruler."

"Me, either." I chuckle as I glance over at her. "Are you feeling okay about this meeting?"

"I want to get it over with."

"I understand. It's traumatizing to relive it, especially several times in the same week."

She keeps her gaze directed out the window. "It's not my trauma. It was hers. I just happened to witness it."

"Based on how you've described your reaction to it, I think it's safe to say you were traumatized, too. Anyone would be, Blaise."

"It's nice of you to cut me a break, but I don't deserve that."

"Yes, you do. You were still a kid."

"My mother said the same thing when I told her why I'm here, and don't worry. She won't tell anyone. She said I needed to give myself a break, but I've never wanted a break. I just wanted it to go away. I wanted to go back to that night and not defy my parents' wishes by driving to LE. I wanted not to see things that could never be unseen. I wanted this not to have happened to her. I wanted to go back to my life as it had been earlier that day. I wanted that for her, too."

"I wish there'd been someone you could've talked to about it."

"I was so afraid anyone I told would force me to go public. I saw what they'd done to Denise. I couldn't let that happen to me, too. I was spineless and weak, and I hated myself for that."

"Again, you were seventeen. Old enough to know what you'd seen was terrible, but not old enough to see a way through it."

"It makes me uncomfortable for people like you and my mother to give me a pass."

"We're not giving you a pass. We're saying things happen, overwhelming things that are so big and unfathomable it's impossible to see a way out. That doesn't mean you're a bad person. You aren't the one who committed the unspeakable crime."

"What I did was unspeakable in its own way, especially after she came forward and people trashed her in defense of him. Other than having to leave her alone and hurt in the woods, that was the worst part. It's the only time in my life I've contemplated suicide."

"God, Blaise…"

"Please don't feel sorry for me, Houston. I screwed up royally. All I care about now is fixing it."

"I do feel sorry for you. What you saw and how it affected you make you a victim in this as well."

She shakes her head. "Denise was the victim. The only victim."

I don't agree with her, but I can tell there's no point in arguing with her about it. Hopefully as this process unfolds, she'll see that Denise wasn't the only victim of Ryder's crime.

We pass the remainder of the ride in silence.

In Providence, I lead the way to the AG's conference room. I've only been there one other time since we don't have a lot of cases in our town that rise to this level.

Josh Spurling greets us. He's in his late thirties, with brown skin and dark eyes. He's wearing a sharp navy-blue suit and a platinum wedding band on his left hand. He has a reputation for the successful prosecutions of some of the state's highest-profile cases, which would certainly describe this one, as it involves a congressional candidate.

After I introduce him to Blaise, he offers coffee or water.

"I'd appreciate some water, please," Blaise says.

"I'm all set. Thanks, Josh."

We take seats at the far end of the conference room table.

After he pours a glass of water for Blaise from a pitcher, he places a camera and tripod on the table and turns it on, reciting the names of the people present and the purpose of the meeting.

"Please state your name and age for the record."

"Blaise Merrick, age thirty-one."

"Do you swear the testimony you're about to give is truthful in this matter?"

"I do."

"Would you please describe the events fourteen years ago on the evening of June twentieth?"

"That was the last day of school. We'd had a half day. That night, I drove from my home in Hope to Land's End, against my parents' rules, to sneak into a party that was being held at the Rafferty home."

"Why did your parents tell you not to go?"

"They knew nothing about the party. I was forbidden to drive to Land's End in general. I was still somewhat new to driving, and they didn't want me over there. They said it was too far, too dark, too winding…"

"Did you usually do what they asked?"

"Always. I had a rebellious older sister who was constantly in trouble. The fighting was hard on me. I went out of my way to avoid anything that would upset them."

"So you'd say it was a rare moment of rebellion?"

"My only moment of true rebellion."

"Were you alone in this rebellion?"

"I'd prefer not to answer that. I'm speaking only for myself and what I experienced that night."

"Our case would be stronger with multiple witnesses."

"I understand. I'm speaking only for myself."

"Take me through what happened from when you arrived at the party until you left the area."

Listening to Blaise go through the details of what she saw is no less painful the third time. Her every word is laced with the agony of what she witnessed, what she failed to do and how the events of that evening have haunted her ever since.

"Weeks later, when the victim came forward to police, what happened then?"

"Everyone was talking about it. My brother, Arlo, who was one of Ryder's closest friends, was irate over it. Arlo asked how anyone could accuse him of such a thing. I'd never seen him like that. The Facebook attacks on Neisy, as she was known then, were vicious. It made me sick as someone who knew she was telling the truth. He had raped her."

Blaise pauses and looks down at her hands, which are tightly folded on the table. "I'm sure you must be wondering how I could sit on this information while another young woman went through such a terrible ordeal. I asked myself that question every day. I wanted to help her. I wanted to do the right thing. But all I could see and hear were the people closest to me defending him, talking about how we grew up with him, how she wasn't one of us, but he was. It was a loud roar in my head that I couldn't escape no matter what I did.

"I started taking Tylenol PM every night, so I'd have a prayer of sleeping. I could barely eat or function. My senior-year grades were the worst of my life. I stopped going out. I didn't care about anything. I felt like shit all the time. And I thought of her... Of Neisy and what she was going through, and I was sick over it. When we went back to school, nothing had changed for Ryder. He was the same popular, successful student and athlete."

"How did that make you feel?"

"Deeply, deeply angry. Especially because Neisy had to leave our school and go somewhere else for her senior year. I've thought of her every day, and I hoped...I hoped she'd managed to go on with her life. I was so happy to hear she's married and has four kids."

"Why come forward with this information now?"

"I heard Ryder is running for Congress. That news made me realize I don't care anymore what happens to me. I couldn't live with this for another second while he's out there seeking a prestigious office based on his inherent popularity. After I told Houston my story... That was first time in fourteen years I slept through the night without medication."

"And you're willing to testify in open court?"

"I am."

Josh leans forward to turn off the recording. "Thank you for your candor and for coming forward."

"What happens now?"

"We'll present the case to the statewide grand jury, which will decide whether it's strong enough to pursue charges."

"How soon will you know?"

"In the next seven to ten days."

She nods. "Do you have a sense of which way it'll go?"

"With your testimony and the victim's decision to participate, I'll be shocked if they don't vote to indict."

On the way home, I tell her I'm surprised Spurling said that. "They usually play these things much closer to the vest. It's possible he wanted you to know how critical your testimony would be." Before I leave her at Jack's, I caution her not to get her hopes up. "Just because Spurling has faith in the case doesn't mean the grand jury will vote to indict."

"I've been far more concerned about my conscience than any hopes I might have for what happens next."

"I hope your conscience is feeling lighter."

"It is."

"I need to share something with you." I've had a raging debate with myself over this ever since I heard her story the first time.

"What's that?"

"Over the years, I've been friendly with Ryder. Dallas and I play cards with him and Cam, your brother and some others. I wouldn't say I'm in any way close to him, but I do consider him a friend."

"And yet you're still moving forward with the case."

"I'm doing my job."

"Your job may cost you several friends, not to mention your brother."

"I'm aware."

"Does that bother you?"

"Of course it does, but I believe you. It was shocking to hear what you'd seen, to realize your story matched Denise's description of events almost exactly and to reconcile that information with the man I've known all these years. But that won't stop me from doing what needs to be done to get justice for Denise, who was also my friend once upon a time."

"I wasn't aware of the personal stakes for you."

"Don't forget the incident took place at my party. It's always been personal for me."

"True."

"Like you, I wish it'd never happened."

She looks over at me, seeming tentative. "May I tell you something else that worries me?"

"Of course."

"During the preliminary hearing, the defense introduced an affidavit on behalf of several of Ryder's friends and teammates saying they'd slept with Denise. Do you remember that?"

"I do, and I thought it was bullshit at the time. All she talked about was her boyfriend Kane and how much she loved him. I didn't believe them for a second."

"Both our brothers signed that statement."

"I know. I argued fiercely with Dallas about it at the time. He stuck to his story, but I knew it was a lie." I don't tell her how he eventually admitted as much to me.

"Will they get in trouble for that?"

"It's hard to say. If they're smart, they won't let Ryder's attorney use it as evidence this time around. Since most of them are married with families, they have a lot more to lose than they did then. But Denise mentioned that to me as something else she wanted addressed, and I passed it on to Josh."

I'm sick with anxiety over the thought of my brother getting into trouble because of a chain of events that I started. However, it was his decision to sign on to a lie to protect his friend. If he has to live with those consequences, so be it.

"Thank you for everything you're doing, even though it might cost you, too."

"I wish I'd met you again under different circumstances."

"Why's that?" she asks, seeming confused.

"I might've asked if you wanted to grab dinner sometime."

"Oh, well…"

"I don't mean to make you uncomfortable."

"You didn't. It's nice of you to say that."

"Maybe after all of this is over."

"Maybe."

"Are you planning to stick around until we hear from Spurling?"

"I think I might. My boss said it was okay for me to work from here for a while, so I might take a break from the city while I can."

"I'll be in touch when I hear anything."

"Thanks again, Houston."

"Sure thing."

Chapter 18

Blaise
NOW

I WATCH HIS TAILLIGHTS until his vehicle disappears from view. Did that really happen? Did he say he might like to go out with me if we weren't mired in a potential criminal case together? He did, and it's truly flattering. Houston is a great guy, and I genuinely like and appreciate him, but there's no crackle with him like there is with Jack.

Speak of the devil. He comes out of the house with Fenway on a leash.

"I wondered if you owned shoes," I tell him when I notice he's wearing an old pair of sneakers.

"Hardy har har. I prefer to be au natural. You should be thankful I wear clothes. To hear my mother tell it, I was naked until I was five."

"That could turn up in a Yelp review."

"Which is why I've become such a bore in my old age. What's cute as a five-year-old is apparently weird thirty years later."

"Truer words were never spoken."

"My best girl and I were about to go on a romp. Would you like to join us?"

"What do these romps entail?"

"Trails, sticks, mud, various decomposing animals. Whatever comes our way. We play it by ear."

"Mud and decomposing animals, huh?"

He shrugs as he grins. "What can I say? My girl is unpredictable."

"I'd love to go. Can I have five minutes to change?"

"Take ten. We're in no rush."

"I'll be right out." I quickly change into jeans and a long-sleeved T-shirt and put my hair up in a ponytail. I slide my phone into a back pocket and grab my zip-up sweat shirt and sunglasses on the way out the door wearing my sneakers.

"That was quick." Jack has been entertaining Fenway with the tennis ball while they waited for me.

She runs over to greet me like she hasn't seen me in years.

"Down, girl. Don't get Blaise dirty."

I bend to give Fenway my attention and am rewarded with a wet lick that goes from chin to forehead in a flash and makes me laugh as I sputter.

Jack clips the leash on her and tugs her away from me. "If you laugh, you encourage her naughtiness."

"I can't help but laugh. She's funny."

"This is why she's a mess. Everyone thinks that. Speaking of her getting you dirty, if you need to do laundry, you're welcome to the washer and dryer at my house."

"Thanks. I might need it after mud and decomposing animal day."

Smiling, he leads me to an old white truck with a red stripe on the side that's been lovingly restored. "This was my dad's first and only truck. It's almost fifty years old and still purrs like a kitten." He holds the passenger door for Fenway and me. "You're in her usual seat, and she moved to the middle without a qualm. She must like you."

"I'm easier to lick when I'm sitting next to her."

"That's also true."

"Where're we going?"

"To a trail that ends at the beach. It's her favorite."

"Do you mind if I put the window down? It's so nice."

"Make yourself at home with me, Blaise."

What a nice thing for him to say. "Thanks."

"I love your name by the way. I've never known anyone with that name."

"My mom wanted names that no one else had—Teagan, Arlo, Blaise and Juniper."

"I like them all."

"We didn't when we were kids. I wanted to be Emily or Brooke like all the other girls."

"Blaise is unique and special."

"Until the boys start calling you Ablaze in fifth grade because you have red hair and that name."

He rolls his lips together as if he's trying not to laugh.

"It's not funny!"

"It's kinda funny."

"Not even. They also called me Fire Ant, Fireball, Hot Pants and anything else they could think of to make me aware that my name was weird."

"It's beautiful, and it suits you."

Is he saying he thinks I'm beautiful? And what if he is? I'd be okay with that.

"No work today?" I ask, eager to stop talking about myself.

"I got it in earlier. I try to quit early on nice days like this, especially when it's about to get nasty for a bunch of months."

"I hate the winter."

"I don't mind it. Gives us an excuse to chill out and do nothing after the frantic pace of the summer. My mom used to call it Crock-Pot season."

"I like that."

"She'd say it was time to get cozy, light the fire and watch football."

"Sounds a lot more pleasant than winter in the city."

"That's gotta be a drag."

"It really is. We walk everywhere, and there's no way to stay warm and dry when you're slogging through slush and ice and snow that turns black within a day. And then you add the trash piled up on the sidewalks on pickup day and the cars that fly by spraying you with ice water, and it's a real treat."

"What keeps you there?"

"I work in theater, and that's the hub."

"What do you do?"

"I manage Wendall Brooks, who's starring in *Grey Matter* right now."

"My friend saw that in New York. She loved it."

"It's a great show. Everyone loves it."

"Is it a fun job?"

"It should be, but Wendall is a bit insufferable. He takes the fun out of it with his endless demands."

"How's he getting by without you?"

"I'm still keeping him organized and on schedule from here, but I can't deny it's nice to have a break from dealing with him in person every day."

"Sounds like it would be. What'd you tell him about why you're here?"

"I said it was a family emergency, and he shocked me by saying family comes first. I didn't expect that at all."

"Did you study theater in college?"

"Yep. I graduated from NYU's Tisch School of the Arts with a bachelor's degree in performance."

"Did you do any acting?"

"Quite a bit, actually. It was one of the ways I survived, by losing myself in other people's stories so I could be free of my own for a while. But I got tired of barely making the rent, so when I had the opportunity to work for Wendall, I grabbed it thinking it would solve all my problems. Instead, it created new ones."

He pulls into a dirt parking lot and shuts off the truck.

When we get out, Fenway follows me. I grab her leash.

"Hey, so guess what?" he says as we head for the trail.

"What?"

"We both graduated from art school."

"So we did."

"And we're both making a living at it despite a million people telling us we'd starve to death if we pursued these careers."

"I'm barely scraping by on what I make."

"Still… You're in the game, and that's more than a lot of our fellow grads can say."

"I suppose."

"What would you do if you could do anything you want?"

"I think about that a lot, but I don't really know. I still haven't found the thing that makes me excited to get up and go to work every day. That's been sorely missing in the years I've worked for Wendall. He drives me nuts."

"So why don't you quit and find something that makes you happy?"

"Says the guy with crazy-ass talent who can do whatever he wants."

"You think my talent is crazy ass?"

I nudge my shoulder into him and nearly knock him over, which makes us laugh like little kids. We're holding each other up as Fenway gives us a puzzled look while we try to pull ourselves together.

Jack brushes himself off dramatically. "Didn't see that coming."

I can't stop laughing. "I'm so sorry."

"You didn't tell me one of your nicknames is Bruiser." He quirks a brow. "Did you play football?"

"Not once in my whole life."

"Whatever you say."

He takes my hand smoothly and casually, as if it's not the biggest of deals. It's a thrill to hold hands with a handsome, funny guy on a gorgeous trail that's popping with fall color as Fenway dashes ahead of us. She returns every minute or two to make sure we're still there.

"I can see why it's safe to let her off the leash."

"She wants me in her sight at all times. The second she realizes she can't see me she comes running back. She's chipped and air tagged, just in case."

"Good call."

"I'd go mad if I couldn't find her."

"I would, too, and I've only known her a few days."

As promised, the trail ends at a sandy beach.

Fenway goes crazy when she sees the water and takes off in a sprint.

"Did I mention she's wet on the ride home?"

"I don't think you did."

"Thus the laundry offer," he says with an irresistible little grin. "She loves it here so much that she entertains herself, splashing and chasing the gulls." He leads me to a log on the sand. "Have a seat to watch the Fenway Show."

It's the best show I've seen in a long time, especially when she comes over to check in with us and then takes off to continue her performance.

"This is fun. Thanks for asking me to come."

"It's much more fun with you along."

"A girl could get used to being with a nice guy like you."

"Could she? That'd be awesome."

"Things are about to get very weird for me."

"I know."

"A smart man would keep his distance from that."

He slips an arm around me and kisses my temple. "I guess I'm not as smart as I thought I was."

"That's a pretty big statement to make."

"Is it?"

"Uh-huh."

"Well, let me make an even bigger one then. I like you. My dog likes you, which is really the most important thing. We want to spend as much time with you as we can, and we want to offer our support during this difficult time."

I turn to look at him and he sneaks in a sweet kiss I don't see coming. My hand rises to his face, and I lean into the kiss, which goes from sweet to sizzling in a matter of seconds.

We're interrupted abruptly when wet, stinky Fenway crashes into us, nearly sending us backward off the log.

Jack manages to keep us from falling as we fend off the dog's wild tongue. "For crying out loud, Fenway!"

She plops her butt down and smiles as she pants, clearly pleased with herself as she now has our full attention.

"Sorry about that."

"Don't be. She's so funny."

"No, she isn't."

"Yes, she is."

Fenway barks, wanting in on the debate, and we laugh at her shame-lessness.

"This is why she's unmanageable," Jack says. "She uses her cuteness to get away with murder." He takes my hand and helps me up to walk the length of the beach with Fenway leading the way before we head back to the trail.

As we ride home with the windows down, I realize this has been the nicest afternoon of my adult life. I decide to tell him that.

"I'm glad you enjoyed it."

"Everything is more enjoyable when you're not harboring a hideous secret."

"I'll bet."

"Even knowing the shit could hit the fan at any second isn't as bad as the secret was. I wonder all the time about how my life might've been different if I'd done the right thing then. Maybe everyone would've hated me, but I wouldn't have had to carry a thousand-pound weight around with me."

"Having everyone hate you doesn't look as terrible now as it would've been then. Who knows what kind of damage that would've done, you know?"

"Yeah, I guess."

"It was a no-win situation for you no matter what you did. Still is. But you're doing the right thing regardless of what it might cost you. That's admirable."

I'm still not ready to take praise for what I'm doing. Maybe someday I'll get there, but that won't happen today.

After a quiet minute, he says, "You want to grab some dinner?"

"What're you thinking?"

"I know a place out at the point with great food. An old friend of mine is the owner."

"Would it be a date?"

"Something like that."

"I'd love to."

Chapter 19

Ryder
NOW

MY KIDS ARE WILD tonight. They're resisting bedtime with everything they've got. I resort to blackmail to get them into bed.

"Anyone who gets in bed right now will get a special surprise tomorrow."

Three little bodies go hurtling toward their beds.

That worked better than expected.

Seven-year-old Miles, five-year-old Grace and three-year-old Elise are in bed in two seconds flat.

"What will our surprise be?" Grace asks.

"You'll have to wait and see. And everyone has to *stay* in bed, or there's no surprise."

"You hear that, Elise?" Miles asks. "Don't mess it up for the rest of us."

We keep saying we need to put the girls in their own room, but Miles wants "his babies" with him. He's been the best big brother to them from the day we brought each of them home from the hospital.

I kiss them all goodnight and advise them to go to sleep, so they'll earn their surprise, and then I head for the shower.

Since I declared my candidacy, I've missed a lot of bedtimes. I hate that. I never want to miss a second with them, but I'm determined to do whatever it takes to win this special election in November. Our longtime representative resigned his seat, which gave me an opening that I jumped on. The opportunity to serve the community I grew up in on the national stage is something I've long aspired to do.

If I win, Caroline and the kids will move to DC, so we can be together most of the time. I'll have to be back in Rhode Island a lot, but our goal is to keep the family together as much as we possibly can. Thanks to the job I left to run for office, we've got some savings to set up a second household in Washington.

It's all a huge risk, in more ways than one, but it's been an exciting time for our entire family.

I keep waiting for my opponent to dig up my past and the accusation that nearly ruined everything, but so far, that hasn't come up.

Cam told me not to run, that I'd be opening myself to having the case relitigated in the press, but I was undeterred. The case was thrown out for a lack of evidence. I refuse to live my life as if I were convicted of a crime. He thinks the reason the opposition hasn't made a thing about the charges that were eventually dropped is the fear of a civil defamation suit. You can't go around accusing people who were never convicted of a crime without opening yourself up to exposure, according to my brother, the lawyer.

That said, I'm deeply ashamed of that night and what I did to Neisy. I was out of my mind with grief for Louisa. When I think of that time, all I recall is the agony. That's no justification for what I did. There is no justification. I've devoted myself to being a better person, but that's been a struggle.

I suffered from deep depression after Louisa died that was compounded by what I did to Neisy. No matter how I try, I simply can't explain why I did it. I've hated myself for it every second of every day since. It was a struggle to pull myself out of that deep spiral and try to get back on track.

I lost my Naval Academy appointment after I was charged. It didn't matter that the case never went to trial. The accusation alone was enough. Captain Sutton saw to that. Not that I blame him. I don't. It was my fault, and I own that. All of it was my fault. My dad getting arrested, losing his job and dealing with financial and emotional hardship that lasted for a long time was my fault.

After a hellish few years of grief, remorse and depression, I met Caroline in college. She helped me turn things around. I told her soon after we met that I'd been accused of rape. She asked me if I did it.

I lied.

I wanted her in my life so badly that I lied to her face.

It's the only time I've ever lied to her, but the lie eats at me. She married me thinking I was innocent of the charges. Our whole life together is built on a lie.

On the night before our wedding eight years ago, Cam asked me if she knew the truth.

I said no.

"Ryder... How can you marry her without telling her?"

"If she knew, she'd never marry me. She put me back together, Cam. I can't be without her."

"I hope you know what you're doing."

Since the night I told him the truth, things between my brother and me have been strained. We're still close, but not like we once were. I tell myself that would've happened anyway as we left home, went to different colleges and weren't together every day anymore. But that's not why things changed. It's because I told him, and only him, the truth about what happened with Neisy. I put an awful burden on him. I made myself feel better at his expense. I never should've done that. It's another thing I deeply regret.

As I shave in the shower, I think about how the saying, "the truth sets you free" is bullshit.

The truth would ruin me.

I'm thankful to Cam, Arlo and Dallas for leaving perfectly good jobs to run my campaign. I'll never forget the chance they all took to ensure my freedom years ago, and there's nothing I wouldn't do for any of them. I owe them everything.

I learned after the fact that Arlo was the one who suggested they swear as a group to having had sex with Neisy, to confirm the widely spread rumors about her promiscuity. If I'd known about it, I would've told them not to risk themselves for me. But I believe the affidavit made the difference in the case getting tossed. I've never forgotten what they did, and I never will.

It makes me sick to think about what we did to an innocent young woman who didn't deserve any of it. I wish I could apologize to her for everything, but there's no way I can do that without putting myself in legal jeopardy.

So I live with regret that gnaws at me even after all this time. That's the least of what I deserve for inexcusable behavior.

Caroline is in bed when I emerge from the bathroom.

She's so beautiful—inside and out.

Her long dark hair shines in the light of the bedside lamp and her warm, brown eyes look at me with nothing but love and affection. I'm so lucky to have her in my life, and I make sure she feels my love every day. I give her everything she wants or needs, and she gives right back to me in spades. Sometimes I wonder what my marriage to Louisa would've been like and whether it would've been as amazing as what I have with Caroline. Comparing them adds to the guilt that's always with me, so I try not to do that. But I still think of Louisa every day and miss her, even after all this time.

"What'd you promise to get them to go to sleep?" Caroline asks when I get into bed.

"A surprise tomorrow."

"Which will be what?"

"Haven't decided yet."

"So we've been reduced to blackmail now, huh?"

I put an arm around her and rest my head on her chest. "Whatever works to give us an hour or two of peace and quiet to ourselves."

She runs her fingers through my hair. "Marty called about the fundraiser. We're sold out for the tenth year in a row."

"That's amazing news." Along with Louisa's beloved brother we've raised more than a million dollars for Hodgkin's research in Louisa's name. Caroline took over the coordination of the annual fundraiser the year after we got married. She retooled the event, and it's thanks to her that we've raised so much money. When I say she's the best thing to ever happen to me, I mean it.

I exhale a deep breath, overwhelmed with gratitude for her, our kids and this life I don't deserve.

Cam
NOW

"WE HAVE A PROBLEM," Sienna says as she gets into bed next to me.

I'm exhausted and have no patience for her drama of the day. "What problem do we have?"

"Blaise Merrick is back in town."

"So?"

"From what I've heard, she's hanging out in LE, which is bizarre to say the only time she's been home since high school is when her father died."

"Maybe she has friends there."

"Or maybe she's decided it's time to ease her conscience."

I sit up straighter. What the hell is she talking about. "What?"

A guilty look crosses her super expressive face. "I need to tell you something I should've told you years ago."

My entire body goes cold with dread. Sienna doesn't keep anything to herself. Her mouth runs overtime, which is one of our biggest issues. She talks about things she shouldn't at inappropriate times. I tell her she's a liability that way, which infuriates her. So the possibility that she might know something she hasn't already told me is terrifying because it must be something huge. "What do you need to tell me?"

"That night in LE… Houston's party."

Dread shifts to terror. I'm afraid to ask. "What about it?"

"Things between you and me had been weird that summer. You were acting like you weren't into me anymore, and I was feeling insecure. So Blaise and I snuck over to LE to spy on the party."

My mind races, trying to figure out what she might've seen me do or who she saw me talk to and why that might be coming up now.

"We were there when Ryder raped her. We saw it."

The bottom falls out of my entire life. There were witnesses, and one of them is my own wife. The implications are so huge I have no idea what to do with this information.

"Cam. Say something."

I stare at the far wall, trying to resist the overwhelming urge to scream at her. "You never thought you should mention this to me?" She doesn't know Ryder told me the truth. I love her, but I don't entirely trust her to keep something like that to herself. Besides, Ryder and I swore we'd never tell anyone else, and he didn't even tell Caroline.

"I know how much you love Ryder! I'd never want to do anything to cause a rift between you guys. I made sure Blaise kept her mouth shut."

"This is why you stopped hanging out with her." At the time, she wouldn't tell me what had come between them. She said it was girl stuff, and I wouldn't understand. Arlo and I talked about it a few times, but eventually it didn't matter anymore why two teenaged girls had fallen out a long time ago. It had nothing to do with us.

"She made me so mad with her holier-than-thou act and how we were bad people for leaving Neisy there alone…after it happened. She said we should've helped her. I told her everyone, including Arlo, would hate her the way they hated Neisy, and that she'd better keep her mouth shut or else."

My head is spinning, and I feel like I might be sick.

There were fucking witnesses, and one of them is my own wife.

I know nothing about Blaise or what she's been up to all this time. Arlo rarely mentions her except to say it's weird that she left home and never looked back. This is why. Because she *saw* my brother rape Neisy. She ran away and never came back, taking this secret with her.

And now she's in LE doing God knows what.

Fucking hell.

"Are you mad?" Sienna asks me in a soft voice that's so not like her.

"No."

"I did what I thought was right, Cam. I was protecting you and your family, like always."

"I know."

"You knew, didn't you?"

I look over at her. "Knew what?"

"That he did it. You weren't surprised to hear me confirm it. You were only surprised to hear I saw it."

My head aches as I try to figure out how I should reply. And then I decide to go with the truth. "Yes, I knew."

"For how long?"

"From the beginning."

"What does it say about us that we've never told each other what we knew?"

"It says we both realized we were sitting on a powder keg and chose to keep our mouths shut, even with each other."

"It makes me sad that you felt you couldn't trust me with what he'd told you when you know I've always been loyal to you and your family."

"I know that, Sienna, but I didn't want you burdened with this."

"Is that what you've been? Burdened?"

It's the deepest conversation we've had in a while, which says something about the state of our marriage. "I hate that he made himself feel better by telling me he did it. I've been angry with him about that for years, not to mention he did it in the first place. That's the part I still can't believe. What the hell could he have been thinking?"

"Can I ask you something else and will you tell me the truth?"

I'm suddenly as tired as I've been in years. "Yeah, I'll tell you the truth."

"The affidavit you all signed. Was that true?"

I ache when I think about being part of that. "No, it wasn't."

Her expression is so relieved that I realize she's wanted to ask me that for years.

"What're you going to do about Blaise?"

"I have no idea."

"You've got to do something before she ruins everything."

"I'll take care of it." I look over at her. "Don't you do anything about her. Do you hear me?"

A guilty look crosses her face. "I might've already texted her and reminded her to keep her mouth shut."

"Goddamn it, Sienna! Why would you do that? Maybe she's wavering and you pushed her right over the edge."

"I wanted her to know people are watching her."

"Stay out of it from now on. You got me?"

"Fine. Whatever. You don't have to be so nasty to me when I sacrificed my lifelong best friend to protect you and your brother."

Because I'm afraid of what she might do if I piss her off, I turn to face her. "I appreciate what you did. I truly do. But promise me you'll stay out of it from now on."

She gives me a defiant look, and just that quickly the closeness I felt with her a few minutes ago evaporates.

"Sienna, I mean it. You'll do much more harm than good by getting involved."

"Fine. I promise I'll stay out of it. But I want to know what you're going to do about it."

"I'm not sure yet."

"But you'll do something, right?"

"Yeah." I've got to do something before the past blows up in our faces and ruins our lives.

I CALL RYDER FIRST thing in the morning.

"Hey, how's it—"

"Ryder."

"What's wrong?"

"Sienna told me something last night that I didn't know."

"What did she tell you?"

"That she and Blaise Merrick witnessed what happened with Neisy."

"*What?*" he gasps. "They *saw* it?"

"They saw it."

"And she never told you that before now?"

"She said she was protecting us by keeping it to herself."

"Why'd she tell you now?"

"Because Blaise is back in town and hanging out in LE, according to Sienna."

"What the fuck, Cam? How can we find out why she's here?"

"We could ask Arlo."

"Wouldn't he have told us if he knew?"

"I would think so."

"So what can we do?" he asks with a hysterical edge to his voice.

"There're a million reasons why Blaise could be in LE. Maybe she met a guy on a dating app, and he lives there. Maybe she got a job over there. Who knows?"

"Can we ask Houston?"

"You want me to call him and ask if Blaise reported seeing you rape Neisy fourteen years ago?"

"Don't even say it out loud. Someone might hear."

"My wife already knows what you did. She saw it."

"You're angry."

"You're goddamned right I am! If Blaise comes forward, it'll wreck us all. Remember how we laid ourselves on the line to defend you? If it gets out that I committed perjury, I could be disbarred."

"What do we do? We can't just sit here and do nothing."

"I don't think we should do anything. We could be totally wrong about why she's here, and the last thing we'd want to do is alert Houston that we're worried."

"How am I supposed to function after hearing this?"

"You need to stick to your schedule and keep your cool."

"How in the hell can I do that?"

"Ryder… It could be nothing."

"Or it could be the end of me."

Chapter 20

Blaise
NOW

OVER THE NEXT TWO weeks, Jack and I fall into the habit of having dinner together every night. Sometimes he cooks. Sometimes I do. Other times we go out. I like him more with every passing day. We have the best time together, laughing, talking, kissing. There's been a lot of that. The kissing, I mean. We make out like teenagers, or like I imagine teenagers do. I never did that. I've never had anything like what I do with him, and as October slips into November and the days start getting chillier, all I think about is how I can make this moment with him last forever.

And then Wendall will call me with some unreasonable request that'll send my day spiraling out of control, reminding me I have a job and a life four hours from here, which is my reality. This interlude with Jack isn't real life, even if it feels better than anything ever has.

"When will you be back in the city, Blaise?" Wendall asks for the third time this week. "It's getting harder all the time to manage things here without you. I don't want to pressure you while you're dealing with family stuff, but I *need* you."

"I understand, and I'm working on resolving things here." That's a lie. I'm working on the most exciting romance of my life and haven't seen anyone from my family since the lunch with my mom a couple of weeks ago.

She did as I asked and didn't tell the others I'm home and has been checking in every day to see how I'm doing.

We're waiting to hear from the AG about the grand jury. Until then, I'm enjoying the break from my regular life. I didn't realize how burnt out I was until I got away from Wendall, his endless demands and the relentless pace of the city.

"I want you to know, Blaise," Wendall says, "I appreciate you so much. I know I don't always show that, but I really do. You make everything run so smoothly for me, and I'm lost without you."

His kindness continues to floor me. "Thank you, Wendall. That's nice to hear. I'll try to get you an ETA for my return to the city in the next week or so."

"That'd be great." He sounds relieved. "I hope everything is getting better with your family."

"It is. Thank you. I'll be in touch in the morning with your schedule."

"Very good. Talk soon."

After I end the call, I see a new text from Jack. *Come visit me. I'm lonely.*

You're working.

I'm on a break that might last the rest of the day for the right incentive…

What about your deadline?

My what?

Jack…

Blaise… Fenway misses you.

I've never felt anything like the giddy excitement that floods my entire system any time I see him or talk to him or even flirt with him by text. I have a million things I should be doing for Wendall, but I can't bring myself to care about any of that when Jack wants me to come visit.

I brush my teeth and hair, pull on a sweatshirt and head out the door.

The grass on the path across the yard from my little cottage to his house has begun to be worn down from the many times we've gone back and forth in recent weeks. The time here has been the most exciting and relaxing of my life. No matter what happens with the grand jury, I feel free and unencumbered for the first time since that long-ago night.

When I walk through Jack's back door, I find him in the kitchen holding a cup of coffee. He smiles when he sees me and pours a mug for me, adding the cream he bought for me.

"Thank you."

"You're welcome."

"Where's Fenway?"

"Out cold on the third floor. I snuck out so she wouldn't know I was leaving."

I sip from the mug. He makes the best coffee. "Why aren't you working?"

"Because I have better things to do than stupid old work."

"You love your stupid old work."

"Yes, I do, but it's not as much fun as you are."

It's a heady thing to have a wildly talented and successful man say such a thing to me. He comes to stand in front of me, putting both our mugs on the counter so he can kiss me.

Smiling, he tucks a strand of hair behind my ear. "Hi."

"Hi there."

"How'd you sleep?"

"Like a dead woman." Since my first meeting with Houston, I haven't needed medication to sleep. "You?"

"I tossed and turned a bit."

"How come?"

He runs his fingertips lightly over my cheek, and goosebumps erupt throughout my whole body. That hint of a touch is more of a turn on than sex has been with other men. "You left me in quite a state when you insisted on going back to your cabin."

"Did I?"

"You know you did."

"I was in a similar state."

He leans in and kisses my neck.

My hands land on his hips as I try to keep my knees from buckling.

"I have a secret."

"What's that?"

"I know the cure to this problem we both seem to have."

My eyes close as my head falls back in complete surrender to what he's doing to my neck. "There's a cure?"

"A very pleasurable cure."

"I thought we agreed to keep things casual since I'm not sure where I'll be in a week."

"Did we agree to that? I don't recall."

I poke him in the belly, making him gasp and laugh.

His head lands on my shoulder. "This isn't feeling casual for me, Blaise."

"No?"

"Not at all."

"What should we do about that?"

"I have a few ideas."

The press of his erection against my abdomen has me pulling him closer.

He groans. "Blaise…"

"It scares me."

His head comes off my shoulder so fast, I nearly stumble. Only because he's holding me so tightly against the counter do I remain in place. "What does?"

"All of it."

"Sex?"

I have a feeling that sex with him wouldn't be like anything I've had in the past. "That, but I'm more afraid of the big feelings."

"You're having big feelings for me?"

"Yeah."

"That's the best thing I've ever heard."

"It's scary."

"No, it's amazing. I feel like I've been waiting for you for my whole life."

"Jack…" I sound as breathless as I feel.

I used to think it was preposterous that someone's breath could be stolen by a romantic partner. Now I know it's not preposterous at all. I just needed this man to show me how it's done.

"Yes, Blaise?"

"I, um…I can't talk when you're doing that."

"Doing what?" He cups my breasts and runs his thumbs over my nipples. "This?"

I'm on the verge of begging him to take me to bed when Fenway comes running down the stairs from the third floor, barking her head off.

Jack pulls back from me to look out the window. "Houston is here."

I feel like a balloon that's been stuck with a pin as desire is replaced by anxiety that has my brain pinging from one thing to another so quickly I'm left a bit dizzy. It takes several deep breaths to get myself together enough to feel like Houston won't be able to tell exactly what he interrupted.

"Do you want me to come with you?"

"Would you mind?"

"Not at all."

"I'm sorry about…"

"Don't be. It'll keep."

The promise in those four little words propels me forward, out of the house to the yard where Houston is playing with Fenway.

Houston immediately notes that Jack and I were together in his house. "Sorry to drop by without calling first."

"That's okay," I tell him. "What's going on?"

"I heard from Spurling. The grand jury has voted to indict."

Jack's hand lands on my back in a private show of support that I deeply appreciate.

"What happens now?"

"Ryder will be arrested and charged. He'll be held until an arraignment at which he'll probably be released on bail and asked to surrender his passport. The AG's office will hold a press conference this afternoon to announce the case has been reopened due to new evidence."

"Will they say what that evidence is?"

"No, they won't want to tip their hand yet, but it won't be long before they'll be required to turn over discovery to Ryder's defense attorney. That discovery will include your sworn statement."

I swallow hard. I have a matter of days, maybe not even that long, before everyone will know the case is being reopened because of me. Sienna knows I'm home in Rhode Island. She won't see this as a coincidence.

"I received a threatening text." I'd debated whether to tell him and had decided not to bother him with it. But now that shit's getting real, I'm worried.

"From whom?"

"Sienna Elliott." I show him the text. "She knows I'm back in town. When the case is reopened, she'll know why."

"I'll increase patrols around here today." He hands my phone back to me. "Was she the other witness?"

"I can speak only for myself, but that was the first text I've received from her in fourteen years."

"Understood. Would you like me to have a word with her?"

"I don't think that's necessary. She'll find out soon enough that her threats didn't have any effect on me."

"Because the crime took place at a party at my house, I've asked the

State Police to handle the arrest. I'm taking every precaution to make sure no one can impugn the reopened investigation."

"Thank you, Houston. I know this is complicated for you."

"It is, but I don't want you to worry about that."

"When will I be needed? My boss in New York is making noise about me getting back to the city."

"In the next two weeks or so for the preliminary hearing."

"I'll be there."

"See you then."

"Thanks again for coming by."

"No problem."

It seems like there's something else he wanted to say, but he turns back to his SUV, giving Fenway a pat on the head before he gets in.

After I wave him off, I turn to Jack. "So."

"So. How're you feeling?"

"Anxious but determined."

"What's this about your boss wanting you back in New York?"

"He's been great about me being here this long, which is wildly out of character for him, but I have to go back eventually."

"Do you?"

"What do you mean?"

He rests his hands on my shoulders. "Do you have to go back to the city?"

"I live there. My job is there."

"But I'm here."

"Remember when we said this was casual?"

"Remember when I said it's not casual for me anymore?"

"Since when?"

"From about the first time I ever talked to you."

"Jack…"

"Blaise… Don't go."

"I need to work. I have an apartment. I have—"

He kisses me, and I forget what I was going to say. "I've never felt like this."

"Like what?"

"Like if I let you go, I'll regret it for the rest of my life."

I've never felt like this either. There's nowhere else I want to be than wherever he is, but I'm not ready to decide anything more than that. "I don't have anywhere to be today." I put my arms around him. "Maybe we could go back to what we were doing before Houston arrived?"

His hands slide down my arms to take my hands. Walking backward, he leads the way inside and upstairs to his room. I haven't been in there before. I want to look around, but he has other ideas as he unbuttons my top and pushes it off my shoulders.

"Softest skin in the whole world," he whispers as he kisses my neck.

Fenway comes barreling into the room and crashes into us, sending us sprawling onto his bed.

We crack up as her tongue goes on a mission to lick anything she can reach.

He gently pushes her away. "Thanks for moving things along, girl, but I've got it from here. Go lay down."

She acts like he didn't say anything.

"Fenway," he says more sternly. "Go lay down in your bed." He gives her another push to get her moving.

The dog finally jumps off the bed and lands with a thump and an indignant grunt.

"Now, where were we before we were so rudely interrupted?"

I want to focus on this moment with Jack, but all I can think about is what's happening across the river in Hope where Ryder will be arrested. The word will get out that the case is being reopened and Sienna will know why.

"Hey," he says as he kisses my face and lips.

I shift my gaze to meet his. "I'm sorry. My brain is racing."

"I know." He gathers me into his warm embrace. "What can I do?"

"This helps. I'm sorry to check out on you."

"It's okay. Things are tense, and you can't help wondering what's happening."

"Or when it's going to explode in my face."

He caresses my cheek. "I won't let anything explode anywhere near this gorgeous face. Don't worry."

"Thank you, Jack. I really need a friend right now, and I'm thankful for you."

"I'm here, and I'm not going anywhere."

There's nothing he could've said that would've meant more to me.

Chapter 21

Ryder
NOW

"KEEP YOUR EYE ON the ball, Miles. Wait for your pitch."

The umpire calls a ball.

Watching my son play fall ball and helping to coach his team are among my favorite things. I've missed more games than I've made this season, so I'm thankful to be here for his last game.

"That's the way. Wait him out."

"Who's on deck, Coach?" Petey Johnson asks.

"Jalen. Get out there and take some swings. Come on, Miles! You got this."

The crack of the bat connecting with a ball has the whole team cheering as Miles grabs a standup double and an RBI. We're now up four to one. *"That's the way to do it!"*

"Mr. Elliott?" The voice comes from the right side of the dugout.

I give the man a distracted glance. "Yeah?"

"I need you to come with me, sir."

I give him another look and do a double take. A state cop. No. No fucking way. My stomach drops to the ground.

"Sir?"

The kids in the dugout immediately realize something big is happening and turn their innocent stares my way.

I put down my clipboard and walk toward the cop. "I'll go with you but please don't make a big production of it in front of the kids."

"I'm sorry, sir, but we're under orders. Put your hands behind your back."

"Please. My wife and kids are watching."

"Put your hands behind your back."

As the cuffs encircle my wrists, I glance toward the stands where Caroline is watching with a confused expression. She hands Grace and Elise off to a friend and comes down the bleachers to the fence. "What's happening?"

"Where are you taking me?"

"Wickford Barracks."

"Call Cam. Tell him I need him in Wickford right away."

"Ryder... What's going on?"

"Call Cam, Caroline. Right now."

They lead me out of there as everyone watches in stunned silence. The game has come to a complete halt. As we walk to the State Police SUV, one of them tells me I'm under arrest for first-degree sexual assault and sexual assault of a minor. They recite my Miranda rights.

My son comes running in from second base. "Dad! *Wait.* Where're you going?"

"Stay with Mom," I tell him over my shoulder. "Just stay with Mom."

"*Ryder!*" Caroline's hysterical cry breaks me.

Tears fill my eyes.

They don't know yet that I've ruined their lives.

Cam
NOW

I'M EATING DINNER WITH Sienna and the kids when I get a call from Caroline. I'd hoped to make it to Miles's game, but I got home late and was starving. "Hey, what's up?"

"Cam! They arrested Ryder! Just now at the ballfield. No one will tell me anything. He said to call you."

Her every word hits me like a knife stabbing me in the heart.

"Cam!"

"I'm here. Did they say where they're taking him?"

Sienna gasps, immediately putting two and two together from what she can hear me saying.

"The Wickford Barracks. What's happening, Cam?"

"I'll find out."

"What should I do?"

"Take the kids and go home. I'll update you as soon as I know anything."

"Miles will want to finish the game."

"Then finish the game."

"What do I tell people?"

"Just say you don't know what's going on, which is the truth. I'll be back to you as soon as I can."

"Cam…"

"I know, Caro. I'll take care of him. Try not to worry."

"My husband was just arrested in front of our children and half the town. Why would I worry?"

She's understandably distraught, and I wish I could say something that would soothe her. But things will get a whole lot worse when she hears the rest. "I'll see what I can find out and get back to you. Try to stay calm for the kids."

"He's my whole life, Cam," she says on a whimper.

"I know. Let me go so I can get on it."

"Okay."

The phone goes dead, and I glance at Sienna.

Her expression is hard with anger. "Why would she do this after all this time?"

"Because he's running for Congress." I have no doubt that's why she came forward.

Sienna is less convinced. "What?"

"This is why I told him not to run, Sienna. Because I knew something like this would happen."

"You knew a witness would come forward?"

"No, I couldn't have known that, but I knew it might be relitigated and could smear him and the rest of us with shit from the past. Goddamn it!" I pound my hand on the table, causing my kids to startle. "I'm sorry guys. Dad's upset. I need to go back to work."

"Finish your dinner," Sienna says to the kids as she gets up to leave the room with me. "That fucking bitch. *That motherfucking bitch!* How can she do this to us?"

"It doesn't matter at this point why she did it. The fact is she did, and now he's totally fucked."

"There has to be a way to keep this from ruining him."

"There isn't. He'll stand trial for raping Neisy, who's probably agreed to testify. With a witness backing her story, he'll lose."

"No. That's not possible."

"It's not only possible, but also probable. Now pull it together for the kids while I go see what I can do to get him out of jail."

I'm on the road to Wickford when my mother calls. "Camden! Your brother has been *arrested*. What is going on?"

"I'm on the way to figure that out, Mom." I don't have the heart to tell her a witness has come forward who saw Ryder rape Neisy. She'll find that out soon enough.

"What in the world could he have done to warrant such treatment? They hauled him away from the baseball game like a common criminal! Caroline is beside herself, and the children are hysterical."

"I'm getting another call. I'll get back to you when I know more."

"Please do something, Cam."

"I'll do what I can." I juggle the phone to take the call from Rich Morton, my law school friend who works for the AG. I'd texted him to tell him Ryder is my brother and to ask what he could find out. "Hey, Rich. Thanks for calling me back. What've you got?"

"The grand jury has issued a true bill on first degree charges of sexual assault and sexual assault of a minor."

Oh fuck. He's been indicted. That means this has been in the works for weeks.

"Cam? Are you there?"

"I'm here."

"You didn't know about this?"

"No, we hadn't heard a word about a grand jury or any of that."

"Oh, wow, sorry it came as a total shock. I assume it was handled very carefully due to his campaign. Prosecutors never want to be accused of trying to influence politics."

"Was the grand jury verdict unanimous?"

"I believe it was."

Son of a bitch.

"Why did the state cops arrest him?"

"Apparently, the LE chief has a conflict of interest as the alleged assault took place at a party at his former home. He turned the case over to the State Police."

Of course I already know about Houston Rafferty's party because I was there, but Rich doesn't need to know that. It's also a shock to learn Houston has been involved in this for weeks and never said a word. "Okay. Thank you, Rich."

"No problem. I'm sorry about your brother."

"I am, too."

"Did he do it, Cam?"

There's no way I can tell someone from the AG's office, even a friend, the truth. "I don't know."

"Well, good luck to you and your family."

"Thank you for calling."

"Of course."

I feel worse than I did before Rich filled me in on the details. This is bad. As bad as it gets and about to get so much worse. I'm furious that Ryder didn't take my advice about running for office. I'd told him it was a huge mistake, and I hate to say *I told you so*, but... If someone had been sitting with this information for all this time, hearing Ryder was seeking that kind of office would've been enough to push the witness into doing something about it. I'd bet my life that's what happened.

And now I also have to worry about what'll happen if it gets out that we lied about Neisy in a sworn affidavit when the original charges were filed.

I've no sooner had that thought when Arlo calls. "What the fuck is happening?"

"Ryder's been indicted on rape charges."

"Who are they saying he raped?"

"Neisy."

"That was fourteen years ago! How is this coming up again now?"

"Apparently a witness has come forward who can corroborate her story."

"*What?*" Arlo asks on a long exhale. "A *witness*? Where was this so-called witness all this time?"

"I don't know anything more. I'm on the way to the Wickford Barracks now to see Ryder." Someone else can tell Arlo that the witness is his sister.

"We went out on a limb to save his ass years ago."

"I'm well aware."

"Will that come back to bite us now?"

"I really hope not."

"Christ, Cam. How can this be happening after all this time?"

"I don't know." People would find out soon enough how it happened.

"Let me know what's going on, if you can."

"I will."

On the drive across the bay to Wickford, I take three more calls from guys who signed the affidavit about Neisy back in the day, all expressing the same fears Arlo had. I do what I can to reassure them, even as I'm filled with dread over what this will mean for me and my family. If I'm disbarred, how will I provide for them?

In Wickford, I wait more than an hour before they let me in to see Ryder.

He looks wild in the eyes. "Cam! They came to Miles's game. They arrested me in front of Caro and the kids and everyone we know. They fucking strip-searched me! Is this because of Blaise?"

"Yes."

"So she went to the police after fourteen years of holding onto this secret."

"She did, which means she no longer cares about the implications for herself." I run my hands through my hair as I pace the claustrophobically small room. "Goddamn it, Ryder. This is exactly why I told you not to run. It was fucking arrogant to think the past wouldn't resurface."

"How was I supposed to know there was a fucking witness?"

"She might've stayed quiet forever if you hadn't run for Congress."

"Maybe you could pay her a visit?"

"And say what?"

"Ask her not to testify."

"I'm not doing that."

"Arlo would."

"If you want him to do that, you can ask him yourself."

"How can I do that from in here?"

"I'm sure you'll be released on bond after the arraignment. If you want Arlo to deal with his sister, you can take care of that dirty work on your own."

"I'm sorry, Cam. You were right. I never should've run for Congress."

"No, you really shouldn't have. You know what your problem has always been?"

"What are you talking about?"

"Everyone said you were the shit, and you believed it." I poke his chest when I'd much rather punch him. "You believed you could attack Neisy and get away with it. That you could run for Congress and none of this shit would come back to bite you—and the rest of us—in the ass. You're arrogant and entitled, and you deserve all of this."

"I'm sorry! If I could go back and change everything, don't you think I would?"

I have nothing to say to that. You can't change the past, no matter how much he might wish he could.

"So what now?"

"You'll be arraigned and hopefully released pending trial. And this time, there'll be a trial."

"Not if Arlo can talk his sister out of testifying."

"Do you honestly think she would've done this in the first place if she wasn't determined to see it through to the finish?"

"So you think I'm fucked?"

"Totally fucked."

"You're pissed."

"You're goddamned right I am! Everything was fine the way it was, but you just had to want more. I hope you're not going to take me and all the guys who lied for you the first time around down with you."

"I never asked you guys to lie for me!"

"But we did it anyway and saved your ass!"

"I'm so sorry, Cam." His voice breaks. "I know that's meaningless right now, but I really am."

"I'm sure you are, but you're right. That doesn't mean much to me right now."

"So you won't represent me?"

"I'm not a defense attorney. You need someone who knows what they're doing. I'll ask around and get someone here for the arraignment."

"What about Caroline and the kids? What do I tell them?"

I stare at him, incredulous. "How about the truth?"

He shakes his head. "I can't. She'll leave me and take my kids. I can't lose my family."

"What do you think she'll do when you're convicted?"

"Maybe I won't be."

"Ryder… They have an *eyewitness* who saw you rape her. There's no statute of limitations on sexual assault in this state. The fact that she took fourteen years to come forward won't mean anything to a jury when they hear her testimony in support of Neisy."

"We have to do something. We can't just let this ruin everything."

"It's far too late to *do* anything. This is why I begged you not to run. I was afraid of something just like this."

"Okay, *you were right!* Are you happy now?"

"No, Ryder. I'm not at all happy. What do you want me to tell Caroline? She's frantic and blindsided."

"Tell her…tell her I'll explain everything when I get out of here."

"And you'll tell her the truth?"

"I…I don't know."

"You owe her the truth at this point."

"I…uh…"

"Ryder! You've turned her life upside down! She deserves to know."

"I'll think about it."

"You do that." I slap my hand against the door to call for a Trooper to let me out.

"Cam…"

I turn back to him.

"I'm scared."

I want to tell him he should be, but I say nothing, exiting the room after a cop lets me out. On the way home, I call Caroline.

She grabs the call on the first ring. "Cam. Did you see him?"

"I did."

"Is he okay?"

"He's upset, but otherwise, he's fine."

"What is happening?"

"He's been indicted on rape charges from fourteen years ago."

She gasps. "No. That's not possible. He said he didn't do it."

What can I say to that? She'll need to come around to understanding he lied to her in her own time.

"What do I do?"

"Sit tight until he's arraigned. He should be released on personal recognizance sometime tomorrow."

"He has to spend the night there?"

"Yes."

"How is he being charged with this if he didn't do it?"

"You'll have to talk to him about that."

"What do you know, Cam?"

"I'll text you when I hear what time the arraignment will be in

Newport County Superior Court. He'll need clothes for that."

"That's it? I just have to sit here and wait?"

"I don't know what else to say."

"You could tell me this is a big mistake!"

I wish I could. "Just hang in there, Caroline. You'll see him tomorrow. I'll be in touch."

I've never been more thankful to end a call in my life. I adore her and always have. She came along at a time when I feared Ryder might never recover from the events of that summer. In addition to committing a horrendous crime—and getting away with it—he'd withstood the devastating loss of Louisa, her funeral and deep, unrelenting grief. All before he'd started his senior year of high school.

He met Caroline during his sophomore year at URI, and they've been together ever since. In addition to facing charges, he'll also have to confront the fallout from the lie he's told his wife for all these years. Whether she'll stay with him is anyone's guess.

When I arrive home, Sienna mutes the TV. "How'd it go?"

"As you might expect. He's terrified and worried about Caro and the kids."

"Does she know the truth?"

I shake my head.

"Wow. I always figured he'd probably told her the truth at some point."

"He didn't." I fix myself a glass of bourbon straight out of the bottle and sit next to her on the sofa.

"What happens now?"

"He'll be arraigned tomorrow and hopefully let out on personal recognizance. That's the usual routine for first-time offenders."

"He's still a first-time offender even though he was charged with this before?"

"He wasn't convicted, so yes, he's a first-time offender."

"What about the campaign?"

"I assume that'll be suspended after the arraignment. There's no way he can run now."

"Even if he's acquitted?"

"If that happens, and it's a very big if, it'll take months. The election will be long over by then."

"I feel so bad for Caroline and their kids."

"I know."

"I should talk to Blaise."

"No, you shouldn't."

"Why not? What can it hurt at this point?"

"We don't need to add to his troubles with charges of witness tampering."

"He wouldn't be going anywhere near her. I could go to her and plead with her to have mercy on Ryder's wife and kids."

"Why would she care about them? She doesn't even know them."

"She knows me, and I'd be the one asking."

"It's too risky."

"What do we have to lose at this point?"

"I don't like it, and I don't think you should do it."

"So noted."

If there's one thing I know about Sienna after eight years of marriage and nearly sixteen years together it's that she does what she wants when she wants. I can't stop her from seeking out Blaise.

All I can do is discourage it.

Chapter 22

Blaise
NOW

I WAKE UP SLOWLY after sleeping like a dead woman. It's amazing how well I've been sleeping lately—better than I have in fourteen years. I blink Jack's bedroom into focus and realize we fell asleep in his bed. His arms are around me, my head is resting on his chest, and I feel more rested than I have since I got here.

"Morning," he says in a gruff, sleepy-sounding voice.

"Morning."

"Fancy meeting you here."

"Haha. We fell asleep."

"So we did."

He holds me tighter. "Best sleep I've had in ages."

"Me, too." I'm almost afraid to leave him and his warm bed to find out what's been happening outside our little bubble.

"Whatever it is, it's not your fault."

"So you're a mind reader now?"

"Nope. I just felt you get tense as you recalled the grand jury decision and its implications."

"I wonder if he's been arrested?"

"I'm sure he has by now."

"I can't stop thinking about his wife and kids and how they must be feeling."

"That's not your responsibility, Blaise."

"I know."

"None of this is your fault. Tell me you know that."

"I do, but there's no denying that there would've been no grand jury hearing without me."

"And there would've been no need for you to report it if he hadn't raped that girl."

"Keep reminding me of that, will you?"

"Any time you need to hear it."

"I'm apt to need to hear it a lot in the next few weeks."

"I'm here for you."

I turn on my back so I can see him. At some point during the night, he removed his shirt. I run my hand over his bare chest, which is muscular with just the right amount of soft hair. "I can't tell you what it means to me to have your support. I'd feel really alone with this if it wasn't for you."

"I've felt really alone for a long time now, and the minute I met you, I didn't feel alone anymore."

I look up to meet his intense gaze. "Are you always so honest about how you feel?"

"I never used to be, but losing my parents the way I did was a big reminder that life is short, and there's no time for bullshit."

"I suppose that would change a guy."

"It did, but the changes were needed. I wish I hadn't had to learn the big lessons that way, of course. I'm a better person than I was before I lost them. It's my goal now to make sure they'd always be proud of me."

I squeeze his hand. "They'd be so proud of you."

"I hope so."

"I should get going so you can go to work."

"I'd rather spend this day with you."

"What about your deadlines?"

"They'll keep."

"Are you sure?"

"I work my ass off. I haven't taken a real break in years. It'll be fine."

"In that case, I'd love to spend today with you after I check in at work."

"While you do that, I'll make us some breakfast."

"With coffee?"

"What do you take me for? A savage?"

He makes me smile like no one has in so long. "I'm sorry that things got derailed last night. I promise I'll make it up to you."

"Don't be sorry, and you have nothing to make up to me. When we get there, I want you fully focused on me and us and not worrying about anything else."

"I want that, too."

"Please don't add me to the list of things on your mind. I want to be a positive in all of this."

"You are. You're the most positive thing to happen to me in well… ever."

"Same, babe. Let's just enjoy it, okay?"

I nod and smile as he kisses me.

"I'm off to see about coffee."

"I'm off to see about work."

"Meet me in the kitchen."

"I'll be quick."

I step out of his back door into a cool, crisp autumn morning. I catch a whiff of woodsmoke, and for the first time since that night, the scent doesn't repulse me. That used to be one of my favorite scents. Maybe it will be again now that I've taken this step toward righting the wrongs of the past.

I stop short at the sight of something on the front stoop of my cottage. Leaning in, I take a closer look that I immediately regret. It's a bloody carcass of some sort. Whatever it once was is unrecognizable now.

I must've screamed because Jack comes running. "What happened?"

As I fight back a wave of bile, I point to the dead animal.

"What the fuck?" He pulls out his phone and makes a call.

"Wh-what're you doing?"

"Calling Houston. This is a message."

I was so shocked by the gory sight that I hadn't made that leap on my own.

Jack puts his arm around me and leads me away from the cottage and back into his house.

"It was there when she woke up this morning," he says. "All right. Thank you." He puts down the phone. "He'll be right over. What can I get you?"

I tuck my shaking hands between my knees. "Nothing. I feel like I'm going to be sick."

He pours a glass of ice water and brings it to me. "Drink this."

I take a few sips and put down the glass. "I should go back to New York. They won't know how to find me there."

"Is that what you want to do?"

"No, it's not, but I won't bring this nonsense to your home."

"It's nothing I can't handle, and I'd much rather have you here with me where I can keep you safe than off by yourself in the big city."

"Who will keep you safe if they come for me?"

"I can take care of myself and you."

Houston's SUV comes into the yard and skids to a stop. He's looking at the thing on my stoop when we emerge from Jack's house. "Animal control is coming to clean this up."

I cross my arms, wishing the trembling would stop. "Ryder is indicted because of my testimony and this lands on my stoop the next day. That's not a coincidence, is it?"

"Probably not."

"So people already know it was me who came forward?"

"I haven't seen that reported anywhere, but you know how word gets around."

I also know there's someone else who saw what I did, who'd know exactly who the eyewitness is. Who else could it be? "You should talk to Sienna Elliott." After this, I have no reason to protect her.

"Is that right?"

"Yeah."

"I'll do that. I've stepped up patrols on the street, but I'm not sure how much of a deterrent that'll be. We only have three officers on duty at any given time."

"I'll hire private security," Jack says.

"No. I'll leave. I'll go somewhere else."

He puts an arm around me. "You're safer with me than you'd be alone."

"I can't put you in danger."

"Don't worry about me. I want to be there for you."

Houston gives us a curious look. "It's like that, is it?"

"It is," Jack says with a warm smile for me. "And I have you to thank."

"I'm glad for you guys, but please be careful."

"We will be," Jack says.

"This is the rough part, Blaise. We talked about this. When word gets out that you're the witness, people will pressure you to recant.

People you love will pressure you."

"That won't matter. I won't recant." Nothing could convince me to do that, even threats to my safety.

Jack squeezes my shoulder in a show of support.

"Stay strong," Houston says as he heads back to his SUV. "Animal control will be here shortly."

After he drives off, Jack takes my hand to lead me inside. He pours me a cup of coffee and puts the cream on the counter.

"Thanks."

He gets busy making scrambled eggs and toast that he serves a few minutes later. "Try to eat something."

I take a few bites because he went to the trouble to make it, but it's all I can do to swallow anything with the dead animal image in my head. "Thank you."

"You're welcome. I texted a friend about security."

"I don't want you to take on that expense."

"It's fine."

"No, it isn't. None of this is fine."

"When they realize you won't back down, they'll let it go."

"Will they?"

My cell phone rings with a call from my brother. I take the call on speaker. "Arlo."

"Blaise… What the fuck are you doing?"

"What I should've done fourteen years ago."

"You can't be serious."

"I'm dead serious. I saw him rape her, and keeping that secret nearly ruined me."

"What the hell were you even doing there?"

"Does that matter now?"

"It matters to me! You're accusing my best friend, my *boss*, of a heinous crime."

"Which he committed. Why don't you ask him what really happened? He knows he did it."

"I *quit my job* to work on his campaign. Don't you care about me at all?"

"Don't you dare put that on me! I kept this secret for all this time *because* I love you! If it hadn't been for you, I would've gone to the cops back then."

"You can still fix this by not testifying."

"I'm not fixing anything, and I *will* testify. So you can tell anyone who has a big idea of trying to intimidate me by throwing dead animals on my porch not to bother."

"I thought I knew you, Blaise."

"You don't know me at all. Don't ask me again to protect your friend. I won't do it."

I push the red button to end the call.

Jack fans his face. "That was hot as fuck."

I can't believe it's possible to laugh but leave it to him.

"He had no right to say those things to you. Tell me you know that."

"I do." I'm absolutely certain of that, but my hands are still shaking, nonetheless. "I kept this secret for so long it became part of who I was. I don't want to be that person anymore. I can't go back to living that way, no matter who it might hurt."

"You're doing the right thing."

I nod, appreciative of his support. "You really should let me go back to New York. This isn't your problem."

He comes around the counter to stand in front of me, tipping my chin up so he can kiss me. "Don't you know by now that I want to keep you forever?"

I'm overwhelmed and deeply moved. "That's a really long time."

He kisses me again. "I sure as hell hope so."

Denise
NOW

I'VE PUT THIS OFF as long as I can. Houston called me last night to tell me Ryder has been indicted and taken into custody. I call my dad the minute the twins go down for their morning nap.

"Hey, sweetie. I'm about to tee off on the fourteenth. What's going on?"

"I have to tell you something."

"Is everything all right with you and the kids?"

"Yes, but I have news I need to share with you, and it might be upsetting."

"What news?"

"Ryder Elliott has been indicted on rape charges."

"In your case?"

"Yes."

"How is that possible?"

"A witness has come forward."

"A witness." His tone is hard as concrete. "There was a fucking witness?"

"Yes."

"Where has that person been all this time?"

"I'm not sure, but she heard he was running for Congress, and apparently that's what made her come forward."

"How could she have remained silent when she saw what you went through after he was charged the first time?"

"I don't know. I guess she was afraid of the wolves turning on her."

"That's no excuse. She saw you attacked and *left you there*? What kind of monster does something like that?"

"A teenage kid who feared her whole life blowing up?"

"You can't possibly be defending her."

"I'm not, but she saw what they did to me. Can you blame her for not wanting them to go after her, too?"

"Yes, I can blame her! We could've put that son of a bitch away if she'd done the right thing."

"She's doing it now."

"You must be beside yourself, sweetheart."

"I was, at first, but I'm better now. Kane has been amazing, as always."

"So you'll have to testify?"

"Yes."

His deep breath says it all. "How did you find out about the witness?"

"Houston Rafferty came to see me. When he told me there was a witness, I said I wanted nothing to do with it. But then Kane and I talked about it, and we decided if there's a chance to get justice, I should do whatever it takes."

"Your courage continues to astound me, love."

"I'm a quivering mess on the inside."

"No, you're not. I want to know the details. I'll be right there with you through it all."

"Thank you, Dad."

"Love you so much, Dee."

"Love you, too."

We agree to talk again later.

Kane comes into the room with a steaming mug of lemon tea. "How'd he take it?"

"Like us, he's in disbelief that there was a witness all this time who only just now came forward."

"I heard what you said about why she stayed quiet back then. It's admirable that you can defend her."

"Don't get me wrong. I think what she did was indefensible, from the second she decided to leave me in the woods bleeding and broken. But that doesn't mean I don't understand why she did it. Being a teenager can be hell without everyone you know hating you, including your own brother."

"*He* should've been the one everyone hated."

"Life is never fair like that."

"What's fair is *he* was arrested in public and spent a night in jail. What's fair is *he'll* be arraigned on multiple felonies, forced to abandon his campaign and hopefully pay for what *he* did to you with years of his life behind bars."

"What does it say about me that I ache for his wife and kids?"

"It says you're the best person I've ever known."

Chapter 23

Houston
NOW

I ASK BLAISE TO meet me at my parents' home at nine in the morning to take care of something I should've done days ago. Things have been crazy busy since the flu whipped through the station, taking down half of my officers and three of the admins. In the midst of all that, news of Ryder's arrest has moved like a wildfire through multiple towns, resulting in numerous texts and phone calls from people I've known all my life.

Dallas is outraged that I played a role in having Ryder arrested. He had a lot to say about it on the phone last night.

"How could you do this? I quit my job to help get him elected, while you're building a case to bring him down?"

"I'm not going to apologize for doing my job."

"Fuck that shit. You could've at least given me a heads up."

"No, I couldn't have."

"What if it comes up that we lied about her the first time around? I could end up in big trouble. Do you care about that at all?"

"Of course I do, but there was no way I could sit on this information once it was given to me."

"Arlo's sister of all people. He's losing his shit over that."

"I'm sorry people are upset, but I'm not the one you should be pissed with."

"Believe me, I'm pissed at Ryder, too. I can't believe he actually might've done this. Do you think he'll go down for it?"

"I won't speculate on that."

"But the case is solid?"

"Much more so than it was the first time around."

"Son of a bitch."

My sister, Austin, texts to express her shock at the news. At least a hundred other people from various times in my life have reached out, too. I replied to my sister, but not to anyone else. I don't have time to answer their questions.

I understand why Dallas and others are upset and scared about how this might ricochet back on them. However, I had a job to do, and I did it without prejudice. When I first became a police officer, my dad told me to do the right thing in all my dealings on the job, and I'd never have to explain myself to anyone. It was good advice that I've endeavored to follow at all times, especially during this most challenging situation of my career.

Twenty minutes before Blaise is due to arrive, I go into the garage in search of my dad's metal detector. Once upon a time, he'd loved that thing more than his children, or so we'd told him. He'd taken it with him everywhere we went—camping, the beach, hikes in the woods—always looking to strike it rich with some rare find.

That'd never happened, but he had found some unique things along with hundreds of wedding rings and other valuables that he'd done his best to reunite with their owners. Dad fully embraced social media as a result of those efforts. Thanks to him, I have to make daily updates to the departmental Facebook page Dad started. Like I don't have enough to do.

I locate the metal detector in a corner thick with spider webs that give me the creeps. As I emerge from the barn-shaped garage, I feel like I'm crawling with spiders that I swipe at with wild movements.

That's where Blaise finds me when she gets out of her car and walks toward me, smiling. "Everything all right?"

"I ran into a bunch of spider webs in the garage. Do you see any on me?"

She takes a careful look. "Nope."

I shudder and shake off my clothes. "Ugh, I feel like they're every-where."

"What were you doing in there?"

"Looking for the metal detector."

"How come?"

"Denise told me she lost her car key that night. I want to try to find it, and I need you to show me exactly where to look."

Her hard swallow is visible.

"I know it's a lot to ask you to go back there, but if I can find her key, that would further support her testimony."

Blaise jams her hands into coat pockets and nods, her chin set with the determination she's demonstrated from the beginning. I admire that tremendously. If she wasn't now seeing Jack, I would've asked her out when this is over. "Let's go."

We take a well-worn path from our backyard into the woods that adjoin my parents' property. My siblings and I beat down that path over years of playing every imaginable game in the woods. This was our playground, and it'd been devastating to hear that someone might've been attacked there.

Blaise points to a clearing off the main path, not far from the yard. "There."

"Show me where you were."

We cross the clearing to the far side. "Back here. I'd snuck in from over there." She points to the road that runs behind our place.

I notice her staring at the clearing, probably reliving what happened there.

"That's all I needed if you want to go, Blaise. Thank you for your help."

"No problem."

"Yes, it is, and I appreciate it."

"If it helps to build the case, then it's worth coming back here." She stands for a long time, staring at the clearing. "It's amazing, isn't it, how one person's actions can change so many lives forever."

"Yes, it is."

"What do you think will happen to him?"

"Hard to say for certain. If he's convicted, he'll probably do a long stretch in prison."

"Do you know his wife?"

The question surprises me. "I've met her a few times."

"What's she like?"

"She's very nice."

"Are they happy together?"

"They've seemed to be."

"What about their kids?"

"They have three. A son and two daughters."

She looks over at me. "What'll happen to them?"

"I don't know, Blaise." I study her for a second, but her expression is unreadable. "Are you okay?"

She shrugs. "It's just what I said before about how one person's actions can affect so many lives."

"Like what you're doing?"

"Yes. What're the odds his wife knew anything about this? His arrest will be like a bomb going off in her life. Not to mention what it'll do to innocent kids."

"It's kind of you to have compassion for them. Hell, I do, too. But that doesn't change what he did."

"No, it doesn't. He should pay for that. I just hate that innocent people who had nothing to do with it will pay a big price, too."

"I know. It's upsetting all around, but you're doing the right thing."

"Are you sure? Would it have been better to leave the past in the past?"

I lean on the arm of the metal detector. "What he did was deplorable. It was a crime."

"Yes, it was, but I'll be honest... When I came here and sought you out, I thought only about assuaging my own conscience. I didn't give a single thought to his wife or children or anyone else who might be hurt by me coming forward."

"Please tell me you know you're not the one hurting them. He is."

"I get that, but still... If I hadn't done what I did, they'd be going on with their lives like nothing happened."

"Let me ask you this. If you're his wife, would you want to know you're sleeping with a rapist, or would you rather not know?"

"When you put it that way, I'd rather know than not know. But it must've come as a terrible shock to her."

"I'm sure it did, but that doesn't change the facts of the case."

"Are people giving you a hard time about being involved with this?"

"Here and there. It's nothing I can't handle. I did my job. I'd do it again. Information was conveyed to me, and I passed it along to the proper authorities. If people don't like that, there's nothing I can do about it."

"Would it have been easier for you to tell me there was nothing you could do with the information at this point? Because if you had, I would've believed you."

I can tell she's struggling, so I level with her. "Yeah, it would've been easier. My brother is furious with me over this, but I told him the same thing I told you. I did my job."

"That means he's probably furious with me, too. I'm sure a lot of people are."

"You said you don't care what anyone thinks of you."

"I don't. It's just a lot to process."

"I understand." I really need to get to work trying to find that key, but I wait to see if there's anything else she wants to talk about.

"Do you think I'm in serious danger?"

"I'd like to say no, but people do crazy things when they're desperate, and who knows what'll happen now that he's been arrested. You need to be careful, and if you ever feel unsafe, you can call me. I'll be there within minutes."

"Thank you for that. Maybe I should go back to New York until I have to testify."

"Is that what you want to do?"

She hesitates before she shakes her head. "I'm having a very nice time with Jack." Her face turns bright red as she says that.

"I'm glad for you both."

"It's been a surprising development in the midst of this other stuff."

"I'm sure."

"Well, I'll let you get to work. Thanks for everything, Houston."

"You're welcome. Keep your head down and stay focused on the goal."

"I will."

"Do you want me to walk you back to your car?"

"Would you mind?"

"Not at all."

Fifteen minutes later, I return to the clearing and fire up the metal detector, hoping to find a key that was lost there fourteen years ago. The day is unusually warm for this time of year, and when I start to sweat, I toss my jacket aside and roll up my sleeves. I'm at it for two hours before I get a hit. Crouching over the spot, I put on a latex glove to run my hand over years' worth of leaves and brush and connect with a solid object that I withdraw from under the brush. A Honda key. It's covered in moss and other growth, but the silver H logo stands out, nonetheless.

I hold it up to the light for a closer look and then drop it into an evidence bag.

As I'm heading back to my SUV, my parents arrive home from

dentist appointments. It amuses me that they do such things together as retirees.

Mom gives me a kiss on the cheek as she goes into the house, talking on the phone. "Aunt Betty says hello."

"Tell her hi from me."

"Did you find the key?" Dad asks.

"I did."

"That's good. What's the next move?"

"I'll deliver it directly to the lab at URI."

Dad nods with approval, knowing as I do how important chain of custody is in situations such as this.

"Dallas called last night. He's not happy with me."

"I heard. But don't listen to him or anyone else. You did the only thing you could when a witness came forward. What happens from here isn't your fault or your responsibility."

"Yeah, I know. It's just hard to have everyone pissed at me for doing my job."

"Which is exactly why this woman didn't come forward at the time. Having people turn on you sucks no matter when it happens, but it's particularly rough when you're too young to manage it."

"Very true."

He clasps my shoulder. "I'm proud of how you do the job."

"That means a lot to me."

"I'm proud of a lot more than that when it comes to you. I hope you know that."

"I do. Thanks."

"Hang in there, son."

"I'm trying."

I'm halfway to Kingston, home of the University of Rhode Island and the state crime lab, when my phone rings with a call from a number I don't recognize. "Houston Rafferty."

"Um, hi, Houston, this is, um, Ramona Travers. I'm not sure if you remember me. I was in Dallas's class."

"I remember your name." I can't recall her face, though. "What can I do for you?"

"I, uh, I heard a witness came forward in the Elliott case and he's been indicted."

"Yes." I wait for her to say more as my heart starts to beat faster.

"That night..."

"Were you at the party?"

"Yes."

"Did you see something, Ramona?" I pull off the road, so I won't crash while I wait to hear what she has to say.

"I...I saw them leave the party together."

"Are you willing to testify to that?"

"I want you to know..." She sounds tearful now. "I've agonized over this from the day he was first charged. I wanted to say something, but I couldn't. He was a god in school, and I was nobody. The only reason I was even there that night was because I dated Brody Parker for five minutes that summer."

I exhale a deep breath. Brody is one of the guys who signed the affidavit. "And you're willing to testify to that in court?"

"Would it help the case?"

"Very much so."

After a long pause, she says, "Then yes, I'll testify."

"The prosecutor will want to meet with you. Would it be all right for me to have him call you?"

"Y-yes."

"You'll get a phone call from Joshua Spurling with the attorney general's office."

"Okay."

"Do me a favor, and don't talk about this to anyone."

"My husband is aware of it."

"Please ask him to keep it to himself."

"We won't say anything to anyone."

"Thank you for coming forward."

"I'm sorry it took so long. I've anguished over this."

"I understand. We'll be in touch. Call if there's anything I can do for you in the meantime."

"Thank you, Houston. I appreciate your kindness."

I end that call and reach out to Blaise.

"You won't believe what just happened. Do you remember Ramona Travers from high school?"

"Yes, she was in my class."

"She's come forward to say she saw Ryder leave the party with Neisy."

"Whoa. No way."

"From what she told me, she's had an experience similar to yours, full of guilt and remorse for staying quiet at the time."

"I can't believe this. Would it be possible for me to talk to her?"

"After she gives her statement."

"Okay. Let me know when."

"I will."

After we say our goodbyes, I sit for a long moment processing what Ramona told me and how it'll help to cement the case against Ryder.

He's completely fucked. I wonder if he realizes that yet.

Chapter 24

Ryder
NOW

I'M AWAKE ALL NIGHT in a jail cell, terrified about what comes next. All I can think about are Caroline and my precious kids and what'll become of them if I'm sent to prison. I gave up a lucrative engineering job to run for Congress and sunk a big chunk of our personal money into getting my campaign off the ground. This'll ruin us in more ways than one.

An officer stops in front of my cell. "There's an attorney here to see you."

I get up and run my fingers through my hair.

The officer cuffs me and leads me to the same room where I met with Cam last night.

Before leaving the room, the officer uncuffs me.

The lawyer has grey hair and wire-framed glasses. He's wearing a bespoke suit like the ones my old boss wore. "I'm Bennett Gormley." He holds out a hand to me.

I shake his hand. "Ryder Elliott."

"Your brother asked me to come by. I brought you a change of clothes for court."

One of my suits hangs from a chair and my shaving bag sits on the table. That means someone went to my house to get those things. "How's my wife?"

"I haven't spoken to her directly, but your brother said she's very upset, as you might imagine."

That makes my stomach hurt even more than it already did. "What happens now?"

"You'll be arraigned at ten a.m. in Superior Court in Newport. These are felony counts, so we won't be entering a plea at the arraignment. Since this is your first offense, we can hope for personal recognizance with no outlay of cash."

That's a relief.

He slides a piece of paper across the table. "This is my retainer agreement, authorizing me to act on your behalf. The initial retainer is twenty-five thousand, half of which will be due after the arraignment. The other half is due within thirty days."

A wave of shock rolls through me as I realize how quickly this will burn up our savings. We'll have to sell the house. Immediately. Where will we go?

"Mr. Elliott?"

"I'm sorry. What did you say?"

"I asked if you're able to pay the retainer."

"I, uh… Yes, but not much more than that."

"We'll also need to hire investigators to look into the victim and the witness."

"No."

"Excuse me?"

"I don't want them investigated."

"Do you understand the charges you're facing?"

"Yes."

"In order to mount a defense—"

"What if I plead guilty? Will I still need to pay you?"

He stares at me as if I've lost my mind. "You have young children. You'll spend the rest of their childhood behind bars if you do that. All it takes is one juror to acquit. You'd be insane to plead guilty."

"Even if I did it?"

"Don't tell me that." I'm taken aback by his sharp tone. "Don't say that to anyone."

"I want my wife and kids to have money to survive if I go to prison. If I burn through everything we have defending myself and still get convicted, they'll be left with nothing."

"You don't have to decide anything today. You should be released after the hearing, and you can discuss it with your wife and family. In the meantime, get cleaned up for court and we'll take it from there."

He gets up and leaves the room.

Twenty-five thousand dollars. And that's just the beginning. I'm sick with dread, fear and regret.

That I'm in this boat is entirely my own fault. Not only did I commit the crimes I'm charged with, but I brought this down on myself by not being content with the nice, quiet life Caroline and I had created for ourselves and our kids. I needed more. Cam warned me. He said I was crazy to open myself up to the scrutiny that would come with running for office. But I was so sure I'd left those troubles behind.

Little did I know. There was a witness. A fucking witness. And now my life is in ruins. Tears run down my face as I change into the suit that Caroline sent for me. I try to imagine her standing in front of my closet in our bedroom, deciding what suit to send to jail for me to wear to my arraignment on felony sexual assault charges.

She'll hate me for this.

Who could blame her? The thought of her hating me is far more unbearable than the night in jail was.

When I'm dressed, I bang on the door. A cop comes to cuff me and leads me to a communal bathroom. Thankfully, I've got the place to myself as I shave, brush my teeth and comb my hair.

I'm cuffed again and led to a State Police SUV for transport to court in Newport. The cop tosses a bag with the clothes I was wearing when I was arrested and the shaving bag into the back of the vehicle. I hope that means they don't expect me back after court.

Will Caroline be there, or will she stay far away from this nightmare? I hope she stays away almost as much as I hope she comes. I need her, even if I don't deserve her. I've never deserved her. I always knew that. She's just found out who I really am and must be reeling.

The courthouse is surrounded by media trucks. I'm not surprised. The arrest of a congressional candidate will be big news in this state where political corruption is known to run rampant. Having a candidate accused of sex crimes is a rare occurrence, however. I wouldn't be surprised if it's made the national news.

I'm led in through a side door where Bennett waits for me. "You've drawn a big crowd."

"Is my wife here?"

"I'm not sure, but your parents are. Cam introduced me."

Hearing my parents are here leaves me deeply ashamed for what I'm putting them through. If it wasn't for my kids, I'd end this right now with a guilty plea. Bennett's words from earlier, about spending their child-hoods in prison, has me reconsidering that plan. I need to talk to Caroline before I decide anything.

I've never felt shame like this as I'm brought into court in handcuffs, which are removed when I'm positioned next to Bennett at the defense table.

A sheriff's deputy stands three feet from me in case I get any ideas about making a run for it.

Memories of that long ago summer come flooding back, reminding me of how afraid I was the first time I stood accused of these crimes. That was nothing compared to what I feel now that I have three young children and a wife I love with all my heart—not to mention there being a witness who saw me commit rape.

I'm afraid to look behind me, not wanting to see the disappointment and fear on my loved ones' faces.

The court is called to order, the judge comes in and the lawyers do their thing. Bennett talks about my deep ties to the community as well as my young family as he assures the judge I'm not a flight risk. No one says anything to me. I'm released on personal recognizance and ordered to surrender my passport pending trial.

"You'll be taken back into custody until the paperwork for the PR is signed." Bennett hands me a business card. "Come to my office at four o'clock this afternoon to discuss strategy. Bring a check for fifty percent of the retainer."

I'm cuffed and taken to a cell in the courthouse.

An hour later, a sheriff's deputy comes to the cell with the paper-work I'm required to sign. "You have twelve hours to surrender your passport, or you'll be back in custody."

"I'll take care of that."

"Make sure you do. They don't fuck around with this stuff. This is a no-contact order that prohibits you from having any contact with the victim or anyone associated with the prosecution." He hands me the paperwork to take with me.

The door opens, and Cam is there waiting for me, holding the bag with my possessions as well as my phone, which he hands to me. "We need to go out the back. The front is overrun with media."

Cam's SUV idles outside the door with Arlo at the wheel.

"Where's Caroline?" I ask as we speed away from the courthouse. Getting stopped by the cops is the least of our concerns.

"She stayed home with the kids," Cam said. "We all thought that was for the best."

I want to ask if "all" includes her, but I keep the question to myself. I'll find out what she thinks soon enough.

"I talked to Blaise." Arlo looks at me in the mirror. "She's not backing down."

"We've got another problem," Cam says.

"What's that?" I ask.

"The affidavit could come back to haunt the rest of us."

"How do you know?" Arlo asks.

"A vibe I picked up when I spoke to the prosecutor before court. He said he's going to call me to discuss another matter. There's nothing else it could be."

"Fucking hell," Arlo mutters.

None of us says another word on the ride to my house. I don't look at my phone because I can't bear to see what might be waiting for me there.

As I walk through the door, I feel like a stranger in my own home, like I already don't belong there. I hear the kids' voices and wonder what they're doing home. Then I realize that Caro wouldn't have sent Miles and Grace to school to possibly face ridicule when the whole town knows I've been arrested.

"We'll...ah...give you some time with your family," Cam says as he drops the plastic bag with my belongings inside the door.

"I need someone to take my passport to the courthouse."

"I'll do that this afternoon," Arlo says.

I turn to face the two men who've been my closest friends all my life. "Thank you both for being there for me."

"Always," Arlo says.

Cam leaves without saying anything, which says everything.

I square my shoulders and walk into the family room, uncertain of what to expect.

Miles sees me and lets out a scream as he runs to me. The girls are right behind him. I scoop them up and hug them tightly, inhaling the familiar scents of shampoo, maple syrup and sweetness.

When I put them down, Miles stands to the side, eyeing me warily.

I place my hand on top of his light brown hair. "I'm okay, buddy. Don't worry."

He'll have other questions, for certain, but for now, that seems to satisfy him.

I turn to face my wife, who's seated on the sofa, holding a mug of coffee. Her sister, Maggie, who lives in Philadelphia, is next to her. That Maggie is here says a lot about Caroline's state of mind.

"Could I please speak to my wife in private?"

Maggie glances at Caroline, who stares straight ahead, looking through me rather than at me. The chill in the air sends a shiver through me. "Caro?"

After a long moment, she stands and walks upstairs to our bedroom.

"Stay with Auntie Maggie, guys," I tell the kids as I follow Caroline.

Inside the bedroom, I close the door and lean back against it. My gaze darts to the bed where we made love like passionate newlyweds only two nights ago.

She has her back to me, arms crossed, head down in a position of defeat that makes me ache for having done that to her.

"I'm sorry."

She spins around, her eyes flashing with outrage. "You're *sorry*? Well, that fixes everything. Apology not accepted." She's never spoken to me or anyone like that, and it takes me aback.

I take a step toward her. "I understand that you're—"

"*You understand nothing!* I've been married to a lying rapist for *eight years*. I've slept next to a lying rapist for ten years and had three children with him only to find out *I didn't know him at all*."

"You do know me, Caro."

She shakes her head and puts out her arm to keep me from coming any closer. "You're a complete stranger to me."

"I'm not. I'm the same man I've always been."

"*You're a liar!* And a rapist. I want you out of here. I don't care where you go or what you do, but you're not welcome here."

"Caroline, please. Listen to me."

"I never want to see you again. Take your stuff and get out so your children and I have a chance of salvaging our lives."

"You can't take my kids away from me."

"Have you lost your mind? Of course I can. *You've been charged with sex crimes!* There's not a judge out there who'd let you near those kids."

"Please... They mean everything to me. You know that."

"I have nothing else to say to you. Get your shit, get out and stay gone, or I'll take you to court to keep you away from us."

She brushes past me on her way out of the room.

The door slams shut on our marriage.
I fall to my knees and weep.

Caroline
NOW

"I NEED YOU TO get us out of here," I tell my sister after the confrontation with Ryder. My heart has shattered into a million pieces. "Please, Maggie. Get us out of here."

She came running last night when I called to tell her my husband had been arrested in front of our children, their friends and the friends' parents, all of whom looked at me like I'd suddenly gone rancid or something after he was led away in cuffs.

Maggie hops into action, rounding up the kids and taking them to their rooms to pack. "We're going on a fun vacation," she tells them with forced enthusiasm.

"I don't want to go on a vacation," Miles says, sounding tearful. "I want to go back to school and see my friends."

He doesn't know yet that he'll never be able to go back to that school or those friends. How will I ever explain to him that his entire life as he knew it is over, starting with the loss of the man he worshipped from the day he was born?

It's unbearable.

If you'd asked me this time yesterday if I'd be leaving Ryder and taking our children with me to get them away from him, I would've thought you were out of your mind.

What a difference a day makes.

When I saw the police officers walking toward us, I thought they were there for Michael's father, who'd been accused of domestic battery last year and was prohibited from coming within a thousand feet of his wife, Lori, and their children. I'd seen him lurking in the distance and figured the cops were there to keep him from getting any closer.

Imagine my shock when I realized they were there for *my* husband, not Lori's.

As I wait for Ryder to leave so I can pack my things, I don't know what to do with myself. Nothing could've prepared me for a nightmare like this. I'm one of those wives that other women love to hate, still in love with her husband after more than ten years together with never a bad word to say about him. At least I *was* that wife. Now I don't know what or who I am.

Devastated.

Shocked.

Infuriated.

I'm all those things as well as crushingly disappointed to learn the man I've loved with all my heart is a liar and a rapist. He's many other things, too—a loving husband and father, a hard-working provider and a wonderful son, brother, uncle and friend. But what do any of those other things matter now that the truth has been revealed?

He told me about being accused of sexually assaulting a girl he went to high school with. I asked him point blank if he'd done it. He looked me in the eyes and said no. I wonder if I ever knew him at all.

Oh, God... The fundraiser we host every year, dedicated to the memory of Ryder's beloved high school girlfriend... I can't very well reach out to her brother, Marty, and tell him we're not going to be there. I'm sure he's heard about Ryder's arrest by now.

Heavy footsteps on the stairs alert me to him coming down.

I go into the first-floor powder room and shut the door, so I won't have to see him again.

I fear I might beg him to stay since I have no idea what I'm going to do without him. How will I raise three children on my own without his emotional, physical and financial support? I've hardly eaten anything today, but when I recall sinking a huge chunk of our savings into a campaign that's over now, it's all I can do not to vomit.

This'll ruin us both in every possible way, which is so unfair. All I've ever done is love him and our children with everything I have to give.

"Caro."

His voice outside the door has me covering my mouth so he won't hear my sobs.

"Please. I love you. I love our family. Please don't make me go."

"You need to leave, Ryder," Maggie says. "Don't make this any harder on her or your children than it already is."

"I want to talk to my wife."

"She asked you to go. That's what you need to do."

"I'm not going anywhere. This is my house."

"Not anymore."

Thank God for Maggie saying the things I can't bear to.

"I want to hear that from her."

"She's already told you how she feels. Why would you want to make this worse for her than it has to be?"

"I want to see the kids."

"It's better if you don't. Please go and let them try to put their lives back together."

I hold my breath as I listen and weep silently. My heart is shattered. I've loved this man with my whole heart and soul, almost from the day we met.

A few minutes later, Maggie gives a light tap at the door. "He's gone."

I open the door and fall sobbing into my sister's arms. "I don't know if I'll survive this."

"You will. You have to. Your babies need you."

"I can't."

"Yes, you can. I'll be right there with you. I promise."

"Mommy?"

I pull back from Maggie and make a fast attempt to pull myself together for my son's sake. "Hey, honey."

"Why are you crying?"

"I'm sad."

"Where's Daddy?"

"He had to go."

"Where did he go?"

"I'm not sure, but we're going to Aunt Maggie's for a little bit. Did you finish packing?"

His little chin quivers. "I don't want to go there. I want to go back to school to see my friends. I have basketball on Saturday. I can't miss it. My team needs me."

My heart breaks all over again. "Right now, we're taking a vacation."

"But I have school. I don't want to go on a vacation."

The front doorbell rings as I start to fear my head might explode.

"Get that," Maggie says. "I've got him."

I open the front door to find my next-door neighbor and close friend Aimee on my porch. I'm surprised to see her there holding a covered dish. Pushing the storm door open, I force a small smile. "Come in."

"I brought dinner."

She hands me the dish and a cloth bag. "It's the ziti the kids love with salad, garlic bread and brownies."

"Thank you so much."

Tears fill her eyes. "I'm so, so sorry, Caro. We all are. We can't imagine how you must be feeling."

"I'm shattered."

Maggie comes to take the food from me and smiles at Aimee, who she's met a few times in the past.

"Do you remember my sister, Maggie?"

"Of course. I'm glad you're here."

"Me, too."

Maggie leaves me to talk to my friend.

"What're you going to do?" Aimee asks.

"I guess we'll go to Maggie's since we can't very well stay here."

"Yes, you can. Everyone feels awful for you and the kids."

"They do?"

"Yes! My God, Caro. It's not your fault or the kids' fault that this happened. You have so many good friends in this town, who want to support you through this the way you've supported us through everything. You're always the first one there with food and compassion or anything we need. Don't go. Stay here with us and let us help you."

Tears roll down my face as she embraces me. "Thank you."

"I know it's not possible to believe it now, but you'll get through this. I know you will."

"I'm not so sure."

"You will."

"How will I pay the bills without him?"

"You'll start getting paid for the confectionary works of art you make for every birthday party. I've told you before you should start a business."

"I can't do that with three little kids."

"You can, and you will. We'll help you. You're not alone."

As she hugs me again, I feel slightly better to know I have the unwavering support of the friends who've been such a big part of my life in this town that belonged to Ryder when I first arrived. But I've made my own life here, and I'm thankful to know my friends plan to stick by me and the kids.

That, and the push she's given me toward a means of support, makes all the difference in this nightmare.

Chapter 25

Ryder
NOW

OUTSIDE THE HOUSE, I call Arlo for a ride to my car, which must still be at the ballfield. While I wait, I lean against Caroline's new minivan. The payments are six hundred dollars a month. How will we ever pay for everything with a massive legal tab hanging over our heads?

Since Arlo lives nearby, he arrives ten minutes later.

"We need to talk about the campaign," he says on the way to the ballfield where my life changed forever.

"What campaign? It was over the second I was taken into custody last night."

"I'll take care of making it official." He glances over at me, as stressed as I've ever seen him. "I've been getting calls all day from the other guys who signed that affidavit. They're worried."

"We should talk to Cam about it and see if he's heard from the AG's office on that."

As the lawyer in our group, Cam is usually our go-to guy for advice. That he and our other closest friends could get caught up in this mess only compounds the nightmare.

Arlo calls Cam on the Bluetooth. "Hey, I'm taking Ryder to get his car. The decision has been made to suspend the campaign."

"Okay."

"I'm getting calls from the others about that affidavit…"

"We might be screwed on that."

"You think so?" Arlo asks, his voice quite a bit higher than usual.

"My contact at the AG's office told me that Neisy reminded them that the affidavit was complete bullshit and made her cooperation in the reopened case contingent on them doing something about that. He said they're looking into it."

"Son of a bitch," Arlo whispers.

"I'll let you know what I hear," Cam says.

The line goes dead.

"Yeah, goodbye to you, too," Arlo says.

"He's pissed with me, not you. He told me not to run for Congress because of the skeleton in my closet. I should've listened to him."

"You had no way to know my sister, of all people, had seen it and would come forward." He sounds bitter and furious. "I still can't believe she did that."

"Cam was right. I should've left well enough alone. I should've been satisfied with what I had and counting my lucky stars to have gotten off the first time." I glance out the window at the familiar scenery of the town I've called home for most of my life. "I want you to understand why I felt the need to run…"

"I've wondered about that. It sort of came from out of nowhere."

"Not to me. I'd been thinking about it for a while, and then when Altman decided to resign, it felt like a sign, that maybe this was my time."

"I never would've pictured you for politics."

"I've always had that in the back of my mind. After I was charged the first time, the Naval Academy appointment went kaput and then Louisa died… It took a long time to figure out how to go on. I did my best to be happy at URI, but I was still in such turmoil. I missed Louisa so much. Nothing was ever the same after that summer. I wanted to try to get back some of the magic, you know?"

"I guess." He gives me a tentative glance.

"What's on your mind, Arlo?"

"Jen wants me to stay away from you. She's freaking out about me being unemployed and associated with…."

"A rapist?"

"Yeah."

My heart sinks. My brother is furious with me and now my closest friend is telling me I'm radioactive. "I get it."

"If it was only me, I'd never turn my back on you, man. Tell me you know that."

"I do."

He has a family to protect. I don't blame him for doing what's best for them.

The most important men in my life could end up in big trouble because of me. Of course they'll keep their distance.

Arlo pulls into the parking lot, which is empty except for the silver BMW SUV I can no longer afford. "I'll be pulling for you to find a way out of this, man."

"Thank you."

"I'm sorry it was my sister who caused this."

I look over at him. "She's not the one who caused it." That's as close as I've ever come to admitting the truth to him. "I'm sorry about the job. It was fun to work together, even if just for a little while."

"Yeah, it was."

"Will you tell Dallas about the campaign?"

"I'll take care of it."

I reach for the door handle. "Your friendship for all these years has meant everything to me, Arlo."

"Same, brother."

Before one or both of us breaks down into tears, I get out of the car and wave him off, wondering if I'll ever see him again. I've got fifteen minutes to get to Bennett's office. As I drive there, I think about what the lawyer said about missing everything with the kids if I plead guilty and also about how it only takes one juror to acquit.

I'm so torn over what to do. Before I left the house, I grabbed a check to pay the attorney. I hope there's more than twelve thousand dollars in the account, or I might get charged with passing a bad check, too.

When I get to his office in Newport, I'm shown into a conference room.

Bennett comes in a minute later. "They've got a second witness."

That news leaves me feeling like I've been electrocuted. "Who is it?"

"Does it matter? They've got someone willing to testify that she saw you leave the party with the woman who later accused you of rape. With that added to the person who claims to have seen the actual attack, their case becomes somewhat of a slam dunk."

"You said I shouldn't plead guilty, but it's looking more and more like maybe I should."

"I'll be honest with you. I'm a bit out of my league in this situation."

"My brother is working on getting me someone more experienced in cases like this."

"I think that's a good idea."

"What kind of sentence could I be looking at?"

"Possibly twenty years or more."

Twenty years.

Or more.

My babies will be adults by then, having grown up without me. I'm so devastated by that thought I break down into sobs.

Bennett hands me a tissue.

"I'm sorry. I'll ah…I'll just get going."

"Good luck to you."

"Thank you."

I stumble out of there, heartbroken and terrified. I'm going to prison. Possibly for decades. My family will be left destitute, my brother and closest friends could be in big trouble, and it's all my fault.

Blaise
NOW

THREE MORNINGS AFTER THE dead animal landed on my stoop, I wake to a text message from Sienna.

Can we talk?

I don't open it, so it won't show as read.

"What's wrong?" Jack asks.

He's insisted I stay in the house with him and the Glock he has stashed in his bedside table. He made me aware of the weapon the other night and showed me how to use it, if need be. The possibility that I might need to shoot someone is too big to wrap my head around.

"Sienna texted me."

"She's the ex-best friend, right?"

"Yes, and she's married to Ryder Elliott's brother, Camden. They've been together since middle school."

"What does she want?"

"To talk."

"About you not testifying against her brother-in-law?"

"Probably."

"Delete it. You don't owe her anything."

"Can I tell you something that you can never tell another living soul?"

"Of course."

Because he's shown me I can trust him implicitly, I say, "She was with me that night. She saw it, too."

He props himself up on an elbow. "Does Houston know that?"

"I told him I was speaking only for myself when I initially made the statement, but I think he's figured out from other things I've said that she was with me. She was the one who demanded I stay quiet at the time or else end up a pariah. She said she'd deny she was there."

"Wasn't he going to speak to her about the dead animal?"

"Yeah."

"Ask him how that went."

I send Houston a text to ask if he spoke with Sienna.

He responds right away. *I did. She said she was home all morning and that the other parents on her street could attest to her being at the bus stop that morning.*

Did you tell her why you wanted to know that?

Not specifically. She asked why I wanted to know, and I said it was confidential. Did something else happen?

She texted me and wants to talk.

How do you feel about that?

I don't want to talk to her.

Then don't. You're under no obligation.

Did you find the key?

I did.

That's good, right?

It helps. As does having another witness come forward.

I couldn't believe it when he told me Ramona Travers had seen Ryder and Neisy leave the party together.

Hang in there and let me know if you need anything.

I will. Thanks.

I share the exchange with Jack.

"He's right. You don't owe her anything."

"Is it weird that I'm curious about what she wants to say?"

"Not at all. If you want to see her, see her. But do it on your terms, not hers, and don't ever forget she has a personal stake in this."

"The same stake she's had since it happened. For her it was always all Cam all the time to the exclusion of almost everything else. I was already getting tired of her bullshit before that night, but we'd been friends since third grade. You don't just walk away from something like that."

"No, you don't."

"I wouldn't have even been there if it wasn't for her feeling insecure about things with Cam and wanting to know what he was up to when she wasn't with him."

"If you were to mention to the prosecutor who was there with you, they could subpoena her to testify."

"She'd probably lie."

"Doing that under oath is risky. She could be charged with perjury. Hear me out—Houston said your description of events matched the victim's, almost word for word, right?"

"Yes."

"So they can easily prove you were there. If you testify under oath that she was with you, she'd be hard pressed to lie without exposing herself to possible perjury charges."

"That's true."

"Would she risk being separated from her children to protect her brother-in-law?"

"Probably not. It's interesting to realize the stakes have changed for everyone involved, including her."

"You'd have nothing to lose by passing this information on to the prosecutors."

"No, I wouldn't. Our friendship ended when she refused to let me help Neisy or tell anyone what we'd seen. I own the fact that I could've done it anyway, but she was very convincing about what was at stake for both of us."

"Peer pressure can be a very powerful thing."

"For sure. When you're a teenager, the only thing that matters to you is what your friends think of you. I cringe now at how concerned I was then by what people I didn't even care about would say about me if I reported what I'd seen. I couldn't tell you where most of those people are now."

He twirls a length of my hair around his finger. "Were you in with the in crowd?"

"God, no," I say with a laugh. "Not at all. Sienna was on the fringe because she was with Cam, and my brother was, but I was in the background, basically overlooked by the popular kids. That never really bothered me until Sienna said they'd all hate me if I turned on Ryder."

"I can't imagine you being overlooked."

"Well, I was. No one gave two thoughts to me, which was fine. I didn't like being the center of attention, even on my birthday. It made me uncomfortable."

"And yet you went to acting school?"

"I know, right? It was the ability to disappear into a character, to leave my own story behind for a while, that appealed to me."

"I can see how that would've given you solace. I hope it's okay that you now have my full and undivided attention."

"You're just trying to make me blush."

He runs a fingertip over my cheek. "I hate to tell you it's working."

"Ugh, I hate that more than anything."

"You can't hate my favorite thing."

"Yes, I can."

"Nope."

He kisses me, making me forget why I was "arguing" with him in the first place. The more time I spend with him, the further I seem to get from the life I was leading before him. All I want is to be wherever he is, which is something we should probably talk about at some point. But for now, I'm too drunk on his kisses to think about anything other than what's happening right now.

The T-shirt I slept in moves up and over my head, baring me to his heated gaze.

"You're beautiful everywhere. I can't imagine anyone overlooking you."

He sets me on fire with his words and soft caresses. But more than that, he makes me feel everything in a way I never have before. Maybe because I was never free to enjoy something like this the way I am now. His lips are everywhere as he seduces me one kiss at a time. When I reach for him, he stops me. "Just relax and let me love you."

Relaxing is easier said than done when he moves down between my legs and uses his tongue and fingers to bring me to an orgasm that has me moaning and thrashing from the power of it. That's never happened with a partner before, and it's way better than the solo version.

"Do we need birth control?"

"I'm protected and safe if you are." This isn't the time to tell him my periods had been erratic and painful until I went on birth control to regulate them.

"I'm very safe in all the ways that matter."

"And you know just what to say to me."

Propped above me, he uses his fingertips to brush the hair back from my face. "I want you to be comfortable with me. Always."

"I'm a little *un*comfortable right now," I tell him with a flirty smile and a seductive wiggle of my hips that I wouldn't have been capable of a few weeks ago. It's amazing how my unburdening has changed me so profoundly and made me see what I've been missing for all the years I carried that terrible weight.

"I bet I know just how to fix that." He pushes into me and makes me gasp from the intense pressure, the tight fit and the emotional overload that comes from doing this with someone I truly care for. "Is this okay?"

"Mmm, yes. Very okay."

Because he's got me so aroused and relaxed at the same time, because my conscience is clear and my life is full of new possibilities, I enjoy this more than I ever have before. I'm able to fully let go with him.

"I knew it would be amazing with you," he says after we've made Fenway bark from the noise we're making.

"Did you?"

"Oh yeah."

"Thank you for being patient with me."

"Blaise..." His eyes close as his head falls back. "Tell me you're close."

"I am."

He picks up the pace and takes us both to a finish line that has us gasping and clinging to each other. It's a moment of complete unity that fills me with brand new emotions.

"We need to do that again," he mutters from his perch on top of me. "And again and again and again."

"You didn't tell me you were a fiend that way."

"I never have been before, but I have a feeling I could be with you."

"Oh, lucky me," I say with a laugh.

He raises his head to kiss me. "No, lucky *me*." As he gazes down at me with his heart in his eyes, I feel things I'd all but given up on before him. "This is good between us. Tell me you feel it, too."

"I do."

"What're we going to do about that?"

"I'm not sure yet, but I need to go deal with work before Wendall has a meltdown."

"I don't want to let you go."

"Even if I promise to come right back?"

"Well, I suppose if you're willing to promise."

Smiling, I draw him into a kiss that makes him groan.

"Don't kiss me like that and then tell me you have to go."

"I'll be right back. Promise."

"Fine," he says with an adorable pout as he withdraws from me and rolls onto his back.

Fenway lifts her head off her dog bed to see what we're doing. I hope she isn't scarred for life by what went on in that bed.

Still feeling shy, even after what we just did, I wrap a throw blanket around myself to go into the bathroom to clean up and get dressed.

"Back in a few," I tell him before I go downstairs and out the back door with Fenway hot on my heels.

As we emerge from the house, Fenway barks at a woman leaning against her car.

"Fenway, stop!" I run a hand through my hair, wondering if I look like I've recently been ravished. "May I help you?"

Fenway runs off to pee.

"You probably don't remember me. I'm Mary Elliott."

Oh shit. Ryder's mother. "I, um, I remember you." Even if I didn't immediately recognize her, I do now that she's filled in the blanks for me. Her hair has gone gray, and her face is more lined than it was the last time I saw her. She was one of those people who was at every game and event at the school. She blended into the fabric of our town. "What can I do for you?"

"I think you know why I'm here."

"I can't help you with that."

"Can't you?"

"No, I can't."

"You could tell them you're not going to testify after all."

"I'm not willing to do that."

"Why would you come forward after all this time?"

"Because I should've done it then but wasn't strong enough to deal with peer pressure and the fear of everyone hating me. I don't care about that anymore."

"Ryder is a *good* man," she says tearfully. "He's a loving husband and father to three sweet kids who adore him. His life went off the rails when it became clear he was going to lose Louisa. I don't say that to make excuses for him."

"There's no excuse in the world for what he did that night."

"Maybe you saw it wrong."

"I didn't see it wrong, Mrs. Elliott. I saw him rape her, and I'm going to testify to that. I'm sorry if that hurts you and your family, but it's the truth. You should take it up with him."

"*You think I haven't?*"

The vehemence in her tone puts me on edge. Do I need to be afraid of her?

"That's enough," Jack says from behind me as Fenway runs over to him, greeting him as if she hasn't seen him in days. "You need to be going, ma'am."

She stares daggers at me. "I really hope you'll think twice about what you're doing."

"Are you threatening me?"

"Not at all. I'm asking you to consider how your actions affect others."

That statement is so preposterous coming from her that it's all I can do not to laugh in her face. "My actions aren't what caused this."

"You should've stayed gone. Nobody missed you."

"Get off my property," Jack says. "*Now.*"

She gives me a hateful look and then gets in her car, blowing up dust as she stomps on the gas to back out of the driveway.

Chapter 26

Blaise
NOW

JACK PUTS HIS HANDS on my shoulders. "Are you okay?"

"Never better."

"She had no right to come here and say any of that to you."

"She's a mother trying to protect her son. I don't blame her. Of course she doesn't want to believe it's possible he did this."

"You need to tell Houston she was here and what she said."

"I will." I turn to him and put my hand on his cheek. "I'm okay."

"Have I mentioned that I admire your determination?"

"Don't admire me. If I'd spoken up at the time, there wouldn't be three little kids facing the rest of their childhoods without their father."

"Stop beating yourself up. The past is gone. All you can do is your best today, and that's what you're doing."

"Thanks for the reminder." I give him a kiss and head to my cabin.

"Hey, while you're over there?"

Turning back, I raise a brow.

"Pack up the rest of your stuff and bring it over here."

"Are you asking me to move in with you?"

He shrugs and flashes an adorable grin. "I guess maybe I am."

"I'll think about it."

"You do that."

My phone rings, and I grimace when I see Wendall's name on the screen. "Duty calls," I tell Jack as I take the call. "Hey, Wendall. I'm just getting to work."

"We need to talk, Blaise. I, uh, hate to say this, but… I'm afraid I'm going to have to let you go."

"I understand." I do fast math in my head, and quickly put two plus two together to realize I'll have to sublet my apartment in New York quickly.

"You do?"

"Yes, you need someone there, and I can't be there right now."

"You were supposed to tell me you'd come right back so you won't lose your job!"

As I grasp that the firing was a ruse to force me back to work, I try hard not to laugh. He's such a dope. "I appreciate that you want me there, but I can't come back. Not now." Not when I'm falling in love with the most extraordinary man and dealing with a past that's haunted me. "I can help you find someone to take my place."

"I don't want someone else. I want *you*." He sounds like a petulant toddler who isn't getting what he wants, which is on-brand for him.

"I'm sorry, Wendall. I think I might be done with New York." I let my gaze travel across the yard to where Jack is playing ball with Fenway. This place has started to feel like home to me over the last few weeks. In fact, I'm more at home here than I've been anywhere since the dreadful summer that changed everything.

"You don't mean that. You're New York through and through."

"Not so much anymore. I think it's time for you to get someone else. I'll do everything I can to ensure a smooth transition."

"I didn't mean it when I said I was letting you go! That was supposed to bring you back not drive you away."

This is why working for him has driven me crazy! "You should talk to Kim. She's been looking for something more permanent. And if she needs an apartment, she can take over my place."

"I don't want Kim! I want you!"

"I'm sorry, Wendall. If you can convince Kim to come to work for you, treat her well so she won't hate you. Do you hear me?"

"You're really not coming back?"

"I'm really not."

"What'll I do without you?"

"You'll be fine."

"I'm not sure I will be."

"You will. Kim's great, and she knows the theater inside and out. She'll be a true asset to your career."

"So that's it? We're done? Just like that?"

"It's not just like that. I've already been gone a month, and you're doing fine."

"No, I'm not."

"You are. I've been checking on you, and everyone says you're doing great."

"They don't know how it really is."

"Do you want me to call Kim for you?"

"I guess I have no choice."

"And you'll be nice to her?"

"I'll be nice to her."

"Excellent."

"You were, you know. Excellent, that is. I didn't say it enough, but it's true."

"Thank you, Wendall. That means a lot to me."

"What'll you do now?"

"I don't know yet, but I'll figure it out."

"I hope whatever it is makes you happy."

"I'm sure it will. I'll call Kim and make her day."

"And you'll train her?"

"I said I would. It'll all be fine. Thank you again for the opportunity."

"Keep in touch, okay?"

"I will. You too."

"Oh, you'll be hearing from me."

"I'll look forward to that."

After we say our goodbyes, I let out a giddy laugh. I just quit my job! What the hell was I thinking? Did I do that because of Jack? No. I did it because of *me*. Because I'm happier in this place than I've ever been, and I want more. Do I know for certain he's it for me forever? Nope, but I'd sure like to find out if he might be.

With that in mind, I pack up my stuff, strip the sheets off the bed, gather the towels, put on my backpack and troop across the yard carrying the bundle of laundry in one arm while pulling my suitcase with the other hand.

Fenway runs ahead of me. I wish she could get the door.

I bump the suitcase up the three stairs and stumble into the back door, nearly dropping the laundry on the way in.

"Well, well, well. Look at what the cat dragged in." Jack puts down his coffee mug and takes the laundry from me, dumping it on the floor in front of the washing machine.

"Actually, it was the dog who dragged me in. She convinced me to move across the yard."

Smiling, he kisses me as he removes my backpack from my shoulders. "Remind me to thank her later."

"I have news."

"I'm listening."

"I quit my job in New York."

The smile that stretches across his face makes his lovely golden eyes dance with happiness. "Is that so?"

"That is so."

"What now?"

I shrug. "How do you feel about hosting a homeless, out-of-work freeloader for a little while?"

"I feel very good about that. In fact, if you're looking to earn your keep around here, I could use some help getting my shit organized on the third floor."

"I could help with that."

"Does that mean you're sticking around indefinitely?"

"I believe I will, if you'll have me."

"Oh, I'll have you," he says, waggling his brows.

"I need to return the rental car that's putting me into debt."

"We can go do that this afternoon. You can use my mom's car in the garage. I'm sorry I didn't think of that sooner."

"You're making this far too easy for me."

"Am I?" he asks with the little grin that gets to me every time.

"You know you are. You're sure you're okay with it?"

"I haven't been this okay in a very long time."

Smiling, I kiss him. "Me either."

I STILL NEED TO tell Houston about Mary Elliott coming to see me, so I give him a call.

"Hey," he says. "What's up?"

"Mary Elliott was waiting for me at Jack's this morning."

"She was waiting for you? What'd she want?"

"To talk me out of testifying."

"Are you kidding me?"

"Nope."

"That's witness tampering. I'll pass it on to the AG."

"I don't want her to get in trouble."

"He'll give her a warning. She's got no business bothering you or asking that of you."

"I told her I wouldn't change my mind about testifying."

"That's good. She needs to accept this isn't going away, no matter what she tries to pull. I'll give the AG a call and have them talk to her. I'm sorry that happened. It was wildly inappropriate for her to come there, and we'll make sure she understands that."

"Thank you."

"No problem. Keep in mind if she came there, then word's out about where you're staying. You and Jack need to keep your wits about you, all right?"

"Will do."

"What'd he say?" Jack asks when I put down the phone.

"He'll have the AG's office reach out to let her know it's inappropriate for her to be confronting me and it could lead to witness tampering charges."

"Good. I hope that scares the hell out of her."

"He also said to keep our wits about us now that word's out about where I'm staying."

"Since you wouldn't let me hire security, I ordered cameras to put around the property. I don't like that she was able to sneak up on us this morning. Even Fenway didn't hear the car."

"Probably because we were making so much noise." As I say the words, I feel my face get warm.

"Ah, I love that." He smiles as he caresses my cheek. "So sexy."

"You have work to do, mister."

"I really do, and I hate that I do."

"Show me what I can do to help. I want to make myself useful."

He stirs something on the stove. "I will. After I feed you."

I go to see what he's making. Eggs with veggies and potatoes mixed together. "That looks yummy."

He tosses some spinach into the mix and puts bread in the toaster. "I can't let my new assistant work on an empty stomach."

"I'm not your new assistant. I'm helping you out temporarily."

"We'll see," he says with a smile.

"Yes, we will."

Ryder
NOW

I'M AT MY PARENTS' house because I don't have anywhere else to go. I wouldn't dare go to Cam's right now with things so tense between us. Arlo sent a brief text to tell me Caroline and the kids are staying in town after her close circle of friends rallied around them. That's a relief to me.

Arlo's wife, Jenn, is one of Caroline's best friends, which is probably one of many reasons she told him to stay away from me. Of course she'll take Caroline's side against me. Everyone will, even though most of them were my friends long before they ever met her.

I haven't heard a word from Dallas, which is concerning. Having my friends drop off the radar makes me lonelier than I already am without Caro and the kids.

My mother comes in with groceries that I help her put away.

I remember where everything goes here and ache when I recall Caroline being amused by that once upon a time.

Mom's phone rings, and she glances at the screen. "Who'd be calling me from Providence?"

"No idea."

She takes the call. "Yes, this is she." As she listens to what the other person is saying, her entire body goes tense, her expression conveying anger and maybe fear.

What now?

"I didn't do that. I just wanted to talk to her." After another period of silence, she says, "I understand." She puts down the phone without saying goodbye to the caller.

"What was that about?"

"I went to see Blaise Merrick."

"What? *Why would you do that?*"

"I did it for you! If she doesn't testify, this whole thing goes away!"

"Who called?"

"The guy from the AG's office. That Spurling fellow. He said what I did is technically considered witness tampering, and I could be charged if I approach her again."

I go to her and put my arm around her shoulders. "I appreciate what you were trying to do, but you have to stay out of it. It's bad enough without us making it worse. Remember what happened when Dad confronted Captain Sutton? We don't need more trouble."

"We have to do something! We can't let that woman ruin your life."

"She's not the one who ruined my life. I did that, Mom."

She turns to look at me, seeming shocked. "What're you saying? You never went near that girl!"

"Yes, I did, and apparently Blaise witnessed it."

"No. You wouldn't have done that."

"I did do it, and I've hated myself for it ever since."

She pulls back from me. "*What?*"

"I'm sorry, Mom. I hate that I'm putting you through this again."

In barely a whisper, she says, "You attacked that girl."

"Yes."

She shakes her head as her eyes fill.

I take a step toward her.

"No. *No.*"

Giving me a disgusted look, she leaves the room.

I watch her go with a sinking feeling. I shouldn't have told her. If they kick me out of here, I don't know what I'll do. I'm sick over what I'm putting my family through. Every time I think of that night, I'm filled with revulsion and regret.

Not that it matters now. Who cares if I regret it? Who cares if I've wished every day since that I could go back and undo the hideous thing I did to someone who'd never done anything to me?

I pick up the phone to call Cam. I'm almost surprised when he takes the call. "I, uh…I think I'll plead guilty, so I don't drag you all through the mud of a trial."

"If you do that, you'll never see your kids again."

I close my eyes as the pain of that possibility sears me. "What else can I do, Cam? Maybe they'll go easier on me if I express a willingness to own what I did."

"It's a huge risk. I'm working on getting you a better lawyer. Bennett is good, but you need someone with more experience with this kind of thing. Wait to hear from me before you do something that can't be undone."

"I told Mom the truth."

"*Why would you do that?*"

"Because she went to talk to Blaise Merrick and then received a call from the AG's office telling her witness tampering is a crime."

"Holy hell. What was she thinking?"

"She was trying to protect me. I told her the truth, so she'd stop doing that."

"Don't tell anyone else."

"Why not? It's the truth."

"Ryder… Do you want my help or not?"

"I do."

"Then take my advice and *keep your mouth shut*. Don't talk to anyone and tell her not to tell Dad. God only knows what he'd do with that info. If the AG subpoenas Mom, she has to testify truthfully or land in jail if she's found to be lying. You've just given her information she didn't have before, which is now a legal burden to her. Don't tell anyone else."

"I don't want to put the family through a trial."

"Wait until you have proper representation before you do anything. I'll be back to you soon."

The line goes dead before I can thank him for his help.

I hate the tension between us. We worked long and hard to get our relationship back on track after I initially confessed to him. I put a burden on him, too, with that information. I'd catch him watching me at various times, as if trying to reconcile how I could've done such a vile thing after being raised to respect women and girls, to protect and honor them.

I wish I had the answer to the question of *why* I did what I did, but I don't, and I never will. Right before Caroline and I were married, I tried therapy for a while as I was struggling to deal with the lie I'd told my future wife, not to mention the guilt over what I'd done to an innocent young woman in a moment of evil madness. Without fully confessing to the therapist, I made him understand I'd done something terrible that I deeply regretted and was having trouble living with it. He talked to me about making amends to the people I'd hurt, which wasn't possible in this situation.

But I wish it was. I wish I could tell Neisy that what I did was despicable and wrong, and if I had it to do over again, I never would've gone near her that night. However, if there's one thing I've learned it's that there're no do-overs in life.

I hope the lawyer Cam is talking to calls soon. I want to take a plea to get this over with for my loved ones—and myself.

Maybe if I confess to my crimes and accept my punishment, I'll have a prayer of seeing my kids again someday.

My cell has been ringing off the hook with calls from media who want a statement about my suspended congressional campaign and the criminal charges. I've ignored every one of them.

I get a text from Cam. *Take the call from the 617 area code.*

The phone rings half a minute later with a 617 number.

"Hello?"

"Ryder Elliott?"

"Yes."

"This is Bridget Doyle. I'm a defense attorney. Is this a good time to talk?"

"It is." I run my fingers through my hair as the sleepless nights suddenly catch up to me in a wave of exhaustion.

"Your brother briefed me on your situation."

"They have a very strong case."

"They do, but there're things we can do to fight back."

"If those things include besmirching the reputations of the victim or the witnesses, that's a nonstarter for me. I'd like to discuss a plea."

"I'll contact the prosecutor."

"You aren't going to try to talk me out of it?"

"Not if you're unwilling to mount a full-throated defense. There isn't much I can do for you without that. I'll reach out to them and get back to you."

"Thank you."

I put down the phone as despair and exhaustion come at me from all sides.

Cam calls a few minutes later. "How'd it go?"

"She's going to talk to them about me pleading guilty."

"That's it? You aren't going to fight it?"

"Not if it means going after Neisy and Blaise, which is what Bridget would do to mount what she called a 'full-throated' defense. Besides, how do I fight two eye witnesses?"

"There's a *second* one?"

"Ramona Travers saw us leave the party together. After I was charged, she came forward."

"Oh my God. This gets worse by the minute. Don't do anything right away. Let the hysteria die down a bit."

"It won't change how I feel. I'm choosing not to put myself or my family through a trial that I'll lose anyway. At least this way, there'll be some money left for Caroline and the kids."

"I don't know what to say."

"There's nothing to say. The past has caught up with me, and now I have to pay the price."

"You sound shockingly calm about this."

"What else can I do?"

"Nothing, I suppose."

"What're you hearing about the situation with you guys and the affidavit?"

"I asked Bridget to look to into it."

"I really hope nothing comes of that."

"You and me both, brother."

Chapter 27

Denise
NOW

ALL FOUR KIDS ARE sick, and I'm going slowly crazy from tending to them on my own while Kane is in DC for three days. Thank God he's due home tonight because I think I've got a fever, too. I wouldn't blame him if he ran for his life from our germs rather than coming home, but he'd never do that.

The phone rings, and I jump on it, so it won't wake the twins, who've been cranky and miserable for days now.

"Hello," I whisper.

"Is this Denise?"

"It is."

"This is Josh Spurling from the Rhode Island Attorney General's office."

I get up and take the phone into the kitchen. The twins crashed on the sofa while watching *Baby Shark*, which is another reason I'm losing what's left of my sanity.

"What can I do for you?" I ask him. My heart is in my throat as I wait to hear what he has to say. With my life so busy and chaotic, it's easy to forget for a minute or two what's going on in Rhode Island.

"Mr. Elliott has expressed an interest in pleading guilty in exchange for a lesser sentence."

I have an immediate, visceral and negative reaction to the words "lesser sentence."

"Denise?"

"I'm here. What would his sentence be?"

"We'd propose five years in prison with three years of probation after he's released. It's likely he'd do fewer than five years if he behaves himself in prison. He'd be a convicted felon and required to be on the state's sexual offender registry for life. The deal is contingent upon approval by the judge overseeing the case."

"Doesn't it have to be approved by me as well?"

"We'd prefer to have your support when we take it before the judge."

"What if that outcome isn't enough for me?"

"It would spare you from having to relive the attack in open court."

Until he says that, I hadn't realized how much I've been looking forward to the opportunity to testify, to make *him* understand the full extent of what he put me through.

"What would be enough?" Spurling asks.

Without hesitation, I say, "I want him to sit in a courtroom, with his many supporters behind him, and hear that not only did he rape me, but he stole my virginity and left me pregnant. I want him to hear about my horrendous miscarriage and how I needed transfusions because I lost so much blood. I want him and all the people who supported him without question to listen to Blaise testify that *she was there*, and she saw what he did. I want all the men who lied about me being promiscuous to be scared senseless of what's going to happen to them. I want *vindication* for what they did to me."

I'm shaking from the surge of emotion, but resolute in my determination to see this through. Charlotte walks into the kitchen and gives me a concerned look. She's not used to hearing me speak that way to anyone. I hold out my hand to her and wrap my arm around her. The heat of her body against mine has an immediate calming effect.

"I'll speak to the AG and be back in touch."

"Thank you."

"What's wrong, Mama?"

"Nothing, honey. Everything's fine. How're you feeling?"

"Better."

"That's great news. Daddy will be home in a few hours. Why don't we snuggle on the sofa with the boys and watch a movie?"

"It's my turn to pick."

"Anything but *Frozen*. I'm having dreams about snow because I've seen it so many times this week."

She giggles. "How about *Cinderella?*"

"The boys will love that."

"Not Levi."

"We'll watch *Cars* after for him. Go get it ready. I'll be right in."

After she scoots off toward the family room, I lean back against the counter and close my eyes, breathing in through my nose and out through my mouth. Am I crazy for demanding my day in court when I could've made the whole thing go away by agreeing to the plea?

No, I'm not crazy.

The last time I faced off against these people in court, I was a broken seventeen-year-old with no idea how to fight back against the evil that was done to me by him and everyone who supported him.

I'm not a girl anymore. I'm not afraid of them like I once was. I want them to pay for what they did to me, not just criminally, but in the court of public opinion, where they've reigned far too long as kings.

I will be their downfall.

Blaise
NOW

I RECEIVE THE TEXT Houston told me to expect from Ramona Travers Silvia, asking if we can get together to talk. *I've given my sworn statement to the AG, and they said it would be okay if I reached out to you.*

I'd like that, but it can't be in public.

Can you come to my house in Bristol? I'm free any time after 5 pm on weekdays. Would tomorrow around 5:30 work?

Perfect. I'll see you then.

She includes her address, which is about thirty minutes from Jack's place, over two bridges.

I put down my phone and return to what I was doing in Jack's studio, trying to create a filing system for his work that makes sense to someone other than him. That's turning out to be a far more complicated proposition than I first thought, but I love a good challenge.

Every time I glance up from what I'm doing, I catch him looking at me.

"I'm not an artist, but it seems to me that you need to put your eyes on what you're doing and not on me."

"You're much more fun to look at. Come visit me."

"I'm right here."

"You're all the way over there."

Rolling my eyes at his sad pout, I get up and go over to him. "Is this better?"

"It is, but this would be even better." He brings me onto his lap and wraps his arms around me. "There we go."

Fenway sees us snuggling and lets out a perturbed grunt that makes us laugh. She's so put out by us, but thankfully she's not holding it against me that she's gotten less attention from her favorite guy since I came along. I still get plenty of wet, sloppy kisses from her.

"It's hard to get anything done with you and your pouting distracting me."

"You've gotten so much done in just a couple of days. That whole side of the room is actually useable again."

"I've made the smallest of dents."

"You can see why I needed you, right?"

"It took about two seconds of really digging in to see you need a full-time keeper."

"Are you volunteering for the position? It comes with *amazing* benefits." To make his point, he kisses my neck and makes me shiver. "I'd love nothing more than to be kept by you full time."

He's made me breathless and brainless with his words, lips and hands, which never stop moving.

A huge boom sends me flying from his lap.

I land hard on the floor.

"What the fuck?" He spins to look out the window. "Holy shit! Are you all right?"

I take the hand he offers to help me up as Fenway barks frantically. "What was that?"

"The cabins are on fire. Call 911."

He takes off running down the stairs as I follow on shaky legs while trying to press the numbers with fingers that won't cooperate.

"Nine-one-one. Please state your emergency."

"There's a fire." I struggle to remember the address and eventually manage to convey it to her.

"Fire department is on the way. Is anyone inside the structure?"

I stand at the back door in shocked disbelief at the size of the inferno consuming the cottage where I'd been staying until a week ago.

"Not that we know of."

"Stay on the line until they arrive."

Jack has pulled a hose across the yard and has it trained on the building, but that's not making a dent on the flames.

Barking frantically, Fenway pushes at me, trying to get out to "help" Jack.

"No, girl. You stay here. It's not safe."

What if the fire was intended to draw Jack away from me so someone could harm him? Fear overtakes me in a wild wave of panic. I grab Fenway's collar as I open the door and yell for him.

He drops the hose and comes running to me.

When I see the terrified look on his face, it occurs to me, right then and there, with the fire blazing behind him, that I love him.

Before I have a second to process that development, he comes storming up the stairs.

I open the door for him.

"What happened? What's wrong?"

I let go of Fenway and hug him. "Nothing. I was afraid it was a ruse to get you out in the open."

He smells of smoke and sweat. I love him. "I'm sorry if I scared you. My brain is running away with me."

His arms are tight bands around me. "I get it. No worries."

"I'm sorry about the cottage."

"Fuck the cottage. As long as you're okay, that's all that matters."

"As long as we're all okay." I include our beloved Fenway. "That's what matters." I want to tell him I love him. Now that I know, the urge to share it with him is huge.

But the fire department comes in hot, no pun intended, and the next hour is occupied by dealing with them.

After Jack tells them I'm a witness in the criminal case against Ryder Elliott, they call in an arson inspector. We're told the investigation will take a while and we should go about our business in the meantime. How am I supposed to do that after someone might've *torched* his property because of me?

"I...I should go." My heart aches at the thought of leaving him after what we've shared, especially now that I'm certain I love him, but I can't put him, Fenway or his property at risk.

"No, you shouldn't."

"They did this because of me. What'll they do next?"

He puts his hands on my shoulders and looks into my eyes. "I want you here with me where I can help keep you safe."

I'm so torn between what I should do and what I want to do. Where else could I go that they wouldn't find me? I'd be in the same situation if I stayed with my mother.

"It doesn't feel right to stay here. They *burned* your property."

"The arson inspector?"

"What about him?"

"He was a close friend of my dad's. They went through the fire-fighting academy together. He's excellent at what he does. He'll figure out who did this and make them sorry they were ever born."

"Your dad was a firefighter."

"That's right. He was medically retired as a captain after his diagnosis. Probably would've been chief if he hadn't gotten sick."

Jack puts his arms around me.

Snuggled into his embrace, breathing in the earthy, woodsy scent of him that's become so familiar, I almost can't recall why I thought it was a good idea to go. But then I remember the feeling that came over me when I saw him standing in the yard, fully exposed to anyone who'd want to do him harm to hurt me. "It's not fair to you. I brought this madness to your peaceful home."

He tips my chin up to kiss me. "That's not all you've brought. Do you know how lonely I was before you showed up? I didn't even realize how bad it had gotten until you were here to make it all better. And don't go thinking any random guest could've done that for me. I've had tons of people stay in the cottages since I opened them last year. It was *you* who changed everything for me."

"You've done the same for me. I had no idea how lonely I've been, either, until I met you."

"So then why in the world would we ever let them drive us apart when we've waited so long to find each other?"

"I don't want you or Fenway to get hurt or your property attacked again."

"The only thing Fenway and I truly care about is keeping you safe. If you want to leave here, we'll go together, but there's no way we're letting you leave alone, unless you want to."

"Of course I don't."

"Then let's pack up and take off somewhere together until this is over."

"But your work is here and—"

"I can work anywhere. Let's get in the truck and just go."

"I have one thing I have to do tomorrow."

"Then we'll go after that. The place is crawling with cops and firefighters. No one will come near us tonight."

For the first time in hours, I release the deep breath that's been stuck in my chest from the second I understood what was happening outside.

"Are you okay?"

"No, I'm not okay. None of this is okay."

"Keep reminding yourself it's temporary. Once you testify, it'll be over."

"Not if they somehow get to you or Fenway. It would never be over if that happened."

"We'll be fine, and so will you. We'll make sure of it, right Fenway?"

The dog barks and then sits with a smile on her goofy face and her tongue hanging out as usual.

"See? It's unanimous."

I want so badly to tell him how I feel, but not right after his property was damaged because of me. I've never come close to telling a man I love him, so I'm not at all sure of the proper timing for such a thing. But I know this isn't it. I want it to be special and not done out of duress.

He makes dinner for us—delicious pasta with chicken and broccoli—that he serves with crusty bread and the crisp rosé he introduced me to.

"This is delicious. Thank you."

"My pleasure." Taking his wine glass off the table, he sits back in his seat. "Where should we go to escape this nonsense?"

"I don't know. What do you suggest?"

"A friend of mine from RISD runs a seasonal place on the Cape that goes dormant this time of year. You want to check that out?"

"That sounds amazing. I'd love to."

He puts down the glass, reaches for his phone and sends a text.

My phone rings with a call from Providence, which gives me a pit in my stomach. "Hello?"

"Hi, Blaise, this is Josh Spurling from the AG's office."

"Hi, Josh."

"I wanted to give you a couple of updates. First, Ryder Elliott was interested in a plea agreement that would've had him pleading guilty and serving five years with three years of probation and lifetime registry as a sex offender. However, Denise expressed her displeasure with the deal, so we're going forward with a trial."

My first thought on hearing that is *wow, good for her.*

"A preliminary hearing will be held next Friday at Superior Court in Newport. I'm not sure of the time yet, but I'll need you to testify."

"I'll be there."

"Excellent. Thank you."

"I should let you know what's happened here."

"What's up?"

I tell him about Sienna's text, the dead animal on the stoop, Mary Elliott's visit and the apparent firebombing of Jack's property.

"Houston has informed me of the earlier incidents, and they're completely unacceptable. We've made clear to Mr. Elliott and his family."

"What if it's not them doing it?"

"Who else would it be?"

"A number of men are implicated in the cover-up that was part of the original case. They might think getting rid of me would simplify things for them."

"We're investigating that aspect of the case and will put them on notice as well. If anything else happens, I want you to call me immediately. In the meantime, I'm asking the State Police to keep an eye on the place where you're staying."

"My friend and I are planning to leave tomorrow for the Cape for a few days."

"Please text me the address where you'll be, and I'll ask Mass State Police to increase patrols in the area."

"You really think that's necessary?"

"I don't want to take any chances with your safety."

"Okay, well... Thank you."

"Thank *you* for putting yourself through this."

"It's no problem." That's not true, but I'm not interested in discussing the psychology of this situation with him. "Are the men who signed the original affidavit in trouble?"

"We'll require each of them to issue a public statement that what they said then about Denise was false. Because they were minors at the time, they won't be charged."

"That seems ridiculously unfair to me, even though one of them is my own brother."

"I understand and I agree, but our hands are tied by the law. There's nothing stopping her from suing them in civil court."

"I hope she does."

"I guess we'll see what happens. I'll be in touch next week to confirm the time."

After we say our goodbyes, I'm left with unsettled feelings. I update Jack on what Josh had to say. "I should feel bad for hoping Denise sues my brother and the other guys who made up outrageous lies about her to protect Ryder, but I don't feel bad at all. They deserve it. They might've been minors, but they were old enough to know better. We all were."

"They certainly knew exactly what they were doing when they lied about her, and I don't think you should feel bad for hoping they get their comeuppance. Their lies probably influenced the judge."

"No doubt they did. Ryder might've already served his time by now, and all of this would be a bad memory for the people involved. But they risked everything to protect him because they thought there was *no way* he could've done such a thing."

"Small towns are like that. They close ranks around people they've known all their lives and make assumptions based on what they think they know."

"I remember something my mom said that summer, after Ryder was charged. Arlo was furious about it and wanted us to be as well. He said we knew Ryder because he'd practically grown up in our house, which was true. But my mom said we would have no idea how he behaved when the parents weren't looking. Arlo didn't appreciate that. He expected blind loyalty from us, because he thought he knew how Ryder would behave in any situation."

"No one knows how someone is one-on-one except for the other person they're with."

"Exactly."

"It must've been so hard for you to hear him defending Ryder when you knew what'd happened."

"It was torturous. I felt sick twenty-four hours a day for months. I couldn't eat or sleep or think about anything other than what I saw and what I'd failed to do."

He reaches for my hand across the table.

I link my fingers with his.

"It's almost over," he says.

"Sometimes I wonder if it'll ever be over."

Chapter 28

Houston
NOW

I RETURN FROM A routine appearance at District Court in Newport to someone waiting for me outside my office. Her head is down, so I can't see her face, only her long, shiny dark hair.

"Ryder Elliott's wife," Marge says quietly.

Oh, shit. "Thanks." I go over to her. "Caroline?"

She looks up at me, and it's all I can do not to gasp at the way grief and sadness have ravaged her face. "I'm sorry to bother you. Ryder and Dallas always spoke so highly of you, and… I…"

"Come in."

I hold the door while she goes into my office ahead of me.

After I close the door I take a seat behind my desk while she takes one of my visitor chairs. "What can I do for you?"

"I'm not sure, exactly. I…I guess I want to understand…" She looks up at me with brown eyes swollen and red with dark half-moon bruises under them. "Why is this happening now?" Her voice is barely a whisper.

"Because a witness came forward who saw the attack."

"Where has that witness been for all this time?"

"She grew up in Hope, but she's lived away for most of her adult life."

"Why confess to it now?"

"I believe it was because she heard he was running for Congress."

"So for all these years, she knew he'd done this, but she didn't tell anyone?"

"Yes."

"*Why?*" Her tone is full of despair.

"Because he was her brother's close friend, among other reasons."

"Arlo's sister."

"Yes."

I pause, feeling uncertain about whether I should say more. But she came to me looking for answers. The least I can do is tell her what I know. "You have to understand what it was like when Ryder was charged the first time. As an outstanding student and athlete, he was enormously popular with the other kids. He'd been widely admired for standing by Louisa during years of serious illness. People were shocked when he was charged with such a crime."

"Did you believe he'd done it?"

"I didn't know what to believe. Denise was a friend of mine. All she talked about was the boyfriend she loved, who lived overseas at the time. I found it hard to believe she'd make up a story like this, but it didn't fit with what I knew of him, you know?"

"I guess."

"It got really ugly for her after news of his arrest got out. His friends attacked her on Facebook and in court, basically forcing her out of town. Blaise would've seen how it went for Denise and feared the same thing happening to her if she reported what she'd seen. I'm not excusing what she did, but having once been a teenager myself, I understand why she was afraid to speak up."

"It's very hard for me to believe that the man I've loved with all my heart, the father of my children, is capable of such a thing."

"I can't imagine how difficult this has to be for you."

"It's like someone has died, even though he's very much alive. He's dead to me, I suppose, because how could I ever forgive him for something like this? Not only did he lie to me for all those years, now there's someone saying he *did* attack that poor girl..." She doesn't seem to notice the tears sliding down her cheeks. "Before we were married, he told me he'd been accused. He looked me in the eyes and told me he didn't do it."

I get up and go around the big desk that was once my father's and take a seat in the chair next to hers, handing her a tissue. That's when she seems to realize she's crying.

She takes the tissue from me and wipes her face. "Thank you. I appreciate your kindness."

"I'm sorry this is happening to you and your family."

"Are you allowed to say that?" she asks with the first hint of a smile.

"Maybe not, but I've known Ryder a long time. The witness account came as a huge shock to me, too."

"When he was charged the first time, you didn't think he did it?"

"I couldn't reconcile the charge with the kid I knew. He'd been close friends with Dallas for years by then."

"Dallas came by the house this morning. He's devastated, too."

"I know."

"Is he angry with you?"

"He's not happy with me, but hopefully he'll come around to understanding I have a job to do."

"So our family isn't the only one being torn apart by this?"

"No, you're definitely not alone."

"The party where the attack happened… It was at your house?"

I nod. "My parents' place. They were out of town, and I took full advantage of the opportunity. If I had it to do over, I never would've had the party."

"No one blames you."

"I know, but I was responsible for providing alcohol to underage kids. I was lucky I wasn't charged for that."

"I suppose we all have our regrets."

"Indeed."

"My friends in town… They've been amazing, rallying around the kids and me and bringing food and support and so much love."

"I'm glad you have that."

"Me, too, but I keep thinking I should move the kids away from here, so they don't have this as part of their story."

"Is that what you want to do?"

She shakes her head. "I love it in Hope. We have such a wonderful group of friends and neighbors, and Ryder's family is there, too. The kids are close to their cousins. I know it would be an added trauma for them if we moved somewhere else, but what happens when they're in high school and the other kids resurrect this crap?"

"Maybe you should worry about that then. Focus on right now. If it's easier for you to stay put, then do it. Doesn't have to be forever."

"You're right. That's true. I'm sorry to have taken up so much of your time."

"It's no problem at all."

"Ryder always spoke so highly of you. I can see why."

"That's nice to hear." I reach for the business cards I keep in a little stand on the desk and hand one to her. "My cell number is on there. If I can ever do anything for you, even just listen, give me a call."

"Thank you for being so kind to a distraught wife."

"It's no problem at all."

"Ryder's mom came to stay with the kids, so I could have some time to myself. I got in the car and ended up here."

"I'm glad you did."

She gives me a wan smile. "You're very kind."

Her heartbreak has touched me deeply. "That's nice of you to say." I wish there was more I could do for her than simply listen.

"I'll let you get back to work."

I walk her out to her minivan and hold the driver's side door for her. "Call me. Any time you need to talk. I'll always be here to listen."

"I will. Thank you again, Houston."

"Of course."

I watch her drive off, feeling somewhat stunned by the encounter with a woman I'd only met in passing and barely knew before she came to see me. Dallas and his wife, Jane, have been great friends with Ryder and Caroline forever, so I'd certainly heard about how much they adore her. But this is the first time I've talked to her one-on-one.

My heart goes out to her. No one should have to go through what she is.

Blaise
NOW

AFTER A RESTLESS NIGHT plagued with dreams about fires, Glocks, dead animals and people chasing me through the woods, I'm a wreck in the morning. Judging from the barking, I determine Jack is outside with Fenway. I wonder how long they've been up.

I stare at the ceiling for a long time, thinking through the events of recent days and coming to the same conclusion I reached yesterday—I should get out of here until this is over. Jack didn't sign on for all this drama when he rented his cottage to me. Now that gorgeous little cottage is a pile of smoldering wreckage and most likely a crime scene.

Because of me.

I can't bear to think about what else might happen before this is over.

If anything ever happened to him or Fenway or the home his parents left him…

What if they'd tried to torch this house where all his priceless art is stored?

I've spun myself into a full-blown panic when he appears in the doorway holding two steaming mugs.

Just that quickly the panic is replaced with a deep appreciation for this incredible man, who came into my life under the strangest of circumstances and has never once wavered, despite many reasons to.

"Morning."

Fenway comes bounding into the room and up on the bed to give me relentless morning kisses that make me giggle.

"Down, girl," Jack says.

She actually sits.

"Wow. Miracles do happen."

I stroke her silky ears. "She's a very good girl."

"No, she isn't."

Before Fenway, I wouldn't have thought dogs could smile. She's proven me wrong. I'm as crazy about her as I am about her daddy.

Jack sits on what's become his side of the bed and hands me one of the mugs.

"Thank you."

"How'd you sleep?"

"Not great. Lots of weird dreams."

"You were restless."

"Did I keep you awake?"

"Not at all."

"I was thinking…"

"Uh-oh."

The thought of leaving him and Fenway is painful, but I want to do the right thing. I know how it feels not to, and I never want to be in that place again.

"What's on your mind?"

"I should go."

He shakes his head. "No, you shouldn't."

"Jack, listen to me. This could get much worse before it gets better, and while I love the idea of running away to the Cape with you, we'd be leaving your home unprotected. If they're watching me, by now they know that you mean something to me. I wouldn't be able to bear it if they hurt you in any way."

"It would hurt me if you left. I've waited my whole life to feel this way, Blaise."

His sweetness is my undoing. Tears fill my eyes. "Me, too, but—"

He leans across the pillows to kiss me. "No buts. We're in this together to the bitter end."

"I don't want the end to be bitter. That's what I'm saying."

"That's a figure of speech, and you know it. I spoke to my friend Cory this morning, and he's coming today to install cameras and a security system."

"How much will that cost?"

"It's worth every penny, and I've been meaning to do it for a while now anyway, especially since we now have guests here in the summer." He caresses my face. "I don't want you to worry about anything where I'm concerned."

"I am worried. This could go on for months."

"Does that mean you're planning to be here for months? Maybe years or decades?"

"I'm being serious."

"So am I. If I could have anything I wanted, I'd want you to stay forever."

"It's like that, is it?" I ask, smiling. He can make me forget all my worries and fears like no one else ever has.

"It's been like that for a while now, in case you haven't noticed."

"I've noticed."

"So what do you say?"

"What's the question again?"

"Would you please stay forever and make my life complete?"

I shocked nearly speechless. "Uh… Is that like a…um…proposal?" Does my voice sound high and squeaky, or is that just me?

Laughing, he says, "Not quite yet. It's more of a statement of intention." He kisses me. "When I propose, it'll be a heck of a lot more romantic than sitting in bed with coffee."

"That's pretty romantic if you ask me. No one has ever brought me coffee in bed before."

"If I promise to do that every day for the rest of your life, will you consider sticking around?"

"Yes."

His eyes go wide, which makes me laugh. "That's all it takes?"

"Yep."

"You're easy."

"That's what you like about me."

"I like so many things about you it would take the whole day to tell you all of them."

"I'm free all day."

"In case you haven't noticed, I love you, Blaise."

"I love you, too." I'm so relieved to be able to tell him that. "When I came here to right a terrible wrong from the past, I never imagined for a second that I might find my future."

"When I built the cottages, I never imagined that one day the woman of my dreams might rent one of them."

"You give a good compliment."

"Even with the trouble you're dealing with, I've never been happier in my life than I've been since you arrived."

"I feel the same way, but how can I be so happy in the midst of the craziness going on in my life?"

"The craziness is out there. Let's keep it there, okay?"

"That sounds good to me."

"So we're staying put here and toughing it out together?"

"I guess we are."

"We'll do the Cape after the trial."

"I'll look forward to that."

He takes my mug and puts it next to his on the bedside table. "Now how should we celebrate this somewhat major decision?"

"I can't think of a single thing."

"Really?"

His surprised expression makes me laugh, which happens a lot with him.

I hadn't realized how much I missed laughing until Jack made it part of my daily life again.

"You just got serious on me." He kisses my neck and makes me shiver. "What gives?"

"I was thinking about how much I've missed laughing until you reminded me what it's like to laugh all the time."

"I'll do my best to keep you laughing every day."

"Sometimes I wonder how this can be real. I didn't even know you six weeks ago, and now I can't imagine life without you."

"Then my work here is nearly finished."

"No way! Your work here is just beginning."

"Oh damn, what am I signing on for?"

"A lifetime as my favorite person."

"Yes, please." When he kisses me, I forget the many worries and fears I woke up with and am thinking only of him as he quickly has me clinging to him. The flashpoint of desire that happens with him is new to me, and I can't get enough of it. But I want to give him as much as he gave me, so, I push on his chest to get him to turn over.

When he's settled on his back, he looks up at me with a curious expression. "What's going on?"

"Just a little of this." I kiss his chest and nuzzle his chest hair, making him groan.

Fenway barks, and we laugh.

"He's okay, girl," I tell the dog.

He twirls my hair around his index fingers. "Am I, though?"

"Let's see, shall we?"

"Oh yes, please."

Keeping my gaze connected with his, I kiss a path to his well-defined abdominal muscles as my chin nudges his erection.

He sucks in a sharp deep breath and gives a gentle tug on my hair.

Who knew that could be arousing?

I break the eye contact as I wrap my hand around his thick erection and take him into my mouth.

I'll never forget the sound he makes or the way his hands wrap around my hair or how his hips come off the bed. I've done this a handful of times and never enjoyed it. Not like I do now with this man I love and who loves me. His excitement is mine. His pleasure is mine. Love makes everything different.

I pull out all the stops for him.

"Blaise… Wait…" He gasps as I apply some suction before letting him pop free of my lips. "Let's do this together."

I straddle him and do some serious teasing.

His gaze darts over my body with full appreciation. "Sexiest thing I've ever seen."

I take him in, so slowly his eyes roll back in his head. "That can't possibly be true."

"Oh, it is very true."

His hands slide from my hips to my breasts, his thumbs gliding over my nipples. "Mmm, so hot."

Being with him is like the best kind of fever dream.

I hope it never ends.

Chapter 29

Blaise
NOW

WE SPEND THE ENTIRE day in bed.

"I've never done this before," I tell him around three.

My head is on his chest as he runs his fingers through my hair. He's obsessed with the silky feel of it.

"Done what?"

"Spent a whole day in bed with someone."

"What do you think of it so far?"

"I can't wait to do it again."

"We'll do it as often as you want."

"You'll get fired."

"I'm self-employed. I can do what I want."

"You've got looming deadlines."

"It'll get done. It always does. Don't worry about it."

"I need to find a job if I'm going to stay here."

"I could use a manager."

"I'd do that for free. I need to find something to help pay the bills."

"How to say this..."

I shift so I can see him. "Say what?"

"So the work brings in quite a lot of money. Like enough that we're set. You don't need to worry about helping to pay the bills. You can do whatever you want to."

"You said you built the cottages to help pay the taxes on the property."

"I did, but it wasn't as if I couldn't have paid the taxes without the cottages."

"Oh."

"If I'm being honest, it was getting kind of lonely living here with just Fenway, even though she's very good company. I thought it would be nice to have some people around. That's the real reason I built the cottages." He adds a sexy smile. "Look how it turned out."

"With you lazing away an entire day in bed."

"Best day I've ever had."

"Me, too."

"I still need to get some sort of job."

"You're crazy good at organizing things, right?"

"So I'm told."

"I need that. Badly. I have like six hundred emails I've been ignoring for weeks. My agent has called three times, and I don't want to talk to him because he makes my head hurt. There's talk of a show of my work at RISD that I don't want to deal with. I've been thinking about hiring someone to manage it all for a long time. The job is yours if you want it, and it would be a paid gig with full benefits."

"What does your package include?"

The look on his face is priceless. "I'm being serious, and no matter what you might think, I'm not creating a job for you. I need you, in every possible way."

"I'll think about it."

"Really?"

"Yes, really." I lean over him to check the clock on the bedside table. "I need to shower and get to Bristol."

"Do you want me to come with you?"

"That's ok. I won't be gone long. Are you sure you don't mind if I take your mother's car?"

"I'm sure. I take it out at least once a month to keep it running, and it's got plenty of gas."

"I'll take very good care of it."

"I'm not worried."

He walks me to the garage a half an hour later and hands me the keys. "Be careful."

"I will. Get some work done before you get fired."

Smiling, he kisses me. "Hurry back. I already miss you."

"No one has ever said the kinds of things you say to me."

"That's good to know. I'll have to stay at the top of my game."

"You're doing great so far."

"Let me know if that changes."

"You'll be the first to know." I have to tear myself away from him when leaving is the last thing I want to do. "I'll text you when I'm on the way back."

"I'll be here."

I kiss him one more time before getting into his mother's burgundy Volvo SUV where a lingering scent of something light and floral makes me miss a woman I'll never meet. I want to know more about both his parents, so I'll feel like I know them.

The drive to Ramona's takes me over two bridges—one of them new and spacious, the other old and rickety. The old one freaks me out like it did when I was a teenager, and first driving over it to get to a soccer or lacrosse game.

I hated driving on that bridge then, and I hate it now. I also hate how early it gets dark now that Daylight Savings Time has ended. It's already dark at five fifteen as I drive into the quaint town of Bristol, known for hosting the nation's oldest Fourth of July parade. We went to the parade every year when we were younger, until we grew up and preferred time with our friends to family outings. Outings with all six of us seem like a million years ago now.

Ramona lives off Metacom Avenue, in a tidy neighborhood made up of raised ranches. Hers is painted white with blue shutters and mature landscaping. I park in the driveway, behind a silver minivan.

She greets me at the door, looking much as I remember her from high school—petite with short hair and wire-framed glasses. "Come in. It's nice to see you after all this time."

"You, too."

Her home is right out of a decorating show. "This is gorgeous."

"Thank you. It's a bit of a hobby, but it's not easy to keep it looking nice with three kids underfoot."

"You're very talented."

"Aw, thanks. It keeps me from going crazy dealing with work and kids and all the other stuff."

"What do you do for work?"

"I run a chiropractor's office."

"I bet that's busy."

"Sure is. Can I get you some coffee, tea, water or Diet Coke?"

"Water would be great. Thank you."

She brings the water for me and a Diet Coke for herself to the table where we sit across from each other. "I really need to give this up," she says of the soda, "but I'm addicted."

"I used to be. I gave it up about five years ago."

"I need to get serious about that, but we're not here to talk about Diet Coke."

"It was a relief to me to hear you'd come forward, too."

"Same. Sitting on that info all this time was tough. What they did to her..."

"I know. It made me sick, but not sick enough to risk tearing up my own life to support her. I hated myself for that then, and I still do now."

"I understand the feeling," Ramona says with a sigh. "I agonized over it at the time, but I just kept reading the stuff they were saying about her and tried to imagine what it would be like if they were coming for me. I just couldn't do it."

I reach across the table to cover her hand with mine. "I totally get it. My brother was one of his best friends. He was outraged that she would accuse him of such a thing."

"That must've made it extra tough for you."

"It did."

"It was bad enough for me having witnessed seeing them walk toward the woods together. I can't begin to imagine what it would've been like to have witnessed the actual assault."

I shake my head. "Horrific and heartbreaking." After a pause, I add, "I was with a friend who convinced me our lives would be hell if we said anything. She practically dragged me out of there."

"I'm so sorry. Is she testifying, too?"

"No. She has personal connections."

"Was it Sienna?"

"I, uh..."

"I understand. She was dating Cam then and is married to him now."

"Right. I've told the prosecutor I'm speaking only for myself."

"I understand. I'd never say anything. Don't worry." She takes a sip from her glass. "When I first heard you'd come forward, I was in such a state. That was the first time I told my husband what I'd seen and how it'd affected me. He encouraged me to come forward, too."

"I'm glad you did."

"I want you to know... Even though I hadn't told him or anyone what I saw that night, I never stopped thinking about it or asking myself what kind of person it made me for staying quiet when another young woman was being dragged through the mud. It haunted me."

"Me, too, and it's a huge relief to speak to someone who truly understands. It made me question everything I thought I knew about myself."

"Yes, exactly that. I wasn't raised to sit quietly in the face of injustice. I've been a very active volunteer at a local sexual assault resource center and with the statewide rape crisis hotline. People have complimented me for my commitment, but I've never felt I deserved that praise. It seems like the least I can do."

"I volunteered in that space in the city for years. It was important, worthwhile work, but it didn't soothe my conscience the way I thought it would. Not like finally coming forward has."

"Reporting what I saw has been extremely cathartic."

"But not without its consequences. I keep thinking about his wife and kids, who had a bomb detonate in the center of their lives when he was arrested."

"You know that's on him, not you, right?"

"Intellectually, yes. Emotionally? I feel for her and her kids. By all accounts, she's a lovely person."

"Who was married to a rapist who probably lied to her about his past."

"True."

"What do you hear about Neisy? I've thought of her so often over the years, but there's nothing about her anywhere online after she graduated from high school in Virginia."

"Houston told me she's married to her childhood boyfriend. They have four kids and live in the Norfolk area. He's a naval officer."

"Oh, wow. I'm so glad to hear she's doing well. This must've been a bomb for her, too."

"It was, and at first she wasn't sure she could be part of it. After she thought about it, she called Houston to say she was in—and she wanted the boys who signed that affidavit about her punished, too."

"That was sickening. I dumped Brody after he told me they were doing that. I hope they all get every bit of what's coming to them."

We hear car doors closing outside.

"That'll be my family coming home from dance class. I have two girls, who are seven and nine and a son who's four."

They come in through the mudroom off the kitchen, a flurry of girlish voices and bags dropping as their father tells them to take off their shoes.

The girls have blonde curly hair and cherubic faces. They rush into their mother's arms and then seem to notice me. "This is my friend Blaise from high school. Blaise, this is Audra and Heidi, my son, James, and my husband, Tony."

"It's so nice to meet you all."

The little boy is shy and hides behind his dad. The girls are super polite as they shake hands with me and tell me it's nice to meet me, too. A pang of yearning hits me out of nowhere. What would it be like to have a little girl of my own someday? I've never had a yearning for children, but now anything seems possible. "I won't take up any more of your time. I'm so glad we got to talk."

"Me, too," Ramona says as she walks me to the door. "Let's keep in touch, okay?"

"I'd love that."

We hug and say our goodbyes. As I drive away from her home, I marvel at how two people who barely knew each other in high school have become central players in this made-for-TV drama. It's crazy dark as I make my way to the bridge. I recall my mother hating this time of year when the New England winter sets in with cold, dreary darkness that lasts for months.

I'm on the bridge, thinking I need to call my mom to check in with her, when bright headlights blind me from behind. I adjust the mirror, but that doesn't help to reduce the glare. As I crest the top of the bridge, I get hit from behind. The impact sends me into oncoming traffic. I slam on my brakes and spin in a circle as I scream at the thought of plunging into the black, frigid water below.

That's my last thought before everything goes dark.

Chapter 30

Jack
NOW

I HAVE A TON of work to do, but I can't concentrate on anything. It's amazing to me how quickly Blaise has become the center of my life. If you'd asked me before she showed up if I was happy, I would've said yes. I love my work, and I've adjusted to life without my parents, settled their estate and gotten through the first few years of birthdays and holidays without them. But now I realize there's a huge difference between content and truly happy.

Blaise has made me happier than I've ever been.

She texted to say she was on her way from Bristol, so I take Fenway outside to play until she gets home.

When we step into the yard, the new floodlights are activated by the movement.

Fenway is taken aback for a second by the light, but she quickly recovers when she sees me holding her favorite ball.

We play for half an hour, until she's so tired she lays down in front of me, a sign the game is over.

I'm reaching for the ball when a police SUV rolls into the yard with the lights on.

My stomach drops to my feet as everything in me goes cold with fear.

Houston jumps out of the car. "Jack... Blaise has been in an accident."

I can't move or think or breathe or do anything other than absorb the wave of dread that comes over me. Please no. Not her, too. I knew I should've gone with her.

"Jack? Come with me. I'll take you to her."

"Wh-where is she?"

"They were transporting her to Charlton."

Fenway barks, as if to ask what's going on. I wish I could tell her.

"I have to bring Fenway. I can't leave her here alone." Not with people torching my property.

"Put her in the backseat. I'll keep her with me while you're with Blaise."

I know I'm supposed to move, to walk, to function, but the fear of losing Blaise so soon after I found her has me rooted to the spot where Houston found me.

"She needs you, Jack."

Those four words finally break through the dread to get me moving toward the house to grab Fenway's leash and my wallet.

Houston drives to Fall River with lights and the siren, which doesn't help my anxiety one bit. "What do you know?"

"Someone hit her on the Mount Hope Bridge, and she spun into oncoming traffic. A truck hit her head on."

I feel sick as I think about what that must've been like. "She must've been terrified."

"She was unconscious when the paramedics got to her."

"Did they get the person who hit her?"

"They took off, but people in the car behind the truck that hit her got the plate, and they're tracking it down now."

"This was intentional. Someone followed her over there and waited to do this to her on the bridge, where it would be scarier than hell."

"Probably," Houston says, sounding as grim as I feel.

"Will she make it?"

"I haven't heard anything since they said they were transporting her, but they took her to Charlton and not Rhode Island Hospital."

"What does that mean?"

"Charlton isn't a level-one trauma facility, and Rhode Island Hospital is."

"So that's good news then."

"I think so, but I don't know for sure."

"I'll take whatever hope you can give me."

Houston's radio crackles to life with a call from Dispatch. "Chief, we received word from Bristol police that the victim transported to Charlton—"

My heart stops when the radio cuts out. "What? What about her?"

"Dispatch, please repeat your last transmission."

I hold my breath and pray like I haven't in years. *Please. Please. Please.*

"Chief, the victim is awake and alert."

The relief is so tremendous, I immediately break down. *Thank you. Thank you. Thank you.*

Houston continues to communicate with the dispatcher, but I tune them out. I've heard the only thing that matters to me. She's alive, awake and alert.

I glance at him. "Something needs to be done to keep her safe until this is over."

"I've already spoken to Josh Spurling at the AG's office. They're putting her in a State Police safe house with round-the-clock protection. They're also putting officers at your house."

"I'll want to be with her, and Fenway goes where we go."

"I told them that. I'll take you home to pack whatever you need."

"Thank you, Houston. For everything, especially for sending Blaise to my place when she needed somewhere to stay. I hope I'll be thanking you for that for the rest of my life."

"That's awesome. I'm so happy for you guys."

"I'm happy for us, too. We can't let anything happen to her."

"I hear you. We're on it."

We arrive at the Charlton ER a few minutes later. He pulls up to the door. "Go ahead. I've got Fenway. Call me when you're ready for a pickup."

"Thank you again."

"No problem."

As he drives off, I go inside through the automatic doors. At the reception desk, I ask for Blaise.

"Are you a family member?"

"Yes." It's the easiest "lie" I've ever told. I'm her family, and she's mine. We don't need a ceremony or vows to make that true.

"Let me check on her status. I'll be right back."

I want to tell the woman to hurry, that Blaise has very quickly become the most important person in my life, that I want to marry her and raise a family with her and have everything with her. But I don't say any of those things. I simply stand there and *will* the nurse to understand what Blaise means to me. I'm so thankful I told her I love her. I'd wanted to tell her that for a while.

How did this even happen? How did a red-headed beauty become more important to me than my own life? One day I was minding my own business, taking care of my home and dog while growing my art career. The next minute she was there, and everything had changed. I've never held much stock in the idea of fate or soulmates or true love or any of that stuff. But now I get it. I understand why perfectly sane people do the craziest things to hold on to love once they find it.

It's the most precious and perfect thing there is, and all I want is to feel this way for the rest of my life.

The nurse comes back and gestures for me to follow her.

I move so fast I nearly crash into her back as she leads me through double doors into the bustling emergency department. We go down a corridor, past multiple patient rooms until we stop outside of hers.

I have to hold back a gasp as I take in the cut on her forehead, the bruises on her face and her arm immobilized in some sort of inflatable cast.

Tears fill her eyes when she sees me.

It's a struggle to hold it together as I go to her. My heart is pounding as I realize I came very close to losing her. "Baby…"

Her chin quivers. "I'm okay."

"Yes, you are." I caress her unbruised cheek and kiss her softly. "You're going to be just fine."

"I was so scared."

"I can't even imagine."

"I've always hated driving on that bridge."

"You'll never have to do it again. I'll take you any time you need to go over there."

"And your mother's car… I hope it's not totaled."

I haven't given it the first thought. "It's just a car. The only thing that matters is you're okay."

Her chin continues to quiver as tears slide down her cheeks. "All I could think of was you."

"Same, babe. From the second you left, I thought of you, and when Houston came to tell me you'd been in an accident…" I shake my head. "I should've gone with you."

"Then you'd be hurt, too." Her eyes widen all of a sudden. "Where's Fenway?"

"With Houston."

"Oh, good. That's good."

"I'd never leave her alone."

"You can't because of all the trouble I've caused."

"Don't do that. You've given me so much. Things I've never had before." I can't stop touching every part of her that I can reach. Her gorgeous face, her silky hair, the hand that holds mine so tightly. "They're going to move us to a safe house until the trial."

"You'll hate that. Your work is at home."

"I can bring it with me."

"This is so disruptive to your life."

"Yes, it is," I say with a smile. "You're the best disruption ever."

"I'm being serious."

"As am I." I kiss the back of her hand. "I've never been more serious about anything."

THEY RELEASE HER AT ten o'clock that night with orders to follow up with an orthopedic doctor tomorrow about her badly sprained wrist.

Houston is waiting for us outside the ER doors.

Fenway goes crazy in the backseat when she sees us coming toward the car.

A nurse is pushing Blaise in a wheelchair while I follow, carrying a plastic bag full of the possessions she arrived with.

I help the nurse get her settled in the front seat and put the seatbelt on her, moving carefully so I won't hurt her. "Are you comfortable?"

"Yes, thank you."

Fenway's nose comes through the space between the headrest and the door, her tongue lashing at Blaise.

"I'm here, baby girl." She reaches up to rub Fenway's nose. That earns her a wet lick to the palm of her hand.

I get into the backseat. "Move over, girl."

She's so happy to see me that she does what she's told for once.

"I hope she hasn't driven you crazy," I say to Houston.

"Not at all. She's been a very good girl. We stopped by to see my parents and played some fetch in the yard."

"She must've loved that."

"She did. She had us laughing with her enthusiasm."

"Thank you again for taking care of her for us."

"It was definitely my pleasure."

"So what's the plan?"

"I'm taking you to the safe house in Cranston for tonight. We've got the basics for you there. Tomorrow, a State Police officer will take you home to pack the rest of what you need. They've positioned two officers at your place in revolving twenty-four-hour watches."

"What do we know about the truck that hit Blaise?"

"It belongs to Ryder's father. We're looking for him."

"What?" Blaise whispers.

"He's not new to trouble." Houston glances at me in the rearview mirror. "He was arrested the first time Ryder was charged for harassing Denise's family."

"I never imagined there'd be so much trouble when I came back." Blaise sounds exhausted. "I knew people would freak out about there being a witness, but not like this."

"None of this is your fault, Blaise," Houston says.

"Feels like it is."

I reach up to put my hand on her shoulder. "It's *not*. You haven't done anything to deserve them lashing out at you this way. This is on *him*. Not you."

She has no reply to that. I'll have to keep reminding her of who committed a crime and who didn't.

The house in Cranston is on a nondescript street made up of neatly kept ranch homes. I expect to see State Police vehicles outside, but there're only unmarked SUVs. I get out and run around the car to help Blaise. "Take it nice and easy."

"That's my only speed right now."

Houston gets Fenway from the back seat and follows us into the house where four plain-clothes officers greet us.

Blaise leans on me as she takes small, delicate steps.

"Right this way." One of the officers leads us to the primary bedroom at the end of the hallway.

They leave us alone as I help to get Blaise settled in bed, propping her up on numerous pillows.

"How's that?"

Her complexion has been bleached of all its usual rosiness. "Okay."

"What can I get you?"

"A glass of water would be great, and I'm supposed to pick up meds from the pharmacy."

"I'll ask Houston to do that." I kiss the uninjured side of her face and go to speak to him. "We need to pick up prescriptions at the pharmacy."

"I'll do it."

I give him the sheet of paper with the info about the prescriptions that're waiting at a twenty-four-hour pharmacy and my credit card. "Thank you."

"I'll be right back."

"Where can I find a glass?" I ask one of the officers.

He points me to the correct cabinet.

I return to the bedroom with a glass of ice water.

Her eyes are closed, so I put the glass on the bedside table.

"I'm not sleeping."

"I wasn't sure. Here's the water."

"Thank you for all you're doing."

"It's no big deal."

"Yes, it is. I've made a mess of your life."

"My life was so boring until you came along." I sit gingerly on the mattress next to her. "The only thing that matters is that you're going to be okay."

"That's not the only thing that matters," she says tearfully.

"To me, it is. Please don't worry about me or my life or my work or anything else. It'll all be fine."

"I should just give them what they want and refuse to testify, so they'll leave us alone."

"No way, Red. You've come too far to give up now. Soon enough, this'll be over, and we'll have the whole rest of our lives together."

"Did you just give me a nickname?"

"Maybe."

"Despite having had red hair my whole life and a million nicknames associated with that and my name, no one's ever called me that."

"Is it okay if I do?"

"Yeah, it's okay. What're you hearing about your mother's car?"

"Banged up but fixable."

"That's a huge relief. I know how much it means to you to have her car."

"I feel like she might've had something to do with keeping you safe."

Fenway comes into the room and jumps up on the bed next to Blaise.

Before I can tell her to be careful, she drops to her belly and inches in slowly and carefully, as if she knows to be gentle.

"Hi, sweet girl." Blaise scratches her ears and earns a soft, sweet lick to her wrist. "She's the best girl."

"It's good to know she can behave once in a while."

"I love her."

"She loves you, too." I kiss her forehead. "Get some rest. I'll be right here."

Twenty minutes later, Houston returns with the meds, which knock her out quickly. That's a relief because she was in pain.

"Is there any word on whether they've arrested the guy who did this?" I ask him.

"Not yet, but everyone is looking for him."

Chapter 31

Ryder
NOW

POUNDING ON THE FRONT door awakens me from a restless sleep. *What now*, I wonder as I go to see what's happening.

My mom tightens the belt around her robe as she answers the door to cops holding up their badges.

"We're looking for David Elliott." The older of the two cops is my high school classmate, Caleb Anders. He doesn't look at me.

"He's not here."

"Where is he?"

"I don't know. He didn't come home earlier."

"Are you able to track his location?"

"No."

That's a lie. She's been tracking us for years.

"Why are you looking for him?" I ask.

"He was involved in a car accident earlier."

"Is he all right?" Mom asks.

"We don't know. That's one of several reasons we'd like to speak to him. Would you mind calling him?"

Mom hesitates.

"Do it," I tell her with a sinking feeling. There's no way they'd be here if this didn't somehow involve my case. We can't do anything to make this situation worse than it already is.

She pulls her phone from the pocket of her robe and calls Dad. "Where are you? The police are here looking for you."

I can't hear his side of the conversation.

"Come home right now." After a pause, she says, "Dave, we need you. Please don't do anything stupid."

"Ma'am, where is he?"

She puts her hand over the phone, so she won't be overheard by Dad. "What's going to happen to him?"

"He'll be arrested and charged with attempted vehicular homicide, leaving the scene of an accident, intentionally causing an accident and suspected arson."

"*What?*" Her shriek pierces the air around me. "He wouldn't do that!"

A click sounds, indicating Dad has ended the call.

"I'm afraid he did cause the accident. We have multiple witnesses as well as camera footage from Mount Hope that shows the moment of impact."

"Who did he hit?" I ask, fearing I already know the answer.

"Blaise Merrick."

"Is she…"

"She survived with injuries."

"Are you sure you don't track his location?"

Mom's hands shake as she checks her phone. "He's shut it off."

I use my own phone to text Cam. *Dad hit Blaise's car on the MH bridge. She survived with injuries. Cops are here now, looking for him for that and suspected arson. One of the cops is Caleb Anders.*

Son of a bitch. What was dad thinking? And arson?? WTF?

No idea. He's shut off his location.

I'll see what I can find out.

"Cam is on it," I tell Mom as I guide her to sit on the sofa.

The glow from emergency lights in front of the house filters in through the curtains. I'm sure the neighbors are gathered in the street.

"How could he have done this?" she asks tearfully. "Didn't he learn his lesson the last time?"

My dad's unraveling is my fault. Everything is my fault. He never would've done any of the things they're accusing him of if I hadn't done what I did.

We received word two days ago that Neisy shot down the plea agreement. She wants the case to go to trial. As a result, the AG has pulled the pending offer, and I'll stand trial. In addition, the ten men—including Cam, Arlo and Dallas—who signed the affidavit fourteen years ago are required to publicly disavow the statement and apologize to Neisy to avoid criminal charges. That'll open them up to potential civil liabilities if she chooses to sue. And why wouldn't she?

Yesterday, I paid the twenty-five-thousand-dollar retainer to Bridget to lead my defense team and prepare for Friday's preliminary hearing. That left just five thousand dollars in the joint account I share with Caroline, which is terrifying with the mortgage and car payments due on the first of the month. There won't be much left to support my family after those bills are paid.

I was still processing those shocking developments, and now this.

My phone rings with a call from Cam. "What's up?"

"In addition to hitting her on the bridge and sending her into oncoming traffic, they think Dad torched the guest cabin where Blaise had been staying in LE."

I'm speechless.

"This is bad, Ry. He'll do hard time for this, and it was all for nothing. He could kill her, and her sworn statement would still be used in court."

How will we pay for yet another defense attorney?

"Are you there?"

"Yeah. I don't know what to say."

"He might be able to mount a temporary insanity defense. His son was charged, he went off the deep end. It's a stretch, but it might get him committed rather than sent to prison."

"Maybe I can talk to him."

"I'll take it from here. Stay out of it. You've got enough to contend with."

Before I can respond to that, the line goes dead.

My wife has left me and taken my children.

Mom is inconsolable.

My brother is furious.

My dad is under arrest—again.

All because of me.

I've never hated myself more.

Cam
NOW

MY FAMILY IS SPINNING out of control, and there's not a damned thing I can do about it.

"What's wrong?" Sienna asks when she emerges from our bedroom.

I got out of bed when I received Ryder's initial text. "My dad's suspected of trying to kill Blaise."

"Oh, God. What can I do?"

"Stay here with the kids and don't talk to anyone about this."

"Where're you going?"

"To try to find him." I go into the bedroom to change into jeans and a sweater, grab my wallet and head for the garage.

"Is Blaise okay?"

"She's injured. I'm not sure how seriously."

"Let me know what's going on?"

"I will." I turn back to her. "Please, Sienna. Don't talk about this to anyone."

"I won't. I never would."

Nodding, I leave her in the kitchen and go into the garage. As I drive around the town where I've lived my entire life, looking for my dad's black Chevy truck, I try to think about where he might be.

The last few days have been the worst of my life. Much worse than the first time Ryder was charged. There's so much more at stake now that we're married with families. More than once in recent days it's occurred to me that I should've come forward when Ryder first confessed to me.

Maybe if I had, we wouldn't be facing ruination now. But I also know I never would've done that then, even if it was the right thing. He's my brother, my closest friend. He was everything to me then. There was no way I'd ever have turned him in.

But I should have.

If I had, he would've done his time by now, and this nightmare would be in the past for all of us. Instead, it's a thousand times worse than it would've been then. Hindsight is indeed twenty-twenty.

I take a call from Arlo. "I just heard that the cops are looking for your dad. What's going on?"

"He tried to kill Blaise."

"He did *what*?"

"You heard me."

"Come on... He really tried to kill her?"

"Possibly twice. The cottage where she was staying in LE was torched."

"I heard there was a fire, but not that it involved her."

"She wasn't in the cottage at the time, but they can still charge him with attempted murder on top of arson if they can prove he was targeting her, which of course he was."

"I've got to say, man... This might be the end of the line for me."

"What do you mean?"

"I've stood by Ryder for all these years, defended him, quit my job to work on his campaign, and then I heard he was willing to plead guilty, which opened the rest of us to potential criminal and civil liability. He was thinking only of himself when he negotiated that deal, and now your dad has tried to *kill* my sister? I don't agree with what she's doing, but he tried to kill her? *Twice?*"

"Arlo..."

"There's nothing you can say. All this time I believed him when he said he didn't do it. I staked my own reputation on his word. But that was all bullshit, wasn't it? He *did* attack Neisy. He *did* rape her. And he lied to us for *years*, and now his lies could cost me and the others everything we have. Your dad tried to *kill* my sister to save a guilty rapist. I'm fucking done."

The line goes dead.

My heart is broken. Arlo has been a brother to us, but I don't blame him for cutting his ties. Our family is disintegrating before my eyes. Why would anyone want to be anywhere near us?

I look for my dad for hours while repeatedly trying to call him.

I'm shocked when he calls me back.

"What the hell were you thinking?"

He breaks down into deep sobs. "I had to do something to save him."

"You've only made everything worse."

"I didn't mean to."

"*What did you think would happen* when you tried to *kill* Blaise Merrick *twice?* That doesn't help Ryder."

"I thought if she couldn't testify—"

"They have her sworn statement!"

"They can use that?"

"Yeah, Dad. They can use it."

"I had to do something before they ruined his life."

"He ruined his own life."

"Why would you say such a thing?"

"Because it's true. He did this to himself, and he's taking the rest of us down with him."

"What do you know?"

"I know the truth, Dad, and if you'd asked me that question before you'd gone after Blaise, maybe you wouldn't have made everything worse for Ryder and for the rest of us."

"How could he have done such a thing?"

"You'll have to ask him that. In the meantime, you need to turn yourself in.

"I'm not doing that."

"You have to!"

"If they want to come after me, they'll have to kill me."

"Dad, are you thinking of Mom or your grandchildren or anyone but yourself when you say something like that?"

"I love you all, but I won't sit by and watch them destroy your brother."

"You can't stop what's happening to him!"

"Watch me."

The line goes dead, filling me with dread at realizing as bad as things are now, it could still get much worse.

I call the Hope Police and ask to speak to Caleb. They say they'll have him call me, which he does a few minutes later.

"I spoke to my dad. He won't turn himself in."

"We've got the whole state looking for him, Cam. We'll find him eventually."

"He said if you want him, you'll have to kill him. He's determined to save Ryder."

"Shit. Okay, thanks for the heads-up."

"Will you keep me posted on what's going on?"

"If I can. This is pretty hot. Trying to kill a witness who's prepared to testify against your son is a big deal."

"I understand, and I'm sorry. I don't know what he was thinking."

"Hang in there, Cam. I'll be in touch if I can."

"Thank you."

I drive home a short time later as it becomes clear our lives are ruined.

That much is clear at this point.

Ryder calls me. "Did you find Dad?"

"No, but I talked to him, and he's a mess. Thought he was helping. And Arlo called, too. He cut ties with us. Dad trying to kill Blaise was it for him, especially after he heard you were going to plead guilty."

"I wanted to end this for all of us. I thought if I took responsibility, it would save the rest of you."

"Instead you opened us up to civil liabilities that could ruin us."

"It's not enough to say I'm sorry. I know that."

"I've got to go."

"Cam—"

I end the call. I can't take anymore right now.

At home, I sit in the car for a long time pondering the horrific mess we're in.

Sienna comes to the garage door, sees me sitting there and comes out to get into the car. "I'd ask how it went, but I can see it wasn't good."

"Not good at all. He thought he was helping by trying to get rid of her, and he says the cops will have to kill him because he's not giving up."

"Oh, God."

"Arlo called, too. He's done with all of us."

"I'm sorry, Cam."

"Everyone is so damned sorry, but if any of us had done the right thing back in the day, none of this would be happening."

She recoils. "Are you blaming *me*?"

"No, I'm blaming myself. I wish I'd done something when he told me he did it."

"You never would have. There's no sense in having that regret. It's pointless. You were Team Ryder from the first second you were placed in his arms as a baby, and there's no way you would've turned on him—then or ever."

"It haunted me." I've never said that out loud before. "That we'd done what we did to her…" I shake my head. "I was sick over it."

"I was, too, but think about who we were then and what was important to us. We did what we thought was right."

"We were old enough to know better, Sienna."

"Yes, I suppose we were. So what now?"

"Now we wait and hope my father doesn't make everything worse."

Chapter 32

Blaise
NOW

BY FRIDAY MORNING, I'VE begun to feel slightly better even though I'm still sore from head to toe. I've never been in a car accident before. I don't recommend it. My face is covered in colorful bruises, and my badly sprained wrist is encased in an inflatable splint. Thankfully, I can shower with it on. Blow drying is a challenge, since it's my right wrist, but I do what I can with my hair. I don't bother with makeup.

Let them see what Ryder's father did to me.

From what I've heard, it's been all over the news that Mr. Elliott tried to kill me, and he torched the cottage where I'd been staying. The police are continuing to look for him but having no luck so far. As long as he's on the loose, I'm in danger, which is why we're still at the State Police safe house days after we were first brought there.

I've talked to my mom every day since the accident, and to both of my sisters as well.

Teagan is beside herself over it. "I hope there're no questions left about why you didn't come forward when this first happened."

"I suppose that's an upside to nearly being killed."

"Don't make jokes, Blaise. None of this is funny."

"No, it isn't, but it's still better than keeping that secret was."

"I give you so much credit for what you're doing. In spite of everything, you're resolute in getting justice for Denise."

"Thank you, but I wish I'd been brave enough to stand up for her back then."

"You're doing it now, and I'm sure that matters to her."

"I guess I'll find out. I'm meeting with her before the hearing."

"Oh, damn. How do you feel about that?"

"I'm okay with it. She requested the meeting. I feel like it's the least I can do."

"You're a badass, Blaise. I'm so proud of you."

"Thank you. That means a lot to me." My big sister is proud of me. How cool is that? Her praise touches me more than I can say.

"I'm going with Mom to court."

"You guys don't have to do that."

"We'll be there to support you. I have my own regrets, you know. If I hadn't been such a selfish bitch back then maybe you would've come to me for help. I'm sorry you felt like you couldn't."

"It's okay."

"No, it isn't. It pains me that you suffered in silence for all this time, thinking everyone would hate you for coming forward."

"Arlo probably does."

"He'll get over it once he figures out that his good buddy is dead-ass guilty. Reminder—none of this is your fault, Blaise. Keep the blame where it belongs."

"I'm trying. Thank you for the support. It means everything."

"You've got my support and my love. I want the chance to get to know you again and for you to know my kids… I want that so badly."

"I do, too. We'll fix that soon. I promise."

"I'll hold you to that."

"Thanks again, Teagan."

"Love you, kid."

"Love you, too."

I sobbed for half an hour after that conversation the other day. My big sister loves me. She's sorry I didn't feel like I could go to her with this when it first happened. What might've been different if that had been an option? And what she said about Arlo gave me hope, too. Maybe he'll come around to forgiving me at some point. Wouldn't that be something?

The State Police drive us to court in Newport and escort us inside an hour before the hearing, past a huge group of media that've been cordoned off to the side of the stone stairs. Having a former congressional candidate charged with sexual assault is a big story in this little state, especially when two eyewitnesses have come forward fourteen years after the fact. The media has picked apart the story from every angle, going so far as to publish the transcripts of the preliminary hearing that was held the first time Ryder was charged.

We're walked through a metal detector. My purse is scanned like at an airport.

Jack's hand on my lower back provides the support I need so badly right now. He's been right by my side as I rested and recovered from my injuries and prepared to testify today.

Josh Spurling is waiting for us inside, and escorts us to a private room. "How are you feeling?"

"Still sore but better than I was."

"I'm glad to hear it. I was told this morning that the U.S. Marshals are being brought in to find Mr. Elliott."

"It'll be a relief to hear he's in custody."

"Indeed. Thank you for agreeing to see Denise before the hearing."

"It's no problem."

"Can I get you anything?"

"We're fine. Thanks."

"Okay, I'll bring Denise in when she arrives."

While we wait, Jack sits next to me and holds my left hand. I so appreciate his insistence on being with me today. His unwavering support makes me love him more than I already did.

About ten minutes after we arrive, the door opens to admit Denise and a tall, handsome man with a military haircut.

She's still strikingly beautiful. Her cheeks are slightly fuller, and there's a maturity to her that wasn't there before, but I would've recognized her anywhere.

They sit across from us. "Thank you for seeing me. This is my husband, Kane."

"Good to meet you, Kane. This is my friend, Jack."

"It's nice to meet you, Jack." She clears her throat and looks directly at me. "I was horrified to hear about the accident. Are you all right?"

"I will be."

"I'm so sorry that happened."

"Thank you, but it's not your fault."

"I asked to see you because I wanted to thank you for coming forward."

That's not at all what I expected her to say. "I, um...I don't deserve your thanks. What I did was despicable."

"I don't blame you. We all know what would've happened to you if you'd reported it then. By coming forward now, you're clearing my name and giving me justice I thought I'd never get."

"It should've happened a long time ago. I'll always be sorry it didn't."

"Better late than never."

I'm amazed by her kindness and grace. "I absolutely abhor the way you were treated, from the first minute you joined our class all the way through that dreadful summer. You didn't deserve any of it."

"I know I didn't. I've had a lot of therapy over the years and have come to see that it had nothing to do with me and everything to do with their insecurities."

"I'm still very sorry for what you endured. I wish I could've been there for you the way I wanted to be at the time."

"You're here now."

"I heard you have four kids. Do you have pictures?"

"Of course I do." She smiles as she hands over her phone with a picture of two older kids holding babies. "That's Charlotte, Levi, Hudson and Hayes."

"They're beautiful."

"They're a handful."

"I'll bet."

"While you have my phone, put your number in my contacts. I'd like to keep in touch if that would be all right with you."

"I'd love that." I put my number into her contacts and return the phone to her. "Thank you for your kindness toward me. I wasn't expecting that."

"Anger got me nowhere. Kindness and understanding for others has been far more productive."

"Words to live by."

After a knock on the door, Josh sticks his head in. "We're ready for you in court, ladies."

"Here we go," Denise says with a grimace. "Let's get it over with so we can get back to more enjoyable things."

"Yes, please."

JOSH SPURLING ESCORTS US into the courtroom and shows us where to sit. "Keep Denise and Blaise on the aisles for when they're called to testify." To Denise, he says, "You remember Judge Denton from the first time, right?"

"I do."

"It's somewhat of a lucky break for us that she's presiding this time, too."

When we're seated, with Denise and Kane in front of us, Jack puts his arm around me in a public show of support.

"Thank you for everything."

He kisses my temple. "Entirely my pleasure, love, except the part about you getting hurt."

A rustle of activity behind us precedes the scent of my mother's familiar fragrance settling over me. "We're here, Blaise," she says.

Jack moves so I can turn—slowly and carefully—to see Mom and Teagan behind me. I wince from the movement. My ribs have been incredibly sore since the accident. "Thank you for coming."

"Of course we came." Mom fixates on the bruises on my face that she's already seen via FaceTime. "How're you feeling, honey?"

"A little better every day."

"It's such an outrage that it happened in the first place."

"Agreed," Jack says.

Mom glances at him and raises a brow.

"Oh, um, this is Jack Olsen. Jack, my mom, Deena, and my sister, Teagan."

"It's so nice to meet you both," Jack says.

"Likewise," Teagan replies. "Blaisey has been keeping some secrets from us."

"Blaisey, huh?" Jack asks with a grin.

"You're not allowed to call me that and neither is she." I give my sister a playful glare that earns me a smile. She knows how much I despise that old nickname. The typical sibling exchange, the first in years, fills my heart with yearning for so much more. I had no idea how much I truly missed her, June and Arlo until right now.

Speaking of my brother, he comes in through the double doors, glances quickly toward the defense side of the room and then shocks me when he tells my mother and sister to make room for him behind me.

What is happening?

"Hi, Blaise."

"Hi, Arlo."

"I'm sorry you were hurt in the accident. Are you doing okay?"

"I'm fine."

He reaches out a hand to Jack. "Arlo Merrick."

Jack shakes his hand. "Jack Olsen."

"Are you the artist?" Arlo asks.

"I am."

"My kids love your crocodile books."

"Oh, thanks. That's nice to hear."

Only because I'm turned around to see my family do I note when Ryder comes into the room. He's wearing a dark suit and looks like he hasn't slept in weeks. His gaze briefly lands on me before he looks away.

Ramona comes in with her husband next, followed by Cam, Sienna and Mrs. Elliott.

Sienna looks at me for a long moment, her expression unreadable, until she finally looks away.

It's the first time I've seen her since we graduated from high school, after keeping our distance from each other during our senior year. So many people asked me why we didn't hang out anymore. I dodged the question every time it was asked.

She looks older and a bit heavier than she did in high school, but she's had four kids since then. She still has curly brown hair and bangs like she had back then.

"Was that the ex-best friend?" Jack asks softly.

"Yeah."

"Can I be your new best friend?"

I turn to him, smiling. "You already are."

"Yes!" He gives a little fist pump that only I can see.

I'm so, so thankful for him, that I get to go home with him after this is over and to spend every day with him going forward. I can't imagine anything better than that.

After this hearing, we're going to New York for a few days to pack up my belongings, so Kim can move in as of January. She's so excited to be taking over my job and my apartment, and I'm glad to be closing the book on that chapter of my life and starting a brand new one, filled with love, adventure and passion.

I just have to get through this hearing and the trial to get to the good stuff.

Chapter 33

Caroline
NOW

I HADN'T PLANNED TO come. What good would it do, I asked myself, to hear the details of what he's accused of doing to that poor girl? But with the kids in school and preschool this morning, I found myself showering and dressing for court. I don't want Ryder or anyone else to know I'm there, so I wait outside until I'm certain everyone else has arrived.

As I stare up at the stone stairs, I question my sanity once again in coming here.

No one would blame me for staying away.

"Caroline?"

"Oh, hi, Houston." Is it weird to think how handsome he is in his uniform when I'm here to watch my husband face rape charges? I'm getting weirder by the day lately.

"I thought that was you."

"It's me, asking myself what the hell I'm doing here."

"Anyone in your situation would be curious."

"Really? You think so? Because it feels somewhat masochistic to me."

"It might help you to get closure, whatever that is."

"So you don't think I'm insane for subjecting myself to this?"

"Not at all. Would it help to sit with a friend?"

I look up at him with gratitude. "It would help very much. I was also wondering what I was thinking coming here alone."

"I'll be happy to sit with you and be there for you as long as you need a friend."

"That's very kind of you, Houston."

"It's no problem at all. Shall we?"

"I guess we shall."

We walk up the stairs together, and he holds the door for me, guides me through security, and directs me to the proper courtroom. He makes everything about this easier than it would've been if I hadn't run into him outside.

We take seats in the back row, just as the prosecutor calls Denise to the stand.

As I listen to her story, I try to reconcile her recitation of the events with the man I thought I'd known so deeply over the last decade. The Ryder she describes bears no resemblance whatsoever to my husband.

I believe every word she says. I can hear the pain and agony in her voice as she relives the horror.

"After the assault, what did you do?" the prosecutor asks.

"I went home and showered. I was shocked, traumatized and injured."

"Can you please describe your injuries?"

I want to cover my ears, so I won't hear her recitation of the many ways the attack left her in pain. "I...I'd never done that before, so it hurt for a long time afterward."

"Was there anything else that took place as a result of the attack by the defendant?"

"Yes, I became pregnant."

"Oh my God," I whisper. Just when I thought this couldn't get worse...

Houston reaches for my freezing cold hand and puts it between his warm ones.

"What happened to the baby?"

"I miscarried right before the baby's DNA could've tied him or her to the defendant."

The courtroom erupts into chaos that's contained by the judge banging her gavel and calling for order. "Outbursts of any kind will not be tolerated in my courtroom."

In the quiet that follows her directive, I hear the distinctive sound of someone weeping.

I lean in for a closer look and see that Ryder has his head in his hands as he listens to Denise's testimony. Is he weeping at hearing more about how she suffered?

"Mrs. Messner, can you please describe your overall state of mind in the months that followed the assault?"

"I was as low as I've ever been. Not only because I'd been assaulted and suffered through a painful miscarriage, but also because his brother and friends rallied around him afterward, claiming I'd slept with all of them, which was a lie."

"Have those men admitted to lying?"

"They have."

That causes another gasp and more intense whispering that has the judge banging her gavel again.

"Thank you, Mrs. Messner. Nothing further." As she leaves the witness stand, Josh says, "The state calls Ramona Travers Silvia to the stand."

Ramona is sworn in and seated.

"Mrs. Silvia, can you please tell us where you were on the night in question?"

"I was at the party held by Houston Rafferty at his parents' home in Land's End."

"While you were at the party did you see Ryder Elliott?"

"Yes, I did."

"Did you see Denise Sutton Messner, who was known then as Neisy?"

"Yes, I did."

"Did you at any time see them together?"

"I saw them leave the party together and walk into the woods."

"Did you report this to the authorities after Mr. Elliott was accused of sexually assaulting Ms. Sutton?"

"No, I didn't."

"Why didn't you report it?"

"Because I was afraid the other kids would do the same thing to me that they'd done to her when she reported it."

"Why did you choose to come forward now?"

"Because I heard someone else had witnessed the assault itself and had come forward. I wanted to do the same. I've always regretted that I hadn't done it before."

"Had you ever known of Ryder Elliott to be inappropriate with girls or women?"

"Objection! Anything she heard from someone else is hearsay and is inadmissible."

"Overruled. I want to hear her answer."

"Mrs. Silvia?"

Ramona licks her lips before she speaks. "Once in the library when we were juniors, he backed me into a corner and told me he thought I was pretty. He got very close. I was afraid he was going to try something more, but thankfully someone else came along, and he backed off."

A gasp goes through the courtroom as people start to whisper.

"Did you report the incident to anyone?"

"No, I was afraid to. He was so popular, and I... well, I wasn't."

"Did you ever hear anyone else say he was aggressive or inappropriate with them?"

"Objection!"

"Overruled. Please answer the question, Mrs. Silvia."

"A few people said things here or there, like he wasn't as devoted to Louisa as he wanted everyone to believe, he was flirty and wasn't afraid to touch them if he wanted to... That kind of thing."

"Objection!"

"Nothing further. Thank you, Mrs. Silvia. You're dismissed."

The courtroom decends into chaos that has the judge repeatedly banging her gavel and demanding order in her courtroom.

I simply cannot believe what I'm hearing about the man I thought I knew so well. I'd never known of Ryder to be inappropriate or out of line with any woman. But I believe Ramona. What reason would she have to lie? What reason would anyone have to testify under oath about something like that if it wasn't true?

After Ramona is excused, Blaise Merrick is called to the stand.

She raises her right hand, which is supported by a splint, and swears to tell the truth.

"Ms. Merrick, would you please explain your obvious injuries to the court?"

"I was involved in a car accident on the Mount Hope Bridge earlier this week."

"Was this accident intentionally caused by someone else?"

"I was hit from behind by truck, which forced me into oncoming traffic, where I was hit head on. I was later told the license plate of the truck that hit me was tied to Mr. David Elliott, the defendant's father."

Josh delivers several papers to the judge. "I would ask the court to note that Mr. Elliott has been the subject of an intense manhunt that now includes the U.S. Marshals. He remains at large. When he's arrested, he'll be charged with two counts of attempted murder of Ms. Merrick as well as arson, after the cottage where she was staying was burned."

"So noted," the judge says with a frown.

"Will you please tell the court what you saw on the night in question?"

The details are no less excruciating the second time I hear them.

"What did you do after Miss Sutton was assaulted?"

"I did all the wrong things. I was worried about myself when I should've been worried about Denise. I should have gone to her, offered help and told the police what I'd seen. I did none of those things because I was afraid everyone would hate me if I told the truth."

"Why were you so afraid?"

"Everyone loved Ryder. He was a star in our class. I was afraid no one would believe me. And he was my brother's closest friend, which made it that much harder to believe what I'd seen." Blaise glances at Arlo, who has his head down. "I love my brother. I didn't want everyone to hate me, so I stayed quiet, and that nearly killed me."

"How so?"

"I had so many health problems. Anxiety, depression, eating disorders. I was literally sick with guilt."

"And you'd had none of these issues prior to witnessing the attack?"

"None of them. I withdrew from my life as a high school senior, and as soon as I was able to, I left for college out of state and never looked back. I'd been back to Rhode Island only once before I returned recently, and that was when my father died."

"When you were growing up together in Hope, did you ever know of Ryder Elliott to be inappropriate or aggressive with girls or women?"

"Objection!"

"Overruled. Please answer the question, Ms. Merrick."

"No, I'd never seen or heard of anything like that, which is why I was so shocked by what I saw him do to Denise. He'd been with Louisa for years."

"Why did you decide to come forward now?"

"I heard Ryder was running for Congress, and I couldn't live with this secret for another minute. I drove home and reported it the next day."

"Ms. Merrick, did anyone else witness the attack on Ms. Sutton, that you know of?"

"I'm speaking only for myself."

"Ms. Merrick," the judge says, "you're under oath. Please answer the question."

"Ms. Merrick," Josh says, "did anyone else witness the attack?"

I can tell Blaise wasn't expecting them to push her on this point.

"Yes."

"Who was that person?"

"Sienna Lawton Elliott."

Once again, chaos erupts.

I'm shocked to my core to hear that Sienna, my sister-in-law and friend, knew all along that Ryder had done this and never told me.

"I think I've heard enough," I whisper to Houston.

He gets up and gestures for me to go ahead of him out of the courtroom.

I'm surprised when he follows me.

"I'd ask if you're all right…"

"Four people giving the same story, including my own sister-in-law, who's known, for all this time, I was married to a rapist." I look up at him, my eyes full of tears. "That's a lot to process."

"I can't imagine."

"At least now I know for certain."

"Does that help?"

"In some ways. Since he was arrested, I've sort of had it in the back of my mind that maybe it was all a big mistake. But denial is no longer an option, is it?"

"No, it's not."

"Thank you for being there for me today, Houston. You really helped me."

"I wish there was more I could do."

"You were exactly what I needed—a friend. So, thank you again."

"Would it be okay if I checked on you later?"

"Sure, that would be nice."

"Let me walk you to your car."

Sienna
NOW

THIS CANNOT BE HAPPENING. If they call me to testify, I'll refuse.

They can't make me, can they? I look at Cam, but he's staring straight ahead.

The judge is pissed as she bangs the gavel and demands order in the court.

The hot stares of everyone in the courtroom burn the back of my neck.

I want to expire on the spot.

"What do I do if they call me up?" I whisper to Cam.

"You go up there and tell the truth."

"I can't do that."

"*You have to.*"

The defense attorney, a frosty blonde with four-inch heels, walks over to Blaise, her arms crossed. She didn't have any questions for Denise or Ramona, but she stares at Blaise long enough that she squirms on the witness stand.

"Fourteen years is a long time."

"Yes, it is."

"And in all that time, you never reported what you saw, not to the police or your parents or anyone, is that right?"

"Yes."

"Why not?"

"I was afraid of what would happen to me if I did. He was a big part of my community, my brother's best friend…"

"But you had no compassion for the woman he allegedly assaulted?"

"I thought of her every day of those fourteen years." She glances at Neisy. "Every single day. I was sick over it."

"Why now?"

"I heard he was running for office, and I couldn't live with the secret any longer."

"What's in it for you to come forward after all this time?"

"Nothing other than the chance to right a terrible wrong. As you can see, it's been anything but easy for me."

"Why should we believe a word you say about something that allegedly happened so long ago, you can probably barely remember it?"

Blaise is unflinching as she stares down the attorney. "I remember every second of it. I remember every detail of that day and the days that followed. According to the Land's End chief of police, my description of events exactly matched that of Ms. Sutton's, and there was no way I could've known what she reported."

I swallow hard. She's very believable.

After a long pause, the attorney says, "Nothing further."

Blaise is dismissed from the stand.

She walks back to her seat without looking at me.

I still cannot believe she ratted me out after she promised she never would.

"The state calls Sienna Elliott to the stand."

I'm rooted to my seat.

"Objection." The defense attorney is on her feet. "This witness isn't on the list we were given."

"Overruled. I want to hear what she has to say."

"Mrs. Elliott?" The prosecutor gives me a pointed look. "You can testify willingly, or we can subpoena you."

Cam gives me a nudge. "*Go.*"

As I get up and walk to the front of the room, my legs are trembling, and I feel like I might faint.

They tell me to raise my right hand and swear to tell the truth, the whole truth and nothing but he truth.

Ugh. I do not want to do that.

"Mrs. Elliott, were you with Ms. Merrick on the night in question? And I'll remind you that you're under oath."

"I was there."

"Did you see Ryder Elliott attack Denise Sutton?"

I hesitate before I nod.

"I need you to answer the question out loud for the stenographer."

"I saw him attack her."

"And you chose not to assist her or report the crime to authorities?"

"Yes." My face burns with shame.

"Why?"

"I was dating his brother, who I later married. I did what I thought was best for my boyfriend and his family."

"At the expense of a young woman who'd been assaulted?"

"I didn't know her at all. I'd grown up with him. It was terrible, what he did. But… I did what I thought was right at the time."

"And do you regret that?"

"Sometimes."

Denise
NOW

SIENNA'S TESTIMONY IS SHOCKING and devastating as I hadn't known before then that someone was with Blaise. *Sometimes* she regretted leaving me in the woods, broken and bleeding. Only *sometimes?*

What kind of monster isn't haunted by such a thing?

Kane's arm tightens around me.

This has to be excruciating for him, too.

"When Ryder Elliott was initially charged with assaulting Ms. Sutton, did people believe it?"

"No, no one did."

"But you knew it was true, right?"

Sienna looks down. "Yes."

"Did you tell anyone that?"

"No."

"Not even your boyfriend?"

"No."

"So you've never told the man you married what you saw his brother do?"

"I told him recently."

"After Blaise Merrick reported what she saw, you *still* didn't come forward?"

"You don't understand!"

"You're right. I don't. Nothing further."

I want to stand up and cheer for Josh's takedown of Sienna. I hope she enjoys the rest of her life in her tiny town with everyone knowing what an asshole she is.

Sienna leaves the stand and goes straight to Blaise, slapping her across the face before anyone can anticipate her intention. "*You fucking bitch!* This is all your fault! Why couldn't you have just kept *your fucking mouth shut?*"

Cam grabs his wife from behind and hauls her away from Blaise.

Sherriff deputies surround them, cuffing Sienna as she screams like a hyena.

The judge bangs the gavel. "I want her charged with assault and contempt of this court. Get her out of my courtroom."

I turn to Blaise. "Are you all right?"

"I, uh, I think so. What's another bruise?"

I can tell she's making light of it for everyone else's sake, but her eyes are glassy with shock.

"I've heard everything I need to hear," the judge says. "Mr. Elliott, you're remanded to trial. You'll remain on bail until your trial, which will begin on February twentieth."

"Wait!" Ryder stands. "I want to plead guilty."

His lawyer grabs his arm. "Ryder, sit down."

He resists her efforts to get him to sit. "No!" He looks over at me, appearing anguished. "I'm so sorry, Denise. I don't know what came over me. I did it, and I want to take my punishment so we can all have some peace."

A roar from behind Ryder precedes a man flying through the air to tackle him.

The man goes crazy, punching Ryder as he screams at the top of his lungs. *"How could you do this to my sister? She loved you with all her heart! She was fucking dying, and this is what you were doing?"*

Oh, God. Louisa's brother.

"You son of a bitch!"

By the time the deputies pull Louisa's brother off of Ryder, he's unconscious and bleeding.

"All these years, he's been lying to us while pretending to care about my sister's legacy?"

The man is completely out of control as he rails against the deputies trying to cuff him.

"Holy. Shit."

Two whispered words from Kane sum things up rather succinctly.

The judge bangs her gavel, demanding order in the court as paramedics arrive for Ryder.

"I want to see the attorneys in my chambers. Right now."

She bangs the gavel again. "Court is adjourned."

The judge leaves the room with Josh and Ryder's attorney following her as Ryder is wheeled out of the room on a gurney.

"What the hell just happened?" Kane asks, seeming as shocked as the rest of us.

"Ryder's girlfriend, Louisa, had entered hospice care around the time of the attack. That was her brother."

"Oh, damn. Wow. So all this time, he thought Ryder was innocent."

"I guess so."

A group of sheriff's deputies make sure the courtroom is cleared in an orderly manner as people talk amongst themselves on their way out, expressing shock at the proceedings.

Cam Elliott appears in front of me. "I wanted to tell you face-to-face that I'm sorry for what we did after Ryder was charged the first time. The other guys and I will issue public apologies and provide the seed money to begin a rape crisis center for teens in the area."

"I accept your apology and appreciate the gesture."

I'm sure they're doing that hoping I won't sue them for smearing my reputation, but whatever. Their center will do a lot of good for kids like me who have nowhere to turn after experiencing such a trauma.

"I'm sorry for everything that happened," Cam adds.

"Thank you."

His apology doesn't change anything, but I can't deny there's an element of vindication to this day.

Josh calls to me.

Kane and I walk over to him.

He gestures for us to come with him to a quiet corner of the room. "The judge is inclined to allow Ryder to plead guilty to end this thing once and for all. I told her you were opposed to that. She wants to know if you still are."

I take a deep breath as I consider what he said. "I wanted what I had today—for people to hear, in open court, that he *did* rape me, that he left me pregnant and shattered. I wanted them to hear from Blaise and Ramona that I wasn't making it up." I glance at Kane, who looks at me only with love and admiration. "I got my day in court—and then some. That's enough for me."

"I'll let them know you're open to a deal."

"Thank you for everything, Josh."

"I wish I could say it was a pleasure, but justice was done here, however messy it got."

"What kind of sentence will he receive?"

"Most likely five to ten years, followed by several years of probation and lifetime registry on the sex offender list. There'll be another hearing to set the sentence in a couple of weeks. He'll be remanded into custody at that time."

Once again I glance at Kane to gauge his reaction. He gives a subtle nod.

"Okay," I tell Josh. "Make the deal."

"I'll be in touch."

After he walks away, I step into Kane's arms and let him wrap me up in his love.

"I'm so damned proud of you."

"Thank you for your unwavering support through it all."

"I love you. I've always loved you, and I always will."

"Love you, too. More than anything. I need to text my dad." He wanted to come to court, but I asked him not to, knowing it would be too upsetting for him hear the details of what happened to me. I send him a quick text to tell him everything is fine, and I'll call him later. Then I put the phone in my pocket and turn to my beloved. "You know what we've got?"

"What's that?"

"Twenty-four hours without the kids before our flight tomorrow."

"Yes, we do. How would you like to spend that time?"

"Let's check into a fancy hotel, get room service and forget about all of this."

"I'm with you, babe."

Blaise
NOW

JACK HAS BEEN TIGHT with outrage since Sienna hit me.

It was a shock to me, too. When she came toward me, I barely had time to react before she'd slapped me so hard I saw stars.

"I can't *fucking believe* she hit you," Jack says when we're in the State Police SUV. We've left my family members with promises to see them soon. I'm already looking forward to that. "I hope they throw the goddamned book at her."

"I'm okay."

"Well, I'm not! That was *bullshit*!"

I've never seen him so worked up, and that it's on my behalf is enormously sexy to me. I've never had anyone who cared that much about me before, except my own family. "Come here."

"I'm right here."

"Come closer."

He releases his seatbelt, scoots across the seat and puts his arm around me.

"I'm okay. You're okay. Fenway is okay. Everything is fine."

"She freaking hit you."

"I know, and it hurt. But it's over now."

"I'm sick of people hurting you."

I lean into his warm embrace. "I can't believe what Ramona said in court. She never mentioned the incident in the library to me when we got together."

"I wonder why."

"She was probably afraid of people turning on her the way they did to Denise when she first reported the rape. I bet Ramona never would've said a word to anyone about that if she hadn't been asked about it while under oath."

"It definitely helped to establish a pattern of sorts."

"Which only adds to the never-ending shock. I had no idea Ryder could be like that until I saw it for myself."

My cell phone rings.

Jack sits up so I can grab the phone from my coat pocket.

"It's Josh." I press the button to take the call, while nearly dropping the phone. Everything is more difficult with my right hand and arm in the cast. "Hey, Josh."

"Well, that was quite a spectacle, huh?"

"Sure was."

"Are you all right?"

"I'm fine."

"Sienna is being charged with felony assault."

"Oh, wow. Okay."

"And we've agreed to a plea deal with Denise and Ryder's attorney. Pending Ryder's approval once he's able to review the terms, he'll serve five to ten years with several years of probation after he's released and lifetime listing on the sex offender registry."

"So it's over then?"

"Pending Ryder's approval of the deal, which he said he wanted, and the judge sentencing him, yes, it's over."

I close my eyes and release a deep breath. It's over. Once and for all, it's really over. "Will I have to testify against his father?"

"I've just received word that he was in a shootout with the Marshals in western Massachusetts. Mr. Elliott was killed."

"Oh God." How is it possible to feel sorry for the Elliotts, even after Mr. Elliott tried to kill me?

"The good news is we can release you from protective custody now that he's no longer a threat."

"Okay."

"Are you all right, Blaise?"

"I will be. In time. I never could've imagined everything that would happen after I reported what I'd seen to Houston."

"No one could've predicted this."

"For what it's worth, I don't think Louisa's brother should be charged with anything. He's already been through enough."

"I tend to agree. I'll discuss it with the AG. We'll do what we can for him."

"Thank you for everything, Josh."

"You're welcome. Thank you for your courage. It made all the difference here."

"It's over," I tell Jack after I end the call and tell him Mr. Elliott has been killed.

"Thank God it's over."

"I want to go home and sleep for a week." I pause and then glance at him, feeling shy all of a sudden. "I'm not sure when it happened, but when I think of home, I think of your house."

"That works out rather well, because when I think of home, I think of you, and I know exactly when it happened."

"When?"

"The day a gorgeous redhead drove into my driveway and turned my whole life upside down in the best possible way."

I lean my head on his shoulder, amazed by everything that's happened. By coming home to right a terrible wrong, I also found true love. "I feel like you're my reward for finally doing the right thing."

"I can live with being your reward for a job well done."

Epilogue

TWO YEARS LATER...

Ryder

I LIVE FOR SUNDAYS, when I get to see my kids, who are now nine, seven and five. They're growing up so fast, which breaks my heart. I'm missing everything with them, but at least I get an hour a week to catch up and to make sure they know I always love them, even when I can't be with them every day.

Kids are amazingly forgiving, and I'm lucky they still love me, too, despite everything I've put them through. They send me pictures and letters in the mail, they bake treats to bring to me, and they always tell me they love me, even if I don't deserve it.

I had a rough couple of months after Marty attacked me in the courtroom, breaking my jaw and leaving me with a concussion that messed me up for a long time. They charged him with a misdemeanor, which was fine with me. I don't blame him for his outrage. I deserved it, but I could've done without having my jaw wired shut for two months. That sucked.

About six months after I began my sentence at the state prison in Cranston, I received divorce papers from Caroline. Though she brings the kids to see me every week, I hadn't heard a word from her in all that time, so I wasn't entirely surprised. But it hurt like hell to sign those papers and return them to her. I did it because it was what she wanted, not because I don't love her anymore.

I'll always love her, but our marriage ended the day I was arrested at the ballfield.

Some things you can never come back from. Lying to my wife for most of a decade is one of them, and I own that along with all my other failings.

I've found God in prison.

That might sound funny coming from me, but after completely tuning out everything that happened in church as a kid, I'm comforted by the forgiveness God offers to all his creations, even the ones like me. I attend a weekly Bible study and have read the good book cover to cover twice now. I learn something new every time I pick it up, and it brings me tremendous peace, which was hard to find for a long time.

Bridget tells me there's talk of an early release for me, perhaps as soon as a year to eighteen months from now. I don't get my hopes up. I've learned to take things one day at a time, knowing if or when I get out, I'll have all new challenges to face. For one thing, I'm not sure how I'll support myself as a convicted felon. For another, Caroline has full custody of our children, so my time with them will still be limited.

That's okay. I'll take what I can get.

The kids always come into the visitation room alone.

Caroline waits for them outside the door.

They hug me and kiss me like they always did, clamor for my undivided attention and share the latest news about their friends, the sports they're playing, their new dog and their cousins.

"Houston is building us a swing set," Grace tells me.

The words hit like a flaming arrow to my heart. "Houston is?"

"He's Mommy's special friend," Elise adds.

It's all I can do to keep breathing after hearing that. Of course she's seeing someone. But Houston, who was my friend? That hurts.

"Are you mad, Daddy?" Miles is old enough to understand how these things work.

"Not at all. Your Mommy deserves to be happy." That much is certainly true.

We play a game of Chutes and Ladders that they brought with them.

Elise wins for the first time ever and is so delightfully excited that it brings tears to my eyes.

Our hour is up long before I'm ready to let them go.

"Hey, guys, give me some big hugs to last me a whole week."

They always deliver.

"Are you safe in here, Daddy?" Grace asks me softly.

"I am, honey. Don't worry about me."

"We miss you."

"I miss you, too. But keep those letters coming."

"I've saved all the ones you've sent me," Elise says.

"That's very sweet."

Miles hugs me last.

"Love you, buddy. More than anything in this world."

"Love you, too, Dad. I can't wait for you to come home."

I hope he knows I won't be coming back to his home, but I'll be somewhere close by where I can see them far more often than I do now. That's my hope anyway."

The door opens, and the guard tells the kids it's time to go.

When they hug me again, the girls are tearful, but Miles is stoic as always. He puts a hand on each of their shoulders to guide them out of the room.

Caroline appears at the door, looking uncertain.

I'm surprised to see her. It's the first time she's tried to see me here.

"Are you doing all right?"

I shrug. "As well as can be expected."

She nods.

"Are you seeing Houston?"

The question catches her by surprise.

"The kids said something."

"I... Uh... Yes, I am."

"He's a good guy."

"He's a very good guy."

"I'm happy for you."

"I...I should go."

"Thank you for bringing them to see me. I live for the time with them."

"They do, too. Take care, Ryder."

"You, too."

After they leave, I ask if I can use the phone. Most of the time they say no, but sometimes, such as now, they say yes.

Cam

I WAIT UNTIL THE tea is fully steeped before I carry the delicate cup and saucer to my mother in the three-season room where we spend most of our time these days. A few months after that dreadful day in court, we sold both houses and moved to Tampa. My mother has her own suite off the main part of our house. The kids love having her living with us, and she's adjusted well to a whole new life after losing her husband so dramatically and then sending her eldest son to prison.

Bridget was able to plead Sienna's assault charge down to a misdemeanor. She had to pay a thousand-dollar fine and was ordered to perform a hundred hours of community service.

We moved right after she completed her sentence.

I'll be honest. I thought about divorcing her after her performance in court, but in the end, I decided to stay with her for the sake of our kids. Our marriage is a work in progress. We have good days and not-so-good days, but we're sticking it out as a family in this new life we're making for ourselves far from the only home we've ever known.

I got licensed to practice law in Florida and landed a job that pays the bills. It's nowhere near what I made in Rhode Island, but I'm hoping I can find something better after I get some time on the job at this firm.

Every day that goes by here without our past coming back to haunt us is a blessing. That wouldn't have been possible at home where everyone knew what my brother, father and wife had done.

"How's the tea, Mom?"

"It's perfect, honey. Thank you."

"You're welcome."

Mom suffers from melancholy that's new since that terrible autumn, but being with my kids helps. She loves to walk them to and from the bus stop, and it's helpful to have her here to watch them any time we get the chance to go out, which isn't often.

It's odd to live such a solitary life when we're used to being surrounded by lifelong friends. If I'm ever lucky enough to have that kind of community around me again, I'll never take it for granted the way I used to before everything went to shit.

My phone rings with a call from the prison in Cranston, Rhode Island.

I accept the charges.

"Hey," Ryder says. "Thanks for taking the call."

I didn't take calls from him for a year after that day in court. My mother asked me to talk to him for her sake, so eventually I did.

"What's up? Isn't it visiting day?"

"The kids were here. They just left."

"How're they doing?"

"They're great. It amazes me how unfazed they are by coming to see me here."

"Hopefully they won't remember much about this time in their lives."

"They told me Caroline is seeing Houston."

"Oh. Really?"

"Yeah, the kids said something about him building them a new swing set and how he's Mommy's special friend."

"That must've been hard to hear."

"I guess it was bound to happen eventually. Just didn't picture her with my friend."

"It's not like he was a close friend, and she didn't know him at all through you."

"Still. It sucks. I know it would be a huge longshot, but I was sort of still hoping we might put things back together after this…"

"That's not going to happen, Ry. With or without Houston in the picture."

"Like I said, it was a longshot."

"What matters is you still have your kids in your life."

"I know. How are you guys?"

"We're fine. Lucy has an art show tonight that she's excited about, and Duncan is becoming quite the basketball player. The little ones are getting so big. I'll send you some new pictures."

"I'd love that. Tell them I miss them and love them."

"I will. Do you want to talk to Mom?"

"Sure."

I hand my phone to her and watch her face light up at the sound of Ryder's voice. Wanting to give them time to talk, I go back inside and head for my home office, where I sit behind the desk and stare at the picture of my parents and siblings from when we were all still living at home.

That seems like another lifetime now.

Caroline

WE GET HOME FROM our weekly visit at the prison—and even after all this time, I still can't believe I'm taking my kids to see their father in prison—to find Houston in the backyard putting the finishing touches on the new wooden playset he built for the kids. The one Ryder installed years ago had begun to rot, which I took as a metaphor for my life.

The therapist I worked with after Ryder's arrest and incarceration encouraged me to take the kids to see him, to keep him in their lives because that was in their best interest, even after everything that'd happened.

At first I balked at the idea of taking them there.

But they missed him so much that eventually I decided to do it.

I'm glad I did. They're happier when they get to see him, which makes things easier for me.

My brothers came from Pennsylvania one weekend, shortly after Ryder left, and converted our basement to an apartment that's now rented to a lovely older woman named Mrs. Dugan. She's become an extra grandmother to the kids and is always happy to watch them for me. Between her rent and the proceeds from my baking business, I was able to hold on to the house. There's not a lot leftover for extras, but we have everything we need.

And I have Houston, who's been the greatest blessing to me and my kids in this strange new life we're building for ourselves.

What started as friendship has recently turned into something more, and I couldn't be happier to have that with someone who's been right there for me during the worst time of my life. Knowing how fragile I was for a long time after Ryder left, Houston never pushed for more than friendship.

He called and texted regularly to check on me, came running once when I had a racoon in my trash can and has been an awesome friend to me.

It took me asking him if he wanted more, and his enthusiastic *yes*, to move us out of the friend zone into where we are now, which is a very nice place to be.

Last night, we got carried away on my sofa after the kids went to bed and nearly ended up going all the way. I giggle at that term from high school. Tonight, he's invited me to dinner at his place, and I'm fully aware that this time we'll seal the deal.

Mrs. Dugan is watching the kids, and I'm going to have sex with Houston Rafferty.

I can't wait.

It's amazing, really, how I once thought I'd found the man I would spend the rest of my life with and how stupidly happy I was with him. I built my entire existence around him, and when he was gone, I was left in pieces. I'll never let that happen again. As much as I think I might be in love with Houston, I'm proceeding with caution.

There's so much at stake with my sweet kids and their beautiful hearts.

But as I watch Houston push them on the swings and laugh at their endless questions while patiently answering them all, I know I have nothing to worry about with him. He's as nice and as dependable as he is sexy.

He catches me watching him and smiles.

A flutter of excitement zips through me.

Houston leaves the kids to play and comes over to see me. "Hi."

"Hi. It looks great. Thank you again for doing all that work."

"I loved every minute of it."

"Including the part where you had to start over halfway through?"

"Even that."

"Liar." I give him a gentle shove as he laughs.

"How'd it go today?"

"Same as usual."

"How are you?"

"Same as usual," I say with a small smile.

He wraps me up in a hug that makes everything better. His hugs have become essential to me. "How soon can we escape?"

"I need an hour to get them fed, and then I'm all yours."

"I can't wait."

"Neither can I."

Denise

HOW CAN MY BABY boys be *three years old* already? I've been asking myself that for weeks as I planned their birthday bash.

They come running into the room together—always together—blond and rosy-cheeked and full of mischief. I love them madly.

I lean over to hug them. "Who's excited for their party?"

"We are!"

"They're beyond excited," my dad says when he emerges from the hallway where the kids' bedrooms are.

We're back to living in Fairfax County, near many of the people Kane and I went to high school with. We have more than fifty kids coming to the party, which is insane, but we couldn't leave anyone out.

Kane comes in from the garage carrying the cake I asked him to pick up for me.

"We wanna see," Hudson shouts as he runs over to Kane, nearly taking him out at the knees.

Hayes is right behind him to see the fire truck cake I ordered three months ago.

I get there just in time to save the cake.

Kane laughs and kisses me. "Just another day in the loony bin."

"This one will be extra loony."

"Fifty kids you say?"

I give him a hapless shrug.

"I need a drink."

My dad comes up behind me and squeezes my shoulders. "You're amazing, Dee."

"Why do you say that?"

"You do it all and make it look so easy."

"Aw thanks, Dad. I'm so glad you and Anita could come for the party."

"We wouldn't have missed it." He turns me to face him. "I want you to know how proud I am of you and Kane and my beautiful grandchildren. You survived, Dee. And you thrived."

"I had a lot of help."

"And now you're paying it forward by helping other young women who've been through what you did."

"It's very rewarding work."

"Another reason why I'm so proud."

I went to school nights and weekends for a year to get trained to work with the girls at the rape crisis center. At first, Kane and Dad were worried that it would be too much for me. At times, it is. But oh how I wish I'd had the kind of resources we make available to teenage girls in crisis. That would've made a huge difference for me, so I know I'm making a difference for them.

Charlotte and Levi come running in from outside to tell me they've finished putting the balloons around the yard.

The doorbell rings.

Kane rubs his hands together. "Let the madness begin."

Blaise

"ONE MORE BIG PUSH, Blaise. You've got this."

I don't have this. Not at all. I'm out of my mind from the pain, the pressure, the exhaustion and I'm freaking *starving*.

"I'm so proud of you, babe," Jack says as he wipes the sweat from my brow with a cool cloth that's the best thing I've ever felt.

"Here we go!" the peppy midwife says. Even her name—Poppy—is peppy.

I want to smack the peppiness right out of her.

Jack supports my shoulders as I give a mighty push that *finally* yields results, nearly twenty-four hours after my water broke at home.

"Your beautiful baby girl is here!" Poppy announces.

Only when Jack wipes them away do I realize tears are streaming down my cheeks.

"You did it, Red. She's gorgeous."

They bring her to me, wrapped in a soft white blanket, and with one glance at her delicate features, I see he's right. She's the most beautiful thing I've ever seen.

"Oh, wow, look at her." He wipes away his own tears. "She's stunning just like her mother."

"You have to say that. You caused all this."

"Yes, I did." He puffs his chest the way he has since we found out I was pregnant. "And P.S., it's the truth. She looks just like you."

I don't see that, but I lack the strength to debate anything right now. I just want to stare at the baby I'd once thought I'd never have, back when my life was a complete mess. Hindsight has shown me that. Everything was a mess for the entire fourteen years I kept that dreadful secret.

The minute I told Houston what I'd seen, it was like my real life was finally able to begin.

Jack Olsen has been at the center of that new life.

We got married a year ago in a small, informal gathering in the yard at home. My entire family was there, along with a few unlikely friends, including Houston Rafferty and Caroline Elliott. I was shocked to hear of that pairing when they went public and wary of being around her at first, but she's lovely. She bears me no ill will for the role I played in the demise of her marriage, which is remarkable.

She's an example of grace and perseverance, and I've come to admire her for the way she's carried on with her life.

Against all odds, Denise Messner has also become a close friend one text at a time over the last couple of years. She's one of many people awaiting word of the baby's arrival.

Life is such a strange and awful and wonderful journey.

I've also happened into a whole new career thanks to Jack, managing him and two of his RISD classmates. The work is fun, interesting and challenging, and that I get to spend most of every day with him is the best kind of bonus.

"What's her name?" Poppy asks.

"Diana Elizabeth Olsen," I reply, "in honor of Jack's mother and my grandmother."

"That's a beautiful name for a beautiful girl."

"Hello, Diana the second," Jack says tearfully.

He was overwhelmed when I told him I wanted to name her after his mother.

"Thank you so much for her, Red," he whispers as he kisses me and then the baby.

I continue to be astounded by the many ways the truth has set me free, but nothing is more incredible than the love of this man and the life we're building together.

He and Diana are worth all the hell and heartache I had to go through to get to them.

I'll never take them or any of my many blessings for granted.

If you or someone you know has been sexually assaulted, please know help is available through organizations such as RAINN, the Rape, Abuse and Incest National Network, which operates the National Sexual Assault Hotline at 800.656.HOPE (4673) and at online.rainn.org. Additional information can be found at the National Sexual Violence Resource Center online at www.nsvrc.org/survivors.

Author's Note and Acknowledgments

Phew. I have NO CLUE where this story came from, but once I had the idea, I was obsessed with writing it. I grew up in a small town and live in one now. Everyone knows everyone. The ties run deep. Not only have the kids known each other all their lives, often their parents have, too. Even their grandparents are close. I wanted to put Blaise in a situation where she felt there was no choice but to keep her mouth shut about what she'd witnessed. And then I wanted her to *suffer*. The rest came from there and had me by the throat every second I was writing it.

I want to note that Hope, Monroe and Land's End are fictional Rhode Island towns that locals will recognize as Portsmouth, Tiverton and Little Compton. I want to say emphatically that while the descriptions of each town are true to life, all the darker edges portrayed in this book are fictional, and that's why I changed the names of the towns. My kids had a wonderful experience growing up in Portsmouth, and we're thankful for an amazing community of friends who are like family in our small town—and most of them have known each other all their lives!

I was torn about whether to include Ryder's point of view in this story, but decided the best way to watch his life fall apart due to his horrific actions was to see it from his vantage point. I was deeply fascinated by the exploration of how a promising life can be ruined and a family changed forever in the scope of a few horrifying minutes.

I was also deeply invested in Denise's story and how she reclaimed her life with the help of her devoted boyfriend and father. But more than that, I enjoyed watching her discover her own power and inner strength as the story unfolded. I shivered as I typed "I will be their downfall."

I expect there may be some controversy about whether Blaise is a sympathetic character or another villain. I hope in the end you'll have more sympathy than disdain for her as a teenager caught in a tsunami that nearly drowned her. As I have in past books, such as TREADING WATER, I enjoy writing about the "grey" area that exists between right and wrong and how we often can't say for certain what we'd do in a situation until we're in it. That's when the black and white of right and wrong fades to grey, where most of life takes place. I love those kinds of dilemmas—in fiction, that is. Not so much in real life!

If you're new to me and my books, WELCOME to the party! IN THE AIR TONIGHT is my 105th book! You can find details about the others at marieforce.com/books. Most of my books are available in

Kindle Unlimited. See the full rundown of what's available in KU at marieforce.com/ku. If you're looking for something with a similar vibe to this book, check out THE WRECK, a single title, and/or the Fatal/First Family Series. Join my newsletter mailing list at marieforce.com/connect to keep in touch. You can also find me @marieforceauthor on TikTok, Instagram and Threads. Like my Facebook page at facebook.com/marieforceauthor.

Join the IN THE AIR TONIGHT Reader Group at www.facebook.com/groups/intheairtonightreaders/ **after you finish the book** to discuss all the twists and turns with other readers. Please note that spoilers are allowed in this group.

Special thanks to Liz Berry, MJ Rose and Jillian Greenfield Stein at Bluebox for all your support and enthusiasm for IN THE AIR TONIGHT. I'm so thrilled to be working with you wonder women to bring this book to readers! Thank you also to the team at Simon & Schuster, for placing the paperback in retail outlets.

Many thanks to Captain Russell Hayes (retired), Newport, RI, Police Department, for his assistance with the details pertaining to Rhode Island law enforcement and court procedures. Russ was instrumental in helping me to determine how the chain of events would unfold when Blaise comes home to Rhode Island to report a crime that occurred fourteen years earlier. Dr. Sarah Hewitt, family nurse practitioner, was a huge help in detailing how Denise's appointment at the clinic would've unfolded and answered my many medical and pregnancy-related questions.

As always, a huge thank you to the team that supports me every day: Julie Cupp, Lisa Cafferty, Jean Mello, Nikki Haley, Ashley Lopes and Rachel Spencer, as well as my beta readers, Anne Woodall, Kara Conrad, Tracey Suppo and Gwen Neff. Thank you to my longtime friend and amazing author, Sarah Mayberry, for her insightful feedback.

All my love to Dan, Emily and Jake, who keep my life full of laughter and tomfoolery, as well as my fur babies, Sam Sullivan and Louie, who are my constant companions along with my "granddog," Tommy.

Finally, to the readers, who follow me everywhere my crazy muse takes me—thank you for giving me the career of my dreams. I love you all so much!

xoxo,
Marie

Book Club Discussion Questions

1. Blaise thinks she'd always do the right thing in any situation—until something happens that causes her to question everything she believes about herself and others. Do you see Blaise as a sympathetic character? Why or why not?

2. The town of Hope is very much a "character" in this book, with ties running deep through generations of family and friends. When one of their own is accused of a heinous crime, people in town close ranks around him. Have you experienced this dynamic in your hometown or known of someone who has? What was it like for you or them?

3. In her note at the end, the author mentions that she debated whether to include Ryder's point of view in the book. In the end, she decided she wanted to show how his life fell apart due to his actions years earlier. How did you feel about having his point of view reflected in the story?

4. Ryder's brother Cam plays a central role in the story. He finds out early on that the accusations against his brother are true and like others, he does everything wrong after learning the truth. He goes so far as to sign an affidavit that sullies the reputation of the young woman who's accused Ryder of rape. Later, we witness Cam's life spin out of control along with his brother's, as a result of actions they took years earlier. Do you have empathy or anger toward Cam for what he did to protect his brother and their family?

5. Denise is minding her own business fourteen years after the night that changed her life when Houston Rafferty shows up at her door to tell her a witness has come forward who can back up her story. How do you think you would feel if something like that happened to you? Later, we learn that she and Blaise have become unlikely friends. If you were Denise, could you have become friends with Blaise?

6. Both Denise and Blaise are partnered with loving, supportive men. What difference do you think the characters of Kane and Jack made

for each of the women and how did their love and support influence the outcomes for the women?

7. Houston Rafferty is in an unenviable position after Blaise comes forward as a witness to a crime that took place years earlier at his party. In addition, his brother signed the affidavit in support of Ryder all those years ago and stands to lose his reputation and livelihood if Houston pursues new charges against Ryder. Do you think Houston handled the case properly? What would you have done differently if you had been in his situation?

8. Dave Elliott crosses multiple lines in his misguided efforts to protect his son. Did you feel for him as a parent or were you disgusted by the things he did to "protect" Ryder?

9. Caroline Elliott is blindsided by the charges against her husband, especially after she learns he lied to her about whether he'd raped Denise. How did you feel about her actions after the truth comes to light, and what did you think of her new romance with Houston?

10. Sienna Elliott comes across as a bit selfish in the story, but she thought about what was best for Cam and his family from the minute she realized what Ryder had done. How important do you think the concept of loyalty is in a situation like this? Is she a hero or a villain in this story?

11. Have you ever witnessed a crime? If so, do you feel you did the right thing with the information? If you witnessed a crime like this one, with all the attending complications faced by Blaise and Sienna, what would you do? Keeping in mind, you're seventeen years old and your friends are the center of your life as they are for most teenagers.

12. The Epilogue shows the main characters two years after the memorable day in court. What did you think of where they are now?

Cast of Characters, In Order of Appearance

Blaise Merrick, 31, from Hope, RI, reddish hair, blue eyes. Lives in NYC and manages Broadway star Wendall Brooks.

Wendall Brooks, Blaise's boss, Broadway star of "Grey Matter."

Deena Merrick, Blaise's mother.

Teagan Merrick, 34, Blaise's sister, expecting fifth child.

Doug, Teagan's husband.

Ryder Elliott, 32, classmate of Blaise, best friend to her brother, Arlo.

Arlo Merrick, 32, Blaise's brother, husband of Jen.

Sienna Lawton, 31, Blaise's former best friend, married to Camden Elliott, Ryder's brother, mother of four children, including Lucy and Duncan.

Juniper Merrick, 28, Blaise's sister, known as June or Junie.

Camden "Cam" Elliott, 31, brother to Ryder, classmate of Blaise, Sienna's husband, lawyer, four children, close friend to Arlo.

Houston Rafferty, 35, chief of police in Land's End, brother to Dallas and Austin, son of Chuck, former chief of police.

Dallas Rafferty, 31, brother of Houston and Austin, married with three kids.

Austin Rafferty, 28, sister of Houston and Dallas, lives in California, married with two little boys.

Brooke, 32, in Arlo's class, one year ahead of Blaise and Sienna.

Denise Sutton Messner, 31, classmate of Blaise, wife of Kane Messner,

31. Known as Neisy as a teenager, mother of four children, nickname is Dee as an adult.

Louisa Davies, died at 18 of Hodgkin's Disease, was the longtime girlfriend of Ryder Elliott.

Kane Messner, 31, Denise's husband, lieutenant commander in the navy.

Captain Rick Sutton, Denise's father, navy captain.

Ronnie, cousin to Denise's mother, owner of The Daily Catch restaurant where Denise and Houston worked together.

Dr. Cummings, navy lieutenant commander, works at navy clinic.

David Elliott, father of Ryder and Camden.

Mrs. Dalton, neighbor to Sutton family, takes Denise's mother to AA.

Neil DeGrasso, Assistant Attorney General, prosecutor of initial case against Ryder Elliott.

Judge Morgan Denton, judge presiding over Ryder's initial case.

Chuck Rafferty, father to Houston, Dallas and Austin, former police chief in Land's End, wife was former elementary school principal.

Mary Elliott, mother to Ryder and Camden as well as two unnamed older daughters.

Jack Olsen, 35, owner of guest cottages in Land's End, friend of Houston's, love interest of Blaise, professional illustrator.

Fenway, Jack's Golden Retriever, three years old.

Joshua Spurling, Assistant Attorney General who prosecutes reopened case against Ryder Elliott.

Victor Roberts, Rhode Island Attorney General, been in office just under three years.

Levi Messner, 6, son of Denise and Kane.

Charlotte Messner, 9, daughter of Denise and Kane.

Hayes and Hudson Messner, twin nine-month-old sons of Denise and Kane.

Gretchen, Denise's neighbor.

Caroline Elliott, Ryder's wife, mother to three children.

Miles Elliott, 7, son of Ryder and Caroline.

Grace Elliott, 5, daughter of Ryder and Caroline.

Elise Elliott, 3, daughter of Ryder and Caroline.

Marty Davis, Louisa's brother.

Petey Johnson, Miles's teammate.

Jalen, Miles's teammate.

Rich Morton, law school friend of Camden's who works for the AG's office.

Ramona Travers Silvia, 31, classmate of Blaise, Ryder, Camden and Sienna, lives now in Bristol with husband Tony and three children, Audra, Heidi and James

Brody, one of the guys who signed affidavit supporting Ryder, briefly dated Ramona.

Bennett Gormley, attorney, handles Ryder's arraignment.

Maggie, Caroline Elliott's sister, lives in Philadelphia.

Michael, Miles's teammate.

Lori, mother of Miles's teammate Michael.

Aimee, Caroline's next-door neighbor and friend.

Jen, Arlo Merrick's wife, one of Caroline's best friends.

Jane, Dallas Rafferty's wife.

Kim, Blaise's colleague who takes over her job with Wendall.

Bridget Doyle, Ryder's defense attorney.

Marge, admin at Land's End Police Department.

Caleb Anders, Hope police officer, classmate of Ryder, Cam, Blaise, Sienna.

Mrs. Dugan, Caroline's tenant.

Anita, Rick Sutton's girlfriend.

Diana Elizabeth Olsen, Blaise and Jack's daughter.

Places:

Hope, Rhode Island, hometown of Teagan, Arlo, Blaise, and Juniper Merrick, Ryder and Camden Elliott, Sienna Lawton, and briefly—Denise Sutton.

Land's End, Rhode Island, hometown of Houston, Dallas and Austin Rafferty.

Monroe, Rhode Island, town between Hope and Land's End, accessible from Hope across a bridge over a river.

The Daily Catch, restaurant in Monroe where Houston and Denise worked together.

Bristol, Rhode Island, across the Mount Hope Bridge from Hope, Rhode Island, home of Ramona Travers Silvia.

Rhode Island School of Design, a premier art school located in Providence, RI, Jack Olsen's college.

Bishop Stang High School, Catholic High School in Dartmouth, Massachusetts, Jack Olsen's high school

New York University's Tisch School of the Arts, Blaise Merrick's college.

Newport News, Virginia, home of Denise and Kane Messner.

Charlton Memorial Hospital, located in Fall River, Massachusetts.

Rhode Island Hospital, located in Providence, Rhode Island, only level-one trauma hospital in the area.

Cranston, Rhode Island, city just south of Providence.

About Marie Force

Marie Force is the *New York Times* bestselling author of more than 100 contemporary romance, romantic suspense and erotic romance novels. Her series include Fatal, First Family, Gansett Island, Butler Vermont, Quantum, Treading Water, Miami Nights and Wild Widows. She has also written 12 single titles, with more coming.

Her books have sold more than 13 million copies worldwide, have been translated into more than a dozen languages and have appeared on the *New York Times* bestseller list more than 30 times. She is also a *USA Today* and #1 *Wall Street Journal* bestseller, as well as a Spiegel bestseller in Germany.

Her goals in life are simple—to spend as much time as possible with her young adult children, to keep writing books for as long as she possibly can and to never be on a flight that makes the news.

Stay in touch!

Join my mailing list at marieforce.com/subscribe

Email: marie@marieforce.com

Social Media:
Facebook: facebook.com/marieforceauthor
Instagram: @marieforceauthor
TikTok: @marieforceauthor
Threads: @marieforceauthor

You can find out more about Marie Force at:
   https://marieforce.com.

Discover 1001 Dark Nights Collection Eleven

DRAGON KISS by Donna Grant
A Dragon Kings Novella

THE WILD CARD by Dylan Allen
A Rivers Wilde Novella

ROCK CHICK REMATCH by Kristen Ashley
A Rock Chick Novella

JUST ONE SUMMER by Carly Phillips
A Dirty Dare Series Novella

HAPPILY EVER MAYBE by Carrie Ann Ryan
A Montgomery Ink Legacy Novella

BLUE MOON by Skye Warren
A Cirque des Moroirs Novella

A VAMPIRE'S MATE by Rebecca Zanetti
A Dark Protectors/Rebels Novella

LOVE HAZARD by Rachel Van Dyken

BRODIE by Aurora Rose Reynolds
An Until Her Novella

THE BODYGUARD AND THE BOMBSHELL by Lexi Blake
A Masters and Mercenaries: New Recruits Novella

THE SUBSTITUTE by Kristen Proby
A Single in Seattle Novella

CRAVED BY YOU by J. Kenner
A Stark Security Novella

GRAVEYARD DOG by Darynda Jones
A Charley Davidson Novella

A CHRISTMAS AUCTION by Audrey Carlan
A Marriage Auction Novella

THE GHOST OF A CHANCE by Heather Graham
A Krewe of Hunters Novella

Also from Blue Box Press

LEGACY OF TEMPTATION by Larissa Ione
A Demonica Birthright Novel

VISIONS OF FLESH AND BLOOD by Jennifer L. Armentrout and
Ravyn Salvador
A Blood & Ash and Fire & Flesh Compendium

FORGETTING TO REMEMBER by M.J. Rose

TOUCH ME by J. Kenner
A Stark International Novella

BORN OF BLOOD AND ASH by Jennifer L. Armentrout
A Flesh and Fire Novel

MY ROYAL SHOWMANCE by Lexi Blake
A Park Avenue Promise Novel

SAPPHIRE DAWN by Christopher Rice writing as C. Travis Rice
A Sapphire Cove Novel

EMBRACING THE CHANGE by Kristen Ashley
A River Rain Novel

IN THE AIR TONIGHT by Marie Force

LEGACY OF CHAOS by Larissa Ione
A Demonica Birthright Novel

On Behalf of Blue Box Press,

Liz Berry, M.J. Rose, and Jillian Stein would like to thank ~

Steve Berry
Doug Scofield
Benjamin Stein
Kim Guidroz
Chelle Olson
Tanaka Kangara
Ann-Marie Nieves
Asha Hossain
Chris Graham
Jessica Saunders
Stacey Tardif
Suzy Baldwin
Dylan Stockton
Kate Boggs
Richard Blake
and Simon Lipskar